continued . . .

SUMMER OF STORMS

AFTER THE FALL

THE
FIRST
STONE

JUDITH KELMAN

BERKLEY BOOKS, NEW YORK

THE BERKLEY PUBLISHING GROUP
Published by the Penguin Group
Penguin Group (USA) Inc.
375 Hudson Street, New York, New York 10014, USA
Penguin Group (Canada), 90 Eglinton Avenue East, Suite 700, Toronto, Ontario M4P 2Y3, Canada
(a division of Pearson Penguin Canada Inc.)
Penguin Books Ltd., 80 Strand, London WC2R 0RL, England
Penguin Group Ireland, 25 St. Stephen's Green, Dublin 2, Ireland (a division of Penguin Books Ltd.)
Penguin Group (Australia), 250 Camberwell Road, Camberwell, Victoria 3124, Australia
(a division of Pearson Australia Group Pty. Ltd.)
Penguin Books India Pvt. Ltd., 11 Community Centre, Panchsheel Park, New Delhi—110 017, India
Penguin Group (NZ), 67 Apollo Drive, Rosedale, North Shore 0632, New Zealand
(a division of Pearson New Zealand Ltd.)
Penguin Books (South Africa) (Pty.) Ltd., 24 Sturdee Avenue, Rosebank, Johannesburg 2196,
South Africa

Penguin Books Ltd., Registered Offices: 80 Strand, London WC2R 0RL, England

This is a work of fiction. Names, characters, places, and incidents either are the product of the author's imagination or are used fictitiously, and any resemblance to actual persons, living or dead, business establishments, events, or locales is entirely coincidental.

THE FIRST STONE

A Berkley Book / published by arrangement with Chapter Three, Inc.

PRINTING HISTORY
Berkley hardcover edition / May 2007
Berkley mass-market edition / January 2008

ISBN: 978-0-425-21788-7

BERKLEY®
Berkley Books are published by The Berkley Publishing Group,
a division of Penguin Group (USA) Inc.,
375 Hudson Street, New York, New York 10014.
BERKLEY® is a registered trademark of Penguin Group (USA) Inc.
The "B" design is a trademark belonging to Penguin Group (USA) Inc.

PRINTED IN THE UNITED STATES OF AMERICA

10 9 8 7 6 5 4 3 2 1

For Caroline and Ryan, with
boundless love and constant
astonishment.

Acknowledgments

Thanks to all the brilliant physicians, scientists, and best kind of doctors' wives (and husbands) who have so graciously welcomed me into their universe. They are the true heroes. The bad guys are purely imaginary.

Thanks as always to Peter Lampack, my remarkable agent, and to his wonderful colleague Rema Dilanyan.

Thanks also to Natalee Rosenstein and Michelle Vega at Berkley.

And, of course, above all, to the world's best physician and so many, many other bests, Peter Scardino.

· O N E ·

Through a slim breach in the blinds, I watched the new neighbors move in with a ticking, four-foot, fifty-pound bomb. The explosive was cleverly disguised as a wispy, slender, glossy-haired, unsmiling girl I took to be seven or eight.

The fierce sun leeched her pale skin to near transparency and bunched her eyes in pained slits. A prim navy dress hung limply to the middle of her calves above lace-capped kneesocks and shiny black Mary Janes. She walked with great deliberation, as if the shoes were stiff and inhospitable, tracking the perimeter of each pavement square.

She struck me as uneasy in the way that any child would be cowed by a move. When I was ten, my father's job had taken us from Oceanside, Long Island, to the alien land of L.A. As if it had happened yesterday, I could recall the knot of terror that cramped my stomach as we bumped up the rutted, gravel drive to our new house. Would I be up to the other kids in school? Would they accept me given that I wasn't a movie star, rich or blonde? Even if they did, could

I ever hope to feel safe in such a place? On the six o'clock news, I'd seen harrowing stories about the choking smog, mud slides, flash fires, and earthquakes. I imagined that the sun dropped each night into the raging nearby Pacific, setting the sea aboil with the angry hiss of a doused cigarette.

My three-year-old son, Tyler, knelt on the couch beside me.

"Mama, look. She's a girl."

"That she is."

"Can we maybe play?"

"I don't know, Ty. She's a lot bigger."

"I'm getting bigger." He stretched his arms overhead, exposing a hammock of pale flesh over the fretwork of ribs. "See?"

"I certainly do."

As her parents huddled on the sidewalk with the movers, the glum girl wandered farther down the block. She kept glancing back with a look of defiance, daring them to notice and protest.

Her father was a short, stocky man, given to grandiose gestures and looks of crushing disdain. The mother, a stylish, attractive brunette, was a head taller, decades younger, and more than made up in studied refinement for the polish her husband lacked. She listened with interest when he spoke and dispensed practiced smiles of approval. Every so often, her manicured hand lit for an instant on his arm.

Their black late-model Mercedes sedan was parked in a No Standing zone behind the moving van. The little girl sidled up, cupped her hands to block the glare, and peered through the driver's-side window. When her parents weren't looking, she opened the door and leaned across the seat. A moment later, she emerged with a smug look and skittering eyes. Her fist was clenched around the secret she held behind her back.

Oblivious, her mother and father trailed one of the movers toward the back of the truck. He released the hatch and produced a sheaf of papers. The father slipped a pen from his suit coat, scrutinized, and signed.

Beneath the building's dark green awning, the little girl slipped out of sight. A moment later, the front door slammed as if it had been tossed by a vicious wind. But the day was dead calm. The leaves on our spindly city trees hung limp against a clear exuberant sky.

Tyler's eyes bugged. "How come the girl's so mad?"

"We don't know that she's mad, cutie. It was just a noise."

"Was not. She broked the door."

"I'm sure the door's just fine."

"Look, Mama." A trio of large men had begun to haul furniture from the huge red truck. "That's the girl's chair."

"Could be."

Garlands of hand-painted pastel flowers graced the small white rocker. The name *Adriana* was stenciled in elaborate pink letters across the back. "Or maybe that's the baby sister's chair."

Tyler was due to have his own baby sibling in two months' time. Gently, I'd been trying to sell him on the idea, but so far, no dice. Since my first mention of the new addition when we learned of it in December, he'd let me know in a variety of ways that he was having none of it.

"She does *not* have a baby sister," he insisted.

I cradled the swell of my abdomen. "Maybe she does, sweetie. Maybe she has a wonderful baby sister that she loves very much."

"No, Mommy. No baby sister. Look. She has a mommy, a daddy, a big girl bed, a clothes place, and a chair."

A grunt-faced mover lumbered toward the building, toting a Chinese Chippendale settee with a brocade seat.

"That's the mommy's chair."

"You think?"

Following close behind the mommy's chair, a burly mover ferried a chestnut leather lounge, oil-stained at the head and arms.

"And that's the daddy's chair!"

Tyler squealed, pleased beyond measure to have the Three Bears set complete. He had a passion for order: videos in their proper boxes, accessories stowed with their action figures, vehicles parked in orderly fashion, puzzles pieced in a satisfying whole. Like my husband, Sam, Tyler was forever trying to impose taming logic on the horribly uncertain world. Practically from birth, he'd been taking inventory, setting categories, counting totals, making lists.

"Mommy chair, daddy chair, little girl chair," he chanted happily. "Everyone in the family has a chair."

I caught him from behind and squeezed. "And you know what I have?"

He giggled. "A mommy chair?"

"Nope. What I have is a yummy little monkey named Tyler James Colten, and I'm going to eat him all up."

I scooped him into my arms. Hiking up his pole-striped shirt, I made snorting gobble sounds against his belly.

"Stoppit!" he shrilled. He was willing to tolerate my silliness to a point, but not when he had more pressing matters to attend. Scrabbling back onto the couch, he perched on his knees and resumed his vigil.

Under the blazing scrutiny of Dr. Douglas Malik, world-renowned cardiac surgeon and owner of the aforementioned daddy chair, two of the movers hauled a large astronomical scope mounted on a tripod.

Tyler tensed. "How come they have an octopus?"

"It's not, sweetie. It's a telescope. It's for looking at very faraway things, like the stars."

"And the sun?"

"The sun is a star. But it's too bright to look at. You'd hurt your eyes."

"No!" he cried with startling intensity. "Don't say that!"

"Shh. It's okay. Calm down."

"I wouldn't hurt them, Mama. No!"

"I know you won't. Don't worry." I stroked his arm, made soothing noises.

"It's not an octopus?"

"No. But it does look a little like one. All those legs."

Suddenly, there was a burst of angry thumping overhead. The racket played out quickly, but after a brief silence, it started up again. Frightened, Tyler pressed his face against my straining abdomen.

"It's okay, sweetie. See? It stopped. Probably the movers putting something together."

At that, the ruckus resumed, so intense I felt seismic trembling. From the street, Dr. Malik peered up. Scowling, he strode toward the building. His wife stayed behind.

Moments later, Tyler eyed the ceiling.

"Is the little girl okay, Mama?"

"I'm sure she's fine."

"Why'd the daddy hit her?"

"Who said he hit her?"

"Bad girl. Smack!"

"Tyler, remember what we said about telling stories?"

"I'm not." Backing off the couch, he made for his action dolls.

The moving men now wheeled dollies stacked with packing boxes. Each one was neatly labeled with a list of contents and its intended destination. Limoges—dining room. Books—library. Table linens—kitchen pantry. Young Mrs. Malik followed the last of them into the building, gliding majestically on high-heeled, pinch-toed pumps.

Shifting the blinds to block the sun's glare, I went to my drawing table, where a nearly finished portrait of my little boy in ink and graphite awaited finishing touches and a coat of fixative. Tyler was my favorite subject, bar none, and I used the time between commissions to chart the striking changes as he grew.

"People are not for hitting," he told Batman, aping a prohibition he'd heard me repeat countless times.

"What makes you think someone hit the little girl, Tyler?"

"Her daddy did."

"I know you said that. But why do you think so?"

"Because he did."

"You can see through the ceiling, can you?"

"Superman can see through walls!"

Squinting at the drawing, I added an extra glint in my little one's eye.

"Bam, kapow!"

Splayed on the floor, he was utterly engaged in a pitched battle between a pliable Superman and Bolshak, the nasty-faced winged dragon.

"Bad dragon! I'm gonna get you for hitting. I'm going to punch you so hard!"

· TWO ·

Not long ago, I learned that God hailed from the tony Cleveland, Ohio, suburb of Shaker Heights. In a cautionary hush, my octogenarian friend, Frieda Kalisher, had informed me that the Almighty was relocating to Manhattan to take charge of the cardiovascular service at New York General, scheduled to arrive this week. He and his family would be living in the apartment directly above me. Now, for better or worse, God was here.

"How well do you know Dr. Malik, Mrs. K.?"

"We've met."

"And?"

She shrugged. "My Leonard knew him. Didn't have much use for him, tell you the truth. Plenty of hotshot surgeons have a bit of a God complex, but from what Leonard said, this Malik character actually believes his own press."

"He does have a pretty amazing reputation. Sam thinks he's a giant like DeBakey. That between the devices he's invented and the advances he's made in surgical technique, he's pretty much revolutionized the field."

She sniffed. "Doug Malik puts his pants on one leg at a time like the rest of us, Emma. I've seen way bigger fall on their face. Set yourself above it all, there's nowhere to go but down."

"Or east, as it turns out."

"He'll hate it here, mark my words. Malik is used to being a big fish in a little pond, not swimming in an ocean full of whales."

"There have been rumors about him coming forever. Sam said no way."

"Plenty thought it would never happen. Malik's spent his whole career at the Cleveland Clinic. Practically owned the place. Or thought he did. Hard to imagine why he'd ever leave."

"God complex or not, Sam's a huge admirer. He'd give anything to get a fellowship with Malik. He says if you want to train in cardiac surgery, it doesn't get any better than that."

Her lip curled in distaste. "Your Sam should watch what he wishes for, darling. I hear Malik can be a great big, unpleasant of work. Unreasonable, demanding. Unwilling to share the glory with anyone else. Some of the giants take pride in bringing the next generation along, training talented successors. With Doug Malik, the whole story starts and stops with him."

Mrs. Kalisher's late husband, Leonard, had been an orthopedic surgeon specializing in children with disabilities at New York General for forty years. The Kalishers had been highly entrenched in the hospital community, and well loved. Though Dr. Kalisher had succumbed to esophageal cancer a decade ago, Frieda continued to volunteer, served on a variety of committees, and remained very firmly in the loop.

"Malik's a star, Frieda. They can be that way."

"They can be lots of ways, including ridiculous. You

should have heard his list of demands: double the usual lab space, fancy title, astronomical salary. He insisted on cleaning house in the department here and bringing in his own people from Cleveland. Plus, the new building."

"The cardiac center they've promised to build for him? Sam thinks it's amazing."

"The *Malik* Center for Cardiothoracic Diseases, for heaven's sake. He wants his name on the building instead of offering the privilege to some donor who'll agree to cover a big chunk of the $200 million cost? What does that tell you about him, Emma?"

I smiled. "That he's important enough to get what he wants."

Mrs. Kalisher puffed her contempt. "The hospital's full of stars. Nothing good ever comes if they get in a shining contest."

"Look, Auntie Frieda," Tyler said. "I drawed you a sun!"

Crouching on the pavement, he added an enthusiastic blotch of yellow to the large spike-spitting orb he had rendered in sidewalk chalk.

"You certainly did, sweetheart. Look at that, Emma. Your Tyler is a regular artist, just like you."

"When I grow up, I'm gonna be an artist guy."

I smiled. "I thought it was a builder man this week."

He nodded firmly. "I'm gonna be an artist guy *and* a builder man."

Frieda ruffled his thick pale hair. "You'll be anything you want, sweetheart, and you'll be wonderful at it."

"I'm gonna be a pirate, too."

"The pirates would be lucky to have you."

"And a dinosaur."

"Auntie Frieda's the dinosaur," she said. "You be the artistic pirate with a successful construction business. Believe me, that's much more fun."

"Look, Auntie Frieda. I made you a tree."

She leaned back on our favorite bench. "Marvelous. Look at all those lovely purple leaves. I think I'll sit right here and enjoy the shade."

Tyler endorsed the idea with a pearly-toothed grin. He adored Mrs. Kalisher, who lived in the neighboring apartment house and hung out, as we often did, in St. Stephan's Park across the street. Though time had shrunk her to a bowed, bird-boned sprite, she found boundless patience and energy to shower on my son. She never tired of pushing him on the swing, extolling his virtuosity in the sandbox, or cheering him through countless intrepid ascents and death-defying landings on the three-foot slide.

I adored Frieda, too. And I blessed her for filling a painful void. She was a caring surrogate for my mother and father, who both worked and lived busy lives on the West Coast and visited rarely. She stood in for Sam's mother, who had died when he was only ten, and for Sam's father, a cool, intimidating man who had little use for children of any age. My husband often quipped that his dad, a cardiologist who had been something of a star at New York General in his own right, did not believe the fetus was truly viable until it graduated from medical school, played a decent game of golf, and was able to make urbane small talk at cocktail parties. Years ago, "Senior," as he liked to be called, had discovered the joys of big money from big pharma and quit the salaried constraints of academic medicine to rake it in.

Tyler eagerly soaked up Mrs. Kalisher's attentions and treated her like a rock star in return. He never failed to greet her with manic enthusiasm and presented her with the cream of his preschool art projects. She displayed them in her gracious classic six: the kraft paper turkey with the tongue depressor tail. The menorah with blazing yellow tissue paper lights. The finger-painted, arrow-pierced Valentine heart sprinkled with gold glitter. Frieda was the first woman to offer serious competition for my son's affections. Watching them gaze at each other with dewy-eyed adoration, I knew how it felt to be displaced.

"You saw the wife?" Mrs. Kalisher asked.

"I caught a peek when they were moving in. Very attractive. Extremely well put together. Verging on unforgivably thin. She looks a lot younger than Malik. Much taller, too."

She rolled her eyes. "Sounds like all the others. This is wife number three for Doug, or four maybe. And I think child number seven, including two that by now have to be older than you. Some men have a trophy wife—Malik keeps up the way he's going, he'll need a whole trophy room."

"No problem. He has the space for it."

"To say the least. Six bedrooms. I ask you."

Before agreeing to relocate, God's wife had insisted on a very large, quiet apartment conveniently located near the new cardiothoracic center, where Dr. Malik would have his office, and the hospital's main pavilion nearby, where he would perform his regularly scheduled miracles. Her housing requirements included an eat-in gourmet kitchen, a large master suite with a working fireplace, spacious living areas, separate child's quarters, including a playroom, and a room off the kitchen for live-in help. Expecting extravagant space, quiet, and convenience in Manhattan was akin to demanding a Starbucks on your corner on the moon. Nevertheless, given sufficient will and funding, almost anything, it seemed, could be done.

Of all the hospital-owned housing they'd been shown, the Maliks had chosen to take up residence in our ten-story brick prewar off First Avenue. Four apartments on the floor above ours had been commandeered, summarily vacated, and hastily combined. The wife of one of the displaced couples, a friend whose husband was a surgical resident with Sam, said she'd felt like a tornado victim, wrenched without warning from their cozy home and suddenly plunked down ten blocks away in a cookie-cutter high-rise with tissue paper walls that trembled with the constant clatter of traffic over the nearby Queensborough Bridge.

A team of contractors had worked nonstop to demolish and reconfigure the space to meet the Maliks' highly particular demands by the deadline. During the construction phase, I'd taken Tyler up several times for a peek at the source of the incessant hammering and sawing.

Thoroughly captivated by the irresistible combination of noise, dirt, and burly workers who made rude noises, said bad words, and had tattoos, my son had added "builder man" to the long list of future professions—hot dog vendor, pilot, dog walker, traffic cop, astronaut—he had already embraced.

Solemnly, he had labored for hours with his brightly hued plastic tools, constructing phantom additions to our cramped one-bedroom. For mere mortals in New York City, excess square footage was the true stuff of fantasy. Since moving here, I've had a recurrent dream in which I happen upon a secret passage in our apartment that leads to à rambling complex of extra rooms. In a joyous delirium, I skip along the endless looping corridor, finding one large, sunny space after another. There's an actual person-sized bedroom for Tyler and another for the child we expect. A courtyard garden where the kids can play. Empty closets. Lots of them. And shelves.

Tyler was drawing a face on the pavement. Dot eyes, an apostrophe nose, and a broad, perky, melon-slice mouth. He launched the word game he and Auntie Frieda played all the time. Know what? No, what?

"You know what, Auntie Frieda?"

"No, what?"

He raised his hands triumphantly. "That's a picture of you!"

"Well, of course it is. Anyone could see."

"And you know what?"

"No, what?"

"The new people have a little girl I can maybe play with."

"Is that so?"

"Yup, and you know what? Her daddy hit her 'cause she made him really mad."

"Tyler, remember what we said about telling stories?"

A fresh wrinkle joined the familiar crowd on Mrs. Kalisher's brow. "I wouldn't put it past him."

Tyler took up the fat turquoise chalk stick and rendered a squat square house with a dunce cap roof. He added port-hole windows and a slim chimney belching pink and lavender smoke. The door, a beckoning red span, had a smiley face on the knob.

"See that!"

Mrs. Kalisher leaned in, squinting through bottle-thick glasses set in spare silver frames. "Lovely."

"The house is all ready. And now the new people are moving in."

"Is that so?"

My son nodded sagely. "The daddy moves in. The mommy moves in; the little girl moves in. And you know what, Auntie Frieda?"

"No, what?"

"Everyone lives happily ever after."

· THREE ·

"We should do something, Em." Sam said this with his head in the refrigerator and the call beeper razzing on his belt.

"Do what?"

Backing out, he checked the source of the call. "Damn. It's the OR. I'm late."

Again, I prompted him. "We should do what?"

The demands of surgical residency left Sam preoccupied and distractible. Rarely did we have time for such luxuries as a complete conversation. Sometimes I imagined our ceiling hung with the sharp little fragments of the thousands of unfinished thoughts he tossed out and left suspended precariously in midair.

Frowning, he ducked into the fridge again. "I'm starved."

"There's leftover chicken, sweetie. Sliced turkey. Want me to scramble some eggs?"

"No time."

Grabbing the peanut butter jar, he downed several heaping spoonfuls. He chased that back with a hit from a quart of Dora the Explorer chocolate milk.

"Daddy, no!" Tyler cried in alarm. "You're not allowed to eat peanut butter except on bread or apples. Plain makes you choke!"

"That's okay, Ty," I reassured him. "Daddy's not going to choke."

"But you said."

"I know. But that's for little children. The rules for daddies are different."

The rules for surgical resident daddies were even more different, verging on bizarre. Part of the eight-year training program (four years of medical school, four in residency) for Sam's chosen specialty, cardiovascular surgery, involved learning how to work incredibly hard for marathon stints, forgoing such frivolities as nourishment, downtime, and sleep. Laws enacted in the 1980s had placed legal limits on the number of hours doctors in training could work in the hospital, but that didn't stop them from plugging away on research, papers, and no end of other work-related enterprises during their so-called time off.

When he was a first-year resident, Sam had stumbled around in a dislocated fog, getting by on little more than terror-induced adrenaline. But eventually, he'd learned to disregard the calls of nature in favor of the far more pressing ones from higher-ups in the hospital hierarchy.

On the rare occasions when he wasn't working, he shifted into manic catch-up mode, determined to eat, sleep, go to the bathroom, watch the game, have sex, call his sister, fix the stereo, play with Tyler, and get back in peak physical condition, all at once.

Tyler looked uneasy, mulling over the daddy exemption to the peanut-butter-on-a-spoon rule as he stared into his bowl of chicken soup with alphabet noodles, searching out the letters in his name. Beside his plate in a neat line were an *L*, an *E*, and a *T*. "No choking, Daddy."

"Don't worry, sweetie. See? Daddy's fine."

Sam was also oblivious, talking on his BlackBerry. "Sure. In a minute. Can you get Ron to prep that? Right. Will do."

Sam stuck the peanut butter back in the refrigerator. The chocolate milk, he set absently in the sink.

"Better run."

He kissed Tyler's cheek and rumpled my hair, getting it backward, but close enough.

"You said we have to do something, Sam?"

At that, he paused. "Right. Thanks for reminding me. About the Maliks."

"What about them?"

"I was thinking we should get them something. A welcome gift."

"Such as?"

"Cookies? Candy? Bottle of wine?"

"What if Dr. Malik's a carb nazi, or a teetotaler?"

"Flowers, then. A plant. Whatever, Em. Would you please just do something? Whatever's right."

"Sure." I snapped my fingers. "I'll just go on that website: What to get God for a house gift dot com."

"Thanks."

"Maybe I can get some nice fresh frankincense. Or you think he's more a myrrh type of guy?"

His eyes had glazed over, already switched to a different frame.

"Or maybe a burnt offering, Sam. How's that?"

Leaning down, he kissed Tyler again and helped himself to a spoonful of alphabet soup.

Tyler's jaw trembled. "No, Daddy. You ate the *R*."

"That's okay, sweetie," I said. "There are plenty more *R*s in the pot."

"But I wanted that one."

Sam blinked. "Tell you what, champ. How about I take you for ice cream later?"

"Vanilla?"

"You bet."

"Deal."

"When, Sam?" I said, recognizing the need to pin him down. Kids were not assuaged by even the loftiest intentions. In case of a messy disappointment, I'd be left to mop up.

"I'm scrubbing in on a cholecystectomy now. There's a morbidity and mortality conference at five. And then there's a welcome reception for the Maliks. Cocktail thing at the faculty club. Should be over by seven, eight the latest."

"Bedtime is seven thirty, Sam. Guaranteed meltdown at seven forty-five. Remember?"

"I'll bring ice cream home then. You can have it with your story, buddy. How's that?"

Tyler wasn't letting him off that easily. "You ate the *R*, Daddy."

Sam hoisted our little one out of his chair and suspended him upside down.

"I stand guilty as charged, sir. And my punishment is to swing you like a whirligig."

"A great big curly whirligig?"

"Huge!"

Sam's cheeks reddened as they twirled. "Okay, tiger. That's it. Down you go."

"More whirligig, Daddy!"

"One."

With a whirring sound, Sam spun. Ty was a blur of flap-haired elation and broad upended smiles.

"That's it. Game's over. Have to go."

"One more?"

"No more."

"Just one, Daddy. Please!"

"Later." He shrugged on his lab coat over soft blue scrubs. "The cocktail thing for Malik, Em? I think it may be spouses, too."

"You think?"

"Check with LeeAnn, would you?"

"Ruthie has class. It's pretty short notice to find a sitter."

"Do it, Em. Please. And try to think of something nice we can get for them. Malik can make or break me. That's the truth."

· FOUR ·

The least little thing could trigger a lethal chain reaction. A butterfly flutters on a tiny Pacific atoll, altering the current of the air, setting the stage through a thousand intervening events for a catastrophic maelstrom thousands of miles away. The toe of a hiker's boot dislodges a pebble that bumps a rotted tree that falls on a precarious rock pile, and in a breath, the face of the mountain slides with monumental force to the sea.

The dozen three-year-olds in Tyler's preschool class sat on the floor in a ragged circle listening raptly to one such harrowing tale. Eager to block out the foolish prattling of a mosquito, an iguana blocked its ears with sticks. This odd sight frightened the other animals, causing them to panic and misbehave, with escalating consequences. At the action-packed conclusion, an owl was in such distress, it forgot its responsibility to wake the sun. According to the tale, from then on, mosquitoes the world over have flown around in a fog of remorseful anxiety, wondering whether people were still angry with them for that tragic day when the sun failed to rise.

"And that's why mosquitoes buzz in people's ears," Siena Gladwell said, closing the book on her lap. "We call that a *pourquoi* story, because *pourquoi* in French means "why." Can everyone say *pourquoi*?"

Most everyone tried. Jake Merson, the child I'd heard one of the mothers cruelly refer to as "Jake the mistake," was off in his own world as usual, inspecting the floor.

In the story circle, an eager hand waved. "Why is it called that, Miss Siena?"

"The story tries to explain why something happens the way it does, Addison. In this case, why mosquitoes buzz in people's ears."

Addison clutched her plump little arms. "Mosquitoes bite."

"Sometimes they do. But that's all part of nature."

"And bees bite," she offered.

"They can," Siena conceded. "But they also make delicious honey."

"And lions bite. And tigers," said a ringlet-studded child named Jean-Michel.

Marissa piped up. "Jake bites, too."

The child in question had predictably refused to sit like the others in the story circle, cross-legged on the floor. Jake scurried, lurched, and howled to a very different drummer. Now he stood at the window, studying his fingers as they flapped in a dusty swirl of light.

"We all try our very best," Siena said.

Marissa's lip jutted. "Jake hits, too. And pulls hair."

And breaks hearts, I wanted to say. Don't forget that.

This was the same Jake who had seemed achingly normal only a year ago. At his second birthday party, his parents had arranged a tour of the Central Park petting zoo. Afterward, there had been pony rides followed by pizza and a fire engine cake. On that crisp October day, Jake had been center stage, and the uncontested star. He'd worn the red plastic chief's hat proudly and sung a reasonable approximation of "Happy Birthday" to himself in clear, certain tones. Bravely, he had perched astride the pony as a young girl whose bouncy hairdo matched the animal's urged it around the corral.

Jake had seemed so wonderfully adventurous then, so self-possessed and secure. He hadn't been the least bit tentative like some of the others. Not thrown in a hot blue panic like Tyler, who had fairly leaped off the saddle screaming into my arms and stayed there, wailing inconsolably, until Jake, in a gesture of truly astonishing statesmanship, had allowed his mother to pass Tyler the chief's helmet.

That day, I'd felt a pang of envy at Jake's equanimity and a sharp twinge of guilt at my failure to make Tyler equally secure. But in a matter of weeks after that, Jake had started to unravel. He'd grown increasingly withdrawn, stopped talking, and slid with frightening rapidity downhill. Top experts had seen him and tested for everything imaginable. In the end they had termed the problem autism. It was "idiopathic," they said—of unknown origin. That easily and cruelly, a pin could pop your dreams.

Siena peered at the cluster of people who had gathered at the door. "Okay, everyone. Tyler's mom is here, and Addison's nanny and Olivia's mom and Jaden's nanny and Taesha's and Jake's and Zachary's dads. Time to get your things."

While the little ones made for their cubbies, Siena drew me aside.

"Tyler told me about Sam, Emma. I'm so sorry."

"What about Sam?"

"The choking. It must have been terrifying. Is he going to be all right?"

"Sam's perfectly fine."

Tyler barreled toward me with Amity Gladwell, Siena's butter blonde daughter, in tow. In class, my son could often be seen holding hands with Amity or sitting contentedly at her side. Though we hadn't discussed it, I strongly suspected that if Tyler were to discover that Mrs. Kalisher was not a serious marriage prospect, Amity Gladwell would do.

"Daddy's fine, Ty. He didn't choke."

"He could of," he said gravely.

"Could have is not the same as did. Save the stories for story time, okay?"

"Okay, Mama. Can Amity come play?"

"Fine with me," I said.

"How about a walk in the park?" Siena said. She was all for fresh air and exercise. My apartment, a juggernaut of shameful commercialism, mind-numbing electronics, violent storybooks, and poisonous processed foods, was a different story.

"A walk sounds perfect. Gorgeous day."

Tyler applauded with splayed fingers. "Can we go to the zoo?"

Siena smiled stiffly. Zoos to her were animal prisons, places where furry and feathered innocents were subjected to unwanted scrutiny and unconscionably restrained.

"We can see beautiful birds in the park flying freely, Tyler. And squirrels scampering happily up the trees."

"And pigeons," I added cheerily. "And if we're really lucky, rats."

Twice most weekdays I saw Siena during pickup and delivery at the door to the Little Ranger, a cooperative neighborhood preschool. Siena was the main teacher, and at intervals, like all the parents, I was scheduled to assist. At some point, against all reason, we'd become friends. Minus the mommy bond, a Krazy Glue of shared concern over ear infections, flammable pajamas, the state of the

city's public schools, and the like, we were about as different as two members of a species could be.

I ordered in, opened cans, shopped at Bloomingdale's
and had my hair cut by a fabulously anal-retentive Japanese
stylist at Maison Beauté. Siena was a passionate vegetarian
who composted on her tiny terrace, belonged to an organic
food collective, and prepared everything her family ate
from scratch. She wore scruffy secondhand clothing and,
on chilly days, a poncho she'd knit from knobby, sheep-
colored wool. A mass of dark frizz spiked with gray spilled
down her back from a sharp center part.

Outside, I steadied the umbrella stroller while Tyler
clambered aboard. To Siena, who had no end of weird con-
victions, a walk meant walking. Amity scurried along in
her mock leather baby Birkenstocks, struggling to match
her mother's robust strides.

"Is everything all right, Emma?"

"Sure, why?"

"You seem tense."

Siena read auras; I read *People* magazine.

"New neighbors."

Her penciled brow peaked. "They finally showed up?"

"Moved in this morning."

"And?"

I shrugged. "Sam's frantic to make a good impression.
Wants me to play Welcome Wagon. He'd give anything to
be accepted as one of Malik's fellows after he finishes his
surgical training next year."

"I can't imagine that would depend on how they feel
about you as neighbors."

"You'd hope not, but Sam says Malik gets a zillion ap-
plicants. I suppose anything could tip the balance."

"Well, I'm sure you're a wonderful neighbor, Emma.
Why wouldn't you be?"

I shrugged. "Who knows? Maybe they'll be put off by Ty's tantrums. Or mine. Maybe they'll think we're too friendly, or not friendly enough. Maybe they'll be offended by the pitiful quality of our trash."

Siena frowned. "You are definitely overthinking this."

"Probably so. Sam asked me to pick up a welcome gift for them, and fair enough. But I've been driving myself crazy, worried I'll screw up. What if I get flowers and someone's allergic? Or I get candy and there's a diabetic in the family? I keep thinking I'll make some idiot move and put a bullet in Sam's career."

"You can't go wrong with homemade baked goods. I can give you a yummy recipe for fruit bars made with pure juice and whole grains. Nothing artificial or refined."

"Thanks anyway. A recipe isn't going to do it."

"It's easy."

"For you maybe. But I can't bake. I'm hopeless at it. If you gave me a ticket to Tokyo, it wouldn't mean I'd be able to speak Japanese."

"I can make them for you if you like."

"You're sweet, but no, thanks. I'm a card-carrying grown-up. I should be able to handle this on my own."

"I'm sure you will, Emma. Just relax and the solution will come to you."

Siena was also prescient. As she made that pronouncement, we came to a gift shop crammed with overpriced, irrelevant things.

"You want to help? Give me a minute in there."

Her nose wrinkled. "Seriously?"

"You look at that window and see nothing but ridiculous junk with no redeemable features. Am I right?"

"Oh my, yes."

"Excellent. Be right out."

From everything I'd seen, Malik and his wife were as

close as possible to Siena's diametric opposite. Something she hated had an excellent chance of pleasing them. I narrowed it down to three possibilities and let Siena choose the one she found most distasteful. The winner was an ornate tin filled with scented soap. She thought it was useless, smelly, precious, and unthinkably expensive. Perfect, in other words.

We continued our trek toward the park. "The new people have a girl," Tyler said. "And no baby."

Siena, who had enlisted in my campaign to prepare him for the new arrival, took the bait. "Maybe they will have one someday."

He shook his head emphatically. "Nope. The girl doesn't want one."

"It's wonderful to have a brother or sister. Someone right there you can play with all the time. Amity loves having Grace for a big sister, don't you, honey?"

"Grace won't let me use her beads."

I smiled. "That's the first rule of cross-examination, my friend. Never ask a question unless you know what the answer will be."

"Tell Tyler who is your best friend, Amity."

"Grace is."

"You see? And I bet your baby sister or brother will be your very best friend, too."

"No."

I sighed. "I don't know. I might have to haul out the big guns. Get the complete three-DVD set of Learn How to Tolerate Your Baby Sibling."

Her smile didn't waver. Siena was impervious to my tweaking, one of the many things about her I admired. She was also wise, grounded, empathetic, thoughtful, and sincere. And she did her level best not to judge, even though I'm sure she believed I was dead wrong about most everything. Her way was to listen and affirm. She heard me. I had a right to my thoughts and feelings, no matter how tragically misguided they happened to be.

Perhaps that's why I found it so easy to confide in her. Letting Siena in on a vexing problem was like lancing a boil. Things didn't seem nearly as threatening or painful once the pressure was released and they were exposed to light and air.

It never occurred to me that buzzing in Siena's ear could set off a chain reaction with consequences so disastrous that even the wisest owl might lose it. The world as I knew it might sink in chaos, and the sun might forget to shine again for weeks.

· FIVE ·

Malik's welcome reception packed the faculty club and spilled onto the sidewalk and down the street. Entering, I searched in vain for Sam. The conversational din was deafening, the room overheated and close. I recognized several hospital luminaries whose pictures graced the cover of the monthly newsletter: the physician-in-chief; the head of development; the billionaire chairman of the board. Yielding to the current of the crowd, I drifted toward the bar and ordered a Perrier.

"Emma, hey."

The voice was thick with an excess of liquid cheer. It belonged to LeeAnn Argenbright, the surgery department's administrator. Among her many responsibilities, LeeAnn arranged for functions like this one and organized academic conferences. She juggled the on-call schedules and saw to it that Sam and the other physicians-in-training got their paychecks, benefits, and a suitable roof over their heads. To the residents, she served as the equivalent of a den mother, though she endeavored never to look the part.

Tonight, the den mother wore a short, slinky bordello red dress and five-inch ooh-baby heels.

"Emma! You're here!" she cleverly observed. "Sam told me he doubted you'd be able to get a sitter."

"Our usual one was busy. So were the backup and the backup's backup. I had to do some serious scrambling."

"Sam honestly doesn't get why you'd be even the least bit picky about who stays with the kid. Like what's the big deal?"

"You heard all that? All those words? From Sam?"

"Not the great communicator?"

"Not exactly."

She snorted. "Typical male."

LeeAnn tossed back her chardonnay and plunked the glass down loudly to summon a refill.

"They never learn," she went on. "Sam told me what happened when Trabert's daughter sat for you during the Christmas party. How the little twit fell so dead asleep you couldn't wake her, and she had the chain on, so Sam had to practically break down the door to get in. Jesus, Mary, and Joseph."

"To say the least."

"And there she was, out cold and snoring on the couch. I said she must have been on something. Sam said he thought it was probably an overdose of ugly pills." She cupped her mouth to catch a burst of inebriated giggles. "Male or no, he can be such a hoot."

The sitter's father was Dr. James Elvin Trabert, General's chief of psychiatry and a brilliant man. Her mother, Evelyn, was an esteemed art historian who lectured on Greek antiquities at the Metropolitan Museum. They were not at all the sort you'd expect to have a child so profoundly irresponsible. The incident had taught me a thing or two about the danger of making neat assumptions.

"It wasn't funny, LeeAnn, believe me. I kept imagining what might have happened if there'd been an emergency, a fire. You'd think after that Sam would understand there's good reason to be picky."

"You'd think, but you'd be wrong. I told you, kiddo. Men don't learn." Reaching out, she plucked a shrimp from a passing platter and popped it, dripping sauce, into her mouth. "Like I said, he's a typical male."

"Speaking of which, how's Rick?"

She blinked slowly. "Rick who?"

"Your fiancé, LeeAnn. That Rick."

Her fingers twirled vaguely. I caught the absence of her round, light-spitting rock.

"I know who you meant. He's history."

"Sorry to hear it."

"Don't be. Turned out he was cheating with one of his paralegals. And this four months before the wedding."

"Ouch."

"Tell me about it. The ink was barely dry on the Save the Date cards. I lost the frigging deposit on the dress."

"I don't know what to say."

"There's nothing to say. It's my own damned fault. I should have learned half a dozen sons of bitches ago." In a gulp, she downed her fresh glass of wine. "Men. Trust me. They're all the same."

"There are exceptions, LeeAnn. For example, Tyler is totally loyal. He would never cheat on Mrs. Kalisher, except with his girlfriend from school."

"You see? They're born that way. Speaking of which, there's yours."

Tracking her gaze, I spotted Sam in rapt conversation with a slim, pretty copper-streaked blonde. A practiced smile framed her sharp little teeth. Preening with raised arms, she tightened the band on her ponytail. Her back arched, baring the pale band of smooth flesh above her tight, low-riding pants. In lieu of stretch marks, her taut abdomen showcased a slim gold navel ring and a dainty blue butterfly tattoo. A ladder of ribs climbed to proud, perky breasts, the kind that beamed like a sign on a flourishing business, beckoning patrons inside.

Sam leaned toward her like a light-seeking plant, glued to her wide blue gaze. I ached to wipe off his broad, foolish grin with a strong solvent and plenty of elbow grease.

Anxiously, I smoothed the shapeless blue tunic that I had ironed, though not well. My cheeks flamed when I came to the elastic extender I had used to tether the gaping waistband of my pants. I had carried Tyler like a hobo's bundle, neatly wrapped in front. This baby had me busting out all over.

"Who's that with Sam?"

"One of our precious little new baby first-years. Name's Suzanne Stitch."

"Dr. Stitch the surgeon? With a name like that, she'd better be good."

"She's the best. Just ask her. Has a CV like you wouldn't believe. She looks even better on paper than she does in living color."

I coughed to clear the static from my voice. "I see."

"Well, I don't. The new residents' class always starts July first, but somehow, she wangled her way into the program a few weeks ago. Mighty strange, wouldn't you say?"

"I don't know. You said she has amazing qualifications."

"That she does." LeeAnn twirled a finger to summon yet another round. "For a snake."

"Why do you call her that?"

"Because that's what she is. Slithers up and sinks those fangs right in. I've seen her at it again and again in just the short time since she came on board."

"She's that obvious?"

She sniffed. "To me, sure. Women are smart enough to realize snakes are dangerous and disgusting. Men find them perfectly fascinating."

The baby kicked. "You think Sam's fascinated?"

She chuckled. "I told you what I think, Emma. Sam's exactly like the rest of them. A typical male. You see a snake around, you'd better lock your dumb puppy up."

I looked at LeeAnn, leaking bitterness through a hard, unfelt smile. She was a typical woman scorned, I told myself firmly. That, and drunk. She was still suffering the fresh sting of her fiancé's betrayal, seeking the comfort of my misery in her despair.

"Thanks for the heads-up," I told her. "See you later."

Cradling my medicine-ball belly, I angled through the crowd to where Sam and the fetching first-year stood.

"Hi, sweetheart."

Looping a hand around his neck, I drew him close. He swerved and offered his cheek. "You made it."

"So I did."

"How? Who?"

"Tyler's at Siena's. In baby detox. Learning the joys of wooden toys and homegrown sprouts."

"Oh." Sam ran a fidgety hand through his thick sandy hair that struck me as far too long and sexy for my own good.

"And you're . . . ?" I asked as sweetly as I could through the band of envy that was squeezing off my air. I had hoped to find glaring flaws at close range, but no such luck.

"Suzanne Stitch." She offered a cool, steady hand. "A surgical resident. And you?"

"Sorry," Sam said. "Suze. This is Emma. My wife."

Suze?

"How great to meet you!" she gushed. "Sam's told me so much about you and that terrific little boy of yours."

"Really? You two work together?"

"We do. My very first rotation and I had the incredible good fortune to land on his team. Sam's been absolutely wonderful, showing me the ropes, helping me settle in."

I swallowed hard. "Isn't that nice?"

"A total sweetheart. Can't imagine what I'd do without him." She peered up through a long fringe of lashes, each one curled and pointed like a hook.

"Oh, I'm sure you'd do just fine, Suzanne. I'm sure you will."

I looped a proprietary hand through the crook of Sam's elbow. His biceps tensed.

"Tyler said to be sure and remind you about his ice cream, Daddy. We're at bedtime minus thirty minutes, and counting."

He scowled. "Malik's scheduled to speak anytime. Won't be the end of the world if the ice cream waits for tomorrow."

"It will be to him, Sam."

I caught the shot of contempt he flashed at Little Suzy First-Year, and the mute promise of boundless forbearance she returned. Everything was so much simpler when you were simply running for office, before you had to do the actual job.

Jarring feedback shrieked through the speaker system. At the podium, Dr. Sterling Lazarus, the hospital's dapper, silver-haired president, raised a commanding hand. Slowly, the din of the crowd died out.

"Esteemed members of the board, staff and faculty, distinguished guests. It is my honor and privilege to present to you the second newest member of the New York General family. The youngest, I'm delighted to announce, is a bouncing baby girl, eight pounds, seven ounces, born less than an hour ago in our state-of-the-art delivery suite.

Mother and infant, I'm told, are doing fine. Dad had a little
rough going for a while, but he is expected to recover
fully."

Lazarus waited out the predicted laugh.

"I can assure you this is the first and last time any one of
us will see the remarkable Dr. Douglas Malik take second
prize at anything."

While Lazarus recited the endless litany of Malik's ac-
complishments, I studied young Dr. Stitch from the corner
of my eye. She had the sure, steady look of boundless confidence that came from a lifetime of easy accomplishment.
I couldn't imagine that she'd ever fallen off a bicycle, lost
the lead in a play, failed to be elected prom queen, had a zit
or a bad hair day, or even considered the possibility of being dumped.

Lazarus was winding down. "And now, without further
ado, it's my pleasure to introduce the new jewel in the
crown of our beloved institution: deputy physician-in-chief
and chair of the newly combined departments of cardiology and vascular and thoracic diseases, Dr. Douglas Anton
Malik."

For over two minutes, Malik basked in a rousing ova-
tion. For the next twenty-five, he held forth. In numbing
detail, he recounted his rise from what he described as
humble immigrant beginnings. He left no doubt that he
now perched in the firmament thanks to his ambition and
ability alone. Having agreed to grace New York General
with his stellar presence, he expected to see his ambitious
vision for the institution fulfilled. Above all, as President
Lazarus had so aptly noted at the outset, he would never,
by design or serendipity, be surpassed. Blessed with extraordinary talent, some people endeavored to build a
legacy. For Malik, nothing less than a major monument
would do.

Frieda Kalisher had come up beside me. Eagerly, she tapped my arm. With a contemptuous curl of her lip, she summed it up. God didn't only live upstairs from Sam and me. He resided above us all.

She beckoned me closer and rasped in my ear, "Don't look at him directly, Emma. It's like you told Tyler about the sun: you'll hurt your eyes."

"He does seem awfully big for a little man," I whispered back.

"Awfully little for a big man, too." With a sly grin, she turned to leave.

Anxiously, I eyed my watch. Almost a quarter to eight. By now, Tyler would be out of steam and self-control, running on noxious fumes. I could all but hear him screaming for his daddy and ice cream, angrily rejecting a substitute of home-cultured yogurt capped by organic raisins and nuts. Poor Siena. I'm sure her kids threw much quieter, gentler, sweeter tantrums.

Finally, Malik relinquished the podium, stepping down to the thunder of frenzied applause.

As he did, I clutched Sam's wrist. "Let's go!"

His eyed rolled. "Christ, Emma. Would you lighten up?"

"All right. Forget it. I'll go."

Young Dr. Perky Boobs gave me the kind of look you'd bestow on a three-legged dog. Then she smiled at my husband adoringly.

"Go on, Sam. It's fine. There's no way any of us are getting anywhere near Malik tonight."

He nodded. When she said it, leaving sounded perfectly reasonable.

"Okay, Suze. See you tomorrow, then."

"You bet," she said. "I'll be at rounds. First thing."

· S I X ·

"**Knock-knock.**"

Through my crimped lids, I made out Tyler's silhouette: a sturdy little fireplug crowned by owl eyes and Prince Valiant hair.

"What?"

"Not *what*, Mama. You're supposed to say Who's there?"

"Whoever's there is supposed to be sleeping."

"Come on. Say Who's there?"

"Who's there?" I croaked groggily.

"Orange."

"Orange who?"

"Orange you gonna give me a big fat smackeroo?"

"It's the middle of the night, baby. Go back to bed and I'll give you twelve big fat smackeroos in the morning. I'll give you all the smackeroos you want once it's light outside."

"But I slept already. I'm done."

"Well, I'm not. Go rest in bed if you can't sleep. Do what they said about Tinkerbell. Think happy thoughts."

Sleep beckoned, urging me back to a clear blue undulating dream. *I'm swimming near a coral reef of huge lacy fans and stately staghorn, surrounded by schools of bright darting fish. Skittering fishlike myself, I feel joyously lithe and buoyant. My spine is a rippling trill, my skin melded with the water, soft as the inside of a baby's cheek, bathed in the sensuous deep. I come upon a dark place steeped in mystery. An irresistible urge draws me to enter. Inside, I'm hopelessly disoriented. Lost in a murky, uncertain space. Something fearsome glides close. Sharply, it raps my shoulder—twice.*

"Knock-knock."

"Whoever is still there had better be back in his bed by the time I count to three. One . . . two . . ."

My count matched the languid tides of Sam's breathing. He lay oblivious, lost in the sleep of the just. Or was it that he just didn't care? I shook him firmly. It was his turn to wrangle our budding little insomniac. Given Tyler's growing recent resistance to an uninterrupted night's sleep, my on-call schedule had far surpassed his.

"Come on, Mama. I said knock-knock."

"And I said night-night."

In the thrumming darkness my voice sounded brittle and outsized. My thin veneer of patience was cracked and crumbling.

"Sam," I urged. "You're it tonight, remember? Come on, honey. Deal's a deal, so deal with this. Please!"

Frowning in his sleep, he flipped onto his stomach and bashed the pillow. I imagined him resuscitating a patient in his heroic imagination, raising a shock-faced flatliner from the dead. How could a nagging blimp and a nocturnal toddler hope to compete with that?

Tyler gripped the sheets and scrabbled onto the bed. In a flash, he was in his favorite spot in the exact center of the mattress between us, burrowed under the blankets, beaming proudly.

"No, you don't, Mr. Monkey Face. You know the rules. As long as it's nighttime, you are to stay in your very own, incredibly cool, big boy bed."

"No."

"Yes."

His chin rumpled. "I can't."

"Because?"

"Because my big boy bed's uncomfortable."

"Since when?"

"Since someone wetted it."

"Someone did that, did they?"

I slipped my hand beneath his round little rump, now plastered with the sodden bottoms of his favorite Thomas the Tank Engine pajamas. "And who, might I ask, would do a rude, inconsiderate thing like that?"

He shrugged. "It wasn't my fault, Mama. Honest. Don't be mad."

"I'm not mad, sweetheart. Don't worry. Happens in the best of families." I shook my husband even harder. "Sam!"

Nothing.

"I call that a highly unfavorable prognosis, Dr. Colten," I said.

"What's that mean?"

"It means Daddy plans to stay asleep."

"That's okay, Mom. I don't mind you."

"Back at you, sweetie. But it's Daddy's turn. Dr. Colten," I said in the crisp nasal twang of the page operator. "Dr. Samuel Colten, report to the nursery *STAT*!"

Still nothing.

Wearily, I slogged out of bed. Tyler's plaid sheets, the

ones I'd washed in the basement that very morning, were still heaped in the laundry basket. Cradling a pillowcase and a pair of his jeans, he padded behind me to his room, a cluttered postage stamp we'd had partitioned from the living room. Wincing at the ripe ammonia smell, I stripped off his soaked linens, wiped down the mattress cover, and remade the bed. Then, as he stood in grudging compliance, I stripped, dried, and redressed him.

"Okay, champ. All set. Hop in."

I drew the quilt to his chin and positioned his prize stuffed Dalmatians, Sebastian and Fred, to guard the pillow. In turn I loudly kissed his forehead, nose, and chin, followed by his left cheek and his right. If I dared any deviation from that sacred pattern, the rules said I'd have to start again.

"Okay, monkey. See you in the morning. Over and out."

"No, wait! I have another knock-knock joke."

"One, and that's it."

"Okay. Here goes." He frowned.

"I'm waiting, Tyler."

"You start."

"Knock-knock."

"Who's there?"

"Tom Thumb."

"Tom Thumb who?"

"It's Tom Thumb-body went night-night."

I flipped off the Yankees logo lamp on his nightstand.

"Wait!" He gripped my hand like someone drowning. "I forgot to tell you."

"We agreed to one more knock-knock joke, and that's it."

"But it's really important, Mama."

I sighed. "It had better be."

"The new big little girl called her mommy a bad word, and her mommy cried."

"Oh, really? And when was that?"

He frowned. "Yesterday?"

"I don't think so."

"Another day, then."

"No stories, Ty. Remember?"

His face lit as he deftly changed course. "Know what Amity gets for dinner?"

"What?"

"Guess."

I tucked him tighter, tracing his compact form. "Hmmm. Let me think. Spaghetti?"

"Nope."

"Fried fillet of elephant?"

"No," he giggled. "Guess again."

"I've got it. Tree stump on a bun with fried potatoes."

"No. Toe food."

"You mean tofu?"

"Ick," he said. "Toe food's gross!"

"No, it's not, Ty. Tofu is made from soybeans. It can be very tasty, and good for you besides."

"Not for me. No way. Yuck!"

"Make you a deal. You go right to sleep and I won't make you eat any tofu."

"I don't want to sleep. I want to watch Backyardigans and Mr. Moose."

"The television's sleeping, cutie. Everyone is."

"Then read me a book!"

"That's it, Tyler! Enough! You're to go to sleep, right now, or I swear you'll be in time-out eating tofu for a year!"

My little psychotic outburst did the trick. He dove under his covers, hiding all but a doubloon of golden hair.

With a weighty sigh, I settled back in bed, next to the warm sleeping lump that was—as Mrs. Kalisher put it— *my* Sam. Normally, we fit together like parts of a contoured whole, but lately, unsettling gaps had formed around my outsized bumps and declivities.

Then again, maybe the off-putting bumps and depressions were his. Medical school had been bad enough. Surgical training was a giant vacuum that sucked you up completely. I understood this. And I'd signed on. But the fact was I missed Sam. I missed us. I hated standing outside his life with my nose pressed to the glass, wishing he'd ask me in.

"Lucky you're cute, Dr. Colten," I said. "Lucky murder is so not my thing."

"You can't get a vein, do a cut-down," he muttered. "Act like a doctor, for chrissakes."

"Bet you don't talk to *Suze* that way, Sam. Bet you're Dr. Sweet and Understanding when it comes to her."

As I turned on my back, assuming the time-honored beached whale position of advanced pregnancy, my heart began thudding strangely. A moment later, I became conscious of the source. A harsh flurry of footsteps sounded overhead. Low rumbling voices followed.

Though the words were indistinct, the fury behind them was unmistakable. A plaintive piccolo clashed with the cold, strident bass. The bass boomed louder, and the piccolo climbed to a plaintive, terrified shrill.

Suddenly everything went still. Through the long, bristling silence that followed, I lay unmoving.

When the voices started up again, I propped on my elbows and strained to make out what they were saying.

The deep voice boomed, "Do you understand me? Do you?"

"Stop!"

"You will do as I say."

"All right," the little girl wailed. "I will, Daddy. I'll be good."

From our visits during the apartment's construction and preliminary decorating phases, I knew that the rooms directly above ours had been converted into the suite for Malik's child. A soft-spoken interior designer had shown me watercolor renderings of the proposed space, a sprawling fantasy filled with ballerina motifs. There would be a popcorn machine and ballet barre in the playroom. Remote-controlled window shades and lights. Speakers buried in the walls would carry surround sound for the sixty-inch plasma TV. The guest room would double as a place for the little girl to do her homework, with a Murphy bed hidden behind ornately framed shelves.

Vividly, I pictured the child's bedroom now, fitted with the antique canopy bed and matching furnishings I had watched the movers haul from the truck. I imagined the Maliks' diminutive daughter huddled in that bed, shrinking against the pillows from her father's terrifying wrath.

"You'll do exactly as I say!" Malik bellowed.

"Hear that, Sam? Sounds like your precious Dr. High-and-Mighty is in no danger of being crowned father of the year."

"What's the hematocrit?" he murmured in fretful delirium. "Better give him an auto unit. STAT."

Yawning, I settled back. "I must say it makes me feel better about merely threatening Tyler with healthy food."

"Don't forget to get a culture from the drain."

"Speaking of sleep deprivation," I said dreamily. "Speaking of becoming a big fat grumpy annoyance to myself and others."

Gently, I leaned over, lifted the thick hair that curled over the collar of Sam's T-shirt, and kissed his neck. My blood froze at the scent of my favorite musky aftershave, the one he slapped on for adult playtime, and never, I'd thought, for work.

A spike of anxious fear shot through me. "Speaking of flat-bellied first-years with flotation tits," I said, "you so much as think of taking up with Little Suzy Home-Wrecker, and I guarantee you'll have to pee sitting down."

Sam rolled to face me and drew me close. "Love you, Em."

"You too, shit head."

His lips smacked. " 'Night, sweetie."

"Sleep tight, Sam. Don't let the snakes bite. Watch those dreams."

· SEVEN ·

A sketched likeness relies on a few basic elements: brights, shadows, angles, planes, and curves. Reticent darks recede while pale tones preen in the foreground. Beauty hinges on simple arithmetic. Ratio and symmetry are either multiplied by the presence of an indefinable spark or divided by its unfortunate absence. The eye and instrument of the beholder simply runs the calculation. My job was to get the equation right.

Normally, I loved studying faces, coaxing their essence onto a broad sheet of bristol board. Only rarely did I feel utterly defeated by a subject. But it happened.

Binnie Palliser was shaping up to be one of those vexing failures. She was a homely little thing with a magpie nose, eyes the murky brown of beef stew, and a mouth reminiscent of a pothole. She would not be still, not even for the instant required to capture a decent reference photo. I was tempted to outline the child in jerky striations to capture her twitchy unease. But of course, I did not. Referrals, small classes, and private lessons had kept me gainfully occupied since Tyler's birth, when I gave up my full-time teaching slot at the Parsons School of Design to spend more time at home. Given college and medical school loans and New York City prices, it would be tough for us to get by on Sam's salary alone.

Awkwardly, I scrambled around the room after Binnie, trying every way I could think of to snap a usable shot, snagging frame after frame of her blurred form or the wisp-haired back of her bulb-shaped head.

"Sorry, Emma. She really hates having her picture taken," her mother said. "Sometimes the sight of the camera is enough to make her scream."

I went to my drawing table and tried to render a rapid sketch, something I could later refine. But Binnie's perpetual motion defeated me again. The lines veered and overlapped in a jumbled mess. Tearing off the sheet, I began again, to no better result.

"I don't know, Jillian. Maybe we should wait until she's older."

"She's an infant. It's not up to her."

"I don't think she sees it that way."

"Then I'll have to convince her."

Jillian Palliser, a brilliant molecular biologist at General with a major research grant from the NIH, dropped to all fours in her tailored tweed suit and did a truly uncanny impression of a truffle-rooting pig.

That propelled her little ten-month-old into gales of hilarity punctuated by extravagant, convulsive hiccups. The baby, who had spent the past hour cruising from chair to sofa to wall to table to chair, lost her balance and flopped backward on the rug. The elaborate skirt and petticoat of her smocked pink dress flew up over her head. Guiltily, I viewed this as an improvement.

Jillian set the child back on her flat, stubby feet. While

she was recovering from the shock of the fall, mustering the breath to express her outrage, I snapped a burst of pictures.

Scrolling through them quickly, I was relieved to find that they would do. Jillian, elegant and attractive by most anyone's definition, wanted a portrait of the baby seated beside her on a slatted garden bench against a background on the order of Monet's Giverny. There would be plenty of lovely distractions from the one little weed.

Binnie started to scream. Jillian scooped her up onto a jutting hip. In soothing rhythm, she jiggled and hummed. The baby quieted, went pale, and spewed her lunch.

Unruffled, the scientist plucked a burp cloth from her diaper bag and blotted the worst of the mess. Rising, she brushed the incident off her graceful hands.

"There. I bet you feel better now. Nasty allergies. Being a baby is no picnic, is it, pumpkin?"

"True, and then you get to grow up."

"When's the new one due, Emma?"

"A couple of months, and I'm so huge. Even my nose looks pregnant. Hard to imagine what I'll be like at the end."

"I was like that, with my first." A shadow crossed her expression.

"I didn't know you had an older child." I'd met her at the gym we'd both belonged to before Tyler was born. We'd gotten to be smiling acquaintances, but our conversation had been typical gym talk, about places to eat.

She averted her gaze. "Gordon died two years ago, of SIDS."

"I'm so sorry."

Now she eyed me guiltily. "I'm the one who should be sorry. Please forgive me, Emma. I used to hate the people who told me horror stories when I was pregnant. And here I've turned into one of them."

"Not at all. It's the fact, not a horror story. You went

through something incredibly difficult. It's natural to have it on your mind."

"Nevertheless, not many people consider it a topic for polite conversation, including me. Don't worry. Yours will be fine."

I touched mine reflexively. "Sure."

Her look was rueful. "Anyway, it's not the kind of thing that makes for good hospital gossip. In the hallowed halls of medicine it's all about who's screwing who."

"Oh? Who is?"

"Nothing new or exciting at the moment. Except for the palace coup in Cardiology."

"Dr. Malik's appointment, you mean?"

"That's Act Two. The opening shocker was when they booted Norm Stryker out the door."

"They did? Sam told me Stryker stepped down."

She chuckled dryly. "As would anyone, if they were pushed hard enough from behind."

"But why? Everyone loved Stryker. The department's in great shape and growing."

The baby started wailing again. Jillian hefted her up in the air like a victor's trophy, and the tears turned to cooing smiles.

"Powers that be aren't talking. I suppose they're anxious to keep it close to the vest," she went on. "But as I understand, Doug Malik was behind it."

"How?"

"He let it be known he wanted to take over the department at General, and it had to be now. Norm Stryker is sixty-three. I suppose Lazarus and company presumed he would be stepping down soon enough, and they didn't want to lose the chance to get Doug Malik here. So bye-bye, Norm Stryker."

Binnie waved bye-bye, too.

"But why the rush? I'm sure the Cleveland Clinic would have done anything to keep Malik on, especially if he had another firm offer to play them against. He could have waited until Stryker retired and demanded the moon in the meantime."

She shrugged. "All true, which is why logic suggests he had some pressing reason to want to get away quickly."

"Like what?"

"There's been plenty of speculation. Malik has quite the reputation as a ladies' man. Also, they say he can play a little fast and loose when it comes to fattening his wallet, but so far, no one's come up with any hard facts."

"Interesting."

"Isn't it, though?" She set the baby down.

"If you hear anything more on that, I'd love to know."

"If I do, you will. Any chance you can have the portrait ready in a month? I'd love to have it in time to give to Graham for a birthday gift."

"Shouldn't be a problem. Do you have time for me to take some shots of you?"

She squinted at her watch. "I'm fine for fifteen minutes or so. If you're okay with more of Miss Hell on Wheels."

"Sure."

I had hauled out a box of Tyler's outgrown toys to entertain the baby, and in record time, she'd strewn the plush and pull toys, baby instruments, and board books all over the room. I tried to imagine what magic I might find to entertain her while I focused on her mother.

Jillian Palliser happened on the answer. From the diaper bag, she extracted a ring of plastic keys, the sort you could buy for a dollar or two in any drugstore.

Eagerly, the little one stretched out a plump dimpled hand. "Kah kee."

"Car keys! That's right. There you go, lovey dove."

Binnie dropped on her bottom and studied the prize intently. Her eyes lit and her mouth stretched in a broad, engaging grin.

Captivated, her mother perched on the floor beside her.

"That's Mommy's little love. That's my precious darling baby girl."

On a fresh sheet of paper, I sketched them quickly with bold, simple lines. They formed the perfect parent/child composition: a cozy bower in the shape of a painfully lopsided heart.

· E I G H T ·

Despite the soft spring weather, Mrs. Kalisher huddled in a thick white cabled cardigan and knit cap. Her bony arms were tightly folded. Her wizened features scrunched against a playful, lilac-scented breeze.

"I'm every bit as modern as the next person, Emma. But trust me, general surgery is not for girls."

"Because?"

"Because general surgeons are a whole different story, a bunch of roosters showing off their cock-a-doodle-doos."

"Worse than other surgical specialties, you think?"

"Definitely." She enumerated on her knob-knuckled fingers. "Gyn is fine for a girl to go into. Also derm. Ophthalmology. Head and neck. Even orthopedics and plastics can be reasonable, depending. Urology, too, though I must say the whole urine thing is not my cup of tea."

"I'm definitely with you on that."

"Mama. Auntie Frieda. Look!"

Tyler sat astride one of the squat brass elephants that passed in our local park for sculpted art. He was having a grand time barking orders, whipping the pachyderm's head with a gnarled little twig.

"Go, Dumbo. Move it, boy! Git!"

"Don't hurt the nice elephant, sweetie. Be gentle."

"I am, Mama." Whack!

"Even neuro, if she happens to be a glutton for punishment," Frieda mused. "Things can get pretty depressing, comes to brains. But not general surgery, for heaven's sake. Mucking around in guts and entrails. You ask me, that's every bit as ridiculous as a girl going off to battle in the Marines."

"I hate to break it to you, Mrs. K., but plenty of women do exactly that."

"The fact that they do it doesn't make it sensible, Emma. People risk their lives doing all sorts of crazy things."

"Practicing general surgery is not exactly life-threatening."

"Maybe not, but life is far from the only important thing a girl has to lose. My mother always told me to consider the consequences. Live as if everything you do could wind up on the cover of the *New York Times*, she used to say."

" 'Woman Becomes General Surgeon'? I don't think that's going to make headlines anytime soon."

"Doesn't matter. That young resident of Sam's is trying to be one of the boys, which makes no sense at all. She has to be drowning in testosterone."

"Not from what I saw."

"That's only the package, sweetheart. Underneath I bet you she has a pair of whatchamawhosies the size of France."

"If she does, Sam doesn't seem to mind in the least."

"Which upset you terribly, Emma. I could see. That's why I'm bringing it up."

"Wouldn't it upset you? Here I am, about as fetching as the Pillsbury Doughboy, and Sam gets to play doctor all day every day with that."

"First of all, you look wonderful. Glowing."

"Sure. Like a great big illuminated blimp."

"Nonsense. Pregnant is beautiful, especially on you. And secondly, it doesn't mean a thing. There's no harm in window-shopping."

"No? Isn't that exactly how people wind up buying things they didn't even know they wanted?"

Tyler was headed toward the swings. Rising from the bench, we slowly trailed him.

"Your Sam's way too smart to buy what he doesn't need and certainly can't afford. Plus, he knows the difference between fancy wrapping paper and what's inside the box. Believe me. I'm a wonderful judge of character, and Sam's not the roving eye type."

I trundled beside her. "Hope you're right."

"I am, Emma. So happens I'm something of an expert on the subject. You may not know this, but my Leonard was extremely handsome in his day. Like a movie star."

"He was. I've seen the pictures."

"Pictures don't do him justice. People used to say he reminded them of a Jewish Tyrone Power. Rugged. And those eyes."

"The eyes will get you every time." Sam's were a steely mesmerizing blue.

"So I'm sure you won't be surprised to hear he got plenty of attention from the ladies. The nurses were all over him like flies. Patients, too."

"Really? I hadn't even thought about patients. A whole new pack of competitors to fret about. Joy, joy."

Her eyes rolled. "Patients were the worst. I'll never forget this one woman, Lila Lenane. Every couple of weeks, she'd make an appointment to come in and see Leonard with a pain in her something or other. Anything to get a little time with him. And let me tell you, she was built. Amazing they could read her X-rays through those giant hoohahs and whoop-de-doos."

"And you honestly didn't feel threatened?"

"For a while, I'll admit I did. But then, one night, I decided to take the bull by the horns."

"Interesting way to put it."

"I cooked up a special candlelight dinner with all Leonard's favorites: baby lamb chops, twice-baked potatoes, creamed spinach, and blueberry pie. While we ate, I had a long heart-to-heart with Leonard about her. I explained how Lila chasing him like that made me uncomfortable. I said I didn't like the idea of him being tempted all the time."

"No. Me neither."

She went coy. "And you know what he said?"

"No. What?"

"He said *good*. He'd been jealous of me plenty of times. He said he'd caught other men giving me the once-over, and it made him nervous as a cat. He was pleased as punch to know that I could be jealous, too. Made him know I cared."

"So talking about it worked."

"Like a charm. A word can be worth a thousand pictures, if you ask me."

"Thanks. But it was different for you, Mrs. K. You were a knockout. Still are, in fact. Ask my son."

She flapped a hand. "What I am is old as dust. So far over the hill, I can't even look back and see it anymore."

"And what I am is big as a house. So big I can't look down and see my toes."

"You're a beauty, Emma. Inside and out." Her hand flew to her mouth. "Oh, my God!"

"What?"

Turning, I saw Tyler charging in a mindless mad dash for the swings. An older boy had just leaped down from a coveted sling seat, and it was veering wildly.

"Tyler, no!" I shouted.

Heedless, he ran all out, legs churning, arms flailing wide.

"Stop!"

Prickling fear washed over me. The swing had sharp metal brackets, lashing chains, cruel edges that could gouge my baby's eye. With ballistic force, the seat caromed off the metal side post and shot toward him on a dead-on, head-cracking collision course.

"Watch out!"

Suddenly, he stopped as if he'd hit a wall. Lurching backward, he crumpled to the ground. Frantically, I raced over and scooped him in my arms. I caught the fearsome preface to a scream: a quivering filament of gathering rage.

"Shh, baby. Easy. Talk to me. Where does it hurt?"

The screech erupted. He went stiff. Angry blotches mottled his skin.

"Let go of me!" He struggled to break free.

"Wait, sweetie. Easy. Let me make sure you're okay." I checked for blood and bruises. I Braille-read his familiar contours and tested his joints and limbs.

"Stop! Let me go!"

"Okay, Ty. Calm down. You seem fine."

In a fury, he wriggled out of my grasp.

"Be careful!" I called as he dashed off.

Trembling, I knelt to retrieve the contents of my purse, which I'd dropped in my haste. The small mirror I carried had shattered. My fractured image looked shaken and pale.

Mrs. Kalisher fanned herself with a hand.

"It's not the years that age you, Emma. It's the children."

The breath I'd been holding escaped in a ragged rush. "That's the truth."

She clapped her forehead. "Oh, Lordy. What's he up to now?"

Tracking her gaze, I watched Tyler running full out with his head cocked like an incensed bull.

"No!" he cried. "Stoppit! It's mine!"

The object of his rage, a diminutive girl with long dark hair, stood with a hand on the now becalmed swing, staring off distractedly. His unexpected shove sent her sprawling. On the way down, her face bashed the metal end post with a sickening thud.

Rushing over, I gripped Tyler's arms.

"No pushing!"

"She was taking the swing away," he said indignantly. "It's my turn!"

"Not anymore, it isn't. Playground's over, mister. People who push are not allowed. You're going home, right now, for a time-out!"

"No time-out," he wailed. "It's not fair!"

Still clutching him, I moved nearer the fallen girl. "I'm so sorry. Are you okay?"

I caught the sharp, pained intake of her breath. A livid swelling bloomed beneath her eye.

"Is someone here with you?"

She stared wide-eyed. Mute.

"Want me to call someone? Do you need a doctor?"

She turned away and buried her face in her hands. Wordlessly, she scrambled to her feet, ran to the gate, and slipped out.

"Wait! Please."

She raced across the street as an oncoming car rumbled by, narrowly missing her. The driver leaned in a fury on the horn.

In a breath, she was around the corner, down the block, out of sight.

"Wait!"

"It's all right, Emma," Mrs. Kalisher soothed. "If she can run like that, she can't be badly hurt."

"Did you see that shiner? I feel absolutely awful."

She shrugged. "Things happen."

Clearly, Tyler had suffered no ill aftereffects. "Look, Mama. There's the ice cream truck. Can I have some vanilla in a cup?"

"Sorry, Charlie. Boys who push do not get special treats."

He giggled. "I'm not Charlie. I'm Tyler."

"Whatever your name is, there'll be no ice cream for you today. Did you see what happened to that girl you pushed? She had a big nasty boo-boo near her eye."

"It wasn't a girl, Mama. She was a lady."

"That's not the issue, kiddo. You pushed, and someone got hurt, which is definitely not okay."

"But it was my turn on the swing. And she tooked it."

"I told you, people are not for hitting or pushing or hurting in any way."

"It was my swing. It's not fair."

"Fair or not, pushing is not the answer. That's what I want you to think about during time-out."

Hopefully, he peered up at Mrs. Kalisher. "Auntie Frieda? Can I come for a play date at your house?"

"When you're not in hot water, absolutely."

"I'm not. Look. I'm not wet at all."

Her kindly smile erased a decade. "That's the thing about hot water, darling. Sometimes, we can be in it up to our eyeballs, and not have the first idea."

· N I N E ·

Drawing on Mrs. Kalisher's wisdom, I set the stage for
a healing heart-to-heart with Sam. I ordered dim sum,
Grand Marnier shrimp, and Peking duck, the most elegant
of the takeout dishes from our favorite Chinese restaurant.
As soon as Tyler fell asleep, I donned the pup tent that now
served as my "little" black dress, dabbed on lip gloss and
mascara, and swept up my hair. Finally, I set our tiny table,
lit candles, doused the lights, and waited for the sound of
Sam's approach.

And waited.

Restless, I straightened the ever-growing stack of un-
read magazines, emptied the dishwasher, and sorted clean
socks. Flipping on the light behind me, I sat at my drawing
table and worked on the Palliser portrait, trying to capture
the baby's soft, seeking hands.

After most of an hour had passed, I dialed Sam's cell
phone. Instantly, I was bounced to voice mail, which meant
he had the ringer off. Next, I sent a text message. When he

was in lectures or conferences, he often checked his Black-Berry. But this time there was no response.

I tried his beeper. When a triple pulse confirmed that the summons had gotten through, I typed in our number.

He didn't call.

Again, I consulted the copy of his schedule taped to the refrigerator and confirmed that he was off tonight. Had he needed to switch with one of the other residents or been held up for some reason, he typically let me know. The food and I were growing rather cold.

Too anxious to work, I turned off the lamp and stared out the window. An ambulance drove by in eerie silence. A shirtless jogger bobbed in place on the corner, waiting for the light to change. A crush of teenagers passed in a loud, edgy mass.

My mood boomeranged between outrage and alarm. I'd long harbored an unspoken fear of something going terribly wrong for Sam in the operating room. He had never lost a patient, but that was an omnipresent hazard of what he did. I worried that he wouldn't be able to handle it if someone died on his watch, that his confidence could be shattered beyond repair. Or maybe I was projecting. I couldn't fathom how anyone actually mustered the nerve to cut through living flesh and probe beyond. I took no small comfort in the thought that no one had ever perished of a lousy likeness.

Then again, plenty of marriages had gone the way of a wandering eye, and that failed to comfort me in the least. Unbidden images taunted me: Sam with "Suze." Limbs twined, shallow-breathed, lust-fogged brains flying on pleasure-driven autopilot. I imagined them in the on-call room, in the supply closet, recklessly groping on a vacant patient bed. I imagined them in a parked car in the lot, pressed in frenzied urgency against a dim, empty corridor wall.

I had Sam paged. An instant later, the summons rever-
berated through the loudspeaker.

"Dr. Samuel Colten. Dial 3158. Dr. Colten."

More than two minutes passed before the operator came
back on the line. "Dr. Colten doesn't answer, miss. Would
you like me to try the resident on call?"

"No, thanks."

What I wanted her to do was find Sam. I wanted her to
track him down immediately, so I could make sure he was
all right, melt in soothing relief, and then shoot him.

The long white candles had burned to guttering stumps.
One and then the other flamed out in the molten wax pool
with a pungent wisp. Thick gloom settled. Standing in the
dark at the kitchen sink, I ate from the paper cartons, trying
to stanch the acid churning in my gut. I swallowed dry-
mouthed, tasting nothing. Dumb sum. Peking yuck.

My eyes pooled with bitter tears. Angrily, I swiped
them away. Feeling sorry for myself wasn't nearly as useful or satisfying as counting all the lovely ways I could dis-
member "my" Sam.

I traded my dress for an outsized T-shirt, washed my
face, and brushed out my hair. Back in the living room, I
curled up on the couch to stew in comfort. A moment later,
Sam's key clacked in the lock.

He loomed in lanky silhouette. "Why so dark in here,
Em? Having a séance?"

"No. Waiting for you. And waiting. And waiting. Where
have you been?"

"Busy, crazy. You know how it is."

"I don't actually. Why don't you tell me?"

"Meetings. Department stuff. Mind if we pass on the
blow-by-blow? Bad enough going through it once."

"Fine. I'd just like to know what kept you so late and why
you didn't bother to call. I expected you two hours ago."

His hands shot up. "Would you stop? Damn it, Emma. The last thing I need right now is an inquisition. I've been going nonstop since six this morning."

Struggling to rein in my runaway temper, I blew a slow, ragged breath. "I know. And so have I. That's why I planned a special dinner. So we'd have a chance to relax and talk for a change."

He flipped the three-way bulbs on the pole lamp to maximum, flooding the room with dislocating light. Scowling, he eyed the row of open takeout cartons on the counter, half-eaten, stained with sauce.

"You make it sound like you spent the whole day sweating over a hot stove, for chrissakes. You made a phone call."

Tyler stirred beyond the thin wall that served as a partition. Quickly, I turned the lamp down.

Sam puffed his lips. "Pardon me for living."

"It was hard enough getting him to bed, Sam. I don't want to wake him."

"You want the kid to sleep? Stop coddling him."

"Coddling him? Tell me you didn't say that."

"You do, Em. You let him get away with murder."

"How in the hell would you know? You're never here!"

"Would you keep it down!" he rasped, tamping the air. "You want Malik to hear you?"

"Disturb His Majesty? Heaven forbid."

"Yes, heaven forbid. You have no idea what I've been through trying to make a good impression on him. I don't need him thinking I've got a screaming nutcase for a wife."

"Is that what you were off doing? Kissing the Lord's behind?"

"I'm not answering that."

"No? If not Malik, who were you with? Suze?"

"Fuck you!"

Speechless, I stared at him.

His jaw twitched. "You want a civil answer? Ask a civil question."

Tyler's door squealed open. In he padded, clutching a stuffed Dalmatian beneath each arm.

"Mama?" His voice was tiny, scared. "How come everybody's mad?"

"It's okay, champ," Sam said. "Everything's fine."

"Sorry if we bothered you, sweetie. Go back to bed."

"But Sebastian and Fred are thirsty."

"It's sleep time. They can have a drink in the morning."

"Fred's throat hurts."

"Stuffed dogs don't have throats."

"Fred does. Look." With an outstretched tongue, he showed me his.

"Daddy knows all about throats. Talk about it with him. I'm going to bed."

I lay awake in the dark, numb, heart thudding sickly, wondering how things could slide so terribly off the rails. Sam and I used to move in easy synchrony. Now we could barely keep from stomping each other's toes.

"But I can't, Daddy," I heard Tyler whine. "There's a ghost."

"There's no such thing. Now back to bed."

"The ghost is *in* my bed. You have to get it out."

"Stop the nonsense." Sam's voice was climbing a rope of frustration, growing sharp and shrill. "I mean it. Either you go to sleep right now, or there'll be no watching videos for a week."

"You know what, Daddy?" he said sweetly. "When I grow up, I'm gonna be a doctor."

"We'll talk about it in the morning."

"I'm gonna be a surgery guy like you."

"I thought you said surgery was icky."

"That's when I was little."

"I see. Well, you know what surgery guys need? Lots and lots of sleep."

"I better sleep with you and Mama, then."

"No way, José."

"But I have to," he wailed. "The ghost keeps waking me up!"

"Then no DVDs for the ghost either."

"Make it go away, Daddy. Please."

"Out, ghost. Get lost now. Scram!" Sam made a low ululating noise. "Okay, tiger. No answer, which means all clear. Now back to bed."

"First you have to get rid of the troll."

"No, Tyler. No more."

"Please!"

A truly magic word. Three more times, Sam went through the bed-cleansing ritual, evicting trolls, goblins, and dragons in turn. Giving orders and then giving in. I could picture him wrapped in his shaggy-haired entirety around Tyler's little finger.

And he said I coddled the kid.

"That's it, tiger. The bed's all empty and ready for you."

"No, Daddy. There's still the gorilla and the kidnapper and the mean guy."

"If you don't get to bed—this minute—the mean guy is going to be me!"

Tyler giggled. I heard the thump as he flopped on the mattress. Sam bid good night to Sebastian and Fred.

Lying on my side with my back to the door, I heard him come in.

"Em? You awake?"

I didn't answer. I couldn't find the words.

Treading softly, he sat beside me. The mattress bowed beneath his weight, and his shadow loomed like a glum, weighty cloud on the wall.

He touched my back. "I'm sorry."

"You certainly are."

"Forgive me?"

His lips brushed my neck, raising a shiver.

"Why should I?"

"Because I'm asking you to." He kissed me again, and again. "Because I'm sorry for losing it and acting like such a jerk."

"Good. You should be."

"I know it's no excuse, Em. But I've had a seriously lousy day."

Rolling onto my back, I faced him. "Lousy how?"

Sadly, he shook his head. "This afternoon, a post-op on my service presented with chest pains. Guy was a VIP. Hedge fund billionaire. Anyway, he'd heard Dr. Malik was on staff, and he pulled strings to get him called in as the cardiac consult. I figured this was the perfect opportunity to get on Malik's radar screen, show him what I could do. Word came back that he was scrubbed in on a quadruple bypass, so I worked the guy up."

"Makes sense."

"That's what I thought. I played it strictly by the book. People have MIs after surgery. Loss of blood and all stresses the heart. It's a known risk and it happens. It's not like I caused the heart attack."

"The patient died?"

He pulled a breath. "No. He'll be fine. I'm the one who's probably terminal."

"I don't understand."

"Join the club. Soon as Malik showed up and checked the chart, he went ballistic. Apparently, he doesn't like anyone touching a patient of his unless the order comes directly from him."

"But the man was having a heart attack."

Standing, he started to pace. "My argument exactly. I told him I'd done a standard workup, and that's all. Nothing interventional that couldn't be undone. Malik wouldn't even answer me. He paged the chief resident and the attending on call. The minute they got there, he started bitching about me as if I wasn't in the room. Calling me irresponsible, hotheaded, green. After a while, I honestly couldn't take it anymore."

"And?"

"I stood up to him. Told him I'd handled the case by the book, exactly according to standard protocol."

"Good for you."

"That's what I thought. Amazingly enough that seemed to please him. He looked amused, said I had gumption. Then just when I was starting to breathe again, feel a little hopeful, he cut my legs off. Told me gumption was no substitute for judgment or skill."

I cringed. "Nice guy."

"He doesn't have to be."

"Sure. Silly me. God's exempt."

"He's not in a popularity contest, Em. And if he was, all he'd have to do is count the landslide vote. Eric Dubrow, the chief resident, wasn't about to lift a finger to help me out. He's angling for a fellowship with Malik himself, so why rock the boat on my behalf? Same with Chi, the attending. He's much more concerned with getting on Malik's good side than standing up for a disposable like me. Everyone is."

"Politics."

"You bet. So I decided I'd better play, too. I told Dr. Malik that's what I was here for: to improve my judgment and skills. I told him I'd give anything for the chance to learn from him. Show me how, and I'll do it your way, I said. There's nothing in the world I'd like more."

"Sounds like gumption to me."

"At that point, I figured things couldn't get any worse, so what the hell?"

"And?"

"And it was amazing. Malik slapped me on the back and sent Chi and Dubrow packing. After they left, he said, 'I respect a man who knows what he wants and goes after it. Tell you what. Soon as I finish with this case, you and I are going to sit down and have a nice, long talk. Meanwhile, I want you to watch me. Take in exactly what I do on this case and remember every bit of it. That's rule number one.' "

Deep inside, the baby fluttered.

"What's the punch line, Sam? I don't see how your getting a private audience with the Almighty qualifies you to use the lousy-day defense."

He raked his fingers through his hair, an anxious habit that dated back to his childhood, when his mother died, and he was left to be raised by his glacier of a dad.

"As it turns out the joke was on me. Malik took his sweet time with the VIP, sucking up, squeezing the poor bastard for a major donation to the new cardiac center. And this while the man was still dealing with the shock of having had a heart attack, still terrified he was going to die."

"Get them while they're hot," I said dryly. "Early bird makes them squirm."

"When he finished his pitch, Malik left the room without a word. At first, I just stood there. Didn't know what to do. But he said he wanted to talk, so I decided I'd better follow along."

"Sure."

"Until the new cardiac center is ready, Malik's using Stryker's old office in the main pavilion. Soon as we got there, he started returning phone calls, reading papers, signing forms. Then his secretary came in. They spent half an hour discussing his schedule and some trip he's about to make to be a visiting professor in Japan. Went on and on about where he's staying. What kind of room. What he needs to pack. Fascinating stuff."

"And you're just sitting there?"

He nodded glumly. "With my thumb up my ass. Feeling like a total fool. When the secretary left, I cleared my throat to catch his attention. I said if he's too busy, I'd be glad to come back another time. He gave me a look that would spoil milk. Said if I'm too busy and important to wait, I'm welcome to get out for good."

I shut my eyes in pained contemplation of the scene. "So you stayed."

"What choice did I have?"

I winced. "Let me guess. He continued to ignore you."

"As if I didn't exist. He planted his feet on the desk and made more calls. Discussed a new will with his estate lawyer. Spoke to a daughter about her wedding. Had an argument with some broker who's listed his boat. He set up golf lessons. Complained about his subscription to the *Wall Street Journal* showing up late. Then finally, he hung up, stared out the window, and picked his teeth."

"You should have walked out, Sam."

"I wanted to, believe me. But how could I? Malik holds all the cards."

"So don't play. No one deserves to be treated like that."

"True, and when I run the world, things will be different. Guaranteed."

"What finally happened?"

"He got up and left. Turned the lights off. He was waiting when I got to the hall. 'That's rule number two,' he told me. 'What I say goes. Your job is to listen and learn.'"

"Arrogant son of a bitch."

Sam shrugged. "That's how he is."

"Then who needs him? There are plenty of other people to train with. Actual human people."

He sat again beside me and cupped my hand, scrawling an inscrutable message on my palm.

"Remember on our honeymoon, Em? That day when we went to the Louvre?"

"Of course."

"They had that exhibit of master sketches, including a few by Leonardo and Michelangelo. I'll never forget how you looked at them, completely enthralled. You said if you could draw a fraction as well as that, you'd die a happy girl."

"It would be pretty amazing."

"That's how I feel about studying with Dr. Malik."

"Are you honestly comparing Malik to Michelangelo?"

"In a way, yes. He's a genius at what he does. Best on the planet. If you had the chance to learn from the very best, would you give it up because he wasn't a prince of a guy? Because his manners sucked?"

I filled my chest. "No. I suppose not."

"Thanks. Means a lot to have you on my side."

"I am. Almost always."

"I have to figure out a way to turn it around with Malik, Em. At least get close enough so he'll give me an honest chance."

"You could ask your father." Though he'd given up his faculty position at General to reap far greener harvests as adviser to a pharmaceutical company, Senior still held sway at the hospital. He had close high-level friends in the administration and on the board. A call or two from him might solve the problem. But a greater problem stood in the way.

"You know I can't do that."

"You won't, Sam. That's different."

"He wouldn't lift a finger to help me. He'd use it as an opportunity to rub my nose in how important he is."

"Maybe this time would be different. It wouldn't hurt to try."

With a pained look, he shook his head tightly, and that said it all. It would hurt. I was wrong.

"It was just an idea."

Sam smoothed a lolling wave from my forehead and looped it behind my ear. "Don't tell me you're honestly worried about Suzanne."

"Okay. I won't tell you."

"She's part of the politics, Em. Malik's fair-haired girl. Apparently she's a friend of some important friend of his, which is probably code for a big contributor. She did a six-month rotation at the Cleveland Clinic under Malik after graduation. He's the reason she's here. His little protégée. That's why I'm being nice."

I searched his face, felt the familiar magnetic pull. "Don't be too nice."

He nuzzled my neck. "I won't, except to you. Sorry I couldn't call and give you a heads-up. But his deal was maximum discomfort."

"Sounds like a lousy deal."

"Leonardos don't come cheap."

"Neither does Grand Marnier shrimp and Peking duck. I bet you're starved."

His leering smile split the darkness. "Actually, that's not what I'm hungry for."

I smiled back. "Good."

Afterward, he fell instantly, heavily asleep. Soothed by the warm press of his familiar contours, I started to drift off myself. A harsh weight of weariness dragged me under as the jarring clash of voices from above started up again. *Stop. No! Don't you dare. Please!*

A furious storm raged in the murky distance. In my dreamscape, fierce electric javelins split the sky. Thunder roared its fury at a safe remove. Nothing to do with me at all.

·TEN·

Tyler frowned at the grainy swirl on the monitor.
"Looks like icky soup."

"Let me help."

My obstetrician, Dr. Carla Piacenza, slowly traced the fetal contours with the tip of a long, blunt finger.

"There's the head, the tummy, and a foot. And look. The baby's sucking its thumb."

The wand slurped across the jellied slick of my abdomen and paused to probe. I craned my neck to get a better view.

"So what do you think, Ty? The baby can suck its thumb. Isn't that cool?"

"That," he said, leveling an accusatory finger, "is not a baby brother. No way."

"It looks funny now because it hasn't been born yet," the doctor said. "But soon, you'll have a new little pal."

"I don't want a new little pal. I want a Krypto Superdog."

"A baby brother or sister is even better," Dr. Piacenza said. "You'll see."

He pointed again at the screen. "Which is that?"

She passed the silent question. With Tyler, Sam and I had opted for gender surprise. During routine ultrasounds, it had been simple enough to keep the focus off the give-away organs while I watched. This time, we had no objection to learning the sex in advance. Having had a child, we understood there would be no shortage of surprises.

I nodded. "Sure. Go ahead. We'd like to know."

Adjusting the wand, she clicked to enlarge the particular view. Behind the gold-framed glasses, her gray eyes lit up.

"Guess what, Tyler. You're absolutely right. It's not a baby brother."

Eagerly, he tugged the pale washed-out sleeve of my examining gown. "You see, Mama? I told you."

"Dr. Piacenza means you're having a sister, sweetie. The baby is going to be a little girl."

My head was spinning pleasantly. I had envisioned a second boy, variations on the now familiar theme. But there was virtue in the matched set. No question.

"A sister?"

"It certainly is," the doc went on. "See there? That's her shoulder and her elbow and her knee and her pretty little nose."

Looking dubious, he edged closer. "What's that big black round thingy?"

"Her eye."

"Can she see me?"

"She'll be right here where she can see you soon enough."

"No! I don't want her to." He tugged his striped shirt overhead and staggered blindly.

"Easy there, slugger. If you want to wear your shirt like that, sit."

Dr. Piacenza was a rangy woman, six feet tall and change, but somehow, she looked entirely appropriate in the company of squab-sized infants and their reluctant little siblings-to-be.

"Everything's right on target, Emma."

"Even that?" I cast a meaningful glance at my little one, on the stool where she'd planted him, still sporting the polo on his head.

She smiled. "Takes getting used to. I prescribe tincture of time."

"You don't think I should be worried?"

"I don't."

"Then why am I?"

"Good question. See you in a couple of weeks."

While I dressed, Tyler pulled his shirt down and glowered at the screen. "That looks like yucky icky soup."

"That's because it's hard for the doctor to take a good picture through my belly. Once she's born, she'll look like a regular baby."

He made a face. Shook his head. No sale.

I tried a different tack. "What do you think we should name her?"

"Soup."

"That's a name for food, Ty. We need a girl's name."

"How 'bout Amity?"

"Amity's nice. Or maybe we'll call her Rae, like Daddy's mom who died."

"I know. Digga dada."

"What kind of name is that?"

"The lady's."

"What lady?"

"The digga dada lady."

The doctor knocked. "I have a picture for you to take home, sport." She handed him a black-and-white copy of the sonogram. Outlined in red, a thought bubble bloomed from the baby's mouth.

He cocked his head. "What's that say?"

"It says, 'Hi, Tyler! Can't wait to meet you.'"

We stopped for lunch at our local bagel store. The counterman, a ruddy elf named Leo, handed Tyler his usual: a buttered plain with a slice of Muenster cheese. At our usual table, my son ate his usual two bites.

"How about one more for Auntie Frieda?"

"I already did."

"One for Daddy, then."

"I did him, too."

With clamped lips, he pushed the plate away.

I rewrapped the remains. "We'll take it home for later, then."

"Digga dada could have it."

"That's sweet, wanting to share with your baby sister."

"Not her. I told you. Digga dada's the lady who talks funny."

I held his wide, innocent gaze.

"Remember what we said about telling stories? If it's an imaginary lady, you're supposed to say it's made up."

"It's not," he shrilled indignantly. "She says digga dada. Digga dada. Shush. And the new big little girl makes bad faces at her and calls her names."

"Tyler James Colten, that does not sound in the least bit like a true thing."

"Is too. Look."

As soon as I freed him from the stroller, he charged into our building. By the time I trundled down the hall after him, he had pressed the elevator down button.

"Wrong way, Corrigan."

Angrily, he pushed my hand away when I tried to send the car up. "No! We have to go near the trash."

"We don't have any trash."

When the doors gaped, he dashed inside and pressed B.

"That's where the digga dada lady lives."

"Fine. We'll put an end to that nonsense right now."

The basement was musty and dim. A confounding weave of exposed pipes cast gloomy silhouettes on the whitewashed walls. The insistent bass thump of a distant boom box mingled with the hiss of steam pipes and the brittle creak of the building's ancient bones.

Treading the long narrow corridor, we passed doors marked UTILITY, LAUNDRY, BICYCLES, and AUTHORIZED PERSONNEL. Through the unmarked door beyond those, a row of rickety cages had been set aside for tenant storage. The cubicles were crammed to bursting with forsaken toys, seasonal and holiday decorations, and excess furniture. Sports equipment. Tools.

"Hey there."

The deep, insinuating voice caught me off guard and set my heart stammering. Anxiously, I searched for its source, but at first I saw nothing. Then he stepped out with deliberate slowness, tracking his looming shadow into the light.

He went by Judge, which was either a name or a commentary. He'd worked in the building for as long as we'd lived here, and probably far longer. Judge was the porter, a lumbering man in a gray jumpsuit, in charge of keeping things operative and clean. Despite his bulk, he passed through the building like a vapor. He appeared when you didn't expect him, and then with the same jarring unpredictability, he'd be gone.

"Hello," I said, pulling Tyler close.

"Get the notice? Water be shut down tomorrow, ten to two. Have to change out some pipe."

"We did. Thanks."

His eyes tracked me boldly. "Want to take your bath early, then." He unlocked a rear door with a key from the enormous ring he carried, and slipped inside. The thought that one of those keys would let him into our apartment sent a bristling chill down my spine.

Two small, narrow halls branched off the corridor's end. To the right, neat rows of recycling bins flanked the larger receptacles designated for ordinary garbage. Bright posters detailed the city's dizzying disposal laws. Sandwiched between them, a desiccated cork bulletin board held notices of items for sale, missing pets, forthcoming events, and help wanted. Most were outdated. Some posted by people who had moved out years ago.

"You see, Ty? No lady."

"Over there."

He raced down the hall to the left. Veering left again, he slipped into a small square room I hadn't known existed.

The lights were out, the air thick and musty. I stood in the doorway, waiting for my eyes to adjust.

"Tyler?"

Crouching, he whispered urgently, "Digga dada. It's daytime. Wake up!"

Tracing the cool cement, I found the light switch. Harsh fluorescents set the space ablaze.

"There you go, Ty. See? No one here."

Damp blotches marked the cement floor and powdery mold trails scaled the walls. In one corner, a threadbare blanket held a small radio, a half-emptied liter-sized soda bottle, and an empty bag of chips. And there was something else.

Tyler homed in on it just as I did. "Look! A balloon."

I caught him before he could retrieve the highly dubious prize: a used condom.

"It's not a balloon, sweetie. It's yucky. Leave it alone."

"But maybe the digga dada lady got it for me."

Firmly, I drew him out and down the hall. Gripping his slim shoulders, I crouched to look him hard in the eye.

"There's no lady. Do you hear me? That's made up."

His lower lip jutted defiantly. "Is not. I saw her when I played hide-and-go-seek with Ruthie. I saw the new big little girl be mean to her."

Ruth Schroeder was our best sitter, reliable, patient, and wise. She'd been a nurse for years. Now she was studying to become a physician's assistant, saving my bacon, part-time, on the side.

"You're saying Ruthie brought you to play hide-and-seek in the basement?"

"Yup."

"Tyler?"

"I went to hide in the room but the digga dada lady got mad. So I got to be it. Then Ruthie read me a book in a tree."

I felt a squeeze of anxious guilt. Why had I pressed for another child? Sam had conceded with reluctance, protesting that our plate and our tiny apartment were already overloaded. But I'd thought it important to give our son a sibling. As soon as I broke the news to Tyler, he'd started sleeping poorly and acting out, crossing the line from charmingly normal imaginings to increasingly preposterous inventions he swore were real.

My guilt spawned a knot of fear. I thought of little Jake, who had slipped away "idiopathically," fading to a hazy shadow of what he'd been in a few months' time. A child could get lost for no apparent reason. Changed beyond recognition. That was the terrifying fact.

"I love you very, very much, sweetheart. You know that?"

He stretched his arms to the limits, an accurate measure of my love.

"Made-up stories are fine when we say they're made up. Otherwise, we have to tell the truth. You understand?"

"Yes, Mama."

He wrapped his arms around my neck and squeezed. That's when I noticed the copy of the sonogram that he had torn to angry bits and tossed on the cold basement floor.

"It's very important to know the difference between what we know for sure and the things we think up, sweetie. Otherwise, things can get terribly, horribly confused."

·ELEVEN·

"That's it. Contraction's over. Now take a slow, deep, cleansing breath. Settle back. Relax."

Sam sat behind me, cradling my hips in the muscular V of his legs, rubbing my back and murmuring encouragements.

"Good, Em. Doing great. Another one down."

Our Lamaze teacher, a leggy, jet-eyed stunner named Rita Powell, studied the outsized stopwatch that dripped from a chain into the perilous abyss of her cleavage.

"Twenty seconds, mommies. Fifteen. Focus. Counting you down. Three . . . two . . . one . . . Contraction begins."

I ordered myself to relax, but my body refused to obey. My muscles tensed and my breathing went sharp and shallow. Women were said to forget the pain of giving birth, but I had the dubious gift of indelible recall. With Tyler, my water had broken a month before my due date in a taxi on my way home from teaching a figure drawing class. That day's exercise involved studying a live nude model for ten minutes and then rendering the essence of the form in bold strokes with eyes closed. The purpose was release from stifling convention, and it worked beyond my wildest imaginings. The students let go, and so, as it turned out, did I.

I'd asked the driver to change course to drop me at the hospital. Skulking out red-faced at the door to Emergency, I'd left a tip large enough to cover the embarrassing puddle.

Sam and I had enrolled in a so-called "natural" childbirth course then, too, but Tyler had made his appearance three weeks shy of graduation. By then, I had learned how to take off and muddle along in ideal conditions at standard cruising altitude, but I had no clue how to deal with unexpected turbulence, make a midcourse correction, or land. I had not yet recovered from the film of a live delivery, captured at harrowing close range, the teacher had shown us the previous week. Though I'd seen plenty of sanitized portrayals of women in labor and giving birth in the movies, I had not been in the least prepared for the living-color, no-holds-barred real thing.

Nor was I prepared for the myriad things that could, and therefore were bound to, go wrong. Four surgical residents on Sam's team had gone out for dinner together the night before at a Turkish restaurant and been felled by a salad with salmonella dressing, so on that, of all days, the remaining staff schedules had been thrown into utter chaos. Everyone was covering for someone else who was substituting on some other service in turn. It had taken hours and a dozen phone calls to track Sam down.

By the time he showed up, I was in a hot blue hyperventilating panic. Every two minutes, my womb humped in a searing boulder of agony. By the time it passed, I had barely a moment to collapse in a wet towel heap before I was whacked again. Meanwhile, a motherly floor nurse who knew Sam came in to fuss over him. She brought him coffee and cookies while I was restricted to ice chips. They were my favorite—toll house: the final straw.

"Looking good, mommies and daddies! How's everyone doing?"

A few of us in the stretch-mark brigade traded sardonic looks. Rita was childless. If she really wanted to know how we were doing, she should waddle a mile in our shoes. She should watch her belly button pop like a turkey timer and see her legs sprout a tarantula's web of veins. She should learn firsthand the myriad joys of hemorrhoids and hormone swings and having to pee with the startling frequency of rush-hour trains.

Of course, the men saw things differently. In their view, Rita had everything it took to be the ideal birth coach: she was extremely easy on the eyes. During the first session several weeks ago, one of the daddies-to-be, a balding investment banker with obvious suicidal tendencies, had commented audibly that she was hot. He still had the pained look of someone forced to sleep long-term on the couch.

Rita reached into her cleavage and held the watch again. "Okay, everyone. Here comes another one. Get ready without getting tense. Remember, conquering pain is all about confidence and control."

I tried to do as she said, though on some level, I couldn't shake the conviction that conquering pain was all about really good drugs. In theory, I loved the idea of bringing a child into the world in a dreamy haze of chemical-free goodwill. Siena had delivered her preternaturally calm daughters in a warm-water bath in a homey birthing center. I pictured them dropping like pond lilies against a backdrop of soothing music and soft light, entering a world that felt gentle and welcoming from the start. In the end Tyler had been tugged by biting forceps into a room of screaming fluorescence and order-barking aliens in masks, passed to a groggy, spent mother who was dead of an epidural from the waist down. Before he was even born, I had scored my first significant failure as a parent.

That's why I'd insisted we sign up to take the course again, hopefully all of it. That's why I was trying so hard to get it right.

While we continued our faux labor, the teacher strode around. When she came to us, she stood cross-armed, frowning down.

"Try to relax, Emma. Focus on your breathing."

"I am," I said, panting like an overheated dog.

"You're working too hard. Ease up."

The couple on the adjacent mat won a smile of approval. The one beside them got the smile and a rousing *good*. Behind us were several latecomers and they received affirming nods as well. Except for me, the praise went full circle.

"Easy, Emma," Rita said, sounding more and more like a drill instructor homing in on her favorite torture subject. "Breathe."

I could do that. Firmly, I reminded myself I'd been breathing quite successfully for thirty years. When Rita called the next contraction, I dismissed the crushing doubts from my mind and focused with all my might. I emptied my lungs and drew the air in like a web of pale gossamer strings. Slowly, I forced the breath out again and took tiny measured sips. Out with the bad air. In with the good. In with the good. In. In.

In.

My head expanded like a plumped balloon. Odd prickling sensations trilled along my limbs. Rita's spiced honey voice dimmed to a shivery breeze. So did the soft gyrations of Sam's hand on my back. The mock contraction was ending. Fifteen seconds, she announced. Ten, nine, eight . . .

Next thing I knew I was splayed on the mat, gazing up at a dizzying assemblage of upside-down mouths, gaping nostrils, and wide, wary eyes.

Crouched beside me, Sam clutched my wrist to read the pulse. When I tried to sit, he eased me down again. "Wait, Em. Take a minute. Do you know where you are?"

"Yes. I'm in Lamaze class, making a fool of myself."

"Does anything hurt?"

"My pride. Otherwise, I'm fine."

Again he offered resistance when I tried to get up. Part of me wanted to crawl off and disappear. The rest wanted nothing more than to stay right where I was and slug Sam.

"You hyperventilated, Emma," Rita said. "You have to get the breathing down. Try to practice every day at home."

One of the faces piped up. "Emma? Emma Krause? I can't believe it."

Krause was my maiden name. Tracking the source of the voice, I couldn't believe it either.

"Emma and Sam? You're still with *him*?"

"Franny? Is that really you?"

She clutched her giant midsection. "And then some."

Francine Goodwin had been my freshman roommate at Cornell, a dear friend and near sister. Junior year, she'd gone abroad and stayed. From then on, her address and occupation were constantly changing. At some point, out of busyness and sloth, we'd lost track of each other.

The sight of her revived me instantly. I clambered to my feet and embraced her, bumping bellies. We were two shmoos hugging in frenzied delight.

Leaving class, we discovered that our lives had run in odd parallels. Franny had gone to medical school and become a child psychiatrist. Her husband, Grant, was a sculptor at heart, but his day job was Internet entrepreneur.

During the dot-com boom, he had launched a successful site where artists could display and sell works internationally online. After that company was bought out by one of the major auction houses, he got involved in a start-up called Gotcha! devoted to celebrity exposés. They lived a mere thirty minutes north in the Westchester town of Larchmont. Their twin sons were two weeks older than Tyler, and the due date for their daughter-to-be was a week before ours.

Shaggy-haired, lanky, and boyish, Grant and Sam had an almost familial resemblance. They were like-minded, too, at least about baseball and beer. They couldn't wait to get to a TV and catch the remainder of the Yankees game. We wandered in to do so at a boisterous Irish pub on First Avenue.

"Twins," I said with reverence. "I can't imagine how you managed."

"For one thing, it's like they all say: I didn't know any better. Plus I had the ultimate secret parenting weapons: work that got me out of the house part-time and plenty of help."

"Help or no, I'd be a basket case."

"You? No way. You were always so sensible, cool and collected, even around exams. I couldn't count how many times you talked me down from the roof."

Sam caught that and snorted. "Emma cool and collected? People certainly change."

"And some don't," she said, scowling. It appeared that Franny still hadn't forgiven Sam for dumping me sophomore year for an unforgivably pretty blonde freshman named Haley Breisblatt. Even before that, what passed between them had always been a little prickly.

I shrugged. "He's right. I'm not exactly what you'd call relaxed, especially when it comes to Tyler."

Franny stirred her Virgin Mary with a celery stalk. "Because?"

"There has to be a reason? Simple neurotic hysteria won't do?"

"It will if that's honestly why."

Someone scored a three-run homer, raising an exultant roar. Grant and Sam bolted from their stools in unison and punched the air.

"Look," I said. "Hairy Rockettes."

Franny held her steady gaze on me. Neither trained psychiatrists nor true friends let you change a painful subject that easily.

"Tyler's a terrific little boy, bright and imaginative. I adore him completely."

Still, she stared.

"Okay, I'll admit I'm a little worried about him."

"Because?"

"Because he keeps making up wilder and wilder stories and claiming they're true. Getting more and more intense and aggressive."

She plucked a cherry from the metal bin in front of her. "Hitting, pushing?"

"Biting, throwing, kicking, mauling, drive-by shooting. You name it."

"Sounds like a typical three-year-old."

"Maybe so. But he's not a typical three-year-old. Poor thing has me for a mother."

"I'll be glad to take a look at him if you like, Emma. If that would make you feel better."

"It would only make me feel better if you find nothing wrong." I tried to smile. "Forget it, Franny. I'm being ridiculous."

Sam could be totally deaf to me, but he had impeccable hearing when it came to my admitting a fault. "You are.

Tyler is willful, manipulative, and exasperating. When he doesn't get his way, he blows like Vesuvius. In other words, a perfectly normal kid."

Franny plucked a kernel from the popcorn bowl and flicked it expertly at Sam's cheek. She had always been brilliant, insightful, and a little off-the-wall. In other words, a perfectly normal shrink.

Sam clutched his cheek. "What the hell was that for?"

She glared at him. "Being concerned about your children is the opposite of ridiculous."

"Oh yeah? What about throwing popcorn?"

"It wasn't ridiculous at all. You deserved it."

Chuckling dryly, Sam rolled his eyes. "You sure haven't changed."

Franny smiled. "Why, thanks, Sam. It's settled then. I'll come in early before next week's class and you'll introduce me to that little guy."

Sam folded his hands on the bar. "Tyler's fine. The last thing he needs is a shrink."

My husband was ardently opposed to psychotherapy and the people who dispensed it. He took the hard-line surgeon's view. If something wasn't right, you either left it alone or cut it out, depending on the benefits and risks. He also blamed the entire psychiatric profession for the horrifying event that had shattered his childhood. After years of intensive therapy, his chronically depressed mother had killed herself with valium and gin. Sam, then a fifth-grader, had discovered her cold on the floor when he came home from school. In typical fashion, his father had been unreachable.

"I'm not suggesting he needs counseling, Sam," Franny said evenly. "All I'm trying to do is help put Emma's mind at ease."

"Fat chance."

"What's that supposed to mean?"

"Worry is Emma's middle name. Putting her mind at ease would take a frontal lobotomy," Sam said.

"You know what they say," Grant said, raising his beer. "I'd rather have a bottle in front of me than a frontal lobotomy."

The announcer's voice boomed from the wall-mounted flat-screen. It was top of the ninth, bases loaded. Batting cleanup, the Yanks' recently acquired megamillion-dollar switch hitter Pete Canisetti faced a full count. Joe Reinharz, pitching for the Padres, dipped and lurched through his dramatic windup and shot a streaking low fastball across the inside corner of the plate.

Canisetti swung away and connected with a jarring crack, launching the ball on a high arching trajectory toward deep left field. The fans erupted as the outfielder readied his mitt.

Sam and Grant leaped up, cheering as the ball bumped the side of the hapless fielder's glove and bounced away. They traded hoots and high fives, as if they'd won the game personally. "Yes!"

Franny held her hand up as well, and I pressed it with my palm.

"I'm so happy to see you," I said, meaning it intensely.

"Back at you, Emma. Pretty amazing coincidence."

"Indeed."

"You know what my mother would say."

I remembered Blanche Goodwin well, a squat, chubby woman with a fixed look of perplexity. She was forever sending care packages that reeked of salami and writing rambling letters filled with hilarious mangled advice based on things she'd misinterpreted or misread. Franny would read them aloud in the dorm to a standing-room-only crowd.

"I remember a few of her gems. That you can get gonorrhea from a toilet seat. And it was possible to get pregnant through clothes."

"But not denim," Franny said, laughing. "So practically every week she'd send me another pair of jeans."

"And those denim underpants she managed to dig up. Don't forget those."

She blotted the tears of hilarity from her eyes. "How could I? But none of that nonsense is what she would say here. Once in a while, by sheer accident, my mother actually comes up with something sensible. In this case, she would tell me we'd found each other again for a reason, Emma. Blanche would tell us it was meant to be."

·TWELVE·

The Maliks' phone number was unpublished. Obie, the dear pewter-haired doorman who mostly worked the day shift and sometimes filled in at night, dialed their apartment for me on the house phone. Hanging up, he nodded.

"Okay, Mrs. Colten. You're good to go."

"What's she like?"

"Mrs. Malik? Oh, she's fine."

Obie saw the good in everyone. For him, calling someone "fine" amounted to a serious indictment.

No one answered when I rang the bell. Then I doubted they could hear over the angry roar of the vacuum. I waited until the noise stopped and rang again.

The door opened to the meager limits of the security chain. Inside, all I could see was part of an ornate console on a jewel-toned oriental rug. A tease of dark hair was reflected in the mirror above the console, the back of a bold print blouse.

"Mrs. Malik?"

"No."

"I'm Emma Colten, a neighbor downstairs. Is she in?"

"Wait."

The door closed again, followed by a sharp twist of the dead bolt. I thought of Sam in Malik's office, being treated like a piece of furniture, or not that well. Feeling more than a bit foolish myself, I stood clutching the fancy little rope-handled shopping bag that contained the expensive scented soap Siena had loathed above all else at the gift shop.

I heard voices inside, and then silence. The phone rang. Someone picked up and had a short, muted conversation. Finally, restrained footfalls approached.

Lena Malik stood in the doorway, elegantly dressed as she had been on moving day, not to mention perfectly coiffed, made up, and bejeweled. She reminded me of a model room, roped off to be admired at arm's length. Challenge sparked in her dark, deep-set eyes. Her crimson lip curled in distaste.

"Yes?"

"I'm Emma Colten, Mrs. Malik. We live downstairs. I wanted to say hello and welcome to the building. This is for you."

Without a glance, she took the bag and set it on the entry console. "Isn't that nice," she said coldly. "Good to meet you."

"If there's ever anything you need. Anything I can do."

"How kind of you, Ms. Cohen."

"It's Colten. My husband, Sam, is a resident at General. He's a great admirer of Dr. Malik."

"I see. Thanks for dropping by. Now, if you'll excuse me."

"Sure. Sorry if it's a bad time."

The door smacked shut before I could finish the sentence. What I longed to say was, *Sorry if it's a bad time,* bitch.

My cheeks flamed. The fourth Mrs. God was every bit as arrogant and imperious as the rude Lord himself.

When I got to the park hours later, I was still caught in the angry aftermath. Frieda Kalisher's impeccable radar picked up on it immediately.

"Whatever it is, Emma darling, the best thing is count to ten."

"I've already done that six hundred and thirty-seven times."

"Tell me what happened, then. Always better to get whatever's aggravating you off your chest."

Anxiously, I looked around, making sure we were in no danger of being overheard by someone who knew the Maliks. Because it was home to the largest hospital complex in the city, our Upper East Side neighborhood had been dubbed "Bedpan Alley." At all hours, the area's streets and shops teemed with white coats, stethoscopes, laminated IDs, and scrubs in sea-foam green or bruise blue. As was true of all hospitals, New York General was a fertile breeding ground for dangerous rumors and germs.

"Malik's wife," I said, summing up the problem in two words.

"Takes one to marry one, Emma. Considering what a horror Doug Malik is, I wouldn't expect his wife to be a doll."

"Then you wouldn't be disappointed. Sam asked me to get them a house gift, so I did. When I dropped it off, she acted as if I was contagious. Wouldn't even let me in the door."

"So she's not the friendly type. So the heck with her. You want my opinion? Better to have nothing to do with her at all."

I blew a long, slow, cleansing breath. Somehow here I was capable of doing that without hitting the deck. Maybe I needed Frieda for a birth coach.

"I can just hear Sam deciding it was all my fault. Telling

me I must have dressed inappropriately or looked at her cockeyed or said the wrong thing."

"Don't worry about it, sweetheart. Life's too short. Anyway, your Sam's not going to do any such thing. Not if he knows what's good for him."

Tyler squatted in the sandbox opposite another like-sized towheaded boy. Armed with plastic shovels, they were gleefully burying a dozen toy children in a yellow school bus. A little redheaded girl spied this and tensed.

"No. Don't." She snatched up two of the tiny round-headed figures in a daring rescue attempt.

Thankfully, Tyler grabbed the dolls she had commandeered instead of a fistful of her tempting fiery hair.

"Stoppit!" he screeched. "They're mine."

"They're not yours, Ty," I reminded him. "The little boy is letting you use them."

"They're not hers, Mama."

"If it's all right with him, she can share, too."

"It's fine," said the boy's mother. "Let her play, too, Gunnar."

Amazingly, Gunnar handed over two of the small figures, neither of them among the ones missing clothing or limbs.

A ginger-haired woman hovered at the edge of the sand. "What do you say, Ophelia?"

"They're being mean to the boys and girls, Mommy. Make them stop."

"They're only playing. Now say thank you for letting you share."

"But they're hurting the children." She scrunched up her face and squeezed out a couple of sympathetic tears.

"It's okay, honey," her mother said, "Nobody's hurt. It's just pretend."

Tyler packed more sand over the head of a bead-headed doll and stomped it, reveling in pure sadistic joy.

Frieda nodded sagely. "You see? That's what I love about the playground. It's preparation for life."

"It is?"

"Definitely. In most every situation, you have two distinct choices."

"You mean suffocate the children or be sweet?"

"That's one good example," she said. "And the business with Lena Malik is another. When it comes to men in academic medicine, there are two kinds of wives."

"Oh?"

"You've got the ones who get out and make a whole separate life. They accept that their husbands are busy men and make sure they have plenty to keep themselves busy, too. They work, volunteer, spend time with friends. They get tickets to things, take courses. They're not about to hang around waiting for their men like bumps on a log."

"Being a bump on a log doesn't sound like much fun."

Now Tyler suffocated the bus driver, not daunted in the least by uniformed authority.

"True. And then there are the ones who get completely caught up in the whole crazy business of their husbands' career. They devote all their time to looking the part, playing the angles, getting friendly with the right people, anything to help their husbands get a leg up."

"Like Lena Malik?"

She made a sour face. "Let's put her on the side for now, Emma."

"Which kind were you, Mrs. K.?"

Frieda dipped her chin approvingly. That was the right question.

"What else? The third kind."

"Naturally."

"The third kind is the wife who makes a life for herself but also does what she can to help the cause. After all, in a way it's her cause, too. You love someone; you want him to do well. He does well; he's happier—and the family is better off. Plus if he's any kind of a mensch, he appreciates the support and responds by paying back with interest. But the third kind doesn't hang on her husband's every move. She has her life, he has his; and when need be, they work together. Everybody wins."

"Makes sense."

She wagged a finger. "Don't be so quick to agree, darling. The truth is it's not so black and white. Your husband's a busy surgeon; there are plenty of trade-offs. He works long hours and travels to endless meetings. His head is so full of research and funding and keeping up with developments in the field, there is barely room for anything else. He means well, but he misses ball games and school plays and guaranteed he's never there when one of the kids gets sick or needs stitches. Guaranteed when that happens either he's in the OR on a case that takes two days or he's off being a visiting professor in Outer Whositstan. Sometimes you wish he would stop being so available to everyone else and pay more attention to you. Sometimes you wish he sold shoes or did tax returns for a living."

I showed my empty palms. "Cardiac surgery is what Sam wants. The only thing he's ever wanted to do."

"So what can you do but try to understand and make the best of it? Help him where you can but not so you lose yourself in the bargain?"

"That's the way I look at it."

"Of course you do. Doug Malik may be a dirty no-good son of a whatsis, but he's very good at what he does. Sam wants to work with him; so you do what you can to help make it happen."

I shrugged. "I'm not convinced Sam's right. The agony of dealing with Malik may not be worth it in the end."

"Maybe not."

"But in the final analysis, it's Sam's career. It's not up to me to decide."

"Exactly. Way back when, I thought Leonard might be making a mistake going into orthopedics. He was so brilliant, and the others made blonde jokes about the orthopods, like they were dummies. But Leonard didn't care. He wanted to work with children with cerebral palsy."

"He was the best. Sam will be, too."

Her lips spread in a puckish grin. "You see? You have all the makings of a perfect surgeon's wife: the third kind out of two."

"I don't know. In this case, I must have screwed up. I must've offended Malik's wife somehow. Otherwise, why would she act that way?"

Her bony shoulders hitched. "Lots of reasons. Maybe she's a born sourpuss, or maybe she has something else on her mind. Sometimes you're just going about your business and you step in a hornet's nest. The bugs may sting, but that's because it's their nature, not because they're particularly mad at you."

"I don't know about that. If someone stepped in my nest even by accident, I'd be pretty miffed."

"You tried, darling. That's the main thing. And you'll keep trying when you can. But the third kind of wife understands that no matter what you do, sometimes it's impossible to win."

· THIRTEEN ·

The kids were bald, steroid-puffed, trapped in a heart-
breaking tangle of carping monitors and venom-dripping
lines. With a catch in my throat, I took it all in: the outsized
casts and bridge strut braces. Twig limbs poking through
limp, washed-out, hospital-issue pajamas. A pie-faced girl
was bound in a flesh-toned shell from hips to chin. Beside
her, a bandage-swaddled mummy of a boy in a back-turned
baseball cap swaggered in a heart-wrenching parody of
pride.

Frieda Kalisher made a slow circuit of the pediatric day
room, greeting the dozen kids who had gathered against
the jarring backdrop of frantically cheerful murals. One
featured cartoon monkeys frolicking in a jungle of
lollipop-shaped trees. On another, stylized fish swayed in
hula skirts to the strains of a one-octopus band. A third de-
picted a crew of astronaut cats and dogs guiding a soup-can
rocket ship to the far reaches of a dazzling galaxy.

"Look at you, Kelly darling," Mrs. K. said to a chunky
girl on a gurney whose head was bound in a draconian halo

of metal spikes. An angled mirror overhead allowed her to look around. "I hope you've been studying those word lists of yours. You keep going the way you're going; I bet they'll have you out in plenty of time for your championship bee."

"Tommyrot," the girl said. "T-o-m-m-y-r-o-t. Means baloney."

"You see that, Emma? That's how you know they're on the mend. They turn right back into their old smart-aleck selves. Kelly's an amazing speller. Last year she won the regionals. Before you know it, she'll be holding the national trophy and you'll be able to say you knew her when."

"Pollyanna," Kelly countered. "That's Mrs. K-a-l-i-s-h-e-r."

"You see? She's not only a spelling whiz, she's a wise apple. Now listen up, everybody. I want to introduce you to the big surprise I've been telling you about. This is my dear friend Emma Colten. She's a wonderful artist, makes the best portraits you ever saw. They look more like the people she draws and paints than the people do themselves. It's amazing. So you should consider yourselves very lucky indeed that she has agreed to come here today and help us do an art project."

The burned boy tucked his bandaged mitts beneath his armpits. "Art project. Sure. See ya."

Frieda barred his stiff, lumbering progress toward the door. "It's definitely your lucky day, Brent darling. You'll tell me what to do, and I'll do it."

"No, thanks. I'm busy. Have to get ready for the freak show later. I'm going for the national championship like Kelly."

Frieda cocked her head coyly. "I can see you haven't heard I'm irresistible, Brent. But I am."

For a true adolescent, it didn't take a face to look snide.

"Besides," she went on, "so happens I have pull with your Dr. McDonough."

"Dr. Frankenstein you mean."

"I bet you think he's all serious business all the time."

"Only about torturing people."

"Think again, my friend. Play your cards right, and I'll get your Dr. McDonough to show you his Dolly Parton imitation."

One sharp laugh escaped the lipless grin. "McDonough? No way."

"Way," Frieda said. "Funniest thing you ever saw. He's got the blonde wig and everything. And I mean *everything*. Now you'd better get back here and start thinking creative. Dolly Parton does not come cheap."

"Kowtow," said the girl in the crown of spikes. "K-o-w-t-o-w. Means suck up to a giant pain in the butt."

"B-u-t-t-f-a-c-e," Brent shot back. "Means Kelly."

Mrs. Kalisher bit back a smile. "I see you're both feeling much better. How nice!"

Given the range of ages and abilities Mrs. Kalisher had described, I'd decided to have the kids do found-object collage. On a medicine cart, I set out cups filled with buttons, empty spools, fabric scraps, feathers, snips of wool, dried beans, macaroni, Q-tips, plastic spoons, and a stack of pictures torn from magazines. For the backing, I'd hit up my dry cleaner for shirt cardboards. The glue was hypoallergenic, nontoxic, odorless, and hospital-approved.

Standing beside the cart, I asked how many of them had ever heard of or done collage. A scatter of hands went up. I explained that this was a work of art made by gluing any kind of material onto a flat surface. The medium dated back to the discovery of paper thousands of years ago, but credit for modern collage as an art form went to Pablo Picasso.

Most of the kids had at least heard the name. One told

me her favorite book was the story of how a cow named Mootise met the porcine artist Pigasso. At first they clashed in a duel of giant egos, but eventually, they became good friends.

A gaunt, jaundiced girl frowned at the items on the tray. "What are we supposed to make?"

I had thought of that. In fact, I'd been up half the night worrying about this almost exclusively. Mrs. K. had advised me not to leave the project open-ended. Low energy and tight scheduling kept these sessions short, and by the time the kids figured out what they might want to design, they wouldn't have time left to finish the work.

The last thing I wanted to do was rub their noses in what they were unable to do. So I'd dismissed the idea of circuses or playgrounds, no picnics or cozy family scenes at home. Finally Tyler, in his relentless night crawling, had provided the perfect inspiration.

"I thought it would be fun to build monsters."

Brent snorted. "Great. I'll do a portrait of Kelly."

A moonfaced bald boy offered, "Cool, Brent. I'll do a portrait of you."

"Well, I certainly won't," Kelly said. "Brent's not a monster, he's a phantasm. P-h-a-n-t-a-s-m. Means nightmare."

Mrs. Kalisher clapped her hands sharply.

"Okay, people. You've got half an hour. Winner of the monster contest gets a special prize. Emma will do a picture of them or anything they choose. On your mark, get set, go."

The kids got to work with the help of the nurses and volunteers who had drifted in while we were setting up. A few were able to construct the collage independently, but most were too limited or weak. Some, like Brent, had limited or no use of their hands.

I circulated while they selected elements, decided on

position, and glued. The emerging monsters had multiple spool heads and long woolen fingers in lieu of ears. There was a button-eyed Cyclops and a stumpy leonine creature with a lima bean mane and kidney bean legs.

Brent's creation was by far the most elaborate. Guiding Frieda's hand, he had conjured an entire scene. Red scraps rose from a dark rectangle at the center of a spoon-bordered room. A figure rendered in Q-tips perched over the rectangle, and a grotesque creature with a button head atop the body of a hawk torn from a magazine hovered menacingly nearby. When I came to him, Brent was directing Mrs. Kalisher to cut up bits of red and yellow fabric and glue them on.

"And put some of those small black feathers on the Q-tip boy," he said. His voice was agitated, and a glint of eagerness brightened his cave creature eyes.

Frieda placed a tiny black quill over Q-tip boy's head. "Like that?"

"Right," Brent said. "Do more. Put them all over. Have some falling down and some flying in the air."

Gazing up at me, she winked. "Did you ever see such excellent leadership qualities in a boy, Emma darling? You hear how he tells me exactly what to do? How he gives orders like a regular boss? Mark my words: one day this one will be a big-time CEO."

I stared at the swirling chaotic scene. "That's wonderful, Brent. Very powerful. Want to tell me about it?"

He said nothing.

"That's okay. Art can speak for itself."

His voice caught me as I started walking away. "I'll tell you."

Behind the bandage mask, his eyes clouded, staring at what he had made. "It's Halloween, late. The kid is dead tired, fast asleep. He was out for hours trick-or-treating with his friends, dressed like Frankenstein with a bolt through his neck, all this black stuff on his face, wearing chains on his hands and feet, looking incredibly cool. He and his friends were stringing trees with toilet paper. Throwing eggs and scaring the younger kids out of their minds. It was perfect, the best. So much fun."

Everyone had gone still, even the youngest ones. Every eye in the room was on Brent.

"Has to be almost midnight. See the moon?" He pointed the bandaged knob of his hand at the large silver button mounted high on the shirt cardboard sky. "His nose starts burning, that's the first thing. Something smells funny, strong. Then all of a sudden it's so bright, he can see a whole galaxy of stars and comets flashing right through his eyelids.

"He tries to wake up, but he can't. He's stuck in this incredible nightmare"—he turned toward Kelly—"this *phantasm*. He needs to scream, but it won't come out. The sound sticks in his throat like a knife. His arms won't move, or his legs. It's like they're frozen, like he is. It's like his brain is a huge block of ice nothing can get through. And the ice is on fire, burning cold."

Brent's bandaged arm rose. "That," he said, pointing at the eerie button figure, "is the phantasm, the monster that drenched me all over with gasoline and lit the match." Tears pooled in his eyes, and a thin wail broke like a wave deep inside him. "That's my father."

Mrs. Kalisher enveloped him in a cautious embrace and broke the bristling silence. "Good for you. So much better to get it out. Such a brave boy. I say that's a prize-winning monster, Brent darling. You get the picture by Emma and the Dr. McDonough Dolly Parton imitation."

"Definitely," I said, forcing the word past the searing lump in my throat. And everyone who had two hands clapped.

Years ago, another monster father had abducted his son and set him afire during a nasty custody dispute. The story had made national headline news. Books were written and TV movies based on the unthinkable true story were made. For a long time, the media observed the grisly anniversary. They ran specials on the father's release from prison and the boy's persistent emotional and physical scars.

Brent's case had garnered no such fanfare. That particular crime had been done and fully exploited before, so it had not been deemed newsworthy. The spotlight was reserved for the new improved monsters, the ones that devised ever more novel and diabolical ways to harm their kids.

The stakes kept escalating. To make the papers today, a monster had to chain a child in darkness and starve her to shadow and bone. A monster had to sell not just one, but several of her children into prostitution to feed a crack habit. A button-headed monster that burned his sleeping, innocent Q-tip child in the midst of a buoyant Halloween-candy dream failed to make the cut.

Brent laughed. "McDonough doing Dolly Parton. How cool is that?"

Mrs. Kalisher set a hand on his bandaged shoulder. "Not, my darling, half as cool as you."

· FOURTEEN ·

Entering the posh Fifth Avenue apartment house,
Tyler hung back and clung to my hand. The staid lobby
with its fancy furnishings, burnished wood paneling,
British hunting scene oils, and stern white-gloved attendant was the perfect antidote for childish glee. So was the
ancient brass and mahogany elevator, manned by an
equally ancient and polished humorless man.

He released us on the penultimate floor into the private
lobby that led to the enormous apartment Sam Senior
shared with Sam's stepmother, Winifred "Freddie" Plascoe
Colten, widow of Carson Plascoe and heiress to a quarter
of his Kansas family's oil fortune.

A uniformed maid answered the door. Freddie, who had
no need to strain herself with doorknob-turning or anything else, stood in the gallery, regally posed in front of a
portrait of my father-in-law that I had not been asked to do.
An enormous Venetian crystal chandelier bathed her in
fractured light.

"Emma, so nice to see you. And look at you, young man. My, how you've grown. How long has it been?"

"Since Christmas. Just before you went to Palm Beach. You asked us to stop by to see the tree." We'd presumed there would be gifts involved, and armed ourselves with that in mind. As was often the case with these people, we'd presumed wrong.

"That's why I insisted you bring the boy. Senior will be so delighted to see him."

That wasn't entirely accurate. Senior would be glad to view Tyler and then see him go. But since she'd asked, make that insisted, I had relented and brought him along.

"Come in, come in. We'll sit in the parlor. Senior is on his way back from a meeting. As soon as he gets here, we'll have lunch. What will the young man drink with his meal?"

"Do you have apple juice?"

She looked mildly shocked, as if I'd asked if she had a sexually transmitted disease. "I can have Maisie squeeze some fresh orange juice."

"Thanks, but he's not a fresh-squeezed sort of person. Milk or water's fine."

The parlor was a large sun-drenched study in floral pastels. Freddie sat with primly crossed legs amid the oversized Fortuny-swaddled pillows on a French settee. I lowered myself with care on a flimsy-looking side chair. I had come to play the third kind of doctor's wife. Smashing one of their precious antiques would not advance Sam's cause.

Neither would Tyler's outbursts, whining, or having him play demolition guy. There was almost nothing in the apartment that my little one could safely touch, much less play with, so I'd brought stickers, "magic" color sticks that worked with water alone, and a stack of his most diverting books. For insurance, I'd tried to inoculate him against misbehavior with my most effective parenting tool: bribery. If he was a model citizen, I would take him out for a double-scoop ice cream cone with chocolate sprinkles.

Early signs were encouraging. He sprawled on the Aubusson rug and started going through his books. Tyler liked to read in his own distinctive way, chanting his version of the text in a tuneful falsetto.

Freddie looked appalled. "Wouldn't he be more comfortable in a chair, Emma? He's welcome to use the desk in my study."

"Thanks, but he'll be happier here with us. Anyway, he likes playing on the floor."

Their dog, Bootsie, a prissy little teacup Maltese, dashed in with the crisp scissor clack of tapping nails. Sam's stepmother lifted her onto the settee, where the dog perched with a bright expectant look, as if she was primed to engage in lively political debate.

Naturally, Freddie had trained the creature to act as little as possible like a dog. Mercifully, she'd never had a child. If she had, no doubt the hapless little thing would have worn Hermès ties in lieu of bibs and had extra starch flowing through its veins. She and Sam's father were two of a kind, a side-by-side refrigerator/freezer combo. Unfortunately, Senior did have a child, and poor Sam and his sister had been left in his so-called care.

As ever, the old man strode in looking trim and fit with improbably dark senatorial hair and blizzard white teeth.

"You're looking well, Emma."

"Thanks. So are you."

"When is the new one expected?"

"Two months. It's a girl."

That caught Tyler's ear. "No baby," he shrieked. "I don't want one."

"We'll have none of that, young man," Freddie said.

"Now stand up and say a proper hello to your grandfather. Gentlemen shake hands."

Tyler regarded her like a curious zoo creature.

Senior eyed his watch. "Shall we have lunch, then? I have a two o'clock."

"Certainly, dear. Emma?"

Freddie led us down the hall to the dining room, a grand gleaming affair with spectacular views. Central Park preened in its leafy spring finery. Sunlight glinted off the solemn face of the Metropolitan Museum.

On the silk-swaddled chair beside me, Tyler perched on his knees. Lunch was cream of asparagus soup followed by seafood salad over baby frisée. Expecting as much, I'd brought peanut butter crackers and grapes.

Freddie was having none of it. "You need to try what we're having, young man. It's simply delicious." She nodded at the maid, who placed a bowl of soup in front of Tyler and served him some of the seafood.

He was the portrait of perfect restraint. "No, Mama. Yuck!"

"He's a little picky." I moved the offending dishes safely beyond the reach of his pitching arm.

Senior sipped his sauvignon blanc. "So, Emma. To what do we owe the pleasure?"

"I haven't seen you in such a long time. I thought it would be nice to visit."

"So it is. And my son?"

"Incredibly busy as usual. He's looking forward to next year, being chief resident and applying for his fellowship."

That raised his patrician brow. "Is that so? Has he settled on a specialty?"

"He hasn't changed his mind. He still wants cardiac surgery."

Tearing an edge off his croissant, he sighed.

"How unfortunate that he couldn't be persuaded to give that up. The medical cardiologists have all but put the surgeons out of business. I've warned him he'd be training for something that's headed the way of the buggy whip, but he's always been far too obstinate to listen."

Which was clearly genetic, I longed to say. "If it turns out to be a mistake, he'll have to live with it. It was good of you to offer your advice."

While Senior stared, gauging my sincerity, I sliced a gargantuan shrimp into bits.

"Has he given thought to where he'd like to do a fellowship?"

Cautiously, I chewed on that. "Naturally, we'd like to stay here. But what he cares about most is learning with the best."

"And who would that be, in my son's opinion?"

Pick up a loaded question, and it could blow up in your face. "I'm sure there are several people he'd be glad to work with. There's no shortage of talent in the field."

Senior snickered. "That would depend on both the yardstick you're using to measure with and whose measurement you believe. In the average room full of cardiothoracic surgeons, you'll have enough hot air for a fleet of enormous balloons."

"Do you think any of them are above average?"

He tapped an impatient cadence on the white linen cloth. "A few, yes, though certainly not as high above as they would have you believe."

"If you were Sam, which of them would you put at the top of the list?"

"Mama look! There's a dog."

Staring out the window, he had spotted an Irish setter in the park. Something was of interest here, at last.

"Yes, sweetie. I see."

Indignation straightened Freddie's spine. "The grown-ups are talking now, Tyler. You mustn't interrupt."

"There's another dog!"

Senior frowned. "If I were foolish enough to make such a misguided specialty choice, I suppose I'd go with Vic Elkins at the Mayo Clinic, Gavin Tremont at Brigham and Women's, Herndon Hart at Johns Hopkins, or Lane Starrett at Duke."

My heart sank. If he was opposed to Malik, he'd be even less likely to help Sam get a shot with him.

Freddie sipped her soup with a raised pinky. For someone who'd been reared in the Midwest on a pig farm, she did an incredible imitation of a woman of high birth. Then, she'd learned her condescension from masters like Senior, a testament to the power of a fortunate apprenticeship. "You forgot Doug Malik, my dear."

Senior frowned. "I did not forget him. It goes without saying that he is the best there is. He's just not for young Sam."

"Because?"

Tyler piped up. "The Maliks live upstairs. They have a big little girl who's bad and no baby."

I pressed a finger to my lips and shushed him. I had come to suck up, after all.

Senior went on. "Because Doug Malik is tough as nails, a demanding, no-nonsense professional. Sam has always been, shall we say, a bit on the sensitive side. Doug would chew him up and dispose of him."

Tyler slid down from the chair. He had eaten his fill: a cracker and two grapes.

Freddie gaped in indignation. "Sit, young man. You have not been excused."

"But I'm through."

"You'll be through when I say so."

"I'm through now."

Senior ignored the exchange. "I hate to have to say it, but Sam simply does not have what it takes to stand up to someone as forceful and exacting as Doug Malik."

I wanted to strangle both of them, but that was not the way to reel a hooked fish in. "You know, I think you're right."

Senior looked startled. He was accustomed to having me battle mightily on Sam's behalf. "You do?"

"Absolutely. Sam would be much better off in a less demanding program with someone who'd be supportive and understanding. After all, we're going to have two little kids to take care of. The last thing I need is to have Sam working nonstop and never around."

His look darkened. "At this point in his training, Sam's career must come first, Emma. Don't make the mistake of thinking you can turn an ambitious surgeon into a house pet. My son may be sensitive and lacking a certain edge, but I can assure you, he won't stand for that."

Normally, I butted heads with Sam's father, but playing him was infinitely more fun. I shrugged. "Maybe you're right, and maybe I am. Unless Sam happens to get a fellowship with Malik, we'll never know."

"Make no mistake. The others I mentioned would not treat him with kid gloves. A fellow in a high-ranking cardiothoracic surgery program is the furthest thing you can imagine from a soccer mom."

"Exactly. That's why I keep telling Sam that if he doesn't get a position with Malik, he can find something else in New York. If it's not high-ranking, as you put it, that's not the end of the world. I'm much more concerned with quality of life."

Senior pressed a napkin to his hard stingy lips. "Be that as it may, Emma, what counts above all is my son's future. I shall not let you stand in his way."

· FIFTEEN ·

Calling a place cooperative does not make the dis-
parate gears mesh. For all its stated goals of harmony and
dedication to the common good, Little Ranger had its
share of clashes, crises, and cliques.

To many New York City parents, education was not so
much the means to a capable, enlightened end as a blood
sport. Children were the jousting sticks, used to muscle
ego-threatening competitors out of the race. My kid's preschool aptitude scores are higher than your kid's. My son
got into Trinity, therefore I am.

Beneath the bright playful surface at Tyler's preschool,
tensions could run absurdly high. What happened there was
seen to determine the eventual outcome of the nosebleed-
high-stakes race for the Ivy League crown. Though most of
the children were still grappling with issues like potty accidents and pacifier dependence, words like *achievement* and
academics often reared their absurd, ugly heads. Major dis-
putes raged over curriculum, ability grouping, and the ab-

sence of grades. It took precious little to set the incendiary undercurrent ablaze.

I had spent the morning teaching a class at the Metropolitan Museum, helping aspiring young artists to learn how to look with a scrupulous eye at selected masterworks and learn what they had to teach. Held up by a raucous parade on Fifth Avenue, I was late to pick up Tyler at the preschool. When I reached her on my cell phone, Siena assured me there was no problem. But as soon as I entered the classroom, the problem was impossible to miss.

At one of the low-slung round tables, Siena sat with Marissa's mother, Jeanette, and a slim, balding stranger in a suit. Out of earshot at the opposite corner of the large space, Marissa and Amity were playing dress-up, draping themselves with beads, lengths of tulle, and bright scarves. Crouching nearby, Tyler neatly positioned row after row of crayons to sabotage a chunky wooden train.

Siena, usually a diehard optimist, bore a slumped look of sorrowful defeat. Jeanette was flame-cheeked and quaking with rage. She spoke in a hiss punctuated by the rabid thump of her fat fist on the little table.

The man in the suit perched uneasily on the child-sized chair with his pale hands folded in his lap. He'd come armed with a fat gold Rolex, a bulging briefcase, and a look of paid-by-the-hour dispassion.

I hung back near the door. "Sorry to interrupt. Get your things, Ty honey. Time to go."

"No, Mama. Not yet. I'm busy."

"You can play train wreck at home."

"I need to finish here."

Siena shot me a pleading look. "Join us for a minute, Emma, would you?"

"She has no place in this, Siena," Jeanette insisted. "It's between you and me."

"That's not true. For one thing, you've included your attorney. For another, this is a cooperative school. Everyone involved in Little Ranger has a stake in this discussion. As a parent, Emma is very much involved."

"Why not call her what she really is: your bosom pal? Why not admit that you're hardly a judge of what's fair or right around here? You have inappropriate relationships with certain people. You have your favorites. I say that's clouded your judgment completely."

The lawyer set a restraining hand on Jeanette's wrist. "Let's try to stick with the issue we're trying to rectify, Mrs. Trevallis."

Siena's look hardened. "I'd like Emma to join us."

"I see no harm in that," the lawyer said.

"Well, I do," Jeanette whined. "All they're going to do is gang up."

"No one is going to gang up on anyone," said the suit. "We're here to have a productive discussion and hopefully a rapid resolution that serves the best interest of everyone."

"Emma?"

Siena patted the empty chair beside her, and I took it reluctantly. My curiosity had been shouted down by a far more compelling inner voice that was counseling me to flee. Sensible people did not step between an angry lioness and the precious cub she was grooming for admission to Dalton and eventual marriage to a Harvard MBA.

Jeanette refused to look at me. She fixed her rabid sights on Siena and thumped the table again.

"Fine. I don't care who hears. I'm telling you that child has no place in this class. His behavior is dangerous and disruptive and getting worse all the time."

My stomach clenched with fear. Could she be talking about Tyler?

"Marissa used to love school, but because of Jake she's terrified and doesn't want to come anymore."

The breath escaped me. "Jake?"

"Of course Jake. Who else? I have to coax her out of the house now. Some days I practically have to carry her here. A school phobia can have a lasting, terrible impact on a child. I will not see my daughter at risk of that because of some absurd bleeding-heart notion that it's fine to put one problem child above everyone else."

"There are many reasons children appear to fall out of love with school," Siena said with a remarkable absence of bile. "Marissa started saying she wanted to leave class as soon as you got the new puppy, Jeanette. She told me she missed being home with Muffin. Her reluctance to come to school had nothing to do with Jake."

A spittle mass had lodged in the corner of Jeanette's mouth. It stretched when she spoke like a security chain, but it didn't stop the ready flow of spleen.

"It had everything to do with Jake. All she can talk about is how Jake hits and bites and carries on. Don't try to tell me you know better than I do what's going on with my own child."

"There's a simple way to find out, Jeanette. Why don't we ask her?" Siena said.

Jeanette puffed out her chest. "You will do no such thing. I will not have my little girl manipulated into saying what you want her to. She is an impressionable three-year-old, entirely at the mercy of what goes on around her. That's the point."

"No," Siena said. "The point is every student in this class has an equal right to be here. We don't dismiss any-one because we don't find him or her to our liking for whatever reason. How would you feel if the parent of some other child requested that we remove Marissa?"

Jeanette shot out of her seat. "That is a terrible, inexcusable thing to say. Don't you dare compare my perfect little girl to that—that—"

"I'm not comparing anyone to anyone. Every child is different, and I respect those differences completely. True, Jake is more atypical in some ways than the other children. He has special challenges and special needs. But like every child, he deserves the chance to learn and grow in the most normal setting possible. We've made a commitment to that. I regret that you don't support that commitment, but it's not going to change."

The lawyer coaxed Jeanette back onto the tiny chair.

"We appreciate that, Ms. Gladwell. Your desire to include 'atypical' children, as you put it, in this preschool is most commendable. No one would argue with that or with the rights of special needs children to be educated in the most normal setting that happens to be appropriate to meet those needs. We are well aware of the Individuals with Disabilities Education Act. We also know that New York State established an early intervention program in 1986 specifically geared for children with special needs aged birth to three."

"I'm glad to hear you're aware of that," Siena said.

"The question here is not whether young Jake deserves an appropriate education. Of course he does. We just disagree with your contention that the appropriate setting for him is here. This is a private preschool with the correct resources for children with normal development. There are excellent publicly funded programs specifically designed for youngsters like Jake."

"And that's where he belongs," Jeanette said. "Not here, ruining things for everybody else."

I stared at Jeanette in horrified disbelief. Marion and Bob, Jake's parents, were supposed to be her good friends. She was well aware that they had gone to look at the available programs in the area for "youngsters like Jake" and come away hopelessly discouraged. For as long as possible, they wanted to keep him in the place he knew with the so-called normal kids, whose progress might somehow rub off on him. Friends were not for smacking in the teeth, I wanted to tell her. I also wanted to smack her in the teeth.

"Jake isn't ruining anything," I said.

She brought her fist down again. "He most certainly is. His behavior is not only dangerous and disruptive, it sets a terrible example for the others."

"The others have learned a lot from Jake," I said. "About acceptance, tolerance. Maybe you should sit in."

"Get off your high horse, Emma. I bet you've had doubts about Jake yourself. I certainly would, watching Tyler."

Somehow, I resisted the urge to lunge for her thick pink neck. Instead, I glanced over as my sweet little boy whacked a loaded passenger car off a towering hill of blocks and then stomped several of the victims with vicious glee.

My heart squirmed. "I feel terrible about what's happened to Jake. I'm worried for him and for Bob and Marion. There's a difference."

"Fine. You be as noble as you like. My concern is my daughter. How am I supposed to explain to Marissa that pushing and hitting are fine for Jake but not all right for her?"

Siena squared her shoulders. "That's easy. I explain it all the time. First of all, no one says it's all right for Jake to be aggressive. I tell them all of us must try to do the very best we can. Developing control and skills vary from child to child. Just because some of the children know all their letters or how to write their names doesn't mean we penalize the ones who don't."

The color drained from Jeanette's face. Marissa was among those who couldn't.

"That's hardly the same. Before Jake's behavior deteriorated so badly, Marissa would never express her frustration by lashing out. His example is the reason she's started reacting physically when she doesn't get her way. Last week, her little cousin took a toy she was playing with, and she hit him. That is so not Marissa."

"Handsome is as handsome does," I muttered.

"I'm sure the school does not wish to be held liable for exposing the other children to a negative influence that might have lasting consequences," the lawyer said in poorly veiled code. If Jake was not expelled, Jeanette and her dweeb husband, Arthur, would sue. She would hold the school personally responsible for any and all of Marissa's future failings.

I smiled sweetly. "Actually, now that I think about it, I believe Tyler learned his lashing out from Marissa."

"That's the most outrageous thing I ever heard," Jeanette sputtered.

"And nose picking. Until he watched Marissa at it, Tyler would never have done anything so rude. That is so not Tyler."

"I do not appreciate you making light of this, Emma. It's serious."

"I agree. Absolutely. Wouldn't you say Marissa picks her nose to an atypical degree, Siena? You're in the best position to judge."

"Every child has areas of strength and weakness," Siena said with a mostly straight face.

"You see," Jeanette whined. "I told you they'd gang up."

The lawyer coughed into his hand. "This line of discussion is obviously not productive."

I glared at Jeanette. "Neither is backstabbing or kicking friends while they're down."

"I'm only trying to do what's right for my child. Any decent parent would."

"You wouldn't know decent if it came up and bit you on the butt."

The lawyer raised his hands. "There's no need for name-calling or acrimony. If everyone will calm down and consider this rationally, I'm sure we can come up with a mutually agreeable solution. Perhaps Jake can be maintained here for a couple of weeks, or even a month, while his parents seek a more suitable placement."

"No," Jeanette said. "This has gone on too long already."

He eyed her sharply. "Or perhaps they'd like to withdraw him for some predetermined period of time after which his progress can be reassessed. In six months or a year, with appropriate intervention, it's highly possible that he'd be able to fit in here with no difficulty. Given the right environment, young children can undergo remarkable changes and growth. Otherwise, I'm sure he'll benefit far more from a school that can better respond to his needs."

"Or else?" Siena said.

"I would hope it wouldn't come to that, but my clients are prepared to pursue legal remedies."

She shrugged. "Do what you will. Jake stays."

"We'll see about that." Jeanette caught her lawyer's eye and stood.

"So we will. As soon as I can arrange it, we'll have a parents' meeting to discuss this in open forum. I hope you and Arthur will join us."

Jeanette looked startled. She had expected to bite and shove and get her way. But like it or not, she was going to be held to a much more rigorous standard.

· SIXTEEN ·

"Em? Tiger? Anybody home?"

The first hint I caught that something was amiss was the cheer in Sam's voice. At the end of a typical thirty-six-hour on-call shift, he was spent and downcast, a ghost of himself, barely there. Most evenings, he slogged home with just enough remaining energy for some gobbled sustenance followed by a nice, long, solitary coma.

"It's Daddy," Tyler exulted, bounding from the tub, sloshing me with a tidal wave of enthusiasm. So delighted was he to have Sam home unexpectedly, he didn't even take the time to line up his rubber ducks, animal bath mitts, and plastic cups in a meticulous line along the rim.

Snatching a towel from the rack, I caught him before he could run out dripping all over the apartment. He was slick as a seal and frosted with bright crackling suds.

"Let go, Mama. It's Daddy."

"Wait one second. You have to dry off first."

Sam burst in, grinning. "I spy with my very own eye . . . a soapy little nude-fish."

Tyler leaped into Sam's arms, soaking his scrubs and lab coat. I would have expected irritated sputtering, but he laughed.

"I'm not a soapy nude-fish, Daddy. I'm a soapy Batman fish."

"You are? What a coincidence."

From the pocket of his lab coat he retrieved a tiny shrink-wrapped Spider-Man figure. It wasn't Batman, but close enough.

More than a minute passed, but still Sam failed to lose interest and drift off in his usual daze. Instead of handing Tyler off to me, he crouched and dried him. He helped our son pull on his Bob the Builder pajamas and combed his hair. Hefting Ty onto his shoulders, he made for the living room.

"I have a big surprise, ladies and gentlemen."

"What?"

"You'll see. Close your eyes."

"How am I supposed to see with my eyes closed?"

Uneasily, I let him lead me. I'd had my fill of recent surprises, one more unpleasant than the next. Not that I was in the least superstitious or pessimistic, but bad things did tend to come in multiples of three.

"Okay. You can look now."

He had set the table with a festive white cloth, but the party mood stopped there. The surface held a shiny array of scrupulously aligned surgical tools and a tidy stack of medical books. *Principles of Anesthesia, Klorman's Annals of Cardiothoracic Surgery, Perioperative Morbidity in the Pulmonary Patient.*

"I give up, Sam. What's going on?"

"Not so fast, Mrs. Colten. Guess."

"Clamps, cautery tips, spreaders, sutures? I can't guess. I haven't got a clue."

"Come on. Try."

"It's doctor stuff," Tyler offered gamely.

Sam ruffled his hair. "Great guess, champ. Now it's Mommy's turn."

I shrugged. "Hmmm. I know. You're planning to do my frontal lobotomy at home."

"Lower."

"Lower? What, Sam? You're planning to do it in the basement?"

"I mean lower in the body."

I clutched my belly. "Forget it. I love you dearly, but there's no way you're delivering this child."

"Not even close, my lovely. Dr. Malik picked me to scrub in on a heart-lung transplant."

"He did?"

"Is that amazing, or what? I was positive he'd written me off for good, that there was no way I'd ever get another chance with him. But now I'm actually scrubbing in on a major case. Can you believe it?"

"I'm glad, sweetie. I know how much this means to you." I also knew that I'd likely had a hand in making it happen, and that this silver lining might contain a big, fat, ugly cloud. I didn't trust the God from Cleveland, not in the least.

"Take whatever you think and multiply it by ten, Em. It's a genuine dream come true."

Our little one was carbonated with excitement, bobbling up and down. "What's the surprise, Daddy? Presents?"

Sam winked. "Batman was your big present, sport. The surprise is Dad's getting to work with the world's most incredible surgery guy. Isn't that great!"

Tyler continued jumping. "Is it ice cream?"

"It's about Daddy's work, sweetie."

That squelched his excitement, though certainly not Sam's.

"The case is on for Thursday. That gives me tonight and tomorrow night to get ready. I thought I'd read up tonight and do a dry run. Tomorrow, I'm signed up to use the simulator. I want to be prepared for every move Malik makes, ready to do whatever he asks."

"Anything I can do to help?"

"There is, Em. Thanks. I really need to concentrate on this and get it right. If I don't, there won't be a next time. Mind if I just find somewhere to hole up and dig in for the duration?"

I swallowed my disappointment. This was my second chance in two days to be the third kind of medical wife and neither had been any fun. If my reward was encounters with Sam's father and sleeping alone, maybe it wasn't for me.

"It's fine. But you're certainly welcome to hole up and work here. We wouldn't disturb you."

"You could read me books, Daddy. We could play airplane. I could help you play surgery guy."

Sam's look said it all.

"All right. Go. Whatever you need."

After I got Tyler to sleep, I dined regally on his rejected green peas and gluey leftover mac and cheese. The Palliser portrait was coming along nicely, and I worked on it for a couple of hours, adding to the bright profusion of tiny watercolor flowers in the riotous garden background until my back ached and a veil of weariness settled over my eyes.

Propped on a mass of pillows, I took up the book for expectant parents on my night table and read the current entry. At week thirty-two, the average fetus had grown to nearly four pounds, the size of a decent chicken, and almost seventeen inches, which outstripped the diagonal measure on my computer monitor. By now, our little girl had begun to sprout a bit of actual gossamer hair to replace the simian fuzz known as lanugo that was characteristic earlier on. She had tiny toenails, and all five senses were fully operative. I couldn't imagine that there was much of interest in there to listen to, sniff, or see, but if she was anything like the pictured example at the head of the chapter, baby girl Colten had quite a lot of weighty issues on her mind.

At this stage, she was starting to dream. Could there also be nightmares? Was that what had her up and squirming in the middle of the night?

How I worried that she'd be a worrier like me. It stood to reason. After all, Tyler was a virtual clone of Sam. He shared his father's passion for order and ice cream and numbers and spectator sports. He had Sam's short fuse and long memory. Like his father, he tended to forgive too easily or not at all. So it made sense that like me this little girl would have a talent for conjuring every conceivable gruesome possibility, using the worst cases to bludgeon herself in the head. No doubt her hair would froth like mine at the first hint of humidity, that she'd have my lousy sense of direction, my love of drawing, and my absurdly outsized terror of even the tiniest of mice.

Pondering names in the next book on my stack, I started to drift off. Abigail, Addison, Agatha, Agnes, Aileen.

I was teetering on the edge of crumbling consciousness when I heard the now too familiar clump of angry footsteps upstairs. Malik's daughter's voice was now familiar, too. Joined by her father's booming bass, she quickly went timorous and shrill.

I tensed. But then, in a pleasant surprise, the conversation took a gentle, soothing turn. The words were indistinct, but there was undeniable tenderness in Malik's tone. The crooning strains of a loving father mixed with his little girl's charmed response.

Soon, I heard a third person speaking, a female. From the few words Lena Malik had deigned to speak to me when I brought the welcome gift, I could not be sure the voice was hers. There had been talk of a live-in nanny. The designer had shown me plans for her room off the kitchen, but I hadn't seen anyone with them when they moved in, so perhaps she had not yet been engaged. Or maybe the Maliks kept their household help locked away Cinderella fashion.

My thoughts swerved to Sam's big alleged opportunity in the OR. Though I knew how much he'd wanted it, I couldn't help but worry about how this encounter with Malik might go. Senior's appraisal of the Lord's incredible swift sword was an understatement. I feared he might perform a radical resident-ectomy and cut Sam off at the knees. What if that happened and Sam discovered I'd had a hand in setting it up? What if that happened and I'd failed to warn Sam? Then again, what if it didn't, and I had?

Nothing like a rousing lose-lose proposition to shift me into screaming red wide-awake alert. Seeking distraction, I read through the *B* names: Barbara, Bathsheba, Beatrice, Belinda, Belle, Beth, Bethany. Though it went against my official regulations, I turned ahead and read about the fetus at week thirty-three. In a mere seven days, our little girl would be spinning an astonishing number of added synapses, preparing for such dazzling feats as being able to breathe and suckle simultaneously.

Cady, Camille, Carly, Caroline, Cassandra, Catherine.

Suddenly, the voices overhead sharpened. Malik's tone took on a fierce edge. Adriana cried out.

"No, Daddy! No!"

I could not hear his response, but the threat of his growling thunder grew.

"No! Stop! I don't want to!"

Suddenly chilled, I drew the covers up and huddled beneath them. Deep in my bones I sensed the approach of something grave and unstoppable. A threat was bearing down like a terrible storm.

"No!" Adriana shrieked again. "No, Daddy. Please! I'm begging you!"

Numbly, I lay there, staring up at the shadows. I wanted to strike something against the ceiling, or cry out to let him know I'd heard.

But what had I heard?

Words could be utterly false to the thoughts and feelings they stepped forth to represent. People said things in haste or in anger. They said things for effect, things they didn't mean. Children, especially.

Tyler was only three, and already he understood what a mighty weapon words could be. Speaking of the manipulative little devil, I heard him padding down the hall. And then I saw him framed in the doorway.

"Back to bed, sweetie. You know the rules. No getting up before the sun."

"But you know what, Mama?" He padded to my bedside, dragging one of his stuffed Dalmatians, Sebastian I thought, by the ear.

"No, what?"

"I have a big, big, big surprise!"

"I'll be glad to hear all about it in the morning."

"I have to tell you now."

"You can tell me on your way back to bed."

Things were quiet now, but I wanted him out of there, in case more frightening fallout rained from upstairs.

"Okay, sir, what's your big surprise?"

He pressed a finger to his lips in contemplation. "I know. My next birthday, I'm going to be four."

"You are indeed."

"And how many will I be after that?"

"Five, six, seven, and on and on until you're a zillion and ten." I pulled back his covers. "Here you go, sweetie. Hop in."

He hung back. "I can't."

"Yes, you can. It's bedtime."

"Fred keeps waking me up, Mama. And there's a bad guy."

"In bed now."

"It's too hot in here. My tummy hurts."

"Now."

"Daddy's not home. Why can't I sleep with you?"

"Because this is where you sleep. In bed, Tyler. Now!"

"No! Don't make me, mama. Please!"

In the end, I left him weeping and pleading, trying to lure me with every thought that crossed his frantic mind. I was mean. The big little girl upstairs was going to hurt someone. The digga dada lady would let him sleep with her. Sebastian was having bad dreams. He had to finish what he'd been coloring. He was desperately hungry for peas.

A child wanted what he wanted with amazing intensity. My little one would have said anything to get his way.

· S E V E N T E E N ·

To some nothing mattered more than location. Others argued that timing spelled the crucial difference between triumph and woe. In my experience, it took both, operating in hair-trigger synchrony, to produce the perfect calamity.

Tyler's prized dump truck, the one he always kept neatly parallel parked at the door of his Little People schoolhouse, had gone missing. After Craig, an art student of mine and our second-best sitter, arrived to spell me while I taught a class, it took us nearly ten minutes to track the toy to the bottom of the laundry basket, where, according to my son's ardent professions of innocence, the truck had elected to hide because it was afraid of the new little big girl who lived upstairs.

Otherwise, I would never have dashed out at that particular moment to press the elevator button. The car arrived and the doors opened to reveal Lena Malik in the company of her daughter and a plump graying woman who carried a large tote and a pink Hello Kitty backpack. My mind raced in search of a plausible excuse to dash off and waddle down the stairs, but I came up empty. Smiling stiffly, I stepped in and turned my back to them, grateful that this was what elevator etiquette required.

The little girl's pleas were a bitter metal echo in my mouth. *No, Daddy! I'm begging you!*

At a glance, I noticed no obvious bruises on her, though I understood that didn't mean much. Abusers had no need or desire to advertise. They simply took what they wished.

What I wished for, above all, was a faster elevator. Ours was old, dimly lit, redolent of cooking smells, creaky, and slow.

Today, it seemed even slower than usual, at least when measured against my jangling impatience. It seemed a small eternity before we reached the lobby. I waited eagerly for the doors to open, but before they did the Lord's wife spoke.

"I'd like to have a word with you, Ms. Colten."

"I'm running late."

"It will only take a moment."

"All right."

"Start walking with Adriana, Luz. I'll catch up with you there."

The woman walked off clutching her bundles and Adriana's bird-boned wrist. Lena Malik led me outside near the edge of the broad green awning. She claimed the remains of the shade, standing with her back to the sun so it shone in my eyes.

A moment later, Obie the doorman stepped out onto the landing behind us. He was a total sweetheart, forever seeking extra ways to help. "You ladies want me to get you a cab?"

"No, Obie. Thanks for asking," I said.

Lena Malik waved him away like a stench. She lit a cigarette with one of the profusion of matchbooks I spotted in her purse, and spoke through the cloying haze of mentholated smoke. "I understand you do portraits, Ms. Colten."

"I do."

"I hear you're quite good, especially with children. Do you work in oils?"

"Rarely. I prefer graphite and ink or watercolor."

"Watercolor suits me fine. Perfectly, in fact. I'm interested in having a portrait done of my daughter."

I shifted uneasily. "I'm flattered that you'd ask, Mrs. Malik. But I'm in the middle of a complex commission right now, and I've agreed to another after that. I'm due in a couple of months, and I can't say how my time will be when the new baby comes. I know some other wonderful portrait artists, though. I'd be happy to recommend someone."

She dragged deeply, sucking in her cheeks. "I like the idea of your being right here, in the same building."

"Most portrait artists today work from reference photos, not live sittings."

"Of course. I'm well aware of that. The last thing I would expect Adriana to do is sit for a portrait."

"So the location of the artist you hired wouldn't matter. They wouldn't even have to be in New York."

"It would matter to me. My husband has been after me for quite some time to have our daughter's portrait done, but no one has seemed right until now, until you. I appreciate that your schedule may seem a bit complicated, but frankly, now that I've made the decision, I'm not prepared to wait. Douglas has been getting rather cross with me on this issue. He wants it done. I'd like to discuss the details and proceed without delay."

"In that case you'd definitely be better off with someone else. As I said, I have no idea when I'll be able to find the time."

"You will, Ms. Colten. I'm completely confident of that."

"Unfortunately, I'm not."

"But you will be. Don't you see?" She laughed mirthlessly at my puzzled frown. "There's no mystery here. It's simple."

"Not to me. I'll be taking care of a toddler and a newborn. I only have two hands and they're going to be full for a while. Once the baby's born, I'm committed to taking a few months off. How soon I decide to return to work depends on how things go."

"Then you'll do Adriana's portrait at once, before the baby comes. A couple of months should be more than adequate to complete it, I'd think."

I dodged a drift of cloying smoke. "I told you. I have other commitments that will keep me busy until the baby's born."

"They can wait. I'll pay double your usual commission, whatever it takes."

"I'm running late to teach a class, Mrs. Malik. I'll think about it and let you know."

"There's only one answer I'm prepared to accept, Ms. Colten. I have a wonderful photograph of Adriana you can work from. I'll slip it under your door, so you can begin at once."

"Please don't. I appreciate your asking, but I honestly don't think it's going to work."

Smoke drifted through her nostrils. "Of course it will. It always does. You'll see."

· EIGHTEEN ·

With a raised pinky, Mrs. Kalisher sipped the air. "How did you make it, sweetheart? In my life I've never had such a delicious cup of tea."

Tyler giggled. "From a dragon. And two scoops of other stuff."

She smacked her lips. "Of course. I should have known. The dragon taste is lovely. And two scoops of other stuff are simply perfect. You think maybe I could have a little more?"

"Here you go." He poured from a huge phantom teapot, staggering beneath its ungainly heft. "Want some dragon tea, Mama?"

"Sure. If it's decaf."

"Uh-oh. All gone. Be right back."

He dashed off toward the pebbles, leaves, and other detritus heaped near the jungle gym to brew another batch. Watching, I mused about the glories of his rich, unfettered imagination and where the crucial boundary lay between that and pathological lies. More than once, I had flashed on a distressing picture of Tyler two or three decades down the road. Given the way he dissembled and manipulated, it wasn't impossible to imagine him growing up to be one of those con man guys who bilk old people out of their life savings.

Frieda's smile faded. "Sounds like Doug Malik found his perfect match this time, Emma. Another one like him who thinks she owns the world."

"She only thinks she owns part of it. The rest she's convinced she can buy."

"The nerve of her trying to boss you around like that. You should look her right in the eye and tell her no. She wants a portrait of her little princess, she can find someone who cares to do the job."

Tyler approached us, treading cautiously with outstretched arms. "Better be careful. It's really hot."

Frieda squinted through the imaginary mist. "Thanks for the warning, darling. I'll blow on it."

"You too, Mama. Don't burn yourself."

"I won't, Ty."

"Blow! It's hot, Mama. Like fire."

"I am, sweetie. I did."

"Don't forget, Auntie Frieda. It's hot."

She spewed a long breath. "Mmm. Delicious. I must say no one makes two-scoop dragon tea like you, sweetheart."

"All gone again. I'll make more."

After he took off, Mrs. Kalisher leaned back, closed her eyes, and tipped her face to the sun. The skin slid over her bones like rumpled silk. Soft folds draped beneath her jaw, and her eyes were set in gentle hillocks. I could read the veins through her smooth papery skin. Marks from the sun's long caress were inscribed on her face like ancient hieroglyphs. I snapped a mental picture, so I could draw her. She was utterly beautiful in so many ways.

"Penny for your thoughts."

A sly smile played on her lips. "Make that three for a nickel, and you're on."

"Deal."

"Number one, Emma. What you did with Brent Elias was simply amazing."

"The boy with the burns? I didn't do anything."

"Nonsense. They've been trying everything they can think of for months to get him to open up, to talk about what happened. Psychiatrists, physical therapists, burn specialists, social workers, you name it. And they got exactly nowhere. Less than an hour and you pulled it off."

"It wasn't me, Mrs. K. It just happened. The time was right. He was ready. Maybe it had to do with the phase of the moon."

"Don't underestimate your part, Emma. He specifically asked when you're coming in to do the sketch he won as a prize."

"He actually wants me to draw him? I'm surprised."

"Brent is full of surprises. You'll see, Emma. You have the capacity to bring them out."

"I told you, it's not me."

"Whatever. It's an important step. So thanks."

I fell silent, watching the kids play, absorbing their buoyant delight. "I don't doubt that it's good for him to talk about it, Mrs. K., but can a child really ever recover from such a thing?"

"You'd be surprised, darling. People are like rubber balls. Some take a couple of hits and that's it. The air goes right out of them and they just lie there. Others you can bat around forever, and they keep bouncing back, high as they ever were or even higher. You'd be amazed at what some recover from, especially children."

"You honestly think any ball is strong enough to keep bouncing after what happened to Brent?"

"I do," she said. "I can't tell you how many times I've seen it happen. A child goes through a terrible, unimaginable thing, and comes back good as new. Abuse, neglect, horrifying loss. You name it. We had this one little girl who lost her mother and two little brothers in a car accident, and she was badly hurt herself. Six months later, she's a kid again. Wisecracking. Spelling as well as she ever did."

"Kelly?"

Her look went mock innocent. "I couldn't possibly identify the patient. Privacy rules, you know. But you should have seen this patient I couldn't possibly identify four months ago. She wouldn't speak, wouldn't relate to anyone. Her father would come in and she wouldn't even look at him. Then one day, it was as if she'd been in a blackout for all that time and someone had finally figured out how to turn the lights back on. No one had any idea what made the difference. But there it is. Now her father comes every day and they have dinner together. They're sad, sure. But they can laugh. They can hug each other. They can even get mad and tell each other off. Can you imagine anything better than that?"

"Not really."

"That's why I so enjoy volunteering at the hospital: the bouncing."

I held the firm, reassuring swell of my belly, felt the skittering squirm of my little girl swimming inside. I hoped she'd have that magical capacity to sense the impending edge of possibility, flip away before she crashed into it headlong, and push off in a more promising direction. Bouncing, I thought, had to be innate.

"Seeing what those kids have to put up with makes me feel pretty idiotic, Mrs. K. Here I've been worried sick about Tyler being able to deal with the trauma of having a new baby in the family, sure I'd done something terrible and damaging to him that he'd never bounce back from."

"That's no problem at all, sweetheart. Your Tyler doesn't like having a baby sister, you'll send her back."

"Why didn't I think of that?"

He barreled toward us, heedless this time of spilling the phantom tea. Mrs. Kalisher savored another cup and then hefted him onto her lap.

"So what's this I hear about you getting to have your very own baby sister, sweetheart?"

He made a sour face. "Am not. I don't want to."

Mrs. K.'s eyes gaped. "Oh, my. That's too bad. If you don't have one, you can't get to join the People Who Have a Baby Sister club."

"What's that?"

"Something very special. For select people only. I'm a member, and your mother is."

"That's right. Aunt Charlotte is my baby sister. And Daddy has Aunt Lorraine."

"How 'bout Amity?"

I shook my head. "Nope. She *is* a baby sister, but only her big sister, Grace, can be a member of the special club. Unless Siena and Joe have another baby girl, of course. Then Amity can join, too."

"So she's out of luck, but you can join. I'll see you get the club's T-shirt and membership badge as soon as this baby comes along," Mrs. Kalisher said.

He wriggled off her lap and eyed her with suspicion.

"And of course, you'll get the person with a baby sister membership coupon book. Each coupon entitles you to a very special treat."

His wary look didn't waver as he backed away. "Time to find more dragons."

"Good try, Mrs. K." I handed her a nickel. "You still owe me two more thoughts."

"Indeed. I was thinking about what they say about keeping your friends close and your enemies closer."

"Yes."

"Maybe doing this portrait for Mrs. High-and-Mighty is an opportunity in disguise."

"Maybe. But how do you keep someone close enough to keep an eye on without having them close enough to twist the knife?"

"Like you handle anything with a skull and crossbones, darling. Very, very carefully."

"Here's more tea," Tyler called as he raced toward us.

"Thank you, sweetheart. The tea you make is so tasty, I can't get enough."

"You know what my daddy makes?"

"No, what?"

"Gas."

She chuckled. "Your daddy's human. How nice. Speaking of which, if you'll excuse me, I have to go to the ladies'."

"Who can blame you?" I said. "All that tea."

While she trundled off to the restrooms at the edge of the park, I watched my little boy. He crouched at the edge of the broad rubber mat, fashioning long snaking parallel trails out of pebbles and twigs. Finished, he navigated deftly between them with a matchbox car, making exuberant vroom sounds. I struggled to remember why I had been so worried about him.

As if in answer, his head snapped up. The cords on his neck bulged, and he shrieked as if he'd seen a raging ghost.

"Wait! No! Stoppit!"

He raced for the gate. Someone had left it open a crack, and he charged through on a reckless beeline toward the street.

I ran after him, lungs searing, frantic to stop time.

Poised at the curb's edge, he stood wavering with uncertainty, head swerving rapidly back and forth.

"Tyler! Don't move!" I cried out.

A sudden misstep sent him sprawling into the street. He lay with splayed arms as a city bus bore down with astonishing speed. The engine roared. Ruts in the pavement rattled its cold metal bones.

In a heartbeat I was through the gate, across the sidewalk, onto the grassy strip beside the curb. My head filled with acrid exhaust and the keening plaint of an approaching ambulance. A searing pain stabbed my middle as I lunged to snatch my baby from harm's way.

I clutched him to me and struggled toward the line of parked cars as the monstrous hulk of the bus roared by, passing so close, the air it displaced tugged me like angry hands. So close, the blazing blur stamped an indelible imprint on my mind.

Mrs. Kalisher's shrill cry broke the shock. "My Lord, Emma! Tyler? What happened? Are you all right?"

I got to my feet, holding him firmly.

With an extravagant yawn, he rubbed his eyes. "I'm sleepy."

That went double for me. My spine was molten wax, my legs gelatinous. The only thing holding me up was quaking rage.

"You must never, ever go anywhere near the street without a grown-up. Do you hear me?"

"I wanted you to see the digga dada lady. But she runned away."

"No nonsense! This is not a joke, Tyler. You could have been badly hurt. Do you understand?"

He screwed up his face. "But I wanted you to see her."

"Stop that right now! I mean it!"

I felt another sharp pain followed by a wash of dizzy fear. It was too early for the baby. I hadn't finished Lamaze class. The book of prenatal development had too many chapters left to go.

"Come, my darlings." Mrs. K. gripped my elbow and clutched Tyler's hand. "Everyone needs to sit a minute and collect themselves."

It took less than a minute for Tyler. Humming happily, he sprawled at our feet, drawing shapes in the dirt with a twig.

The pain was easing, backing off. I dared to draw a deep, sating breath.

Frieda smoothed my hair and nodded approvingly. "Much better. You got your color back. You should have seen yourself, Emma. White as a sheet."

"And mad as a hornet. He needs a time-out the size of Alaska, and he's going to get it."

"No, Mama. Please!"

"Ssh," Frieda soothed. "Everyone's fine. That's what counts."

"You do not run in the street. Not ever again! Do you hear?"

"I won't. I promise."

"You even think about breaking that rule, you'll still be in time-out when you're married with kids of your own."

Mrs. Kalisher patted my hand as he returned to his dirt art. "Which reminds me, I owe you a third thought."

"Good. I could use one. That little episode knocked anything close to a thought right out of my brain."

"So here it is, Emma. We could spend from here until who knows talking about what might happen to Brent and Kelly, talking about what is or isn't bothering Tyler. We could think through every imaginable possibility, and you know what?"

I couldn't help but grin. "No, what?"

"No matter how hard you try to plan and anticipate, the future will go exactly the way it pleases. It's the one thing you never saw coming that always does."

· NINETEEN ·

Scheduled to assist in the preschool, I had to arrive an hour early to help set up. Siena insisted on having supplies replenished and the room restored to perfect order each day, so the children had the chance to trash it anew. Projects left to dry overnight were distributed in the cubbies for the kids to take home at the session's end. Paint jars were filled and chunky crayons sharpened. The biggest task was tidying the profusion of musical instruments, dress-up clothes, blocks, puzzles, puppets, shapes, toys, and books that had been dutifully replaced by the children at the end of the day during cleanup time, though often not in their rightful places.

To Tyler, this was heaven, a chance to sort, fret, and order to his heart's content. He and Amity set to the task with such rhapsodic fervor, there was barely anything for Siena and me to do. Normally, she passed such free time nurturing seedlings, honing her sing-along guitar skills, or concocting organic snacks, but today she was too edgy to concentrate on anything but the storm surrounding Jake.

"I don't get it, Emma. Why couldn't Jeanette and Arthur just come in and talk about their concerns?"

"Because they're idiots."

"Was it really necessary to show up with a lawyer?"

"No. But that's how they operate. They'd rather hide behind a mouth-for-hire Jeanette can pay for with Daddy's money than act like civilized human beings."

Doffing her dark-framed glasses, she pinched the slim bridge of her nose. "But why go to such extremes?"

"Because they're small-minded, self-centered idiots. And those are their positive qualities."

"They're worried about their daughter. That makes sense to me completely. What I can't fathom is how adamant they are that the only solution is to get Jake out of the class. Why can't they see that there's always more than one answer?"

"Because that would take insight, logic, flexibility, and compassion, none of which they happen to have. I hate to break it to you, sweetie, but some people suck."

"You're forgetting I'm a social worker, Emma. I worked at the battered women and kids' shelter for nine years, so I'm well aware that some people suck. But this is different. This isn't a gin-soaked drunk beating his wife or a schizophrenic woman who believes her four-year-old is possessed by the devil. It's not even some idiot, as you put it, losing his temper and busting up the house and whatever or whoever happens to be in his way. This is calculated, premeditated. Plain mean."

"You said you were going to poll the other parents. What's the reaction?"

"I've talked to six so far; all sympathetic to keeping Jake here. With the two of us, that makes eight out of twelve. I still have to contact the other three."

"You see? With odds like that, there's no way Jeanette and Arthur can win."

"Odds are meaningless. Defending a lawsuit could break us, plain and simple."

"We'll figure it out."

"I hope you're right, but I must say, for once I'm not so sure."

She plucked a sickly seedling from the row of tiny plants on the windowsill and tossed it out. Normally, everything she touched flourished, but there were always those depressing exceptions.

Siena had conceived of and founded the school. She had grown it from the germ of an idea to a thriving enterprise. Little Ranger had a devoted following and a lengthy wait list. Unlike most private city schools, this one offered a top-notch learning experience but didn't cost an arm and a leg. On the downside it tended to attract those of us who had no limbs to spare. We had no ultrawealthy parents who could make fat contributions, and precious little money in the bank. The cost of a lawsuit could sink us. Siena could lose this baby. That was true.

In addition to cruel confrontation, Siena had zero tolerance for waste. She gathered scraps of colored paper and began snipping them into confetti with sharp shears. An instant later, she cried out and raced to the sink.

When I got there, the water in the basin was tinged pink. A crimson bead rose on the web of skin between her thumb and forefinger. Her face had the pale, clammy look of raw fish.

"Sit," I told her. "Keep it up." I grabbed a gauze pad from the first aid kit and pressed it on the wound. "Hold it tight."

That caught the kids' attention. They stopped their manic straightening and approached.

Amity's lip quaked. "Are you okay, Mommy?"

"I'm fine, honey. It's nothing."

Tyler gaped. "Scissors are sharp. You have to be careful."

"That's true," Siena said. "I wasn't careful enough. I should have been paying better attention."

"Be careful," urged my little father hen. "Bleeding's bad."

"Everything's all right, sweetie. You guys are doing a great job. Ten more minutes until school starts. Go finish up."

The cut was superficial. I sprayed it with antiseptic and applied a Band-Aid. Siena's deeper wounds called for stronger medicine. I could think of only one surefire means to distract her.

I sat facing her at the little table. "I know you have a lot on your mind, Siena. But I could really use your advice."

"Sure. What about?"

"The whole Malik thing for one. Sam thinks he walks on water, but I don't trust him."

"Because?"

"Because his hobby is humiliation. Because he wields his power like a club."

"But still Sam wants to work with him?"

"He thinks it's worth the trade-off. But I'm not so sure. Sam's father has the highest regard for Malik, and that's more than enough to put me off completely."

"You saw Sam's father? What's the occasion?"

"You really want to know?"

"If you want to tell me."

"I went to talk to him, to get him to put in a good word for Sam with Malik. The good news is it worked. That's also the bad news."

"Sam doesn't know you did this?"

My cheeks flamed. "Seemed like a good idea at the time, but honestly, I didn't think it through. Sam resents his old man like crazy, and I can't blame him. When he finds out Senior had a hand in Malik's sudden attitude change, he'll kill me. And you know how these things go. He's bound to find out."

She shrugged. "You have to tell him, then, Emma. It's better if he hears it from you."

"You're right. I know that. But it's not going to be pretty."

"Maybe not, but it'll blow over."

"Sure it will. Like a typhoon."

Her smile was sympathetic and bemused. Siena was truly in her element when people dumped their problems on her head.

"That's for one, you said. What else?"

"Malik's wife. One day I give her that welcome gift and she treats me like a leper. The next, she's after me to do her daughter's portrait. Won't take no for an answer. Offers me the world."

Siena took some of the paper and started tearing it in ragged bits. There was always, as she'd said, another way. "You don't want to do it?"

"That's not what bothers me. I have no problem sticking my head in a lion's mouth if someone can guarantee it won't get bitten off."

She nodded. "I can see where it could go off the rails. Probably best to discuss that with Sam, too. Once he weighs in, the decision will be easier."

With a few folds and some well-placed cuts, I made her a purple snowflake. She deserved bigger and brighter, but sometimes, you had to make do. "How did you get to be sensible, Siena? You never lose the forest for the trees."

"It's always easier to solve someone else's issues, my friend." She tried to hide her own persistent issue behind a brave, unconvincing grin. "Anything else?"

"Only the Maliks' daughter." I fell silent, questioning whether it might be wiser to keep that particular concern to myself.

"What about her?"

I couldn't resist her cool, steady gaze or the chance to get that worry off my chest. This was Siena after all. In some ancient, stone-carved language, I felt sure that *Siena* meant safe.

"Our room is right below hers. Almost every night, about ten thirty or eleven, Malik comes in. I hear them talking, or maybe battling describes it better."

"About what?"

"Not sure. It's impossible to catch every word, though I admit I try. What I do hear is that he keeps telling her to do as he says, and she keeps pleading for him to stop. I promise I'll be good, she says. Don't, Daddy, please."

"You think he's hurting her?"

"I don't know. But it's certainly troubling. Last night was the worst. She sounded really upset. Stop, Daddy, she said. Please. I'm begging you!"

Her brow furrowed. "This child is how old?"

"Not sure. She's a tiny thing. Looks about eight."

"And those were her exact words? I'm *begging* you?"

I nodded. "It was pretty creepy."

"It's very creepy. I don't like the sound of that one bit. You should report it to Child Protective Services."

That was not what I needed or wished to hear. "They were words, Siena. Nonspecific words with nothing to back them up. Seems a bit much to involve the authorities on the strength of that."

"It doesn't take a huge leap to imagine that little girl was reacting to some kind of abuse."

"True, but blind leaps can be dangerous. I can only imagine what Tyler sounds like some days. When he doesn't get his way, he screams and carries on so you'd think I was murdering him. And he's only three. That doesn't mean I deserve to have Child Protective Services banging on my door."

"They investigate. That's all."

"That's not all and you know it. Suspicion can take on a life of its own. Next thing you know a family is broken up and destroyed, sometimes for no real reason. The system may mean well, but it doesn't always work."

"Fair enough. And you're right, it could be nothing; but what if it's something?"

"I've thought of that, of course. But it seems like pretty flimsy evidence to make such a serious accusation against anyone, much less someone with the power to kill Sam's career."

"I don't like the sound of it, Emma, big shot at Sam's Hospital or no."

"I didn't like it either. Believe me. Gave me the chills. And if I had proof he was abusing her in some way, you know I'd report it no matter what. But he could have been taking away her favorite doll. He could have been insisting that she stop reading and turn off the light. Adriana could be a drama queen, playing a minor disappointment for maximum effect. Grandstanding to get her way. There are a million innocent possibilities."

"True, but—"

I raised a hand to cut her off. "There's no point beating it to death. I'll keep an eye on things."

The door opened to admit a boisterous horde. Olivia's mother wanted to talk to Siena for a minute. Jaden had a potty emergency. Zachary was in manic birthday mode. Jean-Michel was terribly concerned that one of the goldfish looked sad.

Heavily, I stood. "If there's anything solid, I'll pursue it, Siena. Meanwhile, let's drop it, okay?"

· T W E N T Y ·

Franny and I had sat like this a thousand times, facing each other cross-legged on the floor. The difference was that we were now fifteen years older, had careers and husbands, mammoth Buddha bellies, and going on five kids. At thirty-two, we were also considerably wiser, verging on smart enough to begin to appreciate how little we actually knew.

"They should have minimum requirements for motherhood," I said.

"They do. You need a sperm and egg. Of course they don't have to be yours, not anymore, and you don't have to personally go to the trouble of getting them together or hatching the results. So nowadays the requirements are even more minimal than they used to be."

"Lucky thing. Otherwise I certainly wouldn't qualify."

"Why do you say that?"

"Because I'm hopeless. Sam thinks I'm crazy to worry, that everything's fine except my neurotic conviction that it's not."

"Who says Sam's right?"

It took a whole hand to enumerate. "Tyler's teacher; his pediatrician; the obstetrician; my sister, who has three amazing kids; and my friend Mrs. Kalisher. She's eighty-three, and a dozen times saner and more insightful than I'll ever be."

She made a note on the yellow pad she'd pulled from her bulging tote.

"So maybe Sam is right. Let's have a look."

"How? Is there some high-tech, state-of-the-art, scientific instrument you use to pick his brain?"

"Yes. It's called an interview. I ask you things, you answer. We see."

"We can do this here? In front of you know who?"

"I can promise that whatever I say will go right over you know who's head. Tell me about the pregnancy. Was it planned?"

"Sort of. We were just starting to think about trying to conceive when I found out I was pregnant. Or, at least, I was thinking about it. Turns out I'm incredibly fertile. All it takes is the idea."

"And Sam? How was he when he found out?"

"I don't honestly remember, but since it was during his intern year, oblivious is a pretty good guess."

"Would you say he's more connected now?"

"To his work, definitely. There's not much left over for anything else."

She rested the pad on her knees. "Is that how you'd describe your relationship? Unconnected?"

I fiddled with my wedding band. It crouched in a hollow beneath the sausage swell of my finger. Had I wanted to, I couldn't get it off.

"I wouldn't say 'unconnected' is the right word. It's more a matter of distraction, disconnects, trying to squeeze too many things into undersized bits of free time. You went through residency. You know how it is."

If she did, she was not about to admit it. "How was it for you being a mother at first?"

"You mean other than terrifying, strange, intimidating, overwhelming, and exhausting? It was fine."

"Postpartum depression?"

"Only when I made the mistake of looking in the mirror naked. Believe me, it only happened once."

"How long would you say it took you to adjust to having a child?"

I laughed ruefully. "Three and a half years and counting. If I ever get there, I'll let you know."

She smiled. "Sam's wrong about one thing for sure, Em. You haven't changed a bit."

"I have. More than you can imagine. Sometimes I barely recognize myself."

Tyler was showing off his precocious obsessive-compulsive skills, segregating the large marble collection Sam had bestowed upon him into small, precisely ordered groups. A tiny fleck of yellow on an aggie meant it could not go anywhere near a pure gray. The imitation aggies (known as immies) were banished to their own tight, separate clusters. Each color of allies (short for alabaster) had separate standing, and on and on.

"If you want your socks alphabetized or your dust motes arranged in size order, he's your man."

Franny's brow took a curious little hop.

"Have you noticed any change in his eating habits?"

I pondered that. "Not really. He's always subsisted mostly on ice cream and air."

"How is he with his peers?"

"He likes being around other kids. Some he loves, like

this little girl Amity in his class. Some he loves to death, or tries to."

"You mentioned that. Hitting and such?"

"And lots of such. He's not exactly easygoing when it comes to not getting his way."

"Is that new?"

"No, but it's gotten progressively worse."

She made another note. "Sleep?"

"Hmm? I've heard of that. Can't say it happens much around here."

Franny scanned the room with the same look of incredulity she'd attempted to hide when I took her around earlier for the two-minute all-inclusive tour. She'd made the appropriate noises about how bright the place was, how cozy and inviting. But after seeing the sliver of space that passed for our kitchen, the claustrophobic bedroom, and Tyler's two-by-nothing slice lopped off the not so generous living room, she had waited expectantly for me to show her the rest. I can well imagine what she was thinking. How could we possibly hope to pack another clown into this overstuffed Volkswagen, especially a little clown that required considerable equipment? The conundrum had crossed my mind a time or two hundred as well.

"He gets up?" she said.

"Only ten, twelve times. On a good night."

"When did it start?"

"Past couple of months or so."

Tyler studied a marble that defied categorization. He held it above a tight circle of yellow-flecked immies and then tested it next to a clump of aggies marked with blue. Unsatisfied, he pinched it with a grimace of distaste and dropped it in the trash.

"Daddy doesn't want you throwing the marbles away, Ty. Remember?"

"That one's broked."

"It's just different."

"But I don't like it, Mama. It doesn't fit."

"That doesn't mean you have to throw it away."

"Yes, I do." To make the point, he tossed several others in the garbage can.

"That's it. Time to put the marbles away."

He took that extremely well, for a land mine.

Franny waited for the storm to pass. When it did she dipped into her canvas tote and produced a daddy doll in a nerdy business suit, a vintage fifties mommy doll in heels and a shirtwaist dress, a towheaded boy doll in overalls, and an infant doll swaddled in pink.

"I brought some people for you to play with."

Tyler picked up three of the four and began to arrange them. He lined them up in size order and then by hair color, light to dark. Finally, he set the little boy doll between the mommy and daddy figures, touching hands. The baby doll went the way of the unacceptable marbles, in the trash.

Before I could protest, Franny shook her head. She observed mutely as first the mother doll and then the father kissed the little boy good night.

"Night-night. Sleep tight," he chanted happily. "Don't let the bedbugs bite. Night, Mama. Night, Daddy. Night, Tyler. Night, Fred and Sebastian. See you in the morning, guys."

Satisfied, he went in search of a different diversion.

"Look, Tyler. Here are more people."

Franny offered him a gray-haired couple, two other adults, and a teenage boy and girl. She spread them out haphazardly, the perfect draw.

"Toileting, Em? Any problems there?"

"Me, you mean? Or him?"

"That would depend on whose emotional development you want me to take a look at."

"Has to be his. Mine was arrested years ago, charged with attempting to impersonate a grown-up."

She caught her lip in her teeth and stared blankly, a posture she used to take when pondering issues of global import: nuclear disarmament, free trade, whether to have sex with her philosophy instructor, and if so, where.

"What, Franny? I know that look."

"I'm wondering why you feel the need to hide behind sarcasm."

"I don't hide behind it. Obviously, it's right out there where you can pick up on it and rub it in my face."

Tyler stuffed the mommy and daddy dolls in the cab of his miniature Toyota station wagon, leaving the little boy doll behind. He drove them along a road formed by the slim plank edge that bordered our ancient parquet floor to an imaginary parking lot behind his Little People schoolhouse.

Returning to the scatter of figures, he took the gray-haired couple and sat them side by side near the door. "You watch the TV now. Dora's coming on soon." He walked the two other adults in a lurching hobble to sit beside the gray-haired couple and await the scintillating adventures of Dora the Explorer, her talking backpack, and her faithful monkey, Boots.

That left the little boy with the teenagers. Tyler posed the girl to observe from the sidelines and staged a convincing skirmish between the absurdly mismatched boys, complete with karate chops, ninja kicks, and comic-book sound effects.

"Pow! Bam! I got you. Fall down!"

The little one kept pounding mercilessly as the old, larger combatant lay in a cowardly heap.

" 'No. Stop! You're hurting me.' . . . 'Hah. I got you! Got you again! I killed you dead.' "

"Sweet. Don't you think?"

Franny pressed a finger to her lips. The verdict would wait.

Five minutes later, our second-best sitter arrived to spell me, so we could go to our Lamaze class.

I interrupted Tyler's play massacre to kiss him good night.

"Be good for Craig, sweetie."

In a blink, his bravado dissolved. "Don't go, Mama."

"It's okay, Ty. I'll be back later."

"Not later, *soon*."

"Okay, soon."

Frannie trundled down the street beside me.

"So what do you think?"

"He's a cutie," she said. "Very bright, imaginative, and enthusiastic."

"There's a 'but' at the end of that sentence. I can hear it."

"He seems fine, but I can't tell you with absolute certainty that there's nothing to worry about."

"Because?"

"Because if you sense something's going on, I'm not going to write it off that easily. In my experience, most mothers have pretty good instincts when it comes to their kids."

I cradled the swell of my baby girl. "Mrs. Kalisher says no problem. If Tyler doesn't want a sister, we send her back."

"If there is a problem, I don't think it's about the baby, Emma. He may not be keen on the idea, but he's way too young to be distressed by what amounts to an abstraction. Once she gets here, he'll go through an adjustment like every other kid, but that's not what's going on now."

"What then?"

She shrugged. "Could be lots of things."

"Such as?"

"Top of the list: he's fine. There's nothing wrong at all. That's my best guess, no question."

"But you said mothers have good instincts."

"Most. Not all. And not always. It isn't as if you were worried enough to seek professional help. I happened to come along and offered to have a look at him. That's a very different set of facts."

"What's the rest of the list?"

"Not important. I told you. He seems fine."

"Nevertheless, I'd like to know."

"My advice is not to go there."

"You're too late. I'm already there, in spades."

"Then back up. Make a U-turn. Go someplace else."

"Why? It's normal curiosity."

"Normal doesn't make it smart."

I studied her profile. "What's wrong with wanting to know?"

"I'll tell you what's wrong. Someone with a rash and a stuffy head goes for tests and they insist on hearing all the dire possibilities in advance. So the doctor admits that while it's probably a cold, in the worst, most unlikely, rarest possible case, it could be a sign of bubonic plague. Of course, *plague* is all the patient hears. She spends days worrying herself sick, and nine hundred and ninety-nine times out of a thousand, it turns out to be a cold."

We passed a lingerie store. In the window, pouting jut-hipped mannequins were decked out in lace thong panties and matching demicup bras. I had a distant memory of being a girl who could wear such things, a girl whose biggest worry was herself.

"I hear you. But I still want to know."

"Why don't you give it time? See how it goes? Kids are a lot like the weather. Wait ten minutes, and they change. That's what happened with Ben, our younger twin. He refused to be potty trained. Michael was a snap six months earlier, but Ben wasn't interested in the least. I tried everything I could think of. And then just as I was starting to believe he had a serious problem, that I'd have to find diapers big enough to fit him in college, he decided he was ready. And that was that."

"I'm asking you what it could be, Franny. If you don't tell me, I'll go on the Web and get all the misinformation I could possibly hope to obsess about on my own."

She scowled. "Well, for one thing, it could be genetic. He could be a stubborn pain in the butt like his mother."

"Or?"

I won the stare-down. "Okay. If you won't let it go, there are a number of possibilities, but top of the list is trauma. When little kids get off course emotionally, it's usually because they saw or experienced something highly distressing. An illness. The death of a parent."

"Nothing like that happened to Tyler."

"Abandonment," she went on. "Witnessing a natural disaster, war, or violent crime."

I shook my head.

"Neglect. Emotional or physical abuse."

My insides froze. "Or sexual abuse?"

She looped an arm around my neck. "Easy, Vesuvius. No one said anything about that."

"Is that what you think is going on, Franny? Is it?"

"No."

I stared at my hands, furious at their inadequacy. "But how could you know for sure? How could anyone?"

"Take a breath, Emma. I see no signs that Tyler's been abused, sexually or otherwise. And nothing you're telling me raises that kind of red flag."

"Honestly? If there was, do you swear you'd tell me?"

"Of course I would. I'm your friend. I also happen to be

a mental health professional. If I suspect abuse, I have an ethical and legal obligation to report it. If I had knowledge of something like that and let it go, I could lose my license. I could be found guilty of a crime. Friend or no, I'm not about to risk a trip to the big house to put your mind at ease."

"So your diagnosis is Tyler's fine, but I need a rubber room?"

She looped her arm through my elbow. "In the worst and rarest case, my friend, we might just have to commit you to a loony bin for overly fretful mothers. But in my humble estimation, it's probably just a silly little cold."

· TWENTY-ONE ·

Sam was spending the night with the surgical simula-
tor, and Grant had a dinner meeting with a potential in-
vestor in his Internet site, Gotcha!, so Franny and I became
a couple for Lamaze. We took turns playing mother and
coach. I found I far preferred dispensing back rubs and en-
couragement than the role I was doomed to take on.

"I definitely think Sam should have this baby," I whispered to her as a mock contraction approached. "After all,
it's his turn."

"Great idea. Grant, too. We'll elect them in their absence."

"It would serve them right for doing this to us."

"Definitely."

Our teacher the drill sergeant shot us a look. "Focus,
ladies."

"Yes, sir!" I rasped when she stepped out of earshot.

For some reason, that made Franny laugh. Her belly jiggled against my back, which set me off, too. We had met as
thinly veiled adolescents, and we reverted to that with remarkable ease.

Sergeant Rita was not amused. "Laughing is not going to help you when you're in labor." She said this leaning over us with the stopwatch swinging like a bawdy metronome from breast to breast.

The sight triggered a fresh wave of infantile hilarity that rapidly infected the couple to our right. Pops of explosive tittering spread around the room.

Still the teacher trained her angry focus on me. "That's quite enough."

The harder I tried to stop, the harder I laughed. Something deep inside kept bubbling up and spilling over, as if it had been trapped under perilous pressure for too long.

Rita loomed over me with hip-mounted hands and a look of crushing disdain. "You, of all people, need to take this seriously, Emma. Otherwise, I see no point in your continuing with the class."

That was a sobering slap. I so wanted to succeed at this. I swiped the tears of laughter with the sleeve of my giant caftan, and struggled to look suitably grim.

Unsatisfied, Rita threw up her hands. "That's it. I am not wasting any more of my time on the jokers. There are people here who are interested in mastering the technique and I need to focus on them."

The baby was utterly still. Aside from hot creeping shame and my heart stammering, I felt nothing.

Smoothing back her bangs, the teacher took the stopwatch firmly in hand. "Another contraction on the way in ten seconds, mommies and daddies. Nine . . . eight . . . seven. Get ready without getting tense. Get set—"

Behind me, Franny gulped a breath. As the countdown continued, I could sense what was coming.

"Go!"

"With pleasure. Come on, Em. Let's."

Franny slung the strap of her tote on her shoulder and made for the door. The teacher stared at me through cold, narrowed eyes. And I couldn't bear what I saw in them.

Outside, my friend puffed her contempt. "So much for that. Now, where should we eat?"

I could barely speak past the bitter lump lodged in my throat. "Great. I screwed that up, too."

"What are you talking about? You didn't screw up. You laughed, for heaven's sake. That's not even a crime in Singapore."

"I screwed up the class, I mean."

"No way. You handled it beautifully. We both did. Walking out was the only reasonable thing to do. Rita, the Lamaze nazi. For a teacher, she makes a great storm trooper."

"But I wanted to get it right this time. Natural childbirth is better for the baby."

She rolled her eyes. "We need to talk, my friend. And we need to do it over dinner. I'm starved."

Leaning in, she perused the menu mounted in the window of a tiny northern Italian restaurant. "You know this place?"

"Not really."

"Let's try it. Looks perfect. They have food."

The waiter led us to a table in the rear of the narrow space. Between us, a candle flamed in a faceted glass bowl. The warm glow softened Franny's troubled frown.

"What's going on with you, Emma?"

"You mean other than being eleven months pregnant, house-sized, and so hopeless I flunked out of Lamaze class? Everything's great."

"What happened to the Emma I knew, the one who would never let anyone treat her like a doormat?"

"I told you, I just want to do what's best for the baby."

"There's no magic formula, kiddo. No secret handshake

or perfect way. What's best for the baby is to lighten up. Take care of Emma. Personally, I don't buy all that bunk about conquering the pain of childbirth through focus and relaxation. Childbirth hurts like hell. There are drugs for that, and I say, bring them on."

"You didn't do Lamaze with the twins?"

"I took the class, sure, because otherwise, I'd never hear the end of it from my mother. She got it in her fat head that babies whose parents do Lamaze have a lower incidence of nose rings or something equally ridiculous. So I figured I'd take the class, get a nice dinner out in the city in the bargain, and shut Blanche up."

"Doesn't that make you Blanche's doormat?"

She beheaded a breadstick. "Not at all. What I am doing is mother management, not letting Blanche drive me any crazier than absolutely necessary."

"You really plan to take drugs?"

"You bet I do, probably starting as soon as the beginning of the ninth month."

"You don't think natural is healthier?"

"What's natural about agony, I ask you? Plus, where's the hard scientific evidence? Zillions of perfectly healthy infants who grow up to be perfectly normal healthy adults are delivered by C-section or with the help of painkillers. I'm not saying there's anything wrong with Lamaze or hypnobirth or anything else people want to try that doesn't risk harming their baby, but that doesn't mean any of those are right for you or me."

I chewed on that and an olive. "What about breast-feeding?"

"What about it?"

"I tried, but I was hopeless at that, too. Ty was hungry all the time, up every hour, not gaining enough. And my nipples cracked. Finally, the pediatrician said I might be better off giving him formula."

"And let me guess. Things went smoother, easier. You were both better off."

"The feeding wasn't such a struggle, true. But you should have seen the way some of the other mothers looked at me when I bottle-fed him in the park. You would have thought I was giving him arsenic."

"La Leche League nazis. I know them well."

"You didn't breast-feed either?"

Dipping a bread chunk in olive oil, she shook her head. "I gave it a try, too. But I felt like a filling station that was forever running out of gas. I'm aware that studies have shown certain advantages, and all things being equal, I wanted to. But studies are far from the whole story. Turns out all three of us did way better with the arsenic."

"We did, too. So why did I feel so guilty and inept?"

Her finger popped up. "That, my friend, is the question we're here to address. Why did you? Why do you?"

I mulled that over long and hard while I nibbled on a chunk of Parmesan cheese from the antipasto plate Franny had ordered. "I don't know."

"Yes, you do. The answer is in there, somewhere, but you've hidden it from yourself. When you're ready to face whatever it is, you will."

"That doesn't make any sense, Franny. My life has been totally, boringly normal. I can't think of a single thing I went through that I'd need to hide from myself."

She shook her head. "Of course you can't think of it. That's the definition of repressed."

"But what could it be?"

Her hands were empty. "We all go through things, even those of us who'd swear they've led totally boringly normal lives."

"What kind of things? I want the list."

"That one, you'll have to compile on your own, my friend. When it comes to the causes of human pain and suffering, the list goes on and on."

· TWENTY-TWO ·

Sam was flying, though I feared without a net.

"It was amazing, Em. Beyond amazing. Malik's a magician, I swear it. He did the heart-lung without a hitch. Perfect. And then he moves right to the next OR for a laparoscopic valve replacement. He does it freehand, and still takes about half the time most experienced surgeons can do it using the da Vinci robot."

"That's great, honey. He must've been really pleased with you if he had you scrub in on two cases."

"Try three. After the valve, we did a minimally invasive bypass."

"I'm so glad it worked out."

"I'm going to get that fellowship with Malik, Em. I can feel it in my bones."

Bursting with enthusiasm, he grabbed me around the middle. For a harrowing instant, I thought he might be contemplating a suicidal act like trying to lift me, but he settled for the hug.

"Honestly. This could be the day that turns it all around.

I was talking to someone who worked with Malik at the Cleveland Clinic. She said he only has two settings: on and off. If he doesn't like you, you don't exist. If he does, you're golden."

"She?"

He eyed the ceiling. "Don't start that again, Emma. I told you I have absolutely no interest in Suzanne beyond the fact that she's Malik's pet."

I swallowed hard. "I know. I didn't say you did."

"And obviously my being nice to her hasn't hurt. I got on his radar screen. He gave me a chance."

My heart sank. "We have to talk about that, Sam."

"I know, you're going to tell me not to get my hopes up. But it's too late for that. By the end of the day, he was calling me Sam, giving me pointers. I even got a slap on the back and a smile."

"That's because you're good at what you do, sweetie. And hardworking, and a very quick study." Not, I wanted to say, because of "Suze." "Also, Sam . . . You're not going to like this."

"Then save it. Right now, I'm only up for good things. In fact I say we go out and celebrate."

"I'd love to, but it's a little late for the boy wonder."

With a bath towel draped across his shoulders, Tyler had spent the last half hour dashing around the room in manic circles with outstretched arms. Every so often he'd reach his target ground speed and with a fierce grunt, attempt to take off and leap a tall building or, failing that, vault over a throw pillow in a single bound. Watching him, I was exhausted. Hopefully, soon the batteries on his supercharge would run out and he'd spend a nice long night in his big boy hangar, sleeping it off.

"Call a sitter, then. Would be nice for us to have a grown-up night out, just the two of us. It's been too long."

"Sure. It'll be good to go somewhere relaxing where we can talk."

In a public place, Sam would be less likely to scream or strangle me for going to his father. As a civilized soul he would save that to do later at home. "Ruthie has class tonight. I'll try Craig."

That was all it took to send Tyler into orbit.

He went red as fury, screaming, "No Craig. No!"

"Whoa, tiger," Sam soothed. "This is just Mom and Dad going out to dinner."

"No!"

"Ssh, sweetie. It's okay."

"It's. Not. Okay!" He wailed with such ferocity, it pierced my heart. I was fluent in the language of my son's anguish. This was the genuine item.

"Stop, for Christ's sake," Sam demanded. "Hush!"

I picked Tyler up. He looped his arms around my neck, twined his legs around my swollen middle, and clung like someone drowning. Wetly, he cried, wailing in my ear, pulling syncopated scraps of breath.

"Don't go, Mama! Please!"

I stroked his hair and inhaled the scent of little boy sweat and baby shampoo. "You know, now that I think of it, I'm pretty pooped. Maybe we should hang out here and order something in."

The look on Sam's face said it all. I was coddling the kid, making things worse.

Seated on the couch, I held him across my lap like a baby with his head in the crook of my arm. His legs slopped over. He had gotten far too big for me to contain in a neat bundle of protection.

Slowly, the starch of fear went out of him. He wriggled out of my grasp and swaggered off to play with his superheroes.

Sam sniffed. "What the hell was that about?"

"No idea. What's wrong, Ty? Are you angry with Craig?"

Batman was certainly furious with Superman. Tyler had the Caped Crusader beating the Man of Steel mercilessly with a play schoolhouse chair.

"Did Craig hurt you, sweetie?"

"You're putting ideas in his head, Em. Craig's your buddy, tiger. You and he shoot nerf hoops together. Isn't that right?"

In response, he snuffled bravely.

"Did he do anything that bothered you, baby? You can tell us."

He shrugged. "I just don't want you to go."

"That's all? Are you sure?"

"Sebastian's tired."

"Is he, now?"

"Yup. He's tired 'cause the big little girl won't behave."

"Tyler," I warned, "no stories, remember?"

"He is tired, Mama. I promise."

"Would you like to lie down with him awhile until he falls asleep?"

That earned a solemn nod.

While I put boy and stuffed Dalmation to bed, Sam ordered dinner. By the time I tiptoed out of Tyler's tiny room, the food had arrived. Still bent on celebration, Sam popped the cork on a split of champagne.

He poured me a bit, and after a seven-month hiatus, a sip had an instant mellowing effect.

We clinked glasses.

"To getting that fellowship," he said.

"To your success, Sam. Definitely."

"Thanks for understanding about the last couple of days. Meant a lot to be able to go into the OR with a clear head, not to mention prepared."

So there was my big fat opening, the one that led directly to a big, fat trapdoor. "I'd do anything to help you get what you want, Sam. I hope you know that."

"Sure. Me, too."

"Maybe I'd even do something dumb, something you might not be happy about. But it would be out of love, wanting to be supportive. Does that make sense?"

His smile stiffened. "That depends. What did you do?"

"The other day I called Freddie to say hello. It's been months."

A rush of relief escaped him. "You want to be nice to the grand dame from pig farm Kansas, be my guest. Better you than me."

"She asked me to come to lunch. She insisted I bring Tyler. She said your father missed seeing him."

A single sharp laugh escaped him. "I'd never accuse step-mummy dearest of having a sense of humor, but that's pretty damned funny. Imagine my father giving a crap about seeing anyone who didn't pay handsomely for the privilege."

"You're right, of course. Senior barely noticed he was there, and all Freddie could do was criticize his manners. But at least your dad was interested in what's going on with you, Sam. He asked if you still wanted cardiothoracic surgery, where you thought you'd like to train."

Angrily, he popped the staples on the takeout bag. "That's predictable. If he didn't know what I wanted, how could he pick it apart?"

I took another sip, a large one. "He suggested a few top people you might want to work with. I mentioned how highly you thought of Dr. Malik, how much you'd like to do your fellowship with him."

"You *mentioned*?"

My cheeks burned. "Senior knows all the big shots, Sam, including Malik. He could easily put in a good word for you. I figured it couldn't hurt."

"You *figured*?"

"I did."

"Well, you figured wrong, damn it! He's never done a goddamned thing for me, and he's not about to start now. But now that you *mentioned* it to that sanctimonious prick, I'll never hear the end of it. He'll claim credit for every crumb I get from Malik, even though he didn't lift a finger to make it happen."

"You're right. I'm sorry."

He sputtered. "How could you? What the hell were you thinking? Were you thinking at all?"

The lump of sorrow lodged in my throat made it hard to push out the words. "All I was thinking about was how badly Malik treated you, how badly you wanted a chance to work with him. I understand now that it was a dumb idea, but I was only trying to help."

"Great job, Emma! Look what you've accomplished. He'll be shoving this up my butt forever. Every chance he gets, Senior will entertain everyone with the amusing story of how he made my career. How I'd be nothing and nowhere without his incredible power and generosity. How it's lucky for a useless nothing like me that he had the talent and ambition to pave the way."

"I'm sorry, Sam. I was wrong. What more can I say?"

"Nothing! Don't say another goddamned word."

He wrenched off his lab coat and hurled it on the couch. Then he stomped down the hall to the bedroom and slammed the door.

I followed meekly, sinking inside. The door was locked. "Please, Sam. I feel horrible enough already. Don't shut me out."

I heard drawers smacking, a clash of hangers, and a harsh thump as something hit the floor. For a while, there was a rush of water, and I dared to hope he was showering to cool off. Vague noises followed. Finally, the lock turned and he opened the door. But it was not to let me in.

Sam had traded his surgical scrubs for a polo shirt and jeans. The seductive scent of aftershave was enhanced by the heat of his wrath.

"You're going out?"

His hands flew up as if he'd scrubbed and I threatened contamination. "I need space."

I felt sick inside, broken, tiny, scared. "Please, Sam. Don't do this. When you act like a jerk, I forgive you."

His look held nothing but bitter contempt. "I have never, ever done a thing like this to you! Not even close!"

"Fine, then tell me off. Yell at me. Say mean things. Call me names. Talk to me, say anything. Just don't leave."

I couldn't move. He turned sideways, edging along the wall to pass without touching me.

His footsteps faded down the hall. I heard him at the door.

"At least tell me where you're going."

No answer.

"What if I need you, Sam? What if I go into labor? I didn't have a chance to tell you, but I fell yesterday. I had pains."

The knob turned, followed by the familiar squeak of the hinges that for years had been asking for oil. In shocked disbelief I watched as the door slammed behind him. Then I followed him into the hall.

"Wait, Sam. Come on. Let's talk about it."

He was already at the elevator. For once, it came too soon. In a breath, he was in the car with the doors closing in.

"Please, Sam. Don't!" I called after him.

"Good-bye, Emma," he muttered coldly as the gap closed. "Don't wait up."

· T W E N T Y - T H R E E ·

Numbly, I went through the motions: mechanical breakfast, mechanical getting dressed, robotic walking my son to music class and then flopping one leaden foot in front of the other like an artless puppeteer until somehow, I made it home again.

Having neglected to raise the blinds or turn off the lights, the apartment still held the look and sickly feel of the night before. I was trapped in it like a nasty hangover, sick with self-loathing and regret. Endlessly, I replayed the ugly words that had passed between me and Sam, wondering how it was possible for a lethal storm to brew so quickly in a clear promising sky, wondering how long it would take to pass and what would lie in its hazy aftermath, wondering in terror what would happen if it never passed at all.

Feeling a desperate need to blubber, I dialed my sister Charlotte's number in Ann Arbor. Her husband, Hal, was an English professor at the University of Michigan. They'd met when she was an undergraduate at NYU and he was studying there for his doctorate. After college, they had settled near his new job and she'd been functioning happily ever since as the second kind of academic wife. She made dinner parties for Hal's colleagues, charmed his superiors at university functions, and welcomed an endless stream of his adoring students and advisees to the house. Their two girls and a boy, aged six through nine, had been steadily exposed to great minds and great literature. Maybe that was why they were so poised, well spoken, and polite. The specter of Dante's Inferno or Medea's wrath had to pack a far bigger punch than the most onerous imaginable time-out.

Her phone rang three times, four, deepening my dejection. I was about to hang up when I heard her voice.

"Em? I swear you must be psychic. I was just about to call you when the phone rang."

"Saved you the nickel."

"Which means more than you know."

A picture formed in my mind. When she talked on the phone, Char stuffed her free hand beneath her arm and cocked her head like a curious pup. Her hair was the same warm brown shade as mine, but straight and frizz-free no matter how high the humidity. I imagined how it hung like a satiny drape while she spoke, how it shaded her fair skin and bright hazel eyes from the exuberant sunlight that streamed through the French windows in her outsized country kitchen.

I'd caught a catch in her voice. "What's wrong?"

"How about you, Em? You don't sound so fabulous yourself."

"Fair enough. I'll be happy to dump, but you first."

Now I pictured her pacing restlessly toward the cabinet where she kept the cleaning supplies. In times of stress, my sister seized her weapon of choice, a dry Swiffer. She claimed that dusting had a Zen-like calming effect. She'd urged me to try it, to really go for the hidden nooks and crannies that hadn't seen a spray or cloth for ages. For me, the results had not been promising. I trapped a cinder behind my contact lens. My head felt like a backed-up storm drain. I sneezed.

As if she could read my thoughts, she blew her nose. "It's Jared."

My nine-year-old nephew had always been the superstar in her blinding little galaxy. He was incredibly bright, great at sports, terrific with people, and as close as you could get to being a violin prodigy without having the blessing threaten to wreck his young life.

"What about him?"

"He's been having episodes of disturbingly rapid heartbeat. It happens rarely, every six months or so, and never at home. The first time he told me about it, I took him right to the pediatrician. Dr. Sinclair told me not to worry, that he'd probably overdone it during practice. You know how Jared is, always wanting to be the best, always pushing himself. So I didn't take it seriously."

"What happened? Is he all right?"

"Yesterday, he was playing Little League, the opening game, and the rest of us went to watch. Jared was over the moon, pitching a no-hitter. There was one out to go for a perfect game, and this strapping kid on the opposing team popped the ball toward center field. Jared was running back to try to grab it and he collided with his teammate who was rushing in. It looked like nothing. Both of them are skinny as rails and the impact looked like no big deal. But Jared went down clutching his chest. He passed out. Thankfully, one of the dads was an EMT and had come to the game in his van. He made sure Jared was stable and drove us to the hospital. They admitted him through emergency."

"Is he all right, Char? For Christ's sake, tell me what happened."

She spewed air like a blown tire. I realized she was beyond Swiffer therapy. When my sister was in major distress, she scrubbed the sink. Years ago, before Tyler was born, Hal was in a bicycle accident and broke both arms. Charlotte had been left to care for three dependent kids under four and one about to turn thirty. I'd flown out to help for a couple of weeks, and by the time I left, my lungs held a snowdrift of Ajax.

"He has a cardiac arrhythmia. Wolff-Parkinson-White syndrome it's called. It's congenital, which means he's had it from birth. There's an extra bundle of nerves that goes from his atrium to his ventricle. When the electrical impulses run on those nerves instead of the normal ones, there's no safety brake, and the heart can beat incredibly fast. A cardiologist needs to test him to figure out how fast it could be in his case. In some people, it gets so bad, the heart shuts down."

My heart did just that. Clutching my belly, I sank on the couch. "My Lord, Char. So what happens? What do they do?"

"It depends on what they find. Sometimes, it's safe to leave it alone. Or there are medications. But if it's serious enough, they have to go in and get rid of the extra nerves."

"Operate?"

"I'm told that used to be the case, but now they do it with radio waves or freezing."

"That doesn't sound so bad. Or does it?"

"It does to me, Emma. They'd have to put a catheter in through the artery in his groin and thread it up to his heart. The doctor said it's not without risks." The last word cracked in sharp anguished bits, and she broke down completely.

Charlotte had always been the strong and sure one, the

brave one out of two. Though she was a year younger, it had always been Char the Intrepid who went off armed with a determined look and a large-caliber hair dryer to check for burglars when we were alone in the house and heard a suspicious noise. She was the one who killed the wasps and spiders, the one who dared to take the trap outside and release the minuscule field mouse that registered on my skewed psyche as a great, growling beast.

"But it may need no treatment at all. Or a pill may handle it. Or maybe there's a better answer. I'm up to my ears in cardiologists. We'll make sure he gets to the best, Char. We'll figure this out."

"That's what I was hoping you'd say, Em. We'll do anything, go anywhere. All that matters is getting Jared well."

"Of course. Now please, sweetie, I know I'm the last one who has any right to say so, but try not to get ahead of yourself. Take it one step at a time. You don't have to be a raving worrywart like me."

"I'm trying, Em. Believe me. But I keep thinking, it's his *heart*. This thing he has can be life-threatening. What if they don't figure out how bad it is in time and something terrible happens? It's driving me crazy. And I'm driving him crazy. I can barely stand to let him out of my sight."

"I understand. It's scary as hell. But you'll get through it, and he'll be fine. You'll see."

She blew her nose again and drew a ragged breath. "He will. He has to be."

"He will," I said again. "Soon, all this will be behind you, nothing but a bad memory. Fertilizer for the gray hair crop to come."

"I can't wait."

"Yes, you can. Now put down the Ajax, Char."

That brought a nervous giggle. "What makes you think I'm holding Ajax?"

"Just put it down. I want you to back away from the sink slowly and keep your hands in plain sight. Play your cards right, and no one has to get hurt."

The giggle gained steam. "No fair making me laugh, Em," she said, laughing. "Here I am being perfectly miserable, and you have the nerve to spoil it."

"Good. I'll talk to Sam right away. I bet he knows who's the top expert in the field."

"You don't know how much better that makes me feel."

"Can I do anything else? Want me to come?"

"Not now. Let's see how it plays out. For all I know, I may see you in New York."

"Are you sure? It's a plane ride. I could be there today."

"Positive. If I need you to come, promise I'll let you know. Meanwhile, you've got Tyler to take care of, not to mention the one on the way and Sam."

I shoved my own hand under my arm to hold myself together. "Mm-hmm."

"I'm fine now, really, Em. Knowing Sam can help us get to the best in the field means more than I can say. Bless you for marrying the perfect man, someone whose chosen specialty we happen to need."

I swallowed hard. "Glad to oblige. Anything you need, I'm here."

"I know that. Now your turn. What was it you wanted to dump?"

"I forgot, Char. Couldn't have been too important. Let's concentrate on Jared and get this damned thing fixed."

· TWENTY-FOUR ·

When Sam's phone didn't answer, I dialed the department's administrator, LeeAnn.

"Oh, *Emma*, hi! How nice to hear from you, *Emma*." Her voice grew progressively louder and shriller. "What's up, *Emma*?"

"I have to speak to Sam, LeeAnn. It's urgent."

"You're looking for *Sam*? Hmmm. Let me think where he might be."

She had all the subtlety of a hurled brick. In the background I heard muffled voices, giddy laughter, and anxious footsteps scurrying out of her office toward the hall.

And there I was on my cell phone, hanging up.

"Hello, Sam. Suzanne."

With an overwrought look of innocence, Little Miss First-Year trapped Sam's skittish gaze. "Want me to wait?"

His lips pressed in a grim seam. "No need. I'm coming with you. We're late for a meeting, Emma. Whatever it is will have to wait."

I caught his arm. "It can't wait. Jared has a heart problem, an arrhythmia. Charlotte needs to know the top expert in the field, and she needs to know now. Just tell me the name and where to find him, and I'll go."

Sam looked stunned, as if I'd slapped him. He had a special connection with that particular nephew. From the first time Jared fixed him with an adoring toothless grin in infancy, Sam was hooked.

He thrust his hands in his pockets. "You'd better go ahead, Suze."

"You sure? Be glad to wait."

Tightly, he shook his head. "I'll catch up."

He faced me in stony silence as she strutted off, swaying her high, tight behind. After she turned the corner, he assumed a defensive stance, frowning behind a shield of hard-crossed arms.

"How bad?" he said.

"They don't know. They're doing tests."

"Why? What were his symptoms?"

"Some spells of rapid heartbeat. Happened a couple of times, and never when he was home. Charlotte told the pediatrician about it, but he blew it off. Chalked it up to overexertion."

"Typical."

"Yesterday, he was playing in a Little League game and passed out. They rushed him to the hospital and did an EKG." I pulled out a slip of paper on which I had cautiously printed the name of Jared's condition. I'd repeated it to myself over and over again, but I could not persuade my mind to absorb it.

"It's called Wolff-Parkinson-White syndrome."

His chin dipped. "Ancillary nerve bundle. Presents on the EKG as a prolonged delta wave. They're doing tests, you say?"

"Yes."

"Which ones?"

"I don't know. Whatever they do to figure out how serious the problem is."

"Sure, if they know their butts from a hole in the wall. Who's taking care of him?"

"A pediatric cardiologist recommended by their pediatrician. I didn't get the name."

"Of course not," he said, with a nasty smirk. "Why would you do anything that might actually be useful?"

I folded my own arms. "If you don't want to help, Sam, fine. I'll ask someone else. The last thing I need right now is your crap."

"You came here."

"My mistake."

Walking away felt better than being walked out on, but that wasn't saying much. This hospital was full of people who had the answer I needed, but I couldn't think straight, couldn't see where to turn next. Rising tears made it tough to see at all.

And then it came to me. Hurrying toward the elevators, I called their number. Naturally, no one was home at their Park Avenue manse but the maid. "I expect Dr. and Mrs. Colten sometime this evening, ma'am. Would you like to leave a message?"

"No, thanks. I'll call back." I couldn't wait for this evening. I couldn't wait at all. If my insides were roiling with anxiety, imagine my poor sister. "Damn you, Sam!" I rasped aloud.

The doors opened with a cheery ping. As they slid shut, Sam slipped into the car.

"Would you cut it out, Emma? Of course I want to help. Stop acting like such an ass."

"I'm acting like an ass? Look in the mirror, Sam. You're a married man with a little boy and a baby on the way. Now might be an excellent time to grow up."

"I am grown up." He went sheepish. "I just don't always show it."

"That's for sure."

He stared straight ahead. "I was pissed off, extremely. I needed to go cool off."

My gut was churning. "Where?"

"I went to a bar and had a couple of beers, *alone*. Then being up most of the last two nights caught up with me and I crashed in the on-call room, *alone*. That's all."

"That's not all. Not by a long shot. You took a shower, shaved, slapped on *eau de man on the prowl* and walked out. You weren't just doing it to cool off. You did it to make me suffer, to punish me for the horrible sin of trying to help you get what you wanted. Maybe the way I went about it was dopey and misguided. I can't deny that. But I did it out of love. And you know it."

"I suppose."

"You suppose? You think I went to see Senior and Freddie for fun? You think I enjoyed it? Believe me, it's a toss-up between having lunch with those two and a sharp stick in the eye."

He allowed a stingy flicker of a smile. "Really? For me, it's no contest. I'll take the stick in the eye any day."

"Apologize."

"You apologize."

"I did already, but fine. Glad to set the mature example. I'm sorry, Sam. I shouldn't have gone to your father. And believe me, I'll never, ever do a thing like that again. When it comes to you, I'll pretend I don't even have a mouth. Now you say you're sorry."

"Fair enough. I shouldn't have blown my stack and

walked out. And I'm really sorry I did." He dug a knuckle into his lower back. "The bed in the on-call room really sucks."

"You're going to have to work on that apology. And it's going to have to include something about that nonsense of ducking me with LeeAnn and 'Suze.' At this point I give it a big fat F."

"Fine. I'll work on it. Meanwhile, I should talk to Charlotte and get the details. Are they looking for someone near home?"

"They'll go anywhere. All they care about is getting him seen by the best."

We were in the hospital's bustling main lobby now. Uneasily, he looked around. "That's Delavan at Mass General. He's the best bar none. But they never heard it from me."

"Why not?"

"Because a Cadillac salesman who values his job doesn't send customers across the street to buy a Lincoln, that's why not. All I need is for Malik to find out I've been recommending other programs."

"The hell with Malik. This is Jared's life we're talking about. That's more important than your precious career."

"It doesn't have to be one or the other, for God's sake. Jared's health doesn't hinge on me trashing my chance to get a fellowship with Malik."

That softened me, but only somewhat. "I'd just like to see you put something else first for a change."

His eyes narrowed. "Jared's a fabulous kid, and I'll do everything I humanly can to help him. You're not the only one who cares about him. So get off it."

"Fine. Okay. I hear you, Sam. Enough. I'm exhausted. Please let's not fight anymore."

"I'm all for that."

"Think we can be friends?"

"Works for me."

When he drew me in a hug, the tears spilled over, streaming down my cheeks, leaving blots of misery on his scrubs.

"You think they can get Jared in to see Dr. Delavan quickly? Charlotte's terrified something could happen before this thing is treated."

"I think so. A couple of classmates of mine from med school are doing residencies at Mass General. I'll make some calls and see if anyone has a good line to Delavan. I'll do my best, Em. I'll try."

·TWENTY-FIVE·

Mrs. Kalisher held out a cupped palm. "You feel a drop, darling?"

"Nope. There's not a cloud in the sky. Must've been a pigeon."

Her grin was coy. "I didn't say I felt a drop, Emma. I asked if you did. All week on the news they've been predicting we were going to have record rainfall today. Up to three inches, they said. Weatherperson on channel four went on and on about how if it had been snow instead, we'd be practically buried. She talked about such flooding and commotion, you thought you'd better hurry up and book a stateroom on the ark."

"No one ever claimed that weather reporting was an exact science, Mrs. K."

Now she nodded in a way that let me know I was completely off base, not even in the neighborhood of what she was trying to get across.

"Here's the thing, sweetheart. Yesterday I went to the supermarket to pick up a few things: a can of tuna, four rolls of toilet paper, and a pound of coffee. I like the decaf French roast. They grind it fresh and you put it in the freezer. Keeps like new."

"Good to know."

"Speaking of which, have we ever talked about tomatoes?"

"Not that I remember."

"Then good it came up. Whatever you do, don't keep tomatoes in the refrigerator. You do that, they lose all their taste. Might as well have your sandwich with lettuce and potatoes."

"Thanks. I'll keep that in mind."

She patted my hand, her equivalent of a gold star and a smiley face. "So getting back to the supermarket, I expected to run in, grab what I needed, and get on the express line. How long, I ask you, could that possibly take?"

Where my enlightenment was concerned, the rules of engagement with Mrs. Kalisher were crystal clear. I was expected to respond to her questions to the best of my ability, and be totally wrong. "Six hours?"

"You see how smart you are? You're on exactly the right track. It should have taken five minutes, but I didn't get through for almost an hour. The lines were unbelievable. And you should have seen the carts. Piled practically to the ceiling. People were stocking up like nobody's business. Buying canned goods, bottled water, flashlights, first aid kits, huge bags of pet food, you name it. And you see? Is it raining?"

"No."

"Not a drop."

There was a point in this somewhere. "I overreacted, too, Mrs. K. I admit it. I picked up some extra milk and apple juice at the local deli, in case."

She mulled that over. "But not a flashlight."

"No. We have one somewhere. Probably out of batteries, though."

Her head bobbed with huge satisfaction. "You see?"

"Not exactly."

What I did see was Tyler playing sweetly on the elaborate jungle gym with Amity, who was with us for a couple of hours. Siena had an appointment with her osteopath, a holistic medical practitioner she swore by, though Sam placed them somewhere between voodoo and rain dancers in the scientific hierarchy.

"Rumors," she said, with a sniff.

"Let me think, Mrs. K. Weather reports, supermarket lines, flashlights, coffee, tomatoes, and rumors. I'm sure it all comes together somehow."

"Of course. Someone tells you something; you can't help but hear it. But that doesn't mean you have to run out and buy a flashlight. A little extra milk can't hurt, or juice. If the weatherman's prediction turns out to be wrong, you have to drink anyway. You need something to put on your cereal in the morning. And juice is full of vitamin C. Who can argue with that?"

"Far be it from me."

"So having plenty of milk and juice in the house makes perfect sense. But the people who run out to buy flashlights are a whole other kettle of fish. Like those survivalists in Idaho who grow sloppy beards and shoot people."

Fixed to the jungle gym on a broad platform were a steering wheel, a rearview mirror, and a mock ignition with a dangling wooden key. Tyler had been ensconced for the past ten minutes in the driver's seat, but now he backed away and ceded the privilege to Amity. Nothing like the love of a good woman to bring out the best in a guy.

"So the point here has something to do with flashlights?"

"No, darling. Flashlights are just a different kind of

sloppy beard. Overreacting, that's what I'm talking about. A weather report can be totally unreliable, hardly better than a rumor. But still, some people hear a rumor or a prediction of rain and they rely on it as if it's money in the bank."

I shook my head to clear it. "Forgive me, Mrs. K. I'm afraid I'm a little bit dense today. I didn't get a lot of sleep, and then there's the business with my nephew."

"Your sister's Jared will be fine, Emma. Look at how everything is falling into place. You said yourself Sam's classmate from medical school happens to be doing a rotation with the top expert in the field, so he was able to get them an appointment right away. That's what I call a wonderful sign."

I gazed around nervously. "I never told you that. Remember, Mrs. K.? Nobody's supposed to know."

"Don't worry, darling. I understand completely. I wouldn't say a word, except to you."

An ice cream truck approached, trilling the maddeningly irritating theme that was a siren song to my son. Tyler tumbled in a perilous dismount from the jungle gym and rushed toward us.

"Look, Mama. Ice cream. Could me and Amity have big huge giant vanilla cones?"

"Amity is not allowed to have ice cream, cutie. Siena sent special snacks she made that you two can share." I produced the paper bag filled with homemade zucchini bread and another crammed with the odd-looking fruit slices Siena had dried. "Here. Look how yummy."

Backing away, he shuddered. "How come she's not allowed to have ice cream? Was she bad?"

"No, sweetie. Siena only likes Amity to eat things she makes at home. And no sugary things."

"No ice cream?" he said, his face wide with wonderment. "Not even vanilla?"

"Not even any kind."

"Not even strawberry?"

"No. Not even that."

By then, Amity had made her dainty, cautious descent from the driving platform and come to join us. Unconvinced by me, Tyler went right to the source.

"No ice cream," she confirmed. "We have frozen yogurt, though."

That aroused my little one's deepest empathy. "Yogurt. Yuck!"

After they drifted toward the sandbox, Mrs. Kalisher shook her head. "Raising a child without ice cream. What will they think of next?"

"Feeding those same kids tofu."

She laughed. "Tofu? Could you imagine? Mine would have had me thrown in jail."

"Each to his own."

"Exactly. Speaking of which, rumors are not a problem in and of themselves. The problem is the way people react to them."

"Are we talking about rumors in general, Mrs. K.? Or do you have a particular one in mind?"

She stared into the distance, tipping her head toward a large, leafy birch. "You see the bird halfway up on the skinny limb? That's teal. My favorite shade of blue."

"I'm beginning to get the feeling you're trying to tell me something without actually telling me something."

Tyler was back. "I'm allowed to have ice cream. Right, Mama?"

"Not when you're with your friend and she isn't allowed, Ty. That wouldn't be nice."

"Yeah, it would. A vanilla cone would be very nice."

"Tomorrow."

"But I want some now."

"You have two choices, sweetie pie. You can go play with Amity or you can go play with Amity."

"That's silly," he giggled.

Maybe so, but it worked.

Frieda's gesture was as broad as it was vague. "I'm not trying to tell you something without telling you something, sweetheart. We are just talking generalities."

"Are you sure? Because if you've heard a rumor that involves us in any way, I'd much rather you tell me about it."

She waved that away. "All I'm saying is sensible people don't put too much stock in things they hear that aren't proven."

"All right. I won't put too much stock in it. Now what have you heard?"

"People talk, darling. It doesn't mean anything."

Not, I thought, sinking inside, unless the talk was true. "People are talking about Sam?"

She didn't answer. She didn't have to. Rumors might not be bankable gospel truth, but the old dictum about smoke and fire all too often proved true. Sam had sworn his innocence about Suzanne several times, but it was also true that guilty people lied.

I swallowed hard. "They're talking about Sam and that blonde you saw fawning all over him at Malik's welcome reception?"

"Absolutely not. I've heard no such thing. I told you, Emma, your Sam is not the roving type."

"What then? You have to tell me, Mrs. K. If you don't, I'll imagine something worse than the worst thing it could possibly be."

"Okay. But remember, it was only talk."

"Only talk. Got it."

"I was in the elevator with these two girls who looked to be secretaries. They were talking about which of the surgical residents would get to be chief resident next year. One of them said she was really surprised to see Sam scratched off the list."

"You're sure she said Sam?"

"Sam Colten, she said. I'm sure."

"But he's done so well. All the attendings give him great evaluations. And lately even Malik has been partial to him. Had him scrub in on several cases."

"Really? I'm impressed."

"So why would anyone scratch him off the list for chief resident? Makes no sense."

She tamped the air. "Don't get excited. Like I said, it was only talk. Maybe those girls were mistaken. Maybe the list they saw was for something else altogether, or someone scratched his name out to get the ink flowing in a pen. That's the trouble with rumors, what I've been trying to tell you all along."

"I certainly hope it's not true. Sam's worked so hard. All the residents so look forward to the chief year. Residents' spouses do, too. Sam would be more in control of his time. Things wouldn't be quite so busy and crazy. We could certainly use a breather, I'll tell you that."

"I'm sure it's not true, sweetheart. From everything you say, there's not a reason in the world he won't make chief resident."

"But what if it is true? Maybe I should hint at the possibility, give him a heads-up so he's not completely floored if it happens."

She held up her hands, seeking reason. "You see how

talk can make people overreact. You hear a storm might be coming and you happen to pick up a little extra milk and juice, that's fine, dear. Running out to buy a flashlight is another story. No need to rush into anything. Better to wait and see."

· TWENTY-SIX ·

By the scheduled start of the parents' meeting, Tyler's classroom at Little Ranger was packed. People leaned against the toy-lined shelves. Others perched awkwardly on the Lilliputian chairs. When I ducked out for a last-minute run to the bathroom, I found Jake's parents, Bob and Marion Merson, huddled in the hall with Olivia's parents and Jean-Michel's. I stopped to assure them again that I was with them one hundred percent. Sam was, too, though he was on call and unable to attend.

A moment later, Jeanette and Arthur Trevallis strode in, and everyone fell silent. Flushed and tight-lipped, Marissa's parents ran the gauntlet of angry eyes.

When I returned to the room, Siena was poised in front of the bulletin board holding a printed page. Grim-faced, she scanned the room slowly.

"I want to thank you all for coming tonight, for making the time despite the short notice. As I mentioned in the notice I sent out, this is a matter of some urgency, and I felt strongly that we needed to discuss it without delay."

Jeanette set her doughy jaw. "The sooner the better. This has already gone on way too long."

Siena ignored her, which was better than she deserved. "To begin, I'd like to read from a prepared statement. Given the difficult, sensitive nature of this situation, I feel strongly that all of us should take extraordinary care to say solely and precisely what we mean."

"Point of order," Marissa's father called out. "I believe this has been called as a parents' meeting."

"Yes, Arthur. You know it has."

He smirked. "Then it follows that the proceedings should be conducted by the president of the parents' group, not a teacher in our employ." Like his wife, Arthur Trevallis was short of stature and extremely narrow of mind.

Olivia's mother, Monique, was the group's president. "I'm glad to hand it off to Siena. More than glad."

"That's not how it works. If the president can't or won't fulfill her duties, the vice president takes over."

Naturally, the vice president was Jeanette.

Monique took her place beside Siena. "Fine. Meeting is called to order. The chair recognizes Siena Gladwell."

"You can't do that," Arthur said. "That's not proper procedure."

"You're welcome to take it up with our parliamentarian, Arthur, as soon as we get one. Over to you, Siena."

An uneasy hush settled. Training her sights on the text she'd prepared, Siena cleared her throat.

"I have received a formal request seeking the removal of a student from our school. The request was made by a parent, in the company of her attorney. It was stated that if I didn't comply voluntarily, this parent intends to pursue—and I quote—'legal remedies.' I responded without hesitation that removing this student would not be consistent with the philosophy of this school or, in my opinion, the best interests of the children, and I refused. I firmly believe that was the correct answer; and I stand by it unequivocally.

"However, this is not *my* school, it's *ours*. Distasteful though it is, I see no choice but to have an open discussion on this matter. No one will be well served by a divisive, hurtful whispering campaign."

She glared at Arthur and Jeanette, who'd been conducting just such a campaign since the issue reared its ugly head. They had circulated a prepublication draft of an article that detailed a highly provocative study conducted by the venerable Stanton Child Study Center in Chicago. The researchers had found that observing violent behavior had far more profound and long-lasting effects than was previously believed. The article was only one of the blasts in their all-fronts assault. I had personally ducked four calls from Jeanette and two from Arthur. They'd sent e-mails urging me to call them back. They'd sent e-mails urging me to respond to their e-mails. They had left urgent messages for Sam at the hospital, including one they'd called in to LeeAnn, suggesting that it was incumbent upon him as a physician to be more responsive. Despite her lack of medical training, LeeAnn had diagnosed their problem as a classic case of rectocranial inversion. Jeanette and Arthur had their heads firmly wedged up their butts.

Siena went on. "Before I open the discussion, I want to make sure all the cards are on the table. The parent who made the request was Jeanette Trevallis. The child she wishes removed is Jake Merson. Jeanette describes Jake as dangerous and disruptive. She claims he's a negative influence. She holds him responsible for Marissa's reluctance to come to school."

Jeanette thumped her palm on the table. "I do not appreciate your speaking for me, Siena. I am perfectly capable of saying what I think by myself."

"And you'll have that opportunity. All I'm doing at this point is bringing the rest of the parents up to date, Jeanette. The facts are the facts."

"They certainly are. And no amount of your holier-than-thou crap is going to change them."

Siena stared at the paper again. It took a lot to rattle her, but this was doing the job.

"Speaking as a parent, as the founder of this school, and as a teacher who has worked here for the past seven years, I believe in my heart that Jeanette is wrong. Jake's presence at Little Ranger is overwhelmingly more positive than negative. He learns from the others, and they learn from him. It's never too early to start teaching children to respect and tolerate differences, including their own. Wait too long to do so, and you risk producing people incapable of seeing past their own interests and unfounded opinions, people who make it difficult for all of us to peacefully coexist."

While Siena folded the page and tucked it into her pocket, Arthur Trevallis claimed the floor again. He had precisely the legal presence you'd expect of someone who sold building supplies, the Clarence Darrow of toilet bowls and ten-penny nails.

"Frankly, I find your definition of 'overwhelmingly positive' mighty puzzling, Siena. Last week, my wife had to take our daughter to the pediatrician. Jake had bitten Marissa on the hand, and the bite pierced her skin. Dr. Landy cleaned the wound and prescribed antibiotic treatment. The human mouth is teeming with bacteria, and he explained that a bite like that could have had serious health consequences. Thank heavens we got lucky. That doesn't mean I'm prepared to risk having it happen again."

Siena shook her head in disbelief. "You told me you happened to have an appointment with Dr. Landy after school that day, Jeanette. Marissa told me he treated her with salve and a Cinderella Band-Aid."

"I suppose you'd be happier if she'd contracted rabies," Arthur huffed. "And make no mistake. That was hardly an isolated incident. A few weeks ago, Jake pulled Marissa's hair. On her birthday, Jeanette came to class with cupcakes and Jake threw a block into the box and ruined everything. He's torn pages from her favorite book and smeared paint on her clothing. Siena may consider all that violent, aggressive behavior 'overwhelmingly positive,' but in my opinion and the highly respected opinion of the Stanton Child Study Center there is nothing positive about it. Quite the contrary."

Red-faced and trembling, Jeanette got to her fat little feet. "And it doesn't teach tolerance or any of that garbage she said. Marissa's afraid of Jake, plain and simple. All she wants to do when she sees him is run in the other direction. I know how to teach my little girl tolerance and respect for differences. And it's certainly not by letting her be terrorized."

Veronica O'Donovan, Jaden's raven-haired mother, piped up. "Learning tolerance from you would be like taking singing lessons from someone tone-deaf, Jeanette. Like asking a fish to teach you how to ride a bicycle."

"I don't appreciate that. Not in the least. I feel terrible for Bob and Marion. Just terrible. What's happened to Jake is a tragedy." She pouted with an effort that made her look constipated, but the sympathetic tears refused to flow.

Bob and Marion Merson stood stone-faced with linked arms. On the phone earlier in the week, Marion had confessed that one of the hardest things about what they were going through was finding out which of the friends they thought they'd had were not friends at all, learning that if you had the rug pulled out from under you, there were those who would act superior because the misfortune had not been theirs.

Jean-Michel's father, a dapper no-nonsense Frenchman, made no secret of his contempt. "Spare us the noble *merde*, Jeanette. You and Arthur, your only concern is you."

"Don't you see? Tomorrow it could be your child, your family," railed his fiery Italian wife. "People get sick. They have accidents. Much as you'd like to think so, you're not immune."

"Now hold up, everyone." Wanda Beller was a friendly, affable soul with opal eyes and a taffy-pulled southern drawl, all qualities that had passed intact to her son, Zachary. "Every one of us is here because we love our kids and want what we think is best for them, right or wrong. I don't think it's fair to suggest that Jeanette and Arthur are doing this out of pure selfishness or to hurt anyone on purpose."

"Thank you, Wanda," said Jeanette. "At least someone gets it."

"I didn't say I get it, honey. I said I believe you're doing what you think is right, what you believe to be in the best interest of your child, right or wrong."

"Absolutely."

"That's important. But are you absolutely convinced you're going about it in a reasonable way?"

"I am. Arthur and I agonized about this for weeks. The last thing we want to do is hurt anyone, but we see no choice."

Wanda's thick hair was a copper-streaked brown. Eyeing a copy of an e-mail, she tucked a lolling wave behind her ear. "I'm curious about this study you passed around."

Jeanette folded her arms. "The Stanton Child Study Center has an impeccable reputation. The results speak for themselves."

"I'm sure they do. But why don't you just go ahead and

sum them up for those of us who may not have gotten around to reading it?"

Arthur stepped in. "I'll be glad to. The study found that subjects exposed to physical aggression early on became significantly more aggressive than their peers who hadn't been, and they remained so, despite considerable attempts to modify or extinguish those behaviors later on."

"And that's it?"

"In a nutshell," Arthur said.

Wanda held up her thumb and forefinger, walling off a stingy span of air. "The trouble with nutshells, Arthur, is how little you can fit into them."

"What's that supposed to mean?"

From her purse, Wanda extracted a folded sheaf of papers. "Here's the whole study. Those scientists do go on and on."

"How did you get that?" Jeanette demanded. "It hasn't been published yet."

"Same way as you, I suppose, sugar. Got wind of it and made a call," Wanda said. "Nice, accommodating people at the Stanton Center, especially my second oldest brother Michael's youngest boy, Davey. Smart as a whip, that one. Graduated summa cum laude from UVA. Majored in psychology, and tells me he's just happy as a tick on a hound working at Stanton.

"Anyway, that boy's such a sweetheart. Always has been. He was glad to oblige and get me an advance copy of that study. And I can't argue with Arthur's description, though I must tell you, I had to read the thing over half a dozen times to make any sense of it. All that talk about cohorts and case controls and aversive stimuli. Might as well have been written in Greek.

"But I kept it at. And basically, it boils down to what Arthur said: exposure to aggression early on led to persistent aggressive behavior. Blah-dee-blah. Care to tell these good people why the whole thing has nothing in the world to do with the discussion we're having here tonight, Arthur? Jeanette?"

They fumed in silence.

"Guess it's up to me, then." Wanda smiled sweetly. "And it's the damnedest thing. Article happens to be entitled 'Behavioral Effects of Observed Aggression on Immature Brown Capuchin Monkeys.'"

Laughter cracked the tension in the room.

"So as I said, Arthur honey, I'm curious. I can see how that might trouble you and Jeanette, but what in the world does monkey behavior have to do with the rest of us?"

Fury warped Arthur's face. "You can be as dismissive and sarcastic as you like, Wanda, but you're dead wrong. Plenty of behavioral research on lower species has been applied to humans. There's nothing in the least unusual about extrapolating from those studies."

"You know, Davey and I talked about that very thing," Wanda said. "He told me it could turn out to be confirmed five or ten years down the road, if they see similar results in large human studies. Of course, that's if they are able to pull such studies off, which Davey told me is about as likely as a singing hog. Turns out parents don't like having their kids used as guinea pigs, especially when there could be a risk of harm. So basically, they spent tons of time and money on research that doesn't look like it's going much of anywhere. To put the whole thing back in Arthur's teeny-tiny nutshell, this whole thing boils down to mighty troubling news for parents of brown capuchin monkeys, and that's about all."

"I'm not going to argue the merits of the study. Our daughter deserves to be safe and secure at school, not frightened or hurt," Arthur railed. "That's the fact. Jake needs to be in an environment where there's enough adult supervision so that someone can keep an eye on him all the time."

Siena bit back a grin. "You know, Arthur, I agree with you entirely. Having an extra pair of hands in the classroom is a brilliant solution."

"I didn't necessarily mean here," he put in quickly.

"But it's perfect. Exactly the answer we need."

I joined the large chorus of voices that agreed. Arthur and Jeanette were not the only ones who had been conducting strategy sessions and mustering support. Having Arthur propose the idea of an aide for Jake went beyond our wildest imaginings.

"Now all we need to do is figure out how to get that additional help," Siena said.

"We'd be glad to absorb as much of the cost as we can," Bob Merson said. The notion of bringing in an extra person to guide and contain Jake had originated with his parents. They were eager to provide the funding, but two months ago Bob had been laid off in a company downsizing. Six months earlier, Marion had given up her job at an interior design firm to look after Jake full-time. The state's early intervention program would cover Jake in one of the existing classes his parents had turned down, but they'd refused to pay for a support person here. Trying to overturn that would likely involve a long, expensive legal fight that the Mersons could ill afford.

"This is a cooperative," Siena said. "If we need something, everyone pitches in. We can raise the money to cover the extra cost."

"Of course, and Bob and I will do everything we can, but realistically, it's not going to happen overnight," Marion said.

"Waiting is not acceptable," Jeanette insisted. "Something has to be done immediately."

Veronica groaned. "Come on."

"No, you come on," Arthur said. "You said yourself that

Jake needs extra supervision. And I heard plenty of you agree. The only responsible thing is to remove him from class at once until that can be put in place. Otherwise, obviously the school is not acting in good faith."

The rest went without his having to say it. If Jake did not have one-on-one oversight and Marissa broke a nail, they would sue. If she so much as broke wind or a sweat, they'd bring a cause of action, and they'd probably win. We had stuck our collective head in the noose and invited him to kick the little stool.

"Until we raise the money for an aide, why can't we do it?" I said. "We've got twelve sets of parents. It would come down to an extra day every couple of weeks."

There was general agreement, except, of course, from Jeanette and Arthur.

She pounded the little table. "I don't see why we should be penalized because one child needs extra help."

"This is a cooperative, sugar," Wanda said. "That doesn't sit right with you, why don't you and Arthur go find one of those nice uncooperative schools for Marissa? Something tells me you'd find it much more to your liking."

"Maybe we'll do just that," Arthur snapped.

They left in a huff, the best-case scenario. To toast their departure, I raised a plastic cup of lemonade.

"That's the perfect answer. We do it together." Siena's eyes were tearful. "I don't know how to thank you all."

On the walk home, I dared to feel a little upbeat for the first time in days. Sam and I were on the mend. My nephew was in the best of hands. And things were going as well as possible for Jake. What Frieda had overheard about Sam and the chief residency had to be some kind of misunderstanding. Even if that didn't pan out, it wasn't the end of the world.

That, as it happened, was waiting for me at home.

· TWENTY-SEVEN ·

I found Ruthie, our favorite sitter, perched on the couch like a cocked missile. As soon as I walked in, she sprang to her feet. Anxiously, she shrugged into her book-laden backpack and tied the sleeves of a rose-colored cardigan around her waist. During the nearly three years that she'd been helping out, she had seen Tyler through a sudden terrifying spiked fever, an *Exorcist*-quality bout of propulsive vomiting, a head-cracking fall, and any number of nuclear tantrums, all with a cool, level head. But something had her visibly shaken now.

"Ruthie? What's wrong?"

"Sam said I should go, Emma, but I thought I should wait for you."

"Sam's home?"

"In the bedroom. Got here about an hour ago."

"He's supposed to be on call. Is he sick?"

She shot me a pained look and made for the door. When I asked her to wait so I could pay her, she waved me off and hurried out.

Entering the bedroom, I recoiled. Sam was sprawled on the bed with his mouth agape. He looked and smelled like a gin-soaked pile of rags.

I shook his shoulders and urged him to sit. He muttered in delirium and belched loudly. My stomach lurched from the sour stench of booze.

"Sam? Wake up! What's going on?"

"Don't give me that shit, Alston. He's your patient."

"Sam!"

"Did you check his INR? Want the guy to bleed to death, or what?"

"Sam? I need you to wake up right now."

Instead, his drugged rambling worsened, a jumble of murky thoughts tumbling ever more wildly downhill.

"Get up, Sam! Now!"

With that, his arm flailed wildly. It caught me in the gut and sent me reeling. As soon as I got my bearings, I filled a drinking cup in the bathroom sink and tossed the icy contents in his face.

Sputtering, he came awake. "What the hell was that for?"

"I get to ask the questions, Sam. What's going on?"

With an anguished groan, he dropped his head in his hands. "I've been kicked out, that's what's going on. They make up some crazy bullshit, and I'm through."

I sat beside him, and watched the water I'd tossed at him drip from the sodden ends of his hair. Mrs. Kalisher had primed me for this; and I should have warned him. Better to buy an extra flashlight than stumble in the dark. "I'm sure it feels that way, sweetie, but it's not the end of the world."

Angrily, he shook off my consoling hand. "Don't try to feed me any sugarcoated crap, Emma. It is the goddamned end of the world, at least to me. But maybe you're glad about it. Maybe it's what you've wanted all along."

"I have no idea what you're talking about, and I doubt you do either. How much did you have to drink, Sam? And since when did that become the answer to anything that happens to disappoint you?"

"Disappoint me?" he railed. "Four years of med school and four years of residency down the toilet and you call it a *disappointment*?"

"I do," I said gently. "Plenty of doctors have terrific careers without ever being chief resident. I know you were counting on that, and you deserve it, but it's not a tragedy."

He squinted at me. "Chief resident? What the hell are you talking about?"

"You're not upset about being passed over for chief resident?"

"I told you, I was kicked out. I'm no longer a surgical resident at New York General. As of today, I am unemployed—officially." The last word emerged one slurred, exaggerated syllable at a time.

"Why? For what?"

He raked his fingers through his hair. "It's not true. Not a word of it. Sick, crazy accusations. Pack of fucking lies."

"What accusations? You're talking gibberish, Sam. Why don't we talk in the morning after you sleep it off?"

He clutched my hand. "Promise you won't believe them, Em. I swear not a word of it is true."

I pulled free of his crushing grip. "What isn't true? What did they accuse you of?"

A desperate cry escaped him. "Why?" he wailed. "What did I do to deserve this?"

I trembled with a sharp chill of fear. "Tell me what they're saying you did."

With the back of his hand, he swiped his runny nose.

"I never touched her, Em. On my life, I swear I didn't. You have to believe me."

"You never touched who? For the love of God, Sam, tell me what this is about."

He dug into his pocket and pulled out a crumpled note. "It's completely insane."

As I smoothed the paper to make it readable, I saw the hospital letterhead at the top of the page and the signature of Marcus Trilling, the physician-in-chief, at the bottom. The rest, I read in numb disbelief.

Sam stood accused of sexual assault on a colleague. The allegations had been confirmed by the eyewitness account of a senior member of the faculty and by a member of the staff. Effective immediately, his privileges to participate in the hospital's resident training program had been revoked. He was to vacate the premises at once, surrender his ID and all hospital-issued equipment, and consider himself barred from any future professional involvement in the institution. He had ten business days to vacate his apartment. His salary and insurance benefits would be suspended at once, but under New York State law, he was eligible to apply for interim COBRA medical coverage, and he had sixty days to do so. New York General attorneys were reviewing the situation to determine whether formal legal charges should be brought.

Bristling with disbelief, I read it through three times. "Sexual assault? What exactly does that mean?"

"I don't know. I told you, not a word of it is true."

"But what do you think it means?" A hysterical giggle escaped me. "Are they saying you went after this woman with your blunt instrument?"

"All I know is it never happened."

"Which colleague?"

His chest heaved.

"Suzanne?"

With closed eyes, he nodded.

"And let me guess, this was confirmed by your precious Dr. Malik?"

"Malik and Ava, his executive assistant."

My stomach clenched. "Three people say it happened, Sam. Are you telling me everyone's lying except you?"

"Yes, everyone's lying except me," he wailed. "For Christ's sake, Emma. Do you honestly believe I'd sexually assault Malik's protégée? You think I'd do it in front of witnesses? I'd have to be out of my mind."

Again I stared at the paper, trying to make sense of it. "I don't know what to think."

"Believe me, Em. Neither do I."

Heavily I sat. "But why would they make it up?"

"I have no idea. One minute I'm going about my business and life seems perfectly fine, and the next, everything comes crashing down."

"How did it happen?"

"I was making afternoon rounds when I heard my page. The operator said I was wanted in Trilling's office, stat. I actually thought it must be a good thing. That maybe I'd won an award or that Malik had decided to take me on as a fellow and Trilling was going to let me know. Why else would I be called to meet with the physician-in-chief?"

"What did Trilling say?"

"Nothing. He wasn't there. His assistant handed me the letter without a word. Guard from Security was waiting to walk me to my locker so I could clean it out. Then he took my ID, keys, and beeper and showed me the door."

"How awful."

"You can't imagine. I couldn't believe it was happening. Don't even know how I made it to the street. I could barely walk."

"Why didn't you call me?"

"I tried. You weren't home."

I had gone to the meeting early to help Siena set up. I'd had my cell phone with me, but when I checked, I realized it was out of battery.

"I couldn't bear to come home while Tyler was still awake," he said. "I was such a mess; I didn't want him to see me. Truth is I didn't want anyone to see me, so I walked downtown, away from this neighborhood, and when I ran out of steam, I stopped at a bar."

"And got stinking drunk," I said dully. "Don't forget that."

"I'd been up all night. Spent all day in the OR with practically nothing to eat. Didn't take much."

"How could this happen, Sam? Why? There has to be a reason."

His head swung in a rueful arc. "I've been driving myself crazy trying to figure it out, but I can't. These past couple of days, I seemed to be on Malik's good side. And Suzanne? She's the most incomprehensible of all. From day one, she's acted like I walk on water. Why would she turn on me all of a sudden?"

"Because she's a snake," I muttered.

"I guess she is. I didn't see it coming. That's for sure."

"That's what LeeAnn said about her, that she was a snake, that she couldn't be trusted. Maybe this is her way of playing the woman scorned."

He shrugged. "But what about Malik and his assistant? Why would they back her up?"

I puzzled that over, but I couldn't make the pieces add up. "There's no hearing? No due process? It's just done?"

"I don't know how to fight it, Emma. I wouldn't know where to start."

"We'll get through it," I said. "We'll figure it out."

He broke down. "All that work, all those years. I can't believe it's over."

"It's not. It can't be." The words filled me with quiet resolve. "I can feel it, Sam. This is not the end of anything. Not by a long shot."

And sadly, I proved to be right.

· TWENTY-EIGHT ·

The next morning dawned with a ray of hope in the form of a summons from Senta Berger, the physician who oversaw the surgical residents' educational program. She wanted to meet with Sam in an hour. Since he was no longer welcome at the hospital, she'd arranged to do so at a colleague's office in midtown. Sam passed the intervening time fretting and pacing, portrait of a nervous wreck.

His mood was infectious. I felt as jumpy as a tick and so was Tyler. He kept racing in aimless circles, making ear-splitting noises, charging wild.

My snapping nerves made his antics hard to bear. "Stop, Ty. Easy. Why don't you sit and play with your puzzles?"

"I don't want to," he said, still circling.

"How about reading your books, then? Or I'll put on a DVD."

"No. I'm playing helicopter, Mama. Zoom . . . roar!"

"Time to come in for a landing. Now!" He was giving me a headache, making Sam's itchiness worse.

Outside, rain teemed from a dour, tarnished sky. Pelting pins struck our ancient air conditioner with a harsh slapping sound.

"Catch me, Daddy. Roar."

Sam had dressed for his meeting in a white shirt and staid navy tie. Tyler barreled into him, leading with his sticky hands, marking him with murky gray prints.

He'd been teetering on the edge, and that sent him over. "God damn it! Look what you've done."

Tyler shrunk in fear, lip trembling. "I was just landing like Mama said, Daddy. Don't be mad."

"It's okay. Daddy is not mad. He's just busy."

"No more helicopter!" Sam snapped.

"Is too mad." Tyler's chin bunched and his lower lip quaked, prelude to a howling cry.

Quickly, I knelt to put on his shoes. "Tell you what. How about we go next door to Auntie Frieda's? See if she's home."

Mrs. Kalisher was the perfect antidote. The sight of her was a tonic that calmed us both.

"Come in, my darlings. Come in. I was just thinking of you. What a wonderful surprise!"

"I was playing helicopter and my daddy got mad," Tyler whined by way of explanation.

Her brow peaked. "Maybe Daddy has something on his mind?"

I nodded grimly. "Sorry I didn't call first, but—"

She flapped that away. "You know what?"

Tyler grinned. "No, what?"

"So happens you came at the perfect time. If you don't mind, I could use your help."

"I don't mind."

"Wonderful."

She put him to work at her broad kitchen counter, sorting loose change from a mayonnaise jar into a series of small glass bowls. This was my son's idea of heaven. He was instantly, utterly absorbed.

Frieda returned to the living room ferrying a tray laden with a plate of cookies and a pot of freshly brewed tea. I cleared a spot on the burnished wood coffee table, between a stack of magazines and a candy dish filled with red and black licorice. Like their owner, the furnishings were comforting and inviting though they looked a bit faded and frail. The plush maroon fabric on the sofa had worn to a piebald rose and the pictures had worn off the seats of the tapestried side chairs. Framed photographs perched everywhere; evidence of a life richly treasured and lived.

The tea was redolent of ripe peach, mango, and honey. "It's delicious," I said. "Exactly what the doctor ordered."

She watched a ribbon of golden fluid curl into her cup from the honey wand. "I thought something fruity would be better this morning, darling. You look to me like you've had your fill of dragons and scoops of other stuff."

"That's an understatement."

"The business about not making chief resident? It was true?"

"I wish that was all." It was hard to force the words past the painful lump lodged in my throat. "Sam's been kicked out of the program."

Her hand flew to her chest. "Your Sam? No."

"They're accusing him of sexual assault."

"What? That's crazy."

"He swears there's nothing to it, and I'm trying my best to believe him. But the hospital has witnesses."

"What witnesses? Who?"

"Dr. Malik and his executive assistant."

She shook her head as if a mosquito was buzzing in her ear. "They're saying your Sam did this crazy sexual whochamawhatsis in front of people?"

I nodded miserably.

"I never heard anything so ridiculous."

"It doesn't make sense, I know. But why would they make it up? Why would anyone?"

Angrily, she stirred her tea, raising a tiny funnel cloud in the pool of steaming amber. "Not they, he. This is just the kind of thing Doug Malik would pull."

"But why? He was being so nice to Sam."

"Mark my words. Something happened to make the God from Cleveland mad. Maybe Sam looked at him crosswise. Maybe he didn't bow low enough or jump high enough. Who knows?"

"Then why would Suzanne go along with it? Why would Malik's secretary?"

She bit the end off a sugar cookie. "That's easy, sweetheart. When the God from Cleveland speaks, people listen. They don't, maybe he gets mad at them. Next thing, they are accused of some craziness and out on the street themselves. A person has power and he's willing to abuse it like that, plenty will go along with whatever he wants rather than risk having him turn on them."

My throat went tight. "If that's true, Sam's right. It's over. There's nothing we can do."

"Nonsense. There's always a way to fight back."

Tyler scrambled down from the stool with a coin he wanted us to evaluate. It was a penny that had darkened to a dreary slate gray.

"Where does this one go?"

"Wherever you like, darling," Mrs. K. said.

"Can I put it in the garbage?"

"I have a better idea," she said. "It may not be pretty, but it's still worth a penny. And that means you can use it to make a wish."

"How?"

She relieved him of the offending coin. "Close your eyes and think of something you'd like to have."

Tyler grimaced with the effort. "Anything?"

"It's your wish."

"I know—a puppy?"

I met her questioning look with a firm twist of my head in the negative. A real pet would have to wait until we had a real place to live, not to mention far fewer competing complications.

"If the wish fairy can't bring a puppy, what's your second choice?"

"How 'bout a Krypto Superdog?"

"Which is . . . ?"

"A special play dog with superpowers."

"They sell this special play dog on Amazon?"

I shook my head again. "Maybe they do, but just because someone makes a wish doesn't necessarily mean it has to come true. Someone may have all the toys he needs at the moment."

She smiled. "I hear you, darling. But according to the law of wishes, that strictly depends. Okay, my friend. You can open your eyes now. If the penny is gone, it looks pretty good for your runner-up wish."

The penny had vanished into the pocket of her floral housecoat. Eagerly, Tyler returned to his sorting, no doubt in search of more unsightly bargaining chips.

"I'd love to fight back, Mrs. K., but how? Malik has power, status, witnesses. Basically it comes down to three people's words against Sam's. It seems to me the other side is holding all the cards."

"You do it the way all successful battles are fought, darling. You gather all the information you can about the enemy. You try to dope out their strategy and figure out how to beat them at their own game. You muster all the soldiers and weapons you can get on your side and you capitalize on their strengths. What you don't do, under any circumstances, is throw in the towel."

I blew a breath. "It all sounds so simple when you say it, Mrs. K. But I wouldn't know where to start."

Her eyes smiled as she took a sip of tea. "You already started, Emma. You came to me."

· TWENTY-NINE ·

By the time we left Mrs. Kalisher's, the rain had slowed to a shy drizzle and a trace of silvery promise leavened the glum gray sky. I checked my watch. Sam could have left for his meeting, but given five more minutes, I'd be sure.

"Why don't we walk around the block and count puddles?" I said.

"Is that a game?"

"Sure."

"What's it called?"

"It's called the puddle-counting game."

"Okay. One. Two."

That served as a suitable diversion for Tyler, but I couldn't get my mind off the hospital and Sam. Everything loomed as a cruel reminder. We passed an endless stream of people in lab coats and scrub suits, people whose faces were echoed on their dangling photo IDs. A few of those faces looked familiar, and I saw what I took to be traces of smugness, pity, and worse.

"Eleven. Look, Mama. Twelve is a giant one."

A passing taxi wove into the parking lane and zoomed through the giant puddle, kicking up a giant plume of spray. When it hit him, Tyler sputtered in shocked amazement. "That was a great big giant wet splash!" he exulted. In his view, the only thing better than being muddy or wet, was both.

"It certainly was. And we are great big giant wet soaked. Let's go change."

"But we didn't finish."

"The rules say that if you get soaked, you win automatically."

"What's the prize?"

"Two hugs and a snuggle."

"Two hugs and *two* snuggles."

"You drive a hard bargain, sir. But it's a deal."

Obie the doorman hurried to greet us in the lobby. "Dr. Colten just left, Mrs. Colten."

"Thanks."

"Got something for you."

"What?"

"Lady came by to see you last evening when I was covering the night shift for Sanchez. She asked me to hold on to this. Said to make sure I gave it to you personally."

He pulled out the desk drawer. There, behind the master keys, hospital directory, and logbook, was an envelope printed with my name.

"What lady?"

His shoulders hitched. "Older lady. Came with a gentleman to see you and then went up to see Dr. and Mrs. Malik. When I rang up, sitter said you were out, so she left this with me."

"She came to see me and the Maliks? Are you sure?"

"Positive, Mrs. Colten. I called up myself. Sitter told you weren't home, like I said. Dr. Malik asked a bunch of questions when I called up to his place. He didn't want to let the folks up at first. Lady finally had to get on the house phone herself. Told him it was official business. Some other things I didn't hear. Finally, the doc must've said okay, and she went up."

Tyler was at the elevator. "Come on, Mama. We have to change and do our prize."

The envelope was an ivory square, unmarked aside from my name. As soon as the elevator started up, I tore it open. Inside I found a business card and a six-word note. *Sorry I missed you. Please call.*

I changed Tyler's wet shirt and pants and awarded his puddle contest prize. I left him playing with his superheroes and made the call from the bedroom.

"Carolyn Kresge, please. Emma Colten calling."

"Thanks for getting back to me, Mrs. Colten."

"I understand you came to see me?"

"I did. Sorry we didn't get to talk in person."

My heart thumped wildly. "To talk about what?"

"The Malik case. I'm the caseworker who's been assigned to investigate."

I slumped on the bed, clutching my middle, fearful I might explode. "What Malik case?"

"We received a complaint involving their daughter, Adriana. Our department has an obligation to investigate all such allegations exhaustively."

"Who made the complaint?"

"I'm not at liberty to reveal that, Mrs. Colten. We guarantee anonymity to encourage people who have information to come forth."

"What does it have to do with me?"

"Our understanding is that you live in the apartment beneath the Maliks'. Is that correct?"

"Yes. But I didn't make any complaint. This is all a terrible mistake."

"I didn't say you did, Mrs. Colten. But we have reason to believe you may have overheard conversations between Dr. Malik and his daughter. Disturbing conversations."

My stomach cramped as the nightmare scenario came clear. Siena had filed a complaint and cited me as her source. After he was questioned by Child Welfare, Malik must have spoken to the doorman and put two and two together. In this case, two plus two equaled Sam's demise. And mine. When he found out, Sam would kill me.

"All I heard was an argument between a parent and child, Ms. Kresge. It could have been perfectly innocent, and I'm sure it was. I never reported it to anyone as a suspicion of abuse. My friend misunderstood and overreacted. You have to tell the Maliks it was all a mistake. You have to fix this. Now, today. Please."

I heard pages flipping, the background drone of people pursuing other matters of public concern. I pictured a warren of glum claustrophobic cubicles filled with government-issue gunmetal desks, outmoded computers, and overworked, underpaid caseworkers.

The one charged with investigating the Lord from Ohio came back on the line. "Found what I was looking for. Did you hear Adriana Malik plead with her father to stop hurting her, Mrs. Colten?"

"I heard her plead with him to stop, but I have no idea what was happening at the time. He could have been singing, or brushing her hair. I'm sure it was nothing. I told Siena that."

"Did you hear her say, 'Please, Daddy, stop. I'm begging you'?"

"Yes. She used those words. Maybe she doesn't like to

have her hair brushed. Maybe she didn't want him to give her a dose of medicine or turn out the lights. Children object to plenty of things aside from abuse. You don't just run out on the strength of a few words and accuse someone of a terrible thing like that."

Her tone softened. "I appreciate your sensitivity, Mrs. Colten. Nobody likes to stick their nose into what might be someone else's innocent business. But it's never wrong to err on the side of protecting a child, believe me. Some of our best cases are the ones we look into where nothing is wrong. All that involves is hurt pride and ruffled feathers. We don't wind up, as can happen when a friend or neighbor keeps a nagging suspicion to herself, with a seriously hurt or even a dead child."

"You're wrong, Ms. Kresge. It can involve far more than hurt pride and ruffled feathers. My friend Siena meant well. She would never deliberately hurt anyone. But she came to you with half-baked secondhand information, information I specifically asked her not to repeat. Dr. Malik found out that I was involved, and he took it out on my husband, who happens to be a resident in the hospital he practically owns. No, wait. I take that back. Sam *was* a resident. Thanks to this, he's not anymore."

"Are you suggesting Dr. Malik had your husband dismissed in retribution?"

Tyler came in to show me how prodigiously his Spider-Man action figure could fly. "Look, Mama. He can go all the way up to the sky. All the way up to the bad big little girl and the digga dada lady."

I cupped my hand over the mouthpiece. "That's nice, sweetie. But I'm on the phone now. You go play and we'll talk about it soon as I hang up."

"All the way up to the tippy top of the world, Mama!"

"I see."

"Sorry for the interruption," I said. "But yes, that's exactly what happened. Sam was kicked out of the program."

"If that's the case, I can certainly ask our attorney to contact the hospital and protest."

"No. You can't do that. A protest from you might only make things worse."

"Fine, then. You needn't worry, Mrs. Colten. Our sole responsibility is the child."

"What about her? Was there any evidence of abuse?"

She cleared her throat. "Unfortunately, I'm not at liberty to share the results of an ongoing investigation."

"No? But you're at liberty to blow up our life and walk away?"

"All right." Her voice dropped. "I suppose it can't hurt to offer you my personal observation, at least my preliminary impression."

"Which is . . . ?"

"Adriana struck me as extremely bright, serious, and mature for a ten-year-old."

"She looks younger."

"She does, which makes it even stranger."

"What's strange about being extremely bright, serious, and mature?"

"Think about it, Mrs. Colten. All those words are just another way of describing a child who knows and has seen too much."

· THIRTY ·

Though I could barely face Siena, I took Tyler to school. Having him busy for a few hours would give me time I sorely needed to think.

Sam's meeting with the head of the residency program had gone better than I'd dared to hope. Senta Berger thought he deserved due process, and she was not alone. Several members of the faculty planned to join her in urging Physician-in-Chief Trilling to seek broader, more complete information in the case. They would ask that he change Sam's status from permanent expulsion to a suspension, pending that review. Dr. Berger was reasonably confident the request would be granted. Dismissing Sam without due process could invite a lawsuit, not to mention negative publicity for the hospital and damage to its ability to recruit top-notch residents going forward.

While she and her colleagues pushed ahead on that front, she had recommended that Sam hire an attorney. The news in that regard had been encouraging, too. Sam's brother-in-law was a rising star at Henley, Day, a large, powerful firm with offices in several major cities. Gary worked at the branch in San Francisco, but his close friend headed up the firm's labor department in New York. Sam had met with the friend, Andrew Eastham. Eastham had expressed outrage at the hospital's conduct and, in deference to his friend, had agreed to represent Sam at a fraction of the usual cost.

I stopped in the hall at Little Ranger, a comforting distance from the classroom. Shifting my bulk awkwardly, I knelt to say good-bye. "Have fun, sweetie. I'll be here to pick you up."

"Can I play after with Amity?"

"No, Ty. Not today. I think we could use some quiet time alone."

Siena chose that moment to step into the hall. She didn't need keen radar to read my aura today. I was as clear as fireworks, shooting sparks of electric unease.

"Emma? What's wrong?"

"Daddy got mad cause my helicopter messed up his shirt."

I ruffled his hair. "He's not mad, sweetie. Don't worry. Have a great time in school."

With a stiff nod, I turned to leave.

"Wait, Emma, please. Talk to me."

My voice quaked with anger. "I told you I'd keep an eye on things, that if I got anything solid, I'd report it. Why couldn't you just listen?"

"I tried to tell you, but the others showed up. I had no choice but to call Child Protective Services. I'm a licensed social worker. It's unethical and illegal for me to withhold information about possible abuse."

I'd heard the same thing from Franny, the same useless,

defensive excuse. "But it's not unethical and illegal to go off half-cocked and wreck someone's career? You have no idea what you caused, Siena."

She set a hand on my arm. "Tell me, then."

I recoiled from her impossible sincerity. "Not now."

Halfway home, when I had calmed enough to speak again, I called my sister, Charlotte. They had flown to Boston late yesterday and spent the night in a Cambridge hotel. They'd been scheduled to see the arrhythmia specialist at Mass General late this morning.

She sounded exhausted. "Jared's being a total trouper. They've really put him through it, and all he keeps asking is whether Hal and I are okay."

"And are you?"

"Hanging in. Dr. Delavan's wonderful. Please thank Sam again for setting that up."

"He's glad he could." I considered the crushing irony. Sam had been so worried that Malik might discover he'd recommended a program other than his own. But it wasn't his program anymore, so that, at least, had ceased to be an issue.

Charlotte went on. "Delavan said that even if Jared requires treatment to get rid of the extra nerve bundle, he'll be fine. He said the risk of complications is small, that he's never had any serious side effects in twenty years. So whatever it takes, he'll be good as new. All we need to do is get from here to there."

"How is Hal holding up?"

"About like me, Em. Partly cloudy. Pretty good chance of rain."

"I hope both of you are laying off the Ajax."

"Doing the best we can. How about you, big sis? Living large?"

"Extremely. Think beluga whale, going on great blue."

"Good. That's your job. How's Sam?"

I bit my lip to keep from leaking grief. My sister had more than enough to deal with. "Sam's Sam. You know."

"No worries, Em. Give it forty, fifty years, and you'll have him around all the time. That's in the category of watch what you wish for."

"Sure." I felt the tears rising. "I'd better go, Char. Connection's lousy."

"Really? Must be on your end."

"Must be."

In the aftermath of the morning's storm, only a few scattered souls were in the park. A line of puddles dotted the path to my favorite bench, where beads of water shimmied on the lacquered slats.

With a pile of tissues, I cleared a reasonably dry spot. Sitting heavily, I let the thoughts flow.

Given years of determined practice, I had become quite adept at worrying. Experience had schooled me in the nuances of the craft, and the potential pitfalls. Pent-up concerns could form a perilous logjam. If you didn't let them out, the pressure could build beyond control.

So that's what I did. I paraded out all the dire possibilities and held them up to scrutiny in the wan afternoon light. If Sam was finished at General, what would his future hold? What would ours? Could he still have a career in medicine? Or might this episode have some lasting impact on his ability to get licensed? If he couldn't be a doctor, an ambition so ingrained it practically defined him, what then?

Until we had those answers, how would we get by? In the best of times, my income was modest. Even if I could find a full-time teaching position, even if I could bear to commit to that right now, child-care expenses would more than consume the greater sum I'd make.

Where would we live? Our apartment was tiny, but

thanks to a hospital subsidy, the rent was affordable. Without that, I couldn't see any way we'd be able to stay in Manhattan. We'd have to find another place, a different way. And we'd have to do it with gut-churning speed.

A dread sense of loss settled over me as I considered all the comforting familiarity we'd be forced to leave behind. I'd have to find a new school for Tyler, a new obstetrician, new Chinese takeout, a different park. There would be no wise, caring, wonderful Mrs. Kalisher, nothing to lean on but trees.

Even as I thought of that, the teal blue bird Mrs. K. had admired exploded from the nearby tree, unleashing a rain of leaf-borne drops. A girl I hadn't noticed scurried away from the fence at the far side of the park to escape the sudden shower. Until she came closer, I didn't recognize her.

By the time she noticed me, I was blocking the exit. She wore worn jeans and a faded plaid shirt and carried a bundle wrapped in a thin threadbare rug. Gaping at me in alarm, she clutched the burden tight against her chest.

"*Déjame,*" she demanded. *Let me go.*

I had learned Spanish in school and honed it during the college semester I'd spent studying art at El Prado in Madrid. But I hadn't flexed that mental muscle in years. "*Espere un minuto. Tenemos que hablar.*"

I noticed the yellow discoloration beneath her right eye, souvenir of her clash with the swing set after Tyler shoved her off balance. She had tried to mask it with heavy makeup, but the bilious undertone leaked through.

"*De lo que?*" she challenged. What did I want to speak to her about?

I asked her name, and she told me it was Bori. Did she live around here? She hesitated, and then nodded yes. I learned she was from Quito, Ecuador. After high school graduation, I had spent a summer there, volunteering for Habitat for Humanity.

Hearing that, she visibly relaxed. Her country was beautiful, I said: *un país hermoso.*

When she dropped her guard, the weight of her lonely sorrow came clear. Gently, I asked about her eye. Had it hurt badly? Was it okay now?

The question provoked a shy smile. She told me someone had asked if she'd been in a brawl. I couldn't help but smile at that as well. She was about as big as half a minute, barely a decent sparring partner for Sebastian or Fred.

I told her I was glad she was okay, that I'd been worried about her. It was nothing, she insisted, nothing at all. She said this as if she had experienced far worse than being felled like a bowling pin by a rabid three-year-old.

"Lamento eso," I told her nonetheless. I was terribly sorry my toddler had gone berserk.

By then, we were talking like old friends, though I was the old friend with a halting, rusted tongue. I had to pluck the words from the thicket of old memory and I knew I was making mistakes, but perhaps my bumbling helped her to relax. And perhaps that was why she answered without hesitation when I asked where she worked.

"En ese edificio," she said, pointing at my building. *"Para Señora Malik."*

I measured my words carefully. The last thing I wanted to do was scare her off. I told her I lived in the building, too. I didn't really know Mrs. Malik, but I'd met her in passing. I asked what Bori did for her.

"Le ayudo en la casa. Y con la muchacha."

If she helped with the house and Malik's daughter, she had the chance to know and see things, revealing things. I thought of Mrs. Kalisher's advice on the rules of engagement. My first task was to find out everything I could about the enemy. I wondered aloud if she worked for them living in.

That sparked alarm. No, she said with striking vehemence, she didn't live with them. The full-time nanny did, but not her. Bori lived nearby, alone.

The lie might as well have been scrawled on her forehead in flashing neon. It was that obvious.

"Dónde?" I asked softly. Where?

Her dark eyes skittered, and then fell. In a barely audible voice she told me she lived here and there.

That, and the bundle she carried, said it all. *"Vive usted en el parque?"*

With her gaze still averted, she nodded yes. And suddenly, the rest came clear.

What happens when it rains? I prodded. Where do you go when the weather's bad? Where do you go when they lock the park at night?

Her response was a pained whisper. *"En el sótano."*

It's okay, I told her. She could stay in our building's basement. I didn't care at all.

I did care how she'd managed to arrange it. The basement, with all its locked rooms and shadowy secrets, was the province of Judge the porter. He didn't strike me as the altruistic type. Quite the opposite.

And Bori didn't strike me as having the resources to pay Judge in hard currency for the privilege of camping on the cold, damp concrete. I feared he'd demanded more personal payment instead. That would explain the used condom.

It might also explain the desperate terror in her eyes.

"Por favor, señora. No diga nada," she pleaded. *"No diga nada."*

Please! Don't say anything, is what the digga dada lady meant.

· THIRTY-ONE ·

My son was willing to forgive me, for a price.

"I told you she was real, Mama."

"You did, sweetie. I was wrong."

"You said it was made up."

His little face was a mask of innocent outrage. Given the right circumstance, that particular expression could wilt anyone. And this was definitely the right circumstance.

"How about I make it up to you with a sundae?"

"Three scoops?"

"Fine." His stomach would only hold so much, and as it happened, our scoop was pretty small.

"Sprinkles and nuts and whipped cream and chocolate syrup and a cherry on top?"

"We don't have any cherries."

"But I want a cherry."

"Is that so? Well, what I want is a great big bite of monkey."

I picked him up and made gobbling noises in the crook of his neck. He erupted in giggles, sealing the deal.

"Okay, sir. Time for dinner, a sundae, and bed. It's getting late."

"No.

"It is what it is, sweetie. You don't like it, complain to the clock."

I was inclined to do that myself. Sam had filled his day with appointments and told me to expect him at eight. When he got home, I'd have to admit my part in causing this calamity, yet another confession that might drive him out the door.

As soon as Tyler drifted off, I changed into something that looked less like a blimp-skin and combed my hair. From the bathroom, I heard the familiar clack of Sam's key.

He was not alone. I walked in to find him settling a six-pack on the kitchen counter and LeeAnn, in a short black tourniquet of a dress, on the couch. Her lips and nails were hemorrhage red, her dark eyes rimmed with kohl.

"Emma, hi. How are you doing with all this?"

"I've had better days."

"You should try to lighten up. It's actually pretty funny when you think of it."

I thought about it. "Funny how?"

"What was that crack I made again, Sam?"

"You said this time Malik really dropped a stitch."

Doubling over, she roared at her own alleged wit. "Suzanne Stitch. That's the Stitch he dropped. Get it?"

I endeavored to smile. "Good one."

She flapped a hand and popped the lid on a Brooklyn Ale. "Sam will be fine. Trust me."

"I'm sure he will."

"I mean really fine. No lumps or bruises. No harm, no foul. Not a question in my mind."

"I hope you're right."

"I am. The trouble with people like Malik is they think

they can get away with anything. And they can to a point. But *only* to a point. Doug the Ugh, I call him. Don't you love it?"

Her cheeks were aflame, her words slurred. I couldn't tell if Sam had been tippling, too, but I didn't want him doing so on an empty stomach.

"Can I get you two something to eat?"

"No need, Emma. Dark beer happens to be the perfect food." She tipped her head back and drained half the bottle. Sudsy bubbles rose to fill the space.

"Why don't you think Malik can get away with this?" I was eager to finish the conversation, to see her sashay on her spike heels out the door.

"Because he's overplayed his hand, that's why. Plenty of people weren't happy to have him come here. They thought he was way overpriced and not worth all the things he demanded, especially since Dr. Stryker got pushed out in the bargain."

"I heard about that. You think it's true?"

She chuckled. "I don't think, Emma. I know it is."

"How can you be so sure?" Sam opened a bottle for himself.

"That's the advantage of being an administrator, honey. Access to all the dirt all the time."

Sam sniffed. "Sure, LeeAnn. So you have access to dirt about the residents. Big deal."

She wagged a finger. "You're thinking small, Sammy boy. How many times have I told you to look at the big picture?"

"Which is . . . ?" I prompted.

"We keepers of the dirt have a sacred code. I let you peek under my skirt, you return the favor."

Shifting in her seat, she parted her legs to make the point. You could accuse LeeAnn of being many things, but never shy.

"So you know Stryker was pushed out to make room for Malik."

"I do."

"Would you happen to know why Malik was so eager to come to General?"

"Here's the real question, Emma. Ask me if I care."

"It could be important. Stryker would have stepped down in a year or two on his own. So why the big rush to push him out? Why now, especially? Who chooses to take a kid out of school this close to the end of the year?"

"That's easy. Someone who doesn't give a damn about anyone but himself."

"That still doesn't answer the basic question: why was he in such a big hurry to leave Cleveland?"

Sam shrugged. "Who says he was? Maybe he was in a hurry to come here."

"Why?"

"They made him an irresistible offer, that's why. Cleveland hated like hell to lose him, but obviously, they didn't have the wherewithal to build him a major cardiac center with his name over the door. That's not the kind of thing that happens every day."

"No. And it doesn't happen overnight either. From the look of it, the Malik Center won't be finished for quite some time." At this point, the building site was nothing but a cavernous hole in the ground surrounded by machinery and building materials.

"Couple of years, minimum," LeeAnn confirmed.

"So he could have signed a contract with General and postponed his start date until Stryker stepped down and the building was ready. Why the rush?"

LeeAnn strode to our minuscule kitchen and started rummaging through the cabinets.

"Can I get you something?" I said.

"You have peanuts? Pretzels? Something to munch on?"

"Sit. I'll get it for you."

She rolled her eyes. "Thought you'd never ask."

I didn't bother to point out that I had and she'd turned me down. I could imagine Mrs. Kalisher's advice: sometimes you sacrifice a battle to win the war. And anyway, a little undeserved egg on my face was far from the worst of war wounds. LeeAnn might prove to be a worthy ally. In that spirit, I hauled out our premier junk collection: cheddar popcorn, mixed nuts, cheese sticks, corn chips, chocolate-covered raisins, and jelly beans.

LeeAnn and Sam set on the junkfest eagerly.

"Back to why Malik was so eager to get out of Cleveland."

LeeAnn puffed her lips. "It's Cleveland, Emma, for heaven's sake. Who wouldn't be in a hurry to get out?"

"He was there for twenty years. That's hardly a hasty exit."

She laughed. "So maybe he's a little slow on the uptake. Just because he knows how to slice and dice in the chest cavity doesn't guarantee he's a rocket scientist across the board."

Sam frowned. "What Emma says makes sense, LeeAnn. Why was he in such a hurry to come to General? There wasn't only Stryker and the unfinished building; he had another year to go on a major research grant he'd landed at the Clinic that he couldn't bring here. Why not stay and finish that out?"

In the pensive hush that followed, I stared at my own nails. They were ragged and gnawed to the quick.

LeeAnn broke the silence, waving her empty bottle. "You want answers, Sammy boy, better hurry up and grease this girl's wheels. I've still got a wicked bad thirst."

Sam pulled another bottle from the six-pack. "What, LeeAnn? Think you're going to find the answer under the bottle cap?"

She wagged a red-nailed finger. "You haven't been listening, now, have you? I told you, it's all a horse trade."

"It's been a long day. Mind running that by me again?"

Picking through the jelly beans, she stuffed her mouth with a fistful of red ones. "The code of the dirt-keepers, Sammy boy. I let you peek a little, and you show me yours in return. With any luck, they have skirts in Cleveland, too."

· THIRTY-TWO ·

After LeeAnn left, I watched Sam closely, trying to gauge his mood. I was tempted to turn a fresh page in my sketchbook and take up a pointed charcoal nib. I would draw the cocked oval of his head as it nestled between the shoulder hills and sinewy sprawl of his outstretched arms. I'd render the cantilevered lean-to formed by his crossed leg, and the hairpin curve of his hip. I wanted to trap his image like a firefly and read him by the glow of its light. To me, the worst thing was having no idea what to expect, diving blindly into a sea of dread possibilities.

I pulled up a chair from our tiny table and sat facing him. "We have to talk, Sam."

Settling back against the armrest, he shut his eyes. "Can't it wait? I've been at it all day, Em. Everyone wanting to give me advice. Everyone sure his way is the only way. I should fight it, I shouldn't fight it. I should lie low; I should make a lot of noise. I don't think I've ever been so totally talked out."

"It can't wait, Sam. I can't."

He pulled a sharp, pained breath. "You're leaving me, aren't you? You believe the accusations, and you're bailing out."

"No such luck."

"What, then?"

"The thing with Malik. I know why it happened. I never meant to, but I'm afraid I brought it on."

Sitting up, he leaned in with folded hands. "You brought it on? How?"

I recounted the chain of events, reliving them as I did, wishing I could reclaim the pivotal moment and make a different choice. At the time, discussing my concerns about Malik's daughter with Siena had seemed so harmless and innocent. She was the furthest thing imaginable from a gossip, the least destructive person I'd ever known. Siena hated to step on a blade of grass. She even chewed gently.

His eyes narrowed. "You heard his daughter say that? Begging him to stop?"

"Yes."

"Jesus."

"Made my skin crawl, but then I thought about it, and I realized there could have been a perfectly innocent explanation. Kids can sound pretty dramatic when they don't get their way."

"That doesn't sound like drama; it sounds like a desperate kid crying for help."

"I thought that at first, Sam, but I'm not so sure anymore. It never occurred to me that talking about it could lead to a thing like this. You can't imagine how terrible I feel. How sorry."

"There's nothing to be sorry for. You hear a thing like that, you have to tell someone. Keeping it to yourself would be wrong."

"How could it be right if it got you booted out of the program?"

"Malik tossed that grenade, not you. You don't let some sick son of a bitch get away with child abuse because he has the power to bite back."

"How do we know for sure it was child abuse?"

"You don't have to know for sure. In a situation like this, you give that little girl the benefit of the doubt. You get the authorities to investigate and do what's necessary to protect her. That's their job."

"Didn't do much good. The caseworker thought Adriana Malik was unusually bright, serious, and mature. I seriously doubt that's going to get them to take her father off in handcuffs."

"They're on it. That's the important thing. If we hear anything more, we pass it on. If he's touching that kid, we do what we can to stop it. Whatever it takes."

"That's it? You're not mad?"

"At you? No."

"You're not going to scream and call me names? You're not going to slap on fuck-me aftershave and storm out?"

He lay back again and motioned for me to come closer.

I rested my head on his flat gut. I could hear him churning inside, a grinding scrape as if tiny gnomes were rearranging his inner furniture.

He stroked my hair. "Don't beat yourself up, Em. The truth is I brought the whole damned thing on myself."

"How?"

"By being so determined to get on Malik's good side, so ready to do anything I could to get him to take me on as a fellow."

"You didn't throw the grenade either, Sam."

"No, but I made myself a big, juicy target. I thought I was being so clever, that it was such a great strategy to cozy up to Suzanne. Never occurred to me Malik might see it as a threat."

"Wait. Are you saying Suzanne and Malik . . . ?"

He nodded miserably. "I should have gotten it. The way he looked at her. The way he looked at me when she was around. But until LeeAnn brought it up today, it never crossed my mind."

"You really think that's true?"

"I do. LeeAnn said it's been going on for quite a while, that everyone at the Clinic knew about it, but because it was Malik, the powers that be were willing to look the other way. Plus, it fits. His reputation for chasing skirts, his appetite for young girls, maybe even his own daughter. And why else would Suzanne go along with these crazy accusations?"

"Malik's assistant did, too, Sam."

"Ava's been working for him for a decade. Obviously, she's willing to do whatever it takes to make him happy or she never would have lasted that long." Sam blew a long, slow breath. "I put that creep so high up on a pedestal, I couldn't see him for what he was. For what he is. How could I have been so damned dense?"

"Christ, Sam. If what you're saying is true, if Malik made up charges and got you kicked out of the program because he thought you were coming on to his mistress, he has to be completely out of his mind."

"Or completely confident he can get away with it, with the help of Suze and his trusty executive assistant, of course."

"You couldn't possibly have seen it coming. What sane person would imagine such a thing?"

"A sane person interested in keeping his job."

"Look, sweetie. There's nothing I'd rather do than let you take full credit for this mess. But the fact remains that

Malik didn't bring those charges against you until he got the visit from Child Welfare and traced the complaint to me."

"I'm sure that didn't make him feel any more kindly toward me, Em. But he was out to get me, and he was going to, no matter what. The only questions were how and when."

"Why was he acting so nice, then? Having you assist in surgery. What was all that about?"

He shrugged. "Who knows? Maybe he was giving me a chance to screw up so he could nail me. Maybe he thought taking me down would be more fun if he built me up first."

I traced the line of stubble over the stripe of pale skin on his neck. "You got a haircut."

"Gave me something to do between three forty-five and four."

"Looks nice."

"So do you." He ran a hand over my giant middle. "Both of you."

"So what now, Sam?"

"The best advice I got was to keep busy, try to keep my mind off this thing as much as I can. Dr. Berger says she can arrange for me to moonlight in the ER nights at Southshore. At least it'll help pay the bills."

"Sounds good."

He shrugged. "Better than sitting around, driving myself crazy."

I smiled. "You're not allowed. That's my department."

"Other than that, we wait it out. See what happens. Andrew Eastham, the lawyer, says there's a decent chance the hospital will back down and reinstate me. He's spoken to General's attorney. Eastham's read is they're eager to avoid the kind of headlines this case could generate if it went to court."

"Wouldn't Suzanne have to drop the charges against you?"

"Eastham thinks she might, especially when Malik realizes it could come back and bite him in the butt. If LeeAnn is right about him having an affair with Suzanne, he has to realize we'd try to use that to impeach him as a witness. Can't imagine he'd risk a circus like that."

"Wouldn't you need evidence?"

"Would certainly help if we can get it. But it's possible the threat could be enough."

"If she does drop the charges, what then?"

"I keep my nose clean and finish out my surgical residency. Obviously, I'll have to apply elsewhere for a cardiac surgery fellowship. If I can get one at all."

"Why wouldn't you?"

"Because being on Malik's shit list isn't exactly what his colleagues are going to look for in an applicant. Like him or not, he's at the top of the game. Who's going to take my side at the risk of disaffecting God?"

"You have more than a year to go in surgery, Sam. Plenty can happen between here and there. Let's try to take this one step at a time."

"I'm trying. Believe me. I keep thinking, What if the lawyer's wrong? What if Suzanne insists on going ahead with the case? They could press criminal charges, Em. And it's my word against three of theirs. Finishing my residency might be the least of our worries. I could lose my license to practice medicine. I could go to jail."

The word still hung like a stench in the air when Tyler padded in from his sliver of the living room. He was rubbing his eyes, dragging Sebastian, his stuffed Dalmatian, by the ears.

"Back to bed, sweetie. You know the rules."

"But I had a bad dream, Mama," he whined. "This mean guy was after me. He wanted to hurt me and take all my toys."

"That sounds like a yucky dream. But it wasn't real."

"And the big little girl hitted me right on the head, Mama. And I fell down."

"All just a dream, sweetie."

It was only a figment of his fertile imagination, I thought. Sam and I had to deal with that hurtful, joy-thieving bad guy for real.

· THIRTY-THREE ·

It was almost time for us to leave the park when Mrs. Kalisher showed up in a trim black suit with patent leather pumps and matching purse. A pearl choker graced her neck, and chunky gold door-knocker earrings clung to her lobes. I caught the velvety scent of face powder and lilac perfume, a trace of berry lipstick and pale blue shadow.

"So dressed up, Mrs. K. You look lovely."

Tyler stopped his archaeological dig beside the jungle gym to gape. "Auntie Frieda looks so beautiful!"

"Thank you, darling. You've definitely made your Auntie Frieda's day."

"What's the occasion?"

"The New York General Women's Auxiliary annual luncheon."

"You went? I thought you hated those things."

"I said that?"

"Many times. You said they were all about fancy dull ladies making boring conversation over fancy dull food no one ever touched."

"True, but nothing wrong with that once in a while. I figured, why not use the occasion to catch up with Pauline Lazarus and Edie Trilling?"

"You mean Mrs. President Lazarus and the physician-in-chief's wife."

"Exactly. I haven't seen Pauline or Edie in an age. So I thought to myself, Wouldn't it be nice to have lunch with them today?"

"You just happened to sit at their table, did you?"

"Once I moved around a couple of place cards, I happened to sit with them, yes. How else were we going to catch up?"

I patted the empty space beside me on our favorite bench. "I'm all ears."

Primly, she took her seat and held her purse in her lap. The fancy dullness of the auxiliary luncheon had obviously not worn off yet.

"Nice ladies, Pauline and Edie. Pauline, especially. Given her husband runs the hospital, she's actually pretty down-to-earth."

"Really? What sort of down-to-earth things did she have to say?"

"Mostly, we talked about fund-raising, which is pretty much all people talk about at fund-raisers. How it keeps getting harder and harder all the time. How there are so many competing causes it's hard to get people's attention. How you could spend pretty much your whole life getting dressed up to spend a bundle of money going to fancy, boring luncheons where nobody eats."

"Why don't they eat?"

She fiddled with her pearls. "Who knows? Apparently, it's just not done. If you went and ate, they'd probably have to shoot you."

"Aren't you starved?"

"Of course not. I know how these things go. I ate before I went."

"Good plan."

"It's ridiculous. All of it. But I figured it's for a good cause."

"The auxiliary raises a bundle for the hospital."

She nodded. "True. But my good cause today was you and your Sam. After they finished talking about how they really need to come up with a different kind of fundraiser for next year and then almost immediately started talking about where they should have the very same fancy boring luncheon, I happened to bring up the subject of new recruits."

"Meaning Malik?"

"Naturally, he came up."

"Naturally."

She flipped the clasp on her purse and extracted her wallet. "Now that you mention it, I could use a snack. How about we all have a little ice cream?"

Though he seemed to be engrossed in his digging, Tyler picked up on that immediately. "Can I have an orange ice with vanilla?"

"Good idea," I said. "I think I'll join you. But let me treat, Mrs. K. You just dropped a bundle on a fancy, boring, no-food lunch."

"Doesn't matter, Emma. I called it. Rules are rules."

My mouth was soon stained orange, and pleasantly numb. "So you talked about Malik. What did they think?"

"Edie generally doesn't think. Not independently. Certainly not around Pauline. She's definitely the second kind of doctor's wife, the completely involved political kind who does everything and anything to advance her husband's career. Pauline Lazarus is another story. She wouldn't go against her Sterling, not exactly. But president of the hospital or no, she's not the type to give him a rubber stamp."

"So does that make her the first kind of doctor's wife, or the third?"

Her smile was coy. "Neither. I'd say Pauline is the fourth kind. I think she can influence her Sterling. I think when push comes to shove, she shoves back."

"What was her feeling about Malik?"

"That he's not, and I quote, a 'value-add.' She doesn't think it was worth what they had to offer to get him here. He's not a team player, she said, and that can seriously bring down morale."

"He's certainly brought down ours."

She had licked through the orange ice to expose a creamy vein of vanilla. Patient excavation had its rewards.

"I was coming to that. Naturally, Pauline knew all about the business with your Sam. And she doesn't like it, not one little bit."

"It's not exactly the kind of thing you want associated with your institution."

"I mean she doesn't like how it smells. Edie right away was making noises like it's so awful, such a scandal, can you imagine a young doctor behaving like that, especially a married man? Pauline, basically, told her to stop being a ninny and shut her trap."

"She did?"

She nodded happily. "Saved me the trouble. She's a smart one Pauline. She gets the joke."

"Which is . . . ?"

"That the whole thing doesn't make sense. People don't do such things when there's a risk of getting caught, especially when there's a risk of being caught by your boss. Thinking Sam would push some girl to make hanky-panky is crazy enough. Thinking he'd do it where Doug Malik and his assistant might happen to stumble on them is too ridiculous to even think about. The conference room, for heaven's sake."

"That's where they say it happened?" I hadn't pressed Sam for the details. The sketchy picture had been hard enough to bear.

"Such nonsense. They say he got her in there on some pretense and then tried to force his attentions on her. They say Doug Malik happened to walk in with his assistant in the nick of time. They say the girl was completely shaken up."

"Suzanne shaken up? That'll be the day."

"To accuse him of doing such a thing in the conference room of all things. The doors were unlocked. There was a meeting scheduled five minutes later. It was posted right on the door."

"And they're saying Sam assaulted her anyway? Jesus."

"I can tell you Pauline was pretty hot under the collar about it. She said she'd warned her Sterling not to go any-where near it, that it was going to blow up in his face. But he thought he had no choice. The girl brought charges; wit-nesses backed her up. How could he ignore it? But now, the more the story comes out, the fishier it looks. Word is this Suzanne and Doug Malik are extremely close, if you know what I'm saying. Word is his secretary, Ava, has quite the case for Dr. Big Shot, too. Imagine the red faces at the top if all that comes out and turns out to be true."

"And?"

She licked her pop. "And we'll see. Pauline's talking; the president's listening—can't hurt."

"Thanks for going to all that trouble, Frieda. I can't tell you how much it means."

"It was nothing, darling. For you, I don't mind one bit going to a fancy-shmancy boring luncheon where no one eats. Such a waste like you never saw: hundreds of the cutest little stuffed Cornish hens in the garbage; hundreds of miniature blueberry cheesecakes down the drain. But you know what?"

"No, what?"

She patted my leg. "So happens there is one little something you could do for me in return."

· THIRTY-FOUR ·

Brent Elias shared his hospital room with three other boys. Gesturing with the bandaged knob of his hand, he gave me the rundown.

"Eric, the kid who's fast asleep near the window, is waiting for a kidney transplant. Skinny Kenny has cystic fibrosis. Jamil has some weirdo metabolic thing and a great big ugly bug up his butt."

The boy in question lay staring at a daytime soap. "Takes one to know one, Charbroil."

"Be easy for you to do his portrait, Emma. Just draw a whole lot of nasty on a sea of mean."

"I'm here to do yours, Brent. Where would you like to pose?"

Jamil roared cruelly. "How you gonna draw his picture, lady? Charbroil ain't got no face."

"Let's take it somewhere else, Emma. Something in here reeks."

He led me down the hall to the dayroom, where a small

boy dwarfed by a body cast was playing Chutes and Ladders with a blonde candy striper.

"Hey, Mikey. How is it hanging?"

They traded an awkward high five. "Like usual," the boy said, giggling. "Upside down."

In the opposite corner of the room, I unpacked my drawing board, a sketch pad, pencils, gum erasers, and the wrapped paper tortillons I used for blending. "Okay. All set. Now tell me how you'd like to pose, Brent. Would you rather I draw you sitting or standing? Full on or side view?"

"Standing. Holding a hockey stick. Wearing a helmet and uniform, on skates. Can you do an ice rink in the background?"

"Sure."

"A blue fence covered with ads. Nike, Bud, and Coke. Stuff like that?"

"All right."

"Could you put people in the stands?"

"Adults? Kids?"

"Parents mostly, some brothers and sisters, a couple of grandparents, and a few of the players' friends."

"Sure. I can do that."

"And the scoreboard. Don't forget that. It's the big game between the Hornets and the Hurricanes. Hurricanes are up six goals to three. Four minutes to go in the final period. Hurricanes keep it up, they clinch the championship. So everyone has to look excited. Excited and a little worried, if you get what I mean."

"I think so."

I taped a large sheet of vellum on the drawing board and, as he talked, began to rough out the scene. Brent had a transporting gift for storytelling. I could feel the exhilaration, hear the crisp scrape of metal on ice, see plumes of

vapor stretch like thought bubbles from the players'
mouths.

Rapidly, I sketched the bleachers and rough stylized
outlines of the fans. Moving to the ice, I drew some of the
peripheral players in broad strokes. "Which of the cham-
pion Hurricanes are you, Brent?"

Whatever role he'd played in fact, he would be the obvious star of this piece. I would render him bigger in the
forefront and in greater detail than anything else. Portraits
were all about perception, and to me, this boy loomed
large. I had held him firmly in mind when I came within
sight of the hospital and felt a compelling urge to turn and
flee. What had been Sam's second home was now an
alien, hostile place. I imagined everyone sitting in judgment, feeling smug and superior, whispering cruelly behind my back.

But thinking about the hostile horrors this boy had sur-
vived had given me courage to pass through the automatic
door. A security guard had waved me through with an off-
hand nod of recognition, and I'd tracked the familiar route
over the gleaming tile to the east elevators. Grateful to be
alone in the car, I'd pressed 9 for Pediatrics. Brent had
seemed pleased to see me, if a bit surprised. With a trace of
hurt in his eyes, he told me he was still waiting for Dr. Mc-
Donough to do his Dolly Parton impersonation.

He hadn't answered me, so I repeated the question.
"Which position did you play, Brent?"

"Promise you won't laugh?"

"No way. And if you ever saw me on skates, you'd
know why. The only position I could play is flat on my
back."

He tapped the pocket of his robe. "It's in there. Can you
get it out?"

The folded page in his pocket had been clipped from the

sports section of a Long Island newspaper. The article, dated over a year ago, bore the banner headline: *Hurricanes Take Semis by Storm*. The piece was all about the team's star center, the boy who had spurred the squad through a season of record-breaking victories and would now lead them to the state finals.

"A remarkable young talent," I read aloud. "Brent Elias is a steady presence on the ice, with true grit and determination. Thanks in large part to this extraordinary player, the team is having its best year ever."

My eye went to the tiny caption. The star in question was a strapping boy with a broad smile and wide intelligent eyes. Thick sandy hair peeked out from under his helmet, and the smile framed a chipped front tooth. Probably a souvenir of the sport, I thought, the kind of playful imperfection that made a handsome guy even more appealing.

I swallowed hard. "Look at you. Star center. Led the team to victory. I'm impressed."

He shook his head. "By him, maybe. Not this."

"That is you, Brent. Same kid. Just give it time."

He sniffed. "Afraid my hockey career is over. No worries, though. I can always work as a fashion model."

"You'll do something important, kiddo. I can tell."

"So can you draw that? We can call it my before picture."

"You've got it. Can I take this to work on at home? I'll bring it back."

"You can keep it. I've got about a million copies."

On my way out, I saw Kelly. Her bed had been wheeled to a window so she could watch the street below through the mirror angled overhead. She could also observe people passing in the corridor.

"So I was wondering, is *art* short for *artificial*?"

"Good question. I don't know for sure. But in some cases, it certainly seems to be."

"You came to do that picture Brent won in the monster contest?"

"I did."

"You know, everyone makes a big deal about Brent because they feel sorry for him."

"Maybe they just like him."

"No. They feel sorry, and it sucks. Makes you like one of those pity parties on parade they trot out on the telethons. Exploitation with a capital *E*. People are nice to kids like Brent because it makes them feel so noble. That's why I make it a strict policy to be completely obnoxious, so they won't do that to me."

I smiled. "You do an excellent job."

"You like me anyway. I can tell."

I could also tell how much she enjoyed being treated like a regular kid, getting as good as she gave. "That's true. I do like you. I guess there's just no accounting for taste."

Her grin was trapped in infinite regress on the mirror. "That would explain me liking you, too."

I winked at her. "Go easy on Brent. I think he may have a crush on you."

She blushed. "P-o-p-p-y-c-o-c-k. Means tommyrot or bilge."

I walked away with a rueful smile, shaking my head. Compared to Kelly and Brent, my problems seemed minuscule.

That was the thought that stuck with me as I rode the elevator down to the main floor. Twenty minutes remained until I had to pick Tyler up from school. Given the state of my bladder, there was no way I could make it to the preschool without a bathroom break. In the restroom near the cafeteria I took care of that. I was washing my hands when my worst nightmare strolled through the door.

· THIRTY-FIVE ·

"Well, well. Imagine seeing you here, Emma. Visiting a sick friend? Or are you taking a sentimental journey around the scene of Sam's crime?"

My face flamed. "His only crime was being nice to you."

"Is that what that naughty boy is trying to sell you?"

"Nothing happened and you know it, Suzanne. You made the whole thing up."

"Don't be silly. What do you expect him to do? Confess?"

"He told the truth. I believe him."

"Poor Emma. Married to someone who can't keep his zipper up. Must be so humiliating."

"I don't know what game you think you're playing. But you're not going to win."

Her laugh was hollow. "Silly girl. Of course I'll win. I already have."

"It isn't over, not by a long shot."

She clacked her tongue. "So sad when someone is dead and doesn't know enough to lie down."

"I have nothing to say to you."

Gazing at the mirror, she finger-combed her hair and put on lip gloss. "You have plenty to say, just no nerve. This is your big chance to get things off your droopy little chest. Why pass it up?"

"How can you live with yourself?"

"That's easy. I'm a wonderful person. The best."

"Doesn't it bother you in the least to hurt someone who went out of his way to help you?"

"Hmm. Let me think about that. Does it bother me? Actually, no."

"You don't care who you hurt, what you break, it's all about you."

"Naturally. Who else?"

"You make my skin crawl."

"My, my. So angry. I'd watch that blood pressure if I were you. I hear that can be a major health hazard for a cow."

Cringing, I made for the door.

Before I reached it, she caught my arm.

"Not that you deserve it, but I'm going to give you a little friendly advice. Guys like Sam who can't keep it in their pants aren't worth the trouble. You stick by him this time, there'll only be the next and the next."

"The last thing I need is advice from you."

She clutched me harder. "Nevertheless, you're going to get it. You didn't read Sam right, that's your problem. You expected him to play the dutiful little husband while you blew up like a balloon and waddled around. But what can I say? His hormones got the best of him. Poor guy was so horny, I guess he lost his mind."

"Let go of me. I have no interest in hearing your crap."

I wrenched free and strode out to the hall. She caught up and walked beside me, pressed uncomfortably close. She smelled of coconut shampoo and something else dark and predatory.

"Leave me alone, Suzanne. Get the hell away."

"How strange. I'd think a pillar of virtue like you would want to hear the facts."

"I know the facts. Your boyfriend was jealous. He thought Sam was coming on to you, so he made up a bogus charge and got you to go along."

She laughed in earnest. "My boyfriend? Are you saying Doug Malik? That's hilarious."

"We'll see how funny you find it when that comes out."

"Look. I get that you're desperate. Who wouldn't be, in your situation? But you're barking up the way wrong tree. Doug Malik is an old friend of my father's, and I do mean *old*. He's helped me here and there, and that's all. There is absolutely nothing between us. Never was, never will be. If that's the line of bullshit Sam's trying to hand you, don't buy. You're only going to wind up looking more idiotic than you already do."

"That's it, Suzanne. I've listened to all I can take. You're an excellent liar. Don't forget to put that on your résumé when you find yourself out of a job."

She rolled her eyes. "You know, I truly didn't want to have to do this, Emma. Seems so cruel, under the circumstances. But you leave me no choice. Sam did try to rape me, and I have proof."

"I told you I'm not listening to this."

"Yes, you are. Because if you don't, I'll go right now, today, and tell it to the police."

Glaring smugly, she stood her ground.

"I would have already," she continued, "but to be honest, I felt a little sorry for Sam. Him being so depressed and all, having to go on those pills."

"How did you know that?"

"I told you, Sam's a lonely, lonely boy. Started leaning on me before he tried to lean on me, if you catch my drift. He seemed so desperate and pathetic."

"Sam's going through a minor depression isn't proof of anything. He was working too hard, not taking care of himself. He's fine now."

"That's not the proof I was talking about, honey. Before Dr. Malik and Ava happened to come into the conference room and pulled him off me, Sam tried to—how shall I put this delicately—get in my face. And so I got a real good look at him, up close and personal. I saw the scar where he had that mole removed. Looks just like a crooked little smile."

· THIRTY-SIX ·

As soon as I called and told her I had to get away, Franny said to come ahead. She had plenty of room, and we could stay as long as we liked. She didn't push for an explanation. That could wait. When our Metro North train pulled into the Larchmont station, her black Acura was idling at the curb.

On the ride through her sleepy Westchester town, Tyler more than made up for my numb silence. His arms flapped with excitement. "We took the train, Aunt Franny. The conductor came and did a clickity thing on the ticket."

"How much fun was that?"

"And we saw trees and telephone poles and two fat guys with music thingies in their ears, and a lady eating McDonald's with the paper on. Didn't we, Mama?"

"Yes, sweetie." My voice was a dead ball thwack. It occurred to me that my bouncing days might be over.

"And I get to play with your twins." He tried to bobble in the car seat, but the five-point restraint held him back.

"That's right," Franny said. "Ben and Michael are just

your age. They have blond hair and blue eyes like you do, and they're crazy about superheroes. As soon as they wake up from their nap, they'll be ready to play."

"Twins means two boys." He held up three fingers, he was that overwhelmed.

By the time we bumped into her long, meandering drive, those two boys were running around on the plush lawn under the watchful eye of a plump, pewter-haired woman Franny identified as Alma, the nanny. They trailed a boisterous fur-streak of a sheepdog that they'd named Shedder, because he did. Ty couldn't wait to escape the car seat and join the fray.

Looping an arm around my shoulders, Franny led me inside. "Don't worry," she said when I hesitated. "Alma raised seven kids, including triplets. She can manage those three in her sleep."

Her house was a bright, sprawling Tudor. She deposited my suitcase in a guest room with soft sky-colored walls and ornate white moldings. It reminded me of a Wedgwood plate. Bumpy, blue, and breakable, like me.

"Mind if I lie down awhile? I'm pretty wiped."

"That's fine. But first we talk."

"I don't know if I can talk about it."

"You can, Em. You should. It'll help."

She waited while I used the bathroom, then guided me down to the kitchen like a shaky invalid.

"Is it Sam?"

I nodded.

"Another woman?"

"I guess you could say that. Only worse. He's been fired. Charged with attempted rape."

Her eyes bugged. "Sam? You're kidding."

"That's what I thought at first, that it couldn't be for real. He swore he was innocent, and I believed him. But I found out today it was true."

"Wait. This calls for big guns." She lumbered to the refrigerator for club soda, chocolate syrup, and a gallon of milk. She filled two glasses with the frothy concoction and stirred until the liquid turned deep beige.

She set a glass down in front of me. "When was the last time you had a decent egg cream?"

"Last time you made me one. Must have been sophomore year. I remember you used to call them Brooklyn fat bombs. Said they were guaranteed to cure anything but overweight."

"They are. Drink up. You'll feel better."

I could barely swallow. "Thanks, but I don't think that's going to do it."

"Drink. Trust me. Egg creams are medicinal. It'll do you a world of good."

My tears spilled over, blunting the chocolaty sweetness with salt. "How could he do such a thing, Franny? What's wrong with him?"

She held up a hand. "You're getting way ahead of yourself. Tell me what happened. Start at the beginning."

"I don't know where that is. When does a thing like this start? How does it? He's just sick."

"I mean the beginning of what you know. What happened exactly? How did you hear?"

"I came home from a meeting at Tyler's school. Sam was out cold, drunk. I had to throw water on his face to wake him. He seemed so devastated, as if the whole thing had come as a total shock. He showed me a letter he'd gotten from the physician-in-chief. It stated that he'd been accused of sexual assault, that there'd been witnesses. One of them was Douglas Malik, the cardiac surgeon I told you about, the one Sam wanted so badly to work with. The other was Malik's executive assistant."

"This happened at work? There were witnesses?"

"It gets even crazier. I'd heard things, disturbing things from Malik's apartment, which is upstairs from ours. Late at night, he would go into his little girl's room. He'd demand that she do as he said, and she'd plead with him not to. I mentioned it to a friend, and she reported it to Child Welfare. A couple of investigators showed up at the Maliks' the night before Sam was accused. I thought Malik must have found out the complaint originated with me and invented the charges to get back at Sam. I thought it was all my fault."

"What happened today to change your mind?"

Staring out through the broad bay window, I watched Tyler playing with Franny's twins. The trio of little towheads screeched with glee as they chased the dog over the broad Crayola green lawn. Shedder streaked across the grass and stood panting in the shade of a Japanese maple, pale tongue drooping like a flag of surrender. When the kids came close, he charged off in a different direction to find fresh shade and wait for them again. On the sidelines, Nanny Alma smiled with infinite patience.

Franny urged me back. "Emma? What happened today?"

I struggled to hold on to the innocent, sunny scene outside, desperate to keep the other impossible one at bay. But I could not. My mind filled with the image Suzanne had painted. Sam forcing her head down, giving her the up-close and personal view.

"I went to the hospital to do a portrait of one of the kids on Pediatrics. When I was leaving, I ran into the resident who made the accusation against Sam. She said she could prove he'd tried to rape her. Sam had a mole removed from his penis a couple of years ago. She had seen it. She described the scar."

Franny's lips pressed in a grim line. "Did you confront Sam with that?"

"I couldn't. I can't. I don't think I could look at him, Franny. I barely know who he is."

She folded her arms atop the rise of her belly. "Doesn't sound like Sam, does it?"

"Not like the person I thought I knew. But obviously, I was wrong."

"You know, Em, in a way what we do is pretty similar. You build your pictures with line and shade. I do mine with bits of information."

"Interesting way to look at it."

"One thing I've learned is that when something doesn't fit, it might not be part of the picture I'm trying to understand. It could be an artifact, something that belongs to a different puzzle altogether. You might have to leave out that particular shadow or line if you want things to work."

"It's been many years since you knew Sam, Franny."

"True. But you've known him continually. Does this picture of him make any sense to you at all?"

"There are people you think you know but don't really. What about the nice, quiet family man who turns out to be a serial killer? What about the PTA president with three kids who was a radical, hop-head bomber in a former life?"

"Rare exceptions that prove the rule. We're talking about Sam here, about what makes sense to you."

"Suzanne—that's his accuser's name—said Sam was out of his mind with lust. She blamed it on my being pregnant, on his having to live with a big old sexless cow."

"That's what she said?"

I shrugged. "That and worse."

"Christ, Emma. She sounds like an attack dog, not an assault victim."

"I guess she's the kind of victim who bites back."

She shook her head. "It doesn't compute. If Sam was her assailant, she'd see you as someone who shares a common enemy. She might go for Sam's throat, but not yours."

"I told her I didn't believe her. I said she and Malik were playing a game they weren't going to win. Sam heard from his department administrator that Suzanne and Malik were having an affair, and I repeated that. I was going for her throat, too."

"Doesn't matter. I'm telling you something smells off."

The baby squirmed. "Then how could she know about Sam's scar?"

She sipped her egg cream, capping her thoughtful frown with a chocolate foam mustache. "Sam had the mole removed at General?"

"Yes. We were terrified. They suspected it was a melanoma. Turned out to be benign. Or at least I thought it was. There's nothing benign about evidence they can use to throw him in jail."

"Listen to me, Emma. You know how I feel about Sam since he dumped you for Haley Breisblatt. Sometimes I'd like to wring his neck. And sometimes I think that's too good for him. But he's no rapist."

"What about the scar?"

"There are plenty of ways another doctor in the hospital could have found out about it."

"How?"

"For one thing, people talk. Sam's doctor could have said something to this Suzanne character. Or someone in his office might have."

"Years later they just happen to be talking about Sam's benign mole? You honestly think that makes sense?"

She smiled, stretching the mustache thin. "I don't actually. And with any luck, that's not how it went."

"I don't follow you."

"Do you know someone at General who has access to records?"

"Maybe. Why?"

"It would have to be someone on Sam's side, the kind of person who'd be willing to help without making a noise about it. The kind of person who might be willing to bend the rules."

"Why?"

"I'll get to that. First think."

I could come up with only one person who met those criteria: LeeAnn.

"What's she like?" Franny said.

"Hard to describe. LeeAnn's sort of a cross between a camp counselor and a porn queen. Debbie Does Dorm Mother. Now tell me what you're thinking."

She eyed the clock. "First call her. Maybe you can reach her before she leaves for the day. I'll explain when you get her on the phone."

· THIRTY-SEVEN ·

Andrew Eastham's staid, book-lined office perched on the fifty-fifth floor of the Chrysler Building, a landmark Art Deco jewel on Lexington Avenue and Forty-second Street. I arrived to find Sam slumped in one of the squat burgundy visitors' chairs that faced the lawyer's imposing mahogany desk. Eastham wore an impeccably tailored charcoal pinstriped suit, an ivory shirt, and a cash-green dotted tie. He led with a firm stride, a solid handshake, and a ready smile. He had the polished feel of a kid born to privilege and prep school. Not a rough edge or loose thread in sight.

"Thanks for coming in, Mrs. Colten. I thought it would be useful to discuss this in person."

I settled heavily in the chair beside Sam. His hair was sleep-tousled and his clothes were a rumpled mess. The tail of his wrinkled blue shirt lolled over stained khaki pants. He wore one blue sock, one black.

"Sam? Are you okay?"

"I must have called you a hundred times from Southshore.

I tried the hospitals, the police. You can't imagine what was going through my mind."

"I told you we went to Franny's. It got to be late for Ty, so we stayed over."

"Would have been nice for you to let me know. I rushed home from my shift to find out what in hell happened, and the place was empty. No note. Nothing. The beds hadn't been slept in. I thought, God knows where you could be. I was practically out of my mind."

"I wasn't exactly in the best shape myself after running into Suze."

He scowled. "You didn't have to believe the lying bitch, Emma. You could have given me the benefit of the doubt."

Eastham's smile held steady. Conflict, after all, was his stock in trade. "Thankfully, everyone's fine." He propped his elbows on the desk and wove his fingers in a tidy ball. "Now let's focus on the latest development, shall we? I understand you made an interesting discovery about the complainant, Mrs. Colten."

"Disgusting is more like it. Hard to believe what people are capable of doing."

"I'd like to wring her goddamned neck," Sam said. "Five minutes alone with her. That's all I ask."

"You will not, under any circumstances, spend five *seconds* alone with Dr. Stitch," Eastham said. "Not one second. If you so much as see her, you walk away. You cross the street without a word. You don't even look at her. I hope we're perfectly clear on that."

"Yes," I said. "Me, too."

The lawyer met Sam's stony gaze. "I understand your anger, Sam. Anyone would. But our goal in this is to get you reinstated in the residency program and all damaging allegations dropped. We can't lose sight of that."

Sam's nostrils flared. "What about her? She tries to

slaughter me with a lie and that's it? She doesn't have to answer for that at all?"

"That's not true. I'm sure she'll have some serious explaining to do. Confidentiality is a huge issue in health care right now. The feds are all over it, and cracking down hard. I can assure you the hospital is not going to look kindly on someone who accessed a colleague's medical records without impeccable cause."

Sam's eyes bulged. "She'll have to *explain* herself? That's all? Are you kidding me? If I did something like that, they'd have my head."

Easton tamped the air with firm commanding hands. "I have no way of knowing how the hospital will respond. Once we lodge the appropriate complaint, it'll be in their court."

"Why can't we bring charges against her?" Sam railed. "She invaded my privacy. She perjured herself, slandered me, and came close to wrecking my career. That bitch should be in the hot seat. It should be her, Malik, and his assistant on the line here, not me."

"There are two choices, Sam. We can let the hospital deal with her when the time comes, or we can go to war."

"Make it war then. I want that bitch to get everything she deserves."

The lawyer shrugged. "Of course, in the final analysis, it's your call. But I must advise you that winning that war is by no means guaranteed. In fact, I'd say there's an excellent chance you'd lose."

"How could that be?" I demanded. "She accessed Sam's records. The entry is right there with her pass code. There's no way she can deny doing it, and she had no right. She's not Sam's doctor. His medical records are none of her damned business."

"She doesn't have to deny it, Mrs. Colten. Think about

it. The woman claims to have been sexually assaulted. What if she says she looked up Sam's medical history because she was worried about the risk of contracting a serious sexually transmitted disease like HIV, because she wanted to be able to start treatment immediately if she needed to? That would make a pretty compelling excuse for violating his privacy."

"You're saying she could use her own misconduct to seem even more sympathetic."

"If she's confronted, I think it's likely she would do exactly that, and not unlikely that she'd succeed."

My gaze drifted toward the window and the bustling cityscape that shrunk to a comical miniature by the fifty-story height. Ant-sized people swarmed the slim, gray ribbons of concrete. Toy traffic lurched along as if shot from a popgun, and then stalled in a haze of shimmering exhaust. I imagined each minuscule driver bristling with toe-tapping impatience, eager to get on with his ridiculous little fly speck life.

Turning back to Eastham, I wondered why some of those lives trailed a long smooth course while others jolted cruelly off the rails. Was there any way to spot the looming hazards and swerve to avoid them?

"I thought we had them, Mr. Eastham," I said. "Sorry to waste your time."

"You didn't waste my time. Actually, I think what you've learned may be extremely valuable. We just have to use it prudently, wait for the optimal time."

"When's that?" Sam said. "My next life?"

Eastham leaned back in his outsized chair. "I'm afraid I've gotten ahead of myself. We really haven't discussed strategy."

"Meaning?" I said.

"A proceeding like this is not entirely unlike a poker

game. Whether you win or lose can actually depend less on the resources you have than on how you use them. The last thing we want to do is show our strengths and weaknesses too early. We're far better off holding back, hoping they'll tip their hand, as they did here."

"What if they don't?" I said.

Sam raked his hair. "Simple. I'm toast."

"I don't mean to suggest that we're going to be passive in the meantime," the lawyer said. "There's a good deal of information we can obtain legally."

"What kind of information?" I thought of Mrs. Kalisher, who'd proposed the same approach.

"Any past legal actions involving the complainant or witnesses. Issues in their personal or professional history that might diminish their credibility. If any of them have dirty hands, we'll do our very best to find it."

"I'm sure Sam already told you about the child abuse complaint."

Eastham dipped his chin. "He did, but unfortunately, that particular dirt tracks back to you. We'd need independent corroboration before we could hope to use it."

"What if the corroboration came from his past?" I said. "Dr. Malik left Cleveland in a big hurry. He pulled his daughter out of school when the year was nearly over. He got his predecessor pushed into early retirement, which did not win him any popularity contests. He left a major research grant behind."

The lawyer pressed his fingers together and tapped them to his lips. "That's all very interesting, Mrs. Colten, no question. But to hang the man, we'd need the actual nail."

· THIRTY-EIGHT ·

The knock came moments after Sam left for his emer-gency room night shift, so soon I presumed he had left something behind. Unfortunately, what he'd left behind was me.

Tyler brightened at the prospect of visitors, but on seeing who it was, his face fell. Wordlessly, he returned to the pitched battle between Batman and his trusty Dalmatian Fred. Sebastian, he'd somberly informed me, had come down with an earache.

I simply stared for a moment, not quite believing my eyes. In all the years I'd known them, they had never once deigned to visit us at home.

"My word, Emma. Are you going to stand there all night with your jaw flapping? You might have the courtesy to ask us in."

Sam's stepmother did not wait for an answer. She crossed our tiny living room, trailing the weighty scent of jasmine perfume, and perched uneasily on the couch. She wore a rose silk shantung suit, ivory pumps and a matching clutch purse, and outsized diamond jewelry. Her hair had been teased and lacquered into stern submission.

Senior shut the door and stood with his back to the wall. His arms were crossed, his expression belligerent. Like his wife, he was thoroughly polished and pressed.

"Where's my son?"

"Sam's working."

The old man's brow peaked. "Working? My understanding is he's no longer employed."

"Your understanding is obviously wrong."

I sat on a chair beside Tyler. Our place might be small, but there was sufficient room to draw the necessary lines.

"Don't be cute with me, Emma. I can assure you, nothing about this situation amuses me in the least."

"I wouldn't think so."

"I need to speak with Sam at once. Get him on the phone."

"Sorry. I can't do that."

"Of course you can. Pick up the phone and dial."

"I'm not going to disturb him at work. As soon as he gets home, I'll give him the message. Now if there's nothing else, please excuse me. I was just about to put Tyler to bed."

He reddened. "Here's the message you can give him. You can tell Sam I've worked far too long and hard to build my professional reputation to have my good name damaged by his impulsive weakness."

"What a surprise," I said. "It's all about you."

"Such insolence," Freddie said. "I strongly suggest you mind your mouth, young lady."

Senior motioned for her silence. "Tell him I'm going to dig him out of the mess he's gotten himself into this time, but it had damned well better be his last. I've had my fill of carrying him, cleaning up after him, making things right."

"If you have something to say to Sam, do it yourself."

Senior's wife sputtered. "My word. Have you no manners?"

"My manners are fine when I'm dealing with reasonable people."

"The nerve of you. I've never seen such a rude, horrid girl."

Something streaked at the corner of my eye. Freddie screeched and tilted sideways, clutching the side of her face, spewing four-letter words.

With professional dispassion, Sam's father approached her. "Are you all right, my dear?"

In a fury, she brushed him off, sprang up from the couch, and grabbed Tyler's arm. She flipped him around and smacked his bottom with a sound like cracked wood.

"Bad boy! You *do not* throw things! You hear me?"

That's when I saw the mark on her cheek and Tyler's Batman figure where it had landed on the couch.

I picked up my screaming three-year-old and held him tight. "You *do not* touch my child, you old witch!"

"He threw a doll at me."

"He's three. At sixty-five, you're supposed to have better control."

Freddie's nostrils flared. "I am nowhere near sixty-five. No wonder the boy acts like a wild animal. Let's go, Senior. They don't deserve our help."

"Sam doesn't want your help and he doesn't need it," I said. "He's innocent."

Tyler wailed in misery. "How come she hitted me?"

"She lost her temper, Tyler. She didn't think. She was wrong."

"People are not for hitting, Mama."

"That's right." I stroked his hair. "They're certainly not."

Senior sniffed. "You'd do well to wise up about your precious husband. Sam has never accepted responsibility for his actions. He seems to believe the world owes him because his mother died when he was a boy. I hate to have to say it, but my son is a selfish weakling."

"Sounds like a chip off the old block."

"Your insolence is not attractive, Emma. Nor is it helpful to Sam. I've cultivated many important contacts over the years, people who may be able to dig him out of the unthinkable mess he's gotten himself into. I could speak to Doug Malik, for one. We have an excellent relationship. If I approach him correctly, I think he might be willing to accept Sam's apology and a promise that he'll stay away from that young woman in the future."

"Malik's a damned liar, and probably a child molester as well."

He let out a single laugh of disbelief. "Is that what my son claims? That's a bit far-fetched, even for Sam."

"I told you, Sam's innocent." Tyler was weeping in silence now. I could feel the syncopated tics of his grief against my chest.

"Because he says so?" Senior said. "That's his standard defense: I didn't do it. They're lying. It's everyone's fault but mine. This is far from the first time we've been through something like this."

"No wonder you get along with Malik. You're both big on making things up."

"You don't believe me? Ask Sam what happened his senior year in high school."

I glared at him. "I don't have to ask him. I already know. His girlfriend got pregnant. You treated Sam like a criminal, forced him to leave the school months before graduation and go live with your parents in Chicago. You wouldn't let him see the girl, wouldn't let him say good-bye, nothing. She had a miscarriage. He felt terrible about it for years."

"It was reckless, irresponsible. Typical Sam."

"Your son is human. He made a mistake."

Freddie clutched Senior's arm. The mark from the Batman attack had already faded so it was barely visible. "You have no idea what this man has done for that boy, the favors he's called in, the limbs he's gone out on to help Sam get ahead. I told him he was making a mistake, that both of you are hopelessly self-centered and immature, incapable of appreciating anything."

"Sam appreciates exactly what Senior's done for him, Freddie," I said. "That's why he stays away."

Franny's mother may have been dead wrong about the effectiveness of denim as a contraceptive, but things did seem to happen for a reason, as she'd said.

If not for Senior and Freddie's distressing visit, I would never have taken Tyler out so late for a walk. We would not have wandered into the playground, which was nearly empty at this hour, so I could push him on the swing. Both of us found the repetitive rhythms soothing. In fact all three of us did. Since Sam's parents showed up, the baby had been wriggling inside me nonstop, but now she settled down.

Tipping his head back, Tyler stared at the slowly dimming sky. "How come it gets dark, Mama?"

"Because it's almost bedtime."

"Then how come there's a night-light in my room?"

"To help you see if you need to."

His gaze shifted downward, toward the squat brass elephant. "Does he have a night-light?"

"Statues don't need night-lights. They don't need to see."

"Wait, stop!"

"Why? What's wrong?"

"Look! Over there."

I gripped the side chains and brought the swing to a

halt. Tyler scrambled down, ran toward the sandbox, and crouched beside the low wooden frame.

"Help, Mama! Quick!"

The source of his distress was a dead bird in Mrs. Kalisher's favorite teal blue.

"The birdie's hurt, Mama. We have to take it to the doctor."

"The bird's not sick, sweetie pie. He's dead."

"How come?"

"He just is. There's nothing the doctor can do for him anymore."

"We should bury him, then, like Spark and Mavis."

The bunny named Spark and Mavis the centipede had expired during their tenure in the nature program at Little Ranger. Siena had used both episodes to expose the children to common rituals surrounding death.

"I'm sure the people who clean the playground will take care of the bird."

"No. We can't leave it. When something dies, you have to show respect."

Looking around, I quickly rejected the possibilities. Small piles of leafy debris scattered the ground, but I didn't want some child to find the brittle dead thing there or in the sandbox in the morning.

"There's no place to bury it here, Ty. I'm sure the maintenance guy will show the bird lots of respect first thing tomorrow."

"No," he wailed. "We have to do it now."

"Okay. Ssh. I know. We can take it down to the basement and put it in the trash. That goes to a great big burial place where the bird will have lots and lots of company."

He seemed satisfied with that. I fashioned a tiny bird shroud from a tissue in my purse and crossed the street cradling the stiff little corpse in my palm.

Once again, Obie the doorman was doing a double shift, filling in for Sanchez, who was normally scheduled to guard the door at night but too often phoned in a lame excuse.

"We've got a dead bird," Tyler told him proudly. "And it's gonna have lots and lots of company in the trash."

"Sounds like a plan," Obie said.

According to the indicator lights, both elevators languished on high floors. "Let's take the stairs, cutie."

He raced ahead of me toward the trash bins. Treading the shadowy corridor past the row of locked doors, I heard a light scurrying sound. Imagining mice, I shuddered and quickened my pace. But the closer I got to the garbage receptacles, the louder the noise became.

"Where should we bury him, Mama? Which bin?"

Listening, I pressed a finger to my lips. The scuffling sound intensified. There was a sharp intake of breath. A whimper. A cry.

Tyler's eyes widened and he pressed close. "What's that?" he whispered.

"Stay right here," I rasped. The light was on in the musty little room. Holding Tyler in my sights, I peered inside.

· THIRTY-NINE ·

"Get away from her!"

Judge had Bori pressed against the cold cement wall. He was mauling her like a crazed animal, tearing at her clothes. I caught the urgent rasp of his breathing and his musky feral scent.

"Stop!"

Still, he ground against her, red-faced and grunting. He was oblivious to my presence. I had to grab his bulging arms and wrench him away.

"I said leave her alone!"

Bori's lip looked hot and swollen; her cheek pebbled from where he'd mashed it against the concrete. Several buttons had been torn off her slim cotton shirt.

Hastily, she tried to pull herself together. She begged me not to tell anyone, certain that any trouble, even if it was not of her causing, would get her shipped home. Here, at least, she could work. She could send money back to her family, so they could live.

Judge said nothing as he tucked in his work shirt and zipped his pants. His expression had gone curiously blank, as if he'd ducked behind a drape of disbelief. He stared at his rough calloused hands, flipping them over and back again, acting as if they were alien things that didn't belong to him.

I could barely contain my fury. "Get out and don't you dare come back. If I see you anywhere near this building, I'll call the police."

With a shrug, he turned to go.

"If you ever lay a finger on her again, I'll have you thrown in jail."

He trudged off with his head down, hands thrust deep in the pockets of his stained baggy jeans.

"Where's Judge going, Mama?"

"He's leaving, Ty. Judge doesn't work here anymore."

"How come?"

"Because we're going to get someone nicer."

"Like Obie?"

"I hope so, sweetie. That would be great."

Bori huddled in her ruined blouse.

Tyler giggled. "Digga dada. Digga dada. Ssh."

Blushing, she turned away. In a tiny voice she said she was ashamed, that she hated for the little boy to see her like this. She hated for me to know that she was soiled. She was so sorry.

I assured her that she had nothing to be sorry about. It was his fault. She shouldn't blame herself.

But she did. She should have been stronger, she told me, streaming tears. She should have left this place, but she hadn't known where else to go. The rents were too expensive, even for a room to share. She couldn't afford anything and still have enough money left to send home.

"Come on, Mama," Tyler urged. "We have to do respect."

I asked Bori if she'd do us a favor. I explained that we'd found a dead bird in the park. We had to pay final respects, and it would be good if she could join us.

We formed a tight solemn circle. "Good-bye, little bird," I said. "*Adiós, pájarito.*"

"At a yose," Tyler echoed. "Have fun with all the other dead guys."

Bori crossed herself as I lifted the lid from a rubber bin and gently lowered the tissue-wrapped body inside. Her gaze fell and she murmured a prayer. Doing so seemed to soothe her. She drew a long slow breath.

I asked her to come upstairs, but she refused. She was fine now, she said, thanks to me.

"*Dónde irá?*" I said gently. Where would she go? Getting Judge out solved one problem but created another. It was unlikely that his replacement would allow her to break the rules and camp in that room.

She said it didn't matter anymore. This was the last night she'd have to spend in the basement. The Maliks' regular nanny was leaving and they'd asked her to live in starting tomorrow.

I told her I was glad, though I had misgivings. Working for the God from Ohio and his arrogant, demanding wife could not be easy, and living with them was bound to complicate matters further. I wondered where the other nanny had been late at night while Malik and his daughter had those chilling words. I wondered if those words and the actions around them were the reason she was leaving.

Bori smiled at me shyly. "*Mi amiga.*"

I was the first friend she'd made in this country, she said. She couldn't tell me how much it meant to have me come to her rescue. Many people would have turned away and ignored the noise, she insisted. Many had.

I shrugged. Maybe they didn't know what was going on,

I said. Or maybe they misunderstood. Anyway, that was water under the bridge. Judge wouldn't be here to bother her anymore.

She told me I had to let her thank me. It would make her so happy if there was ever anything, any way she could begin to pay me back.

"No hay necesidad." There's no need for that.

She shook her head firmly. She owed me a debt, and she wouldn't rest until it was repaid.

I took a long time answering. When I did, I carefully measured my words. If I primed her to look for signs of abuse, she'd be predisposed to find them. Instead, I said that if she saw anything strange in the Maliks' house, anything at all, it would be a big help if she'd tell me about it as soon as she could.

"Por supuesto," she said. Anything. Of course.

Tyler issued a broad, squeaky yawn. "We better go, Mama. It's getting late out. Sebastian and Fred will be scared."

"You think so?"

He nodded. "Especially Sebastian. His ear hurts."

"Good point."

The boy needs to go to bed, I explained to Bori. Good luck when you move in with the Maliks tomorrow. I hope it goes well for you.

We were down the hall when I turned back with an afterthought. *"Y tenga cuidado,"* I told her. Take care. What I wanted to say was: Don't let your guard down. Don't trust Malik. Watch your back!

· FORTY ·

On the night of the parents' meeting, everyone had been hopeful we'd seen the last of Jeanette and Arthur, but no such luck. As if nothing had happened, Jeannette had shown up with Marissa for school the following day. Three days later, a certified letter from her lawyer arrived. Now, it was my turn to wrangle Jake, and Siena handed me that letter when I entered the room half an hour before class was due to start.

"I want you to read it for yourself, but basically, it says that by agreeing to look after Jake, you accept responsibility along with the school for anything bad that happens."

I read it twice. "'Adverse consequences including but not limited to physical, psychological, or emotional harm'? What's that supposed to mean?"

"What it says. If you help out, a world of limitless trouble awaits you."

"Not limited to? If it rains while I'm watching Jake, am I on the hook for that, too?"

"Possibly."

"I take responsibility if another Republican wins the White House?"

"Definitely."

"What a load of crap."

"That pretty much describes it."

"Now what do I need to know about managing Jake?"

She blew a noisy breath. "You have no idea how relieved I am, Emma. Yesterday Marie read the letter and left. She felt terrible, but she said she couldn't take on a risk like that without discussing it first with her husband."

"I can't imagine that Jean-Michel's daddy would cave in to blackmail like this."

"That's exactly what Etienne did. He was charming as always, but basically, they were both intimidated enough to back away."

"I'm surprised. Just because those jackasses throw a bunch of words at us doesn't mean they can make them stick."

"No, but they can make trouble. In all good conscience, I have to tell you that."

I peered at her eyes behind the thick corrective lenses. They looked wide and clear as polished glass.

"Right," I said. "You don't keep secrets."

"I understand that you're angry with me, Emma, and I feel awful about that. But I did what I had to do. I had no choice."

"I'm not angry." I was surprised to find that was true. Malik was the cause of Sam's troubles, not Siena.

Now her eyes went liquid. "You mean it?"

"Yes. You're as decent, kind, caring, sensible, and solid as they come, but somehow I can forgive that."

"Thanks."

"What I may not be able to forgive are those dreadful fruit bars."

She laughed. "They're good for you."

"Contrary to what you seem to think, there's such a thing as too healthy."

"You really don't like them?"

"They're fine, just not for eating."

"Seriously?"

"If you want my opinion, they'd make excellent packing material. And you could probably use them to repel bugs. At least, bugs who have any taste."

"You are serious."

"I am. Sorry if that insults you. I wouldn't have told you, but I did what I had to do. I had no choice."

"All right. Point taken. And you're right. I did have a choice. I made the only one I could and still look myself in the eye."

I shrugged. "Tragically, I can respect that."

"Friends?"

"Yes. But your fruit bars still suck."

Tyler was coloring with Amity at one of the little tables. Only three and he already stayed compulsively within the lines. That was yet another thing about him that I found worrisome. Kids were supposed to be sloppy and shameless, drawn to create and revel in chaos. A boy barely out of training pants wasn't supposed to spend his days fretting about health risks and hazards like a pint-sized surgeon general. They'd invented neurotic mothers for that.

"The program with Jake is basic behavior modification," Siena said. "We verbally reward everything positive and use a sticker system he can exchange later for treats. Negative behaviors get a firm time-out. Basically, you hold him in your lap and keep him from hurting himself or anyone else."

I looked down. "What if I don't have a lap?"

"You have patience and a sense of humor, Emma. That's basically what it takes."

She didn't mention the bottomless energy I lacked,

though that's what it took as well. That, and impeccable vigilance. Jake wandered constantly and aimlessly, changing course with startling speed. Forget my frequent need for bathroom breaks. I could barely afford to blink.

Twice in the ten minutes after he arrived, I narrowly averted a disaster. The first time, I caught his hand as he was rearing back to bash Marissa in the head with a heavy wooden *E* from the alphabet block set. I held him until he seemed calm. But as soon as I released him, he made a beeline for Marissa again. This time, he lowered his head and charged like an irate bull. When I trapped him, he was a breath away from knocking the little girl over in her chair.

While I held him, I squinted at Marissa, trying to view Jake's little nemesis through his eyes. What about her in particular set him off?

She was not the only chubby girl in the class, not the only one with brown eyes and dark cropped hair. Like her, Olivia wore a bead bracelet and flower barrettes. Addison and Jaden wore similar sneakers with strip lights that flashed when they walked. Tyler had a similar squash-blossom nose. Jean-Michel sat on his feet like Marissa did. Amity had the same habit of resting her chin on her fist.

I could come up with nothing distinctive, nothing that explained Jake's particular animosity toward Marissa. Yet, he went for her again the moment I let him go.

I tried diversion, holding him so Marissa was not within his view, but no matter what I did, he homed in like a guided missile on that particular child. He tracked her to the sink, where she was washing her hands clean of library paste after gluing tiny colored paper squares on a rainbow. He stalked her to the small outside play area where the children rode in people-powered cars. Like a moonstruck coyote, he howled his indignation when she sang.

Jake was maddening, a puzzle I couldn't solve. But he

was fascinating, too, a puzzle I could ponder indefinitely. He was the sum of all my most perplexing questions. What happened to people? What diabolical tricks did the brain play? And why?

His mother showed up first to collect Jake. The boy had inherited her slim, wiry build, small features, and sallow complexion. From him, she had taken on an air of glum resolve.

"Thanks for helping out with Jake today, Emma. How did it go?"

"We did fine. He's perfectly okay with most of the kids. I keep wondering why he has it in for Marissa."

She showed her empty palms. "If only we had some way to figure out what goes on in his head."

I nodded grimly. "Or anyone else's."

Marion held my gaze. "I hope you don't mind my asking, but how are you holding up?"

"Pretty well. It's not easy, but what is? And I don't mind your asking at all. I much prefer that to the looks."

"I know those looks. I get them all the time. 'Poor Marion and Bob, but then they must have done something to deserve it.' 'The poor Mersons, but better them than me.' "

"It has nothing to do with what you deserve. It rains on the just and unjust alike. Things just happen. The more I see and experience, the more I understand how true that is."

"You know that, and I do. But there are plenty of people who put themselves above it all because they've had a little luck. If things go well for me, it must be a reward. I don't have a sick kid or money problems because I'm a wonderful person."

On cue, Jeanette Trevallis, the queen of smug, appeared followed by Wanda and Veronica. Jeanette bustled over to Marissa and made a great show of her excellence in parenting.

"How's Mommy's beautiful little princess? Did you have a good time in school?"

Marissa displayed her most outstanding talent. She picked her nose.

"Did you make that, Marissa?" Jeanette gushed. "It's the most wonderful rainbow ever!"

"I'm hungry," Marissa whined.

"You are? What did you have for snack?"

"Green stuff. It was gross."

"Don't worry. Mommy will get you something to eat right away." Jeanette glared. "You could try to have something children would actually eat, Siena. Marissa is always starved when I pick her up."

"She sure doesn't look starved." I said this louder than I intended. Or maybe my true intent muscled out the remaining shreds of civilized restraint. I yearned to pummel Jeanette, though people were not for pummeling. Insulting her hardly made a dent.

Turning to me, she puffed up. "I certainly wouldn't be taking potshots at other people if my husband was a rapist!"

The room went dead still. Even the children fell silent.

My cheeks flamed. Stiffly, I took Tyler by the hand and headed for the door. It was one thing to know what everyone was thinking, and another to have it said aloud. Sam's innocence didn't make the cloak of shame any easier to wear.

Wanda broke the silence. "Sam's been accused, that's all. But whatever happens, Jeanette darlin', you'll still be the little piggy who should've stayed home."

Jeannette pouted. "Go ahead. Take her side. You're going to feel pretty stupid when the facts come out and he gets marched off to jail."

"What's wrong, Mama? What's a ray puss? Who's marching? How come everyone's mad?"

My voice broke. "It's okay, Ty. Don't worry. Time to go."

"But I made you a rainbow. I need to get my stuff."

Pulling free of my grasp, he headed for his cubby. Numbly, I watched him, marveling that he seemed utterly unchanged. I wanted to disappear, to go someplace alien and new where we could start again fresh. It wasn't true that you were innocent until proven guilty. Guilt stained you from the moment you were accused.

Siena stood and folded her arms. Her jaw twitched, and wormy veins undulated at her temples. I had never seen her look so cold and hard.

"That's it, Jeanette," she said. "No more. Consider yourselves withdrawn from this school, effective immediately."

"You can't do that."

"I just did."

"But we paid for the year. We put a deposit down for the fall. Marissa loves it here."

"And we'll miss her. It's unfortunate that you've made it untenable to have her stay with us."

"Look. This is silly. I'm sorry I said that. Let's forget it."

Siena held her ground. "We'll send you a refund. You should have it in a week."

"That's outrageous," Jeanette sputtered. "Emma calls my child fat and *we're* asked to leave?"

Veronica O'Donovan smirked. "You said yourself no one belongs in this school who's dangerous and disruptive, no one who's a bad influence. And that would be you."

"You just like to gang up, all of you. You're like a bunch of seventh graders trying to bully me out of some club."

"Good-bye, Jeanette," Siena said.

"You'll hear from my lawyer about this. I'll sue. It's discrimination."

"You're absolutely right, Jeanette," Wanda said. "We admit to being totally unfair to judgmental jerks. You and

Arthur go right ahead and pay your lawyer gobs of money to protest that."

"I told you I'm hungry," Marissa wailed. "I want McDonald's now!"

"Hush!" Jeanette shrieked. "You will not get away with this, Siena. None of you. I'll close this stupid school down. I'll make your lives miserable. You'll see."

· FORTY-ONE ·

Some days have themes, and this one was all about completion. During several restless nights, between visits from Tyler and the time I spent coaxing him back to sleep, I had finished the portrait of Jillian Palliser and her baby against the garden backdrop and the picture of Brent Elias as a hockey star before he sustained those horrible burns.

I went to the pediatric floor to deliver Brent's portrait, but he was not in his room. Jamil, who occupied the bed opposite Brent's, spoke to me with his eyes fixed on the ceiling-mounted TV. In the background I heard the syrupy strains of soap opera music and an actress accusing someone of wrecking her life.

"You here to see Charbroil?"

"Brent, yes."

"'Fraid you're out of luck, lady. Char's out getting a skin change. Hear they just rip off the bad stuff and stick on some new. Hear they cut it off dead folk and slap it on him. Pretty harsh."

I set the wrapped portrait down beside Brent's bed.

"Can you please tell him I dropped this off? He can give me a call if he'd like me to hang it for him."

He hitched his scrawny shoulders. "Could tell him if I want to."

I smiled. "I see that bug of yours is still alive and well."

"The one Charbroil says I got up my butt, you mean?"

"Exactly."

"Getting stuck in this hole enough to give anyone bugs. Tell you that."

"You keep eating the food around here, I bet that bug will give up and leave."

That drew a reluctant smile. "Okay. I'll tell Char you dropped the picture off."

"Thanks."

"That all? 'Cause I got to get back to my show. They's some way big shit going down."

"That's all."

He shrugged. "You ever want to draw the real deal, I'm around."

"I'll keep that in mind, Jamil. Hope you're not, though."

I stopped at Jillian Palliser's office next. Unwrapping the portrait, she beamed. "It's perfect. Exactly what I hoped for, only better. You caught Binnie exactly."

"You were a big help."

"Graham's going to love it, Emma. Thanks."

Completion felt good. Every loose end tied meant one less potential entanglement, one less errant string to trip me up.

On the way home from the hospital, I checked in with my sister. To a point, there had been completion for her, too.

"They finished the tests," Charlotte said. "The good news is there's a cure. The bad news is they need to use it."

"That thing with the radio waves?"

"Right. Sounds pretty awful. They thread a catheter

through one of the arteries to Jared's heart and destroy the extra nerves with a special radio frequency."

"When?"

"Soon as they can. There's no room for him on the schedule right now so we're on hold, but as soon as something opens up, they'll do it. Basically, we're here for the duration. Delavan says it could take up to a week."

"And I know you, Charlotte. You'll spend the whole time abusing Ajax."

"We're staying in a damned hotel room. I don't even have a decent sink to scrub."

"Want me to bring one? Ty and I could come anytime."

"I thought about it. Believe me. But under the circumstances, it really doesn't make any sense. We've been running around, doing everything we can think of to keep Jared busy, trying to keep from going at each other's throats to boot. The folks wanted to come, too, but I honestly don't think more displaced people are going to help right now."

"Whatever you want. But if you change your mind, I'm available."

I was also relieved. I still hadn't told her about the accusations against Sam. The last thing she needed was an addition to her towering worry pile. Being around her, I doubted I could keep up the act. Charlotte would see right through me.

"I know you are, Em. You're always there for me. Means a lot."

"I'm so sorry you have to wait like that."

"Me, too, but you know how it is. No choice; no problem. Wait long enough, everything happens. You just don't necessarily get to pick the time or place."

Her words stuck with me as I hung up and entered our apartment house. And a moment later, they proved to be chillingly true.

· FORTY-TWO ·

As he exited the elevator, the Lord from Ohio straight-ened the cuffs on his starched white shirt and fiddled with his cuff links. They were lapis lazuli set in stripes of gold, shaped like cold, unflinching eyes.

My gaze drifted to his hands. They were broad with dark, leathery skin and thick, blunt fingers reminiscent of clipped cigars. They were not, I thought, a surgeon's hands, nothing like Sam's, which were so graceful and command-ing, I longed to curl up inside them like a kitten in a teacup. Malik had the kind of hands you'd expect to see raking a lawn or hefting an axe to chop wood—crude paddles that would get in a person's way.

Anxious to avoid him, I ducked into the cubicle that contained the mailboxes. I'd retrieved our daily bounty of bills and junk earlier, but I opened our box and ducked to peer in as if I had not. I was somehow reassured by the sight of our name as it appeared inside, misspelled in red marker on a ragged, yellowing strip of masking tape. It confirmed we had a place here, at least for now.

Suddenly, I felt a presence behind me. Looming, closing in.

Turning, I found myself face-to-face with God's stylish wife. She wore a sweater set, a full printed skirt, and quilted gold ballet flats. Her daughter hung back in the entry hall in one of her shapeless dour dresses and stiff-looking shoes, shifting from foot to foot like a rootless bird. Her face struck me as far too hard and guarded for someone so young.

"Oh my. I'm afraid I forgot to bring you Adriana's photo for the portrait. I'll get it to you right away so you can begin at once. There's so much going on at the moment, I can't believe I let that slip my mind."

She was crowding me so the swell of my belly almost bumped her when I straightened.

"I didn't agree to do the portrait, Mrs. Malik. And given what's happened, I honestly can't believe you'd expect me to do it now."

"I don't understand."

"Excuse me." I pushed past her, starving for air. But when I filled my lungs, I caught a sharp, unpleasant odor. Adriana gave off a chemical scent I couldn't quite place, though it struck me as disturbingly familiar.

"What are you talking about, Mrs. Colten? What's happened?"

Malik was out on the street, shadowed by the building's awning, gazing with sour impatience at his watch.

Seated at the entry desk, Obie looked our way. "You ladies need anything?"

"No, thanks."

I faced Lena Malik squarely and searched her eyes. "You honestly don't know?"

"I don't. But whatever it is, I'm sure we can work it out. I can increase the commission. Get you help. I told you, Mrs. Colten, I'll do whatever it takes."

"Your husband is the problem. What he's done."

She sniffed in dismissal. "Hospital politics, you mean? All that nonsense has nothing to do with a child's portrait, for heaven's sake."

"Ask your husband," I said again. "This is different. Much worse than hospital politics."

"Nevertheless, I told you, I need to have the portrait done. We need not concern ourselves about our husbands' dealings at work. That should remain where it belongs, between the men."

Her daughter issued a world-weary sigh.

"Go tell your papa to come here, Adriana. Tell him I need to talk to him at once."

I caught her arm. Beneath the gossamer peach cashmere, her flesh spooled like silk beneath my grip. "I'm not going to discuss this with Dr. Malik. I have nothing to say to him."

Adriana's lip curled. This, of all things, seemed to amuse her.

"I told you to go get your papa, young lady. Now you listen!" Lena Malik's voice had taken on a desperate edge that failed utterly to move her little girl. "I need that portrait, Mrs. Colten. It's to go above the mantel, to fill the proper space. It's only right that it be there. And I must have it soon."

"Then you'd better hire someone else to do it."

Her giggle was tinged with hysteria. Her hands fluttered wildly, sparking light from a huge emerald-cut diamond. "You can't do this. There are too many other things for me to see to. This was all done, all arranged. I even picked the frame. Something has to go smoothly. It would turn things for the better. Start the turnaround. Don't you see?"

She gripped my arm, pinching with her long pink nails.

"I have to go, Mrs. Malik. Now." I pulled away, but she clamped on me again.

"No. You can't. You mustn't. I can get Adriana to sit for you in person if that's what you need. She'll do anything that's required, won't you, my sweet? You'll do exactly as Mommy asks."

Adriana turned her back on us and traced the stuccoed surface of the corridor wall.

"She will. She's really a very good girl. Truly she is. Just a little moody sometimes. Children have their little quirks, after all. They go through stages. And then it's over, finished. Doesn't mean a thing."

"This has nothing to do with her, Mrs. Malik. Not with her or you. I told you I was too busy in the first place. And given what's happened, there's no way."

Mascara-tinged tears coursed down her chiseled cheeks. "You must do the portrait, Mrs. Colten. I need you to. Please!"

I was startled by her intensity, and repulsed. Could anyone really be so convinced of her entitlement that a simple disappointment sent her over the edge? She reminded me of Jeanette Trevallis, of Sam's father, and of his stepmother, another overgrown, spoiled child.

Forcefully, I disengaged my arm. The skin was marked with small white arcs from the press of her nails. "I won't do it. That's final. If you want a portrait of Adriana, find someone else."

·FORTY-THREE·

I craved the hour of solitude that remained before Tyler was due home from a play date. I wanted to go to my apartment, inhale the silence, and cleanse myself of that awful encounter. I ached to do something to ease the fizzing in my gut. Take a nice, hot bubble bath, perhaps. Or put my head through the wall. But Sam was home, and we had company. LeeAnn was curled catlike on the sofa, eating lo mein from a round foil pan. Incompetent with chopsticks, she draped the noodles over the sticks like towels on a rack and rushed them to her mouth as they threatened to slide off. Then she slurped noisily through her collagen-plumped red lips. The lips matched her plunging sleeveless top. The spiked mules, like her miniskirt, were the sticky-looking black of spilled oil.

Sam stared like a seer into his container of fried rice, plucking out the few things he was willing to eat: mostly bits of shrimp and mushrooms. He piled the anemic little pork cubes, the peas, and the droopy sprouts in tidy separate heaps on the side. Tyler had not invented picky eating; he was carrying on the proud paternal tradition.

LeeAnn blotted sauce from her chin and the any-man's land between her breasts. "Hey, Emma. Too bad none for you."

"We didn't know you'd be home, Em. Sorry. You're welcome to share mine."

"That's fine. I just ran into Malik and family. That took care of my appetite."

"Well, this girl needs fuel." LeeAnn slurped again. "I was just telling Sam I've been out there doing the legwork. Turning things up."

"Such as?" I poured a glass of milk, eager to rid my mouth of the bad taste that lingered from the unpleasant encounter with Malik.

"I connected with a terrific source in the HR department at the Cleveland Clinic. Major gossip. Delighted to talk. Hard to get her to shut up, if you know what I mean."

I perched on the arm of Sam's chair, feeling huge. "I know exactly what you mean." There was no risk that LeeAnn would take umbrage. Self-awareness was not her strong suit.

"So I asked Aida—that's her name and don't you love it?—about Dr. Malik. I asked if there had been rumors about why he left. Or other rumors, anything."

"And?"

Sam shook his head sadly. "Nothing."

LeeAnn chided him with a leveled chopstick. "Now, now, Sammy boy. What have I told you about being such a Gloomy Gus? I found out several things. Interesting things, it so happens."

"Such as?"

"Malik never once made a claim through HR for any health expenses for the past two years. Not for him, and not for his family. Mighty strange, if you ask me."

"Maybe he didn't have any medical expenses."

"He had to. Docs are required to have an annual physical, not to mention regular blood tests for hepatitis and HIV. Surgeons, especially. And what about the kid? She had to get checkups for school. Booster shots. Plus kids get sick, hurt. But nothing in the records. Not a thing."

"I guess he wants to keep his medical record private."

"Exactly. The question is why? And why all of a sudden? He wasn't a privacy freak for the first eighteen years he was at the clinic. What happened two years ago to change that?"

Sam pressed his lips. "Could be anything. Psychiatric treatment, substance abuse, sexual problems, a disease. Whatever he might consider embarrassing or something that might get in the way of his career. Wouldn't have to be big. Malik isn't the kind who wants to be seen as having clay feet."

I sipped my milk. "Did anything else happen around that time according to your source?"

She tapped her temple. "You see that? Great minds think alike. I had Aida go through his records for the year before he stopped reporting his medical expenses. The only thing she turned up was a move. Malik sold a house in Shaker Heights and bought a bigger, more expensive one a few miles away. Pool, tennis court, exercise room, solarium, the works."

"They like lots of space. That we know."

"It's like I said." Sam sighed, "There's nothing."

"Don't be so impatient," LeeAnn insisted. "Digging takes time. Work. We'll get there."

"Did you ask her if there were any rumors about Malik's reasons for being in such a rush to move here?"

"I did. Aida said it happened so fast, people were shocked speechless. She said no one saw it coming, not even the brass. When he handed in his resignation, they figured General must have pulled a fast one. Then, when news got out about the Malik Cardiothoracic Center, everyone figured that was the ace we'd played."

"No rumors of an affair?"

LeeAnn found that wildly funny. "Only one affair? Not hardly. Little Dougie the Ughie made quite a name for himself as a ladies' man, and I mean *ladies* plural with a small *l* and at least a double D."

"And his wife put up with this?"

"Depends which wife you're talking about. His first three finally gave up and cashed him in for child support and alimony payments. Number four seems to be hanging in there so far, but time will tell."

"Was Suzanne Stitch one of his ladies, according to your source?"

I ignored Sam's pleading look. Like it or not, she was part of the story that had to be told. Pretending otherwise wouldn't make her go away.

LeeAnn stirred the noodles. "I didn't bother to ask. Seemed so obvious that she was. That she is. What else could explain the kid-glove treatment he gets for her? She starts her residency in May? She scrubs in on major cardiac cases as a first-year? I figure she has to know some position I don't."

"Maybe that's not it at all," I said. "Maybe she has something on him."

That stopped her in midslurp. Noodles trailed from her mouth like a pale stringy beard. "You're talking blackmail. I love that! Much more interesting than boring, old extracurricular nookie." She set down the lo mein and eyed me expectantly. "Do tell."

I showed my palms. "It's just a theory. Suzanne doesn't seem like the daddy-worshipping type. Anyway, she said

Malik was an old friend of her father's. Pretty strange way to describe a lover."

"You don't think it would be just as strange to blackmail your father's old friend as it would be to sleep with him?" Sam said.

"Depends on what she means by 'old friend.' Depends on how she values relationships. Depends on whether she has any scruples, which she clearly does not. Do you happen to know where she's from?"

"Chicago," Sam said faster than I would have liked. I didn't relish him having information about that woman or anything else to do with her on the tip of his tongue.

The laptop we shared was on the kitchen counter. I booted it up and ran a search for people named Stitch in Chicago. There were two residential listings and one in the business directory. Ronald Stitch was an attorney, a partner in the law firm of Cowan, Stitch, & Bragg. Among his listed specialties on the firm's website was criminal law. He had a wife and three children. His daughter Suzanne had graduated with honors from Duke Medical School and was training to be a surgeon.

"Bless Google," I said. "How did busybodies ever manage without it?"

Sam and LeeAnn pressed close and peered over my shoulders. "It's only interesting if Malik happened to be a client," Sam said. "According to Suzanne, he's Malik's friend."

I scrolled through the rest of Ronald Stitch's résumé, brought up Douglas Malik's, and compared them side by side. Suzanne's father was a native of Chicago, born, raised, and schooled there. His relationship to the city spanned generations. His father had founded the law firm, and young Ronald had assumed the partnership when Daddy retired. He was ten years older than Malik, who had been born to an American military family in Germany, reared on a variety of army bases, and gone on to higher education in the East. Ronald Stitch made no claim to military service. An article I found from a midwestern magazine society page said that recently he had celebrated thirty years of marriage to a woman named Dorothy, who had been his childhood sweetheart.

"It's possible they were friends, but it's not easy to see where their lives intersected," I said.

"And from this you conclude . . . ?" LeeAnn cleared her throat.

"I'm not concluding anything. Just speculating. What if Malik met Suzanne's father as a client? Maybe he was arrested for something a couple of years ago, and that's why he's gotten so secretive."

At that, she stretched and faked an extravagant yawn. "It's been fun, Sam, Sherlock. But I'd better haul my ass back to work."

"What, LeeAnn? You don't think that makes any sense?"

"It could, Emma. Anything is possible. There might be polka-dotted elephants, and the moon could be made of fruit Jell-O. But if you ask me, going off in left field like that is like riding in an imaginary car. Sounds like fun, but in the end, it doesn't get you anyplace at all."

· FORTY-FOUR ·

Tyler seemed determined to clinch the Eastern Indoor Up-All-Night championship of the world. Between his frequent nocturnal interruptions, I dropped like a stone into a deep well of horror-infested sleep. Chop off a nightmare, and it grows back like a hydra-headed monster, more fearsome by multiples than the one it replaced.

Somehow, my little one still had the energy to charge in at dawn and declare that it was morning. He'd battled sleep with the force of his titanium will, and he'd won. Somehow, I managed to slog out of bed to face the day. No choice; no problem, as my sister was wont to say.

I was staring disjointedly into my cereal bowl, feeling as soggy as the beige flakes bloating there in their tepid sea of milk, thinking it unthinkably unfair that my pregnancy barred me from mainlining coffee, when Sam arrived home from his night shift. I heard him whistling in the corridor as he flipped the lock. I flinched at the exuberant burst of the door.

"You're in a good mood," I accused.

"I am."

"Well, cut it out. I'm way too tired to be around anything perky."

From behind his back, he produced a paper-wrapped bunch of blush pink sweetheart roses.

"Flowers, Sam? Now you're scaring me."

"Come on, Em. I've brought you flowers plenty of times."

"Oh, yeah?" I found the very idea of the unreasonably lovely little blooms overwhelming. I was running on empty, far too exhausted to contemplate finding a suitable container and filling it with water, much less inserting the stems and crumpling the paper so it would fit in the trash. "Name two."

"Fair enough. But I'm going to get you flowers all the time from now on. You'll see."

For Tyler, he'd brought a pint of vanilla ice cream. The city had no end of all-night delis that sold food, drugstore essentials, and inexpensive bouquets. Toy stores weren't open at this hour, but living in the city meant never having to go without your empty calories.

"Can I have it now, Daddy?"

"After your cereal, Tiger. It's for dessert."

That required my challenge. "Since when do we eat dessert with breakfast?"

"Since today became an extremely special occasion."

Sam was grinning, and of course, this worried me sick. People crack under stress. It seemed only logical that unexpected happiness could be a symptom of something dire.

"I have good news, Em. Great news in fact."

"What?"

"Guess."

"I'm afraid to."

"Go ahead. What's the wildest, most wonderful thing you can imagine?"

"They dropped the charges?"

The crooked grin didn't waver. "No, but close enough. Guess again."

"Just tell me."

"Come on. One more guess."

"Hmm. Let me see. I know. I guess if you don't tell me, right now, I'm going to have to disembowel you."

"Fine, crabby. Be that way. Suzanne left."

"She left?"

"Isn't it amazing?"

"Just like that?"

He snapped his fingers. "She called LeeAnn at home first thing this morning. Claimed it was personal and she had to go immediately."

"And that was that?"

He punched the air with a triumphal fist. "I still can't believe it. I was just leaving Southshore when LeeAnn called to tell me on my cell. At first, I thought she had to be kidding, and believe me, I was in no mood for a joke. You can't imagine how down I was. All I wanted to do was get home, crawl under the covers, and sleep forever. But I heard that, and it's like being reborn, as if a cloud has lifted and I can breathe for the first time in days."

"I'm ready for my ice cream, Daddy."

Tyler's bowl looked pretty much untouched. "Two more bites of cereal first," I coaxed.

"One more," he said.

"Three."

"I hate cereal."

"Why? What did cereal ever do to you?"

"I hate the new big little girl, too."

"You don't even know her, Ty."

"Do too. She's a kitso pitso girl who's mean."

"Now that's a made-up story if I ever heard one."

"Is not. Her daddy said she was a kitso pitso girl."

Ignoring my hard, parental glare, Sam scooped ice cream into Tyler's bowl.

"Did LeeAnn tell you what Suzanne's 'personal' issue was?" I asked.

"She didn't know. Suzanne refused to say. According to LeeAnn, rumor has it Lazarus was having second thoughts. My best guess is the president must have said something to Malik, maybe asked him to reconsider the charges against me, and he figured it was time to give it up. By getting Suzanne out of the way, he can let the thing die a natural death."

I tried not to show it, but I wasn't convinced. That old saw about things that seem too good to be true kept scrolling through my mind.

"So you think this means they'll simply forget the whole thing and reinstate you?"

Sam anointed his ice cream with an airy belch of canned whipped cream and deposited the trailing remains on Tyler's nose. "What else can they do? No accuser, no case, don't you think?"

I did; that was the problem. I thought entirely too much. I couldn't stop my mind from meandering through perilous detours and dark unknowns. "I hope so, sweetie. But there's no guarantee."

He blinked at me as if he'd been dying of thirst and I'd just told him the fresh, cool oasis he was about to reach was a cruel mirage. "It makes the whole thing look like a bunch of crap, don't you see? Suzanne brings bullshit charges, and next thing you know she drops them like a hot rock and takes off."

"I hope you're right, Sam. But I don't want you to be disappointed if it doesn't go that smoothly."

Tyler had licked his nose clean. "More whipped cream, Daddy."

"No more."

"Please!"

"I said *no!*"

Sam's mood had gone dark. When I set my hand over his, he brushed it off. "I get the feeling you don't want it to go away."

"Of course I do. That's ridiculous. I'm just worried that it might not be so simple, that you could be setting yourself up for a letdown."

"So you thought you'd let me down instead. Is that it? You couldn't leave well enough alone and let me enjoy it."

"I want you to enjoy it, sweetie. I'm delighted she's gone. It's wonderful."

He tossed his bowl in the sink, flopped on the couch in disgust, and made a noise like a blown tire. In an instant, his breathing went deep and regular and I knew he'd found refuge in sleep.

Tyler seized the opportunity to squeeze a snowdrift of chemical-infested whipped cream onto his breakfast dessert, giggling at the flatulent sound as he pressed the trigger.

I disarmed him. "No more, Ty. You heard Daddy."

"How come Daddy's mad?"

"He's tired, that's all. He needs a rest."

"But how come he's mad?"

"He's not. He's frustrated. You know, like when you really want something badly, and you have to wait."

"I have to wait for my birthday."

"That's right."

"Is Daddy waiting for his birthday?"

"No, he's waiting for something good to happen. It's like a birthday. Only you don't get to be another age."

Frowning, he planted his hand on my stomach. "How old is the baby?"

"When she's born, your sister will be zero, Ty. It'll take her a whole year to get to be one."

"And how old will I be?"

"When the baby's one, you'll be almost five."

That brought a smile. "Five is big."

"That's right. You'll always be her big brother."

He nodded. And despite Sam's pique and my protective pessimism, something stirred in me that felt suspiciously like hope. Maybe Tyler would come to accept his sister; maybe he'd even enjoy playing the part of her little superhero. You never know.

And maybe Suzanne's departure did mean the end of Sam's troubles. He was right. Why not enjoy the moment? We could deal with the nasty weather when it came.

And so it did. The knock on the door was harsh enough to wake Sam. Rising angrily, he went to see who it was.

· FORTY-FIVE ·

"Sorry to bother you folks so early," the stranger said. "Wanted to make sure you got this while it's hot."

The man looked mildly disheveled, like someone down on his luck. His suit was of a bygone era of broader lapels and boxier cuts, and had seen better days. The fabric shone, and the cuffs lolled like open envelopes over his scuffed brown Oxfords. He had the unhealthy pallor and pink, spongy nose of a seasoned tippler. A grease-stained bag, redolent of coffee and doughnuts, drooped from his hand.

"We didn't order anything," Sam said. "You must have the wrong apartment."

The man looked puzzled. He drew a rumpled slip of paper from his coat pocket and squinted at the writing. "Your name Samuel Colten?"

"Yes."

Reaching behind his back, he produced a folded sheaf of papers and handed them to Sam. "You've been served, Mr. Colten. Have a lovely day."

"Served? What are you talking about?"

By then, the stranger had fled halfway down the hall.

"Wait!" Sam called after him. "What is this?"

He read the document, pacing and raking his hair. Color drained from his face. "That goddamned bitch!"

"What is it?"

Without answering, he took up the phone and dialed. "Sam Colten calling for Andrew Eastham. Is he in? No, it can't wait until ten when the office opens. I have to speak to him *now*!"

A moment later he tossed the phone down, not bothering to hang up. A mechanical voice and a trio of rising tones soon droned through the cast-off receiver.

I hung it up. "What's going on?"

"Suzanne is suing me. Claiming sexual harassment. She says I created a hostile environment that caused irreparable harm to her ability to pursue her medical career. She's claiming psychological damage. Post-traumatic stress. That's why she left, the manipulative little—"

I noticed Tyler, hanging on his every word, bug-eyed with mischievous delight. "Please, Sam. Watch your mouth."

"And Malik. If that son of a bitch can't ruin me one way, he'll keep at it until he finds another."

"She's claiming you've ruined her career? What does that mean, Sam? She sues you for all the money she could have made as a surgeon for the next forty years and then spends the rest of her life polishing her toenails on the Riviera?"

"Something like that."

"That's ridiculous."

"Ridiculous or not. That's exactly how it could go." He raked his hair again, whipping it in peaks and spikes so he looked mildly deranged.

"Well, they'd better have Motel 6 on the Riviera then,

Sam. Our pockets aren't exactly what anyone would call deep."

"Doesn't matter. They could put a lien on my future earnings. We could be in the hole for this forever. Remember what happened to Albertsen?"

Theodore Albertsen, Sam's anatomy professor in medical school, had been accused of sexual harassment by a student he'd hired to babysit for his three kids. A jury had awarded the girl millions in punitive damages.

"Albertsen was a very different situation. He abused a power position. The complainant was his student, for heaven's sake. She was twenty-two; he was almost fifty. Plus, she slit her wrists."

"What makes you think that won't be Suzanne's next gambit? She'll swallow pills, check herself into a mental hospital, claim she's pregnant. Whatever it takes."

The last sent the blood to my feet. Woozy, I sat down. "Suzanne is pregnant?"

"No, for God's sake. Not that I know of. I'm just saying she and Malik will do whatever they can think of to hurt me. And there's nothing I can do but wait around like a useless fool while it happens."

Tyler's face went glum. Crouching in front of the toy box, he retrieved his entire collection of superheroes. Solemnly, he carried them to Sam. "Here, Daddy. You can have these guys."

Tears pooled in Sam's steel blue eyes. "Thanks, tiger. You're a good sidekick."

"You can use the Batmobile, too. Or you could fly."

Sam blotted his cheek on his shirtsleeve and hefted our son on his hip. "Good idea." He kissed Tyler loudly on the cheek, set him down, and tapped him with affection on the rump. "Go play. And don't worry. Now that Mom and I have these men of steel, we'll figure it out."

"Superwoman, too." My son knew better than to eliminate a person from a rescue operation because of gender.

And just like that, a little lightbulb flipped on in my head. And the answer to our troubles came clear.

· FORTY-SIX ·

She didn't answer at home or on her cell. Her office said she'd gone out but was expected to return in about an hour. That hour loomed far too large.

Reluctantly, Sam agreed to accompany us to the playground. There he slumped on a shade-dappled bench to brood. Perched beside him, I watched a cheeky squirrel flirt with our son, preening at Tyler's feet while it gnawed on an acorn. When Ty edged closer, the creature dropped to all fours and dashed away. As soon as my little one retreated, the squirrel returned and the game began anew.

"It's not going to work," Sam muttered. "Nothing is going to fix this."

"We'll see, Sam. Let me talk to her at least. It can't hurt to try." I said this, though I realized as I did that it wasn't true. Trying could hurt like hell.

"Look who's here! Emma and Tyler. And who could that be with you, sweetheart? Your daddy?"

My little one rushed her. "Auntie Frieda!"

"What a lovely surprise," she said. "I surely thought it

was too early to find you here. I expected to have my coffee with the birds and see you later on."

"The bird got dead, Auntie Frieda," Ty soberly informed her. "We had to bury it in a garbage can so it would have lots of company."

"I see. But look." She pointed at the clear, exuberant sky. "There are lots of other birds."

A dozen dark specks flew west in a ragged V formation. One intrepid adventurer lagged behind for a moment, and then darted at top speed to catch up.

"Isn't that nice? One bird finishes his life, and there are plenty more to swoop right in and take its place."

My son frowned, trying to absorb the gentle object lesson on the circle of life.

"But the dead bird was scared."

"No, he wasn't, darling. Maybe he looked scared, but he was happily at rest."

Mrs. Kalisher sat on the bench on Sam's left side and set her outsized shopping bag on the ground. In addition to her coffee, she plucked out a juice box for Tyler, a light coffee with two sugars for Sam, and my latest morning craving, hot chocolate with miniature marshmallows. She had bagels as well, tailored to suit our little group. Sam favored sesame with a classic New York *shmear* of cream cheese. Tyler remained a blueberry man, though I clung to the hope that he'd outgrow this. The last two had been anointed with everything on the outside and stuffed with smoked salmon and whitefish salad, a taste I'd acquired from Mrs. K.

I looked at her askance. "Surprised, were you?"

She shrugged. "You're never here so early, but I had a feeling something wonderful was going to happen this morning."

Sam winked. "You should invest in the stock market,

Mrs. K. Or play the lottery. Put that psychic talent of yours to better use."

"There is no better use, sweetheart, than friends. Oh, I almost forgot, Tyler darling." She dipped into her bottomless shopping bag. "Here's that whochamawhatsis you bought with your penny wish."

At the sight of the Krypto Superdog, Tyler screeched and started bobbling with joy. "You gotted it, Auntie Frieda. You gotted it for me!"

"You paid for it fair and square, darling."

We ate awhile in companionable silence, while our little one reveled in the new toy.

"So tell me, Emma, Sam. How are things going?"

"Not well, Mrs. K. The woman who accused Sam left. Now she's suing him, claiming she's too traumatized to pursue her medical career."

"She'll never get away with a thing like that."

Sam leaned forward, elbows on his knees, limp with misery. "She has Malik to back her up, and his assistant. All I have is my word."

"Don't diminish the value of that, darling. People know you; they respect you. That's a lot more than you can say for the God from Cleveland."

"He's the leading cardiac surgeon in the country, arguably the best in the world. I'm an unemployed surgical resident with a big fat accusation hanging over my head. Who is a judge or jury going to believe?"

"You'd be surprised. You're thinking black or white. And maybe this isn't a color at all. Maybe it's more like Napoleon."

Sam paused in midbite. "For a second there, I thought you said Napoleon."

"I did. He was another one who thought he could simply walk over everyone and rule the world. All of Europe wasn't enough for him, so he invaded Russia. And that was the beginning of the end. He was exiled to Elba, but tried to make a comeback, and they got him at Waterloo. Then he was sent off to St. Helena for the rest of his life. You see what I mean?"

"Not exactly," Sam said.

"True, Doug Malik is a big-deal cardiac surgeon. But his department at New York General is not the whole world. You forget that, you're liable to wind up on some godforsaken island with a nasty heartburn and no one to order around but your soup."

That rumpled Sam's brow. "You think Malik's overplaying his hand?"

She smiled broadly. "He's forgetting he's the new boy on the block. Big shot or no, he still has to prove himself here. If he adds to the institution, fine. If he creates problems, stirs things up, who needs him? General did fine before he came, and no one's forgetting that so soon. If having him here turns out to be a negative, they'll cut him loose."

"How could they?" Sam said. "He must have a contract."

"True. From what I understand, he signed on for five years. So for that amount of time, General has to pay his salary and benefits, provide him with lab space and subsidized housing."

Sam slumped lower. "That's what I thought."

"You thought right, darling. But as a doctor, maybe you don't make such a hot lawyer."

"Meaning?"

"Meaning the hospital could do all that at one of its satellite facilities. If they don't like how Dr. God behaves here, they could send him to our nice new facility in Beijing."

"Are you serious?"

She inhaled with gusto. "I must say, I so enjoy a good loophole."

I shifted uneasily on the bench. "How did you find out what's in Malik's contract?"

"Have you by any chance met Ricky Dolan, Sam?"

"Sounds familiar."

"I think now he mostly goes by Rick. Wonderful young man. Does a lot of the hospital's legal work. Our families have been close for many, many years. I'll never forget Ricky's bar mitzvah. He was such a puny thing, and so shy. Then a year or two later, he shot up and really came into himself. Went to Harvard and Stanford Law. The firm he's with has been doing General's employment contracts for years, and when they took Ricky on, they got him involved. He's a master with a loophole. Never leaves the hospital on the hook if there's any possible way to avoid it. So happens I had dinner with Ricky, his wife, and his parents just last night."

I smiled. "It just so happens."

Her face brimmed with mock innocence. "I hadn't seen them in such a long time. Anyway, we got to talking about what's going on with you, Sam."

Sam folded his arms. "And?"

"And Ricky said if Malik's trying to pull a fast one with this sexual assault business, he had better be brushing up on his Chinese."

· FORTY-SEVEN ·

Franny seized the idea immediately. "I can't believe I didn't think of it myself, Emma. Grant's tied up in a meeting this morning, but I'll run it by him first thing this afternoon."

"You think he might be willing?"

"If it's at all possible, I'm sure he'll do it."

"And what happens then?"

"It's amazingly simple, and that's the reason the website has taken off. Basically, they put out a teaser: Gotcha! is looking for information on this particular thing to do with whatever subject they have in mind. At this point, they have millions of regular visitors, plus people in the media who follow the items they run and pass the word along. They reach an enormous audience. If there's anything juicy to dig up, they will."

"And this is legal?"

"Completely."

"What ever happened to the right to privacy?"

"Nothing. The Fourth Amendment is alive and well, as far as it goes. The government isn't allowed to go barging into your home or car without cause. They're not supposed to tap your phone without cause or dig into your medical records, though it doesn't exactly stop them in all cases. But this is entirely different."

"Are you sure? Sounds precisely like digging through dirty laundry to me." Much as I hoped it might work for Sam, it also gave me the creeps. If someone else's dirty laundry was available for the asking, what was to stop someone with evil intent or idle curiosity from pawing through mine?

"I'm sure," Franny said. "The company has been challenged in every way imaginable. But each and every time, it's prevailed. There's this little thing called the First Amendment that protects the free exchange of ideas. Sleazeballs today have precious few places to hide."

"Maybe so, but neither do the rest of us."

"That's why my mother always warned me never to do anything I wouldn't want to see printed on the front page of the *New York Times*."

Mrs. Kalisher's mother had offered the same advice. "Unless you were wearing denim, of course, because that would protect you."

She groaned. "Actually, denim underpants can be hazardous to your health. Believe me, don't try that at home without a net."

"Honestly, Franny. That's all there is to it? Gotcha! asks, and people offer up whatever they know?"

"Pretty much. Grant said you can't believe how delighted most people are to rat on each other. And as an extra incentive, anyone who provides useful information is placed in a drawing for prizes they award at the end of the month. Blow the whistle on Gotcha! and you can win a sound system, a flat-screen TV, even a car."

"My mother always told me it wasn't nice to be a tattletale, that it would come back and bite you in the end."

"When Grant first described the idea for the company, that was my reaction, too. I questioned how he could get involved in a company whose business model relied on ruining people."

"And?"

"And he convinced me I was wrong. The truth is they expose criminal activity, not to mention slimy, underhanded characters that would otherwise go on hurting people who don't deserve it."

"They'll solicit information on anyone? Not just the rich and famous?"

"Normally, they focus on big names, but they make plenty of exceptions. Let me talk it over with Grant. I'm sure he'll make an exception for you."

"You can't imagine how grateful I'd be, Franny." Sam was at the end of his rope; I could see it. He had the dull, weary, hollow-eyed look of someone who had surrendered to a terminal disease.

"It's nothing. Let's hope it works."

"You think it will?"

"I hope so. But of course, that depends."

"On what?"

"In this business, it's always the same thing. At the end of the day, it all comes down to whether there is anything to find."

· FORTY-EIGHT ·

Sam kept logging on to the website, waiting for the promised item about Malik to appear. Predictably, he was let down when it did.

"That's it?"

Anxiously, I read it, too.

Calling all Gotcha! watchers. Tell us what you know about Dr. Douglas Anton Malik, formerly of Cleveland, Ohio, now residing in New York, New York.

The two-paragraph entry went on to list Malik's current and past addresses and places of employment. His current and former wives were mentioned as were the names and ages of his children. The piece called for anything of interest regarding Malik's personal, professional, or business dealings and for similar information regarding Dr. Suzanne Stitch.

Sam was wise to be skeptical. According to Franny, they were likely to get hundreds, if not thousands of replies, most of them useless, many nothing more than outrageous lies. As she described it, people were willing to do almost anything to garner a bit of attention. For a site like Gotcha!, one of the most difficult challenges was sifting through the endless glut of trash.

The results were impossible to predict. They might get the answer we were seeking in a matter of hours, or it could take days or even weeks for them to reach the unhappy conclusion that Malik was, in fact, credible and clean. As time went on, they would be overwhelmed with a similar flood of irrelevant information about newer matters the site had chosen to embrace. Grant kept hiring and training all the speed-reading cynics he could find to filter out the useless reports, but there were never enough to keep up.

Sam slammed the lid on the laptop. "Waste of time. I shouldn't even be here. I should be out trying to find a job."

"You can do that when the time comes."

"When's that? After we're out on the street with two kids?"

Panic squeezed my gut, and the baby shifted. "It's not going to happen that way. Malik can't get away with this."

"He can and he will. If he had skeletons in his closet, don't you think they would have come out by now?"

"Maybe not. Maybe nobody bothered to look."

"I'm not the first person he's screwed over, Em. That I know. If there was a way to trip him up, somebody would have done it already."

"Maybe nobody tried this way, Sam. Maybe this way will work."

Tyler was on the floor, slamming his Matchbox cars into the kind of tragic multivehicle wreck that could bring traffic to a maddening halt for hours. Suddenly, he went still.

"Is the little girl better now, Mama?"

"What little girl?"

"The kitso pitso one upstairs."

"She's fine, sweetie. Why do you ask?"

"Last night, her mama said she was very, very sick."

"What did we say about telling stories, Ty?"

"It's not. I heard her mama talking from upstairs."

Sam shrugged. He didn't share my bristling concern that our toddler was fast becoming a pathological liar.

"If you really heard, she must have meant Adriana had a cold, Ty. Or a tummy ache. Something like that."

Mouthing sound effects, he crashed the remaining car, a vintage '60s red Mustang convertible that bore the scars of the many similar pileups he had staged in the past. "She maybe has to go to the hospital and stay there for a long, long time."

"You heard this in the middle of the night, did you?"

"Uh-huh."

"Somehow I don't think so."

"I think so."

"In any event, nights are for sleeping, not listening in on other people's conversations."

"How come she's sick, though? Sick is bad."

What was worse, I wondered: compulsive lying or compulsive fretting? The obvious answer came to me quickly: worse was doing both. "Don't worry about it, cutie. If she is sick, I'm sure it's nothing serious."

"It is," he whined. "It's very, very serious. Her mama said."

"Her daddy's a doctor like yours, Ty. If there is something wrong with her, he'll make sure she gets all better very soon."

"But what if she doesn't?" He was getting agitated, tensing like a bowstring.

"She will. I'm sure she will."

His lower lip shot out, prelude to a cry.

I picked him up, comforted by his solidity. "What's wrong, sweetie?"

"What if the little girl dies?" he wailed. "What if she gets put in the trash like the blue bird?"

"She won't, Ty. Birds are different from girls."

"What if she takes too much medicine like Grandma Rae and falls on the floor?"

Startled, I blotted his eyes. "Where did you hear a thing like that?"

"From Grandpa."

"Tyler?" I chided.

"It's true. Grandpa said."

"Grandpa told you Grandma Rae took too much medicine?"

He sniffed. "And she fell down on the floor because of the baby."

"What baby?"

"Don't be mad!"

"Ssh. I'm not mad at all. When did Grandpa say that, sweetie?"

"At Christmastime when they had those yuck cookies and I spilled the juice."

Sam's brow furrowed. "Senior said someone gave Grandma Rae too much medicine? He told you that?"

Tyler nodded, wide-eyed. "And she got dead on the floor."

Livid, Sam picked up the phone.

"Isn't it better to ignore him, Sam? Isn't that what you always say?"

"I do. I will. But first I need to know exactly what he said. That and why he would do such a thing. What the hell's wrong with him?"

"Where should I start?"

While he made the call, I took Tyler out for a walk. Sam might need to hear the details of what had transpired, but our little one most certainly did not. He had already heard far too much.

· FORTY-NINE ·

The doorman shifted uneasily at the reception desk, keeping a wary eye on us as we waited outside Senior's posh Park Avenue digs. Sam's father had not been home when he phoned, but according to the housekeeper, an architect was expected at the apartment to discuss a kitchen renovation at two thirty, so the elder Coltens would surely return before then.

Straight from dropping Tyler off at school, we had gone to the building. When we arrived, it was ten after two. Nearly fifteen minutes had passed, as had a uniformed nanny pushing a somnolent newborn in an extravagant stroller and a stylish woman burdened by bulging shopping bags from the priciest of shops. But there was still no sign of Sam's parents. Senior had precious few virtues, but he was always unfailingly prompt.

For the third time, Sam entered the lobby and approached the doorman. "Can you try calling upstairs again? Maybe they came in through the back."

"They wouldn't do that, sir."

"Stranger things have happened. Would you please call up and check."

The doorman peered around anxiously. "Why don't you leave them a note, and I'll give it to them as soon as they come in?"

"I don't want to leave a note. I have to speak to my father now. Today. We'll wait."

"Don't know if you want to do that, sir. Could be quite some time."

"That's not true. They have an appointment here in a couple of minutes."

His smile was thin as broth. "Could be his plans changed."

Sam frowned at his watch. "There's no need for us to play guessing games. The housekeeper's in their apartment now. You can call up and ask her."

"Really, sir. Much better if you leave a note. I'll see they get it personally. I've got paper and a pen you're welcome to use."

"You also have a house phone. Now please pick it up and dial the Coltens and tell whoever answers that we're downstairs."

"Sorry, sir. I can't do that."

The phone on his podium was a chunky vintage model in basic black. Sam lifted the receiver. "Sure you can. Just dial."

The doorman scowled. "No, sir. I can't. Wouldn't want to disturb them."

Sam's lips pressed in a hard, grim line. "Fine. Forget it."

I followed him out the door to a spot beyond the doorman's view, and there he stopped me. He waited for the telephone to ring in the lobby and the sound of the doorman's voice. When that happened, he spoke in an urgent whisper.

"Walk with me. Whatever happens, don't stop."

He gripped my elbow and we hurried through the lobby

to the elevator, which sat with its doors agape. Luckily, the attendant was nowhere in sight. Probably on a break.

Sputtering, the man at the desk called after us. "Where are you going? You can't do that!"

Sam pressed twelve and then hit the facing arrows to speed the closing doors. Through the vanishing gap, I could see the doorman rushing toward us. His face was wide with horror; his skin a hot, hypertensive pink. "Wait! Stop!"

The doors made contact, and the motor engaged. My knees bowed with the tug of pressure as the car began its lumbering ascent.

I caught my spooked reflection in the polished brass. "Something tells me we can get in big trouble for this."

"I don't think there's a judge in the world who would blame me."

"You think they're home?"

"I'm positive they are. Senior told the doorman to get rid of us. No question. Why else would he refuse to call upstairs?"

"I don't know. But he could use that same phone to call the police."

"I hope he does. They can clean up the mess after I get through wringing my old man's neck."

"Calm down, Sam. I'm as upset by this craziness as you are, but the last thing we need is more trouble."

"I know that. Believe me. And I'm not really going to strangle the bastard. Much as I'd enjoy it, he's not worth a jail term."

Sam's insistent press on the doorbell brought no response. Pressing his ear to the door, he listened for signs of life inside.

Again he rang. Then he hammered his fist against the polished wood. "I know you're in there. Open the damned door now!"

Nothing. The only sound was the low hum of the approaching elevator. It had to be the doorman, coming to order us out of the building. From the loud rumble of voices, it seemed he was not alone.

Pressing a finger to his lips, Sam grabbed my hand and urged me down the hall. There, set in a dim recess, was the service door to the apartment. A light knock brought a flurry of footsteps.

"Yes?" The voice was unfamiliar, one in the endless, revolving stream of short-lived household help.

"Delivery," Sam said in a vaguely accented singsong.

When the uniformed woman opened the door, Sam held a finger to his lips and whispered urgently. "Hi. I'm Sam, Dr. Colten's son. And this is my wife, Emma. We just got in from out of town and we want to surprise Dad."

"You're the doctor's son?"

"Yes."

"Because he said not to answer the door."

"It was part of the surprise. I told the doorman to call up and say it was this insurance salesman who keeps bothering them. I knew they'd hole up somewhere and pretend not to be home."

Smiling, she tipped her head. "Smart. Sure. Go ahead. They're in the library."

As we got there, the doorbell rang.

Sam led me inside hurriedly and shut the door behind us.

His father stood. "You are not welcome here. I insist that you leave at once!"

"And I insist that you behave like a human being," Sam said. "Too bad we can't always have our way."

Freddie fanned herself with a copy of *Architectural Digest*. "Honestly, Samuel. These children of yours are simply more than I can bear."

Senior's eyes narrowed. "You have always been a disappointment, Sam, but never like this. You've become a liability, a drain, and an embarrassment."

"What a coincidence. I can say the exact same thing for you."

"I'm calling the police," Freddie said. "This is outrageous."

Senior raised a hand. "I have no interest in such drama, though I suspect that's precisely what Sam wants. He's looking for attention as usual. But he's not going to get it. You two are not welcome here, but if you insist on staying, you'll do so alone. We're leaving."

Sam blocked the door. "We'll leave as soon as you tell us exactly what you said to Tyler about my mother's death."

Senior chuckled. "To Tyler? Do you think I have serious discussions with that child? Are you insane?"

"He knew Mom took an overdose. He said he heard it from you at Christmas."

"If he did, he was listening to a conversation that had nothing to do with him whatsoever."

"And you don't bother to notice that there is a little boy around when you say such things?"

With a sniff, Sam's father sat on the couch and crossed his ankle over his knee. He wore fey velvet slippers with gold anchors embroidered on the toe. The velvet smoking jacket and soft silver trousers made him look like a refugee from an old movie. He plucked the business section from the morning paper and began to read.

"I'm talking to you, you arrogant son of a bitch!" In a rage Sam tore the paper from his father's hands. He caught his old man by the lapels and wrenched him out of his seat. "What did you say about my mother? What lies did you spread about her in front of my little boy?"

The cords bulged in Senior's neck. He worked his jaw and spit in Sam's face.

With a swipe of his sleeve, Sam brushed the frothy spittle from his cheek. He tightened his grip on Senior's collar. The old man reddened, and the cruel defiance on his face pinched with fear.

"What did you say about my mother?"

"Nothing. I don't remember."

He squeezed harder, and his father gagged.

"You let him go, you little hooligan," Freddie demanded. "I don't care what he says, I'm calling the police."

"No, you won't," I said. "If you so much as touch that phone, tomorrow there'll be a piece on page six of the *Post* all about how you used to slop the hogs, not to mention how you got knocked up by Ray Bob Ellington and had to drop out of the tenth grade to go live with your aunt in Topeka until your time came."

Freddie gasped. She valued her shaky position in New York society above all. "That's a lie. All of it."

"It's one hundred percent gospel truth, and the papers will have no trouble at all confirming every word."

"Doesn't matter. That person has nothing to do with me. Not anymore."

"No? You know what they say, Winnie Mae. Once a pig farmer, always a pig farmer."

"You wouldn't dare spread that dreadful story."

"Try me."

"Enough!" Senior shouted. "You want to know what the boy overheard. I'll tell you. Our old rector was at our Christmas open house, and he happened to mention how delighted he was to see that Winifred and I get on so well. The conversation turned to that dreadful episode with your mother. I thought I should spare you the reason she took her life, but you're obviously not worthy of my concern."

"What reason? What are you talking about?"

"Your mother had learned that she was pregnant. She

killed herself rather than bear another child. Only afterward, months later when I'd begun to recover from the shock, did I realize that it was probably not my child at all. She was forever seeking the attentions of other men. Dressing provocatively, flirting like a shameless hussy. I never thought she'd act on it, but I was wrong. Obviously, it was part of her pathology."

My mind bristled with disbelief. "You let Tyler hear that Sam's mother died because she got pregnant? What were you thinking?"

"This is none of your concern, Emma."

"Of course it is. He heard that, and then when he learned I was pregnant, he must have thought something terrible was going to happen to me. You gave our son nightmares. He's been worried sick."

"If the child is an anxious neurotic, blame yourself. Don't you dare criticize me for what you brought on, you silly twit."

Sam's hand swung so hard and fast, I only caught the sound. It was a harsh crack of finality, something fractured in a way that might very well be irreparable.

The mark of the blow bloomed on Senior's cheek. "That's it! I've had quite enough of you! Now get out!"

Sam shook his head in disgust. "We'll be glad to."

A burly man still waited outside the front door. "Have to ask you folks to leave quietly."

Sam managed a stilted smile. "Sure. No problem."

The guard called inside. "It's Bill from Security, Dr. Colten. You folks okay?"

Freddie stepped out of the study. "We're fine, Bill. Thanks for checking. Now please escort these horrible people out of the building. Their names are Sam Jr. and Emma. Sam Jr. used to be related to Dr. Colten, but that's no longer true. Write that down in the book, Bill. Make sure no one ever allows them anywhere near our apartment again."

· FIFTY ·

Cuddling Tyler, I tried to picture how life would be in a few weeks' time when I'd have a little one to occupy each arm. Familiar insecurities threatened a hostile takeover. How could I manage two when I was so lacking? Would my love and energies be sliced perilously thin? Having played the dangerous game of genetic roulette, what if we spawned a child who took after Sam's father? Imagine having to look at that face while I sang to my child or to hear Senior's voice when my baby cried.

Firmly, I pushed the thoughts aside and set a hand on the giant bulge of my daughter. This was a good thing, a blessing. Why not start with wonderment and gratitude, and go from there?

"Daddy and I spoke to Grandpa, sweetie. He told us what you heard about Grandma Rae."

He peered up at me doe-eyed. "She felled down on the floor and she died."

"It had nothing to do with having a baby, Ty. She died because she was very, very sick."

A tear welled up and slowly trailed down his cheek. "I don't want you to be like the blue bird, Mama."

"I won't. Don't worry. I'm not going anywhere. I'm going to stay right here with you and Daddy and your baby sister."

"We won't have to put you in the trash?"

"Definitely not."

"How come Grandma Rae took too much medicine?"

"I told you, sweetie. She was sick. But I'm not. I'm fine."

"Then how come you have to go to the hospital?"

"That's not about being sick. This is a different part of the hospital where moms go for a special sleepover when their babies are ready to be born. I went there to have you, too."

"And I jumped out of your stomach?"

I kissed his forehead. "Close enough."

"Will you read me *Goodnight Moon*?"

"Sure. Why don't I tuck you in first?"

I braced for the expected response, the one I'd gotten every night for months. He didn't want to go to bed. He wasn't sleepy. It wasn't nighttime yet. Sebastian was starved. Fred was scared of the dark. I was mean. There was a burglar guy. But this time, he surprised me.

"I want *Goodnight Moon* and *The Three Bears*."

I offered a quick high five. "That's a deal. I'll get the books. You hop in."

Before I reached the second happily ever after, he drifted off, surrendering to sleep without a fight.

Sam had left for his night shift. I ate the remains of Tyler's grilled cheese, downed a glass of milk, and crawled into bed. It was time to read up on week thirty-five in my pregnancy book. At this point, all of my daughter's systems were in full working order. On average, she'd be eighteen inches long and closing in on five pounds. Until she made her debut, her job was to grow and gain weight. I mused that if she needed tips on the weight-gaining front, she could come to me.

Turning to the book on baby names, I read through the *D*s. Dahlia . . . Dale . . . Daphne . . . Darcy . . . Davida . . . Deborah . . . Dee . . . Delia. As I was pondering what it would be like to grow up with a handle like Delilah, the phone rang.

Franny and Grant were both on the line. "We have news, Emma," Franny said. "Are you sitting down?"

I stifled a yawn. "Lying down actually. What's going on?"

"I'll let Grant tell you."

"We had an e-mail about the Malik item this afternoon. Woman named Cheryl Price. Until a few weeks ago, she worked as a receptionist for a Chicago law firm. Her boss was Ronald Stitch, Suzanne's father."

I yawned again. "Interesting."

"It gets more interesting. Ms. Price told us she'd met Doug Malik also. Said he's a client of the firm."

"Malik lives in Cleveland and went to a Chicago law firm? For what?"

"She couldn't say. Or wouldn't. She was worried about violating lawyer-client privilege."

"Then why did she contact the website at all?"

"Obviously, she wants whatever it was to get out," Grant said. "Between the lines, she was pressing us to dig deeper. Plus she gave us a specific time frame we could work from. She was very specific about the date Malik signed on: March twenty-fourth."

"And?"

"And I put a couple of our top people on it. Had them scour the Cleveland and Chicago papers around that date. Told them to keep an eye open for anything to do with the Cleveland Clinic, Malik's practice, his wife's known interests, close friends or family, or his little girl. And they found something."

That snapped me wide awake. "What?"

"Turns out the daughter's private school caught fire and had to be shut down on March twenty-second, two days before Malik went to Stitch's firm."

"How awful. Was anyone hurt?"

"Fortunately not. School was in session, but they got everyone out without serious injuries. Principal said it was accidental. Claimed one of the teachers had tossed a cigarette butt in a trash can full of papers in the lounge. Only that room went up, but there was lots of smoke and water damage throughout the building. They had to move to temporary quarters in a nearby church."

I yawned again and shifted heavily. "Sorry for being dense, but what does that have to do with Malik?"

"Get this," Franny said. "Two days after the fire, the Maliks go out of town to see Ronald Stitch. A week after that, the school announces a major gift from an anonymous donor that will allow them to build a state-of-the-art swimming pool and gym. Stitch happens to specialize in estate planning and philanthropic gifts."

I slumped back against the pillows. "You think Malik made the anonymous gift?"

"The shoe certainly fits," Franny said.

"Okay. Suppose he did. He decided to help his daughter's school in a time of crisis. Exactly how does that make him a bad guy capable of trumping up a sexual abuse case against Sam?"

"Tell her, Grant," Franny said.

"Our investigator spoke to a teacher at the school. Word is that Malik had been carrying on with the school principal. Lots of meetings at odd times behind closed doors," Grant said.

"So a fire leaves the school homeless and in jeopardy, and Malik's squeeze squeezes him for a big, fat anonymous contribution. Otherwise, she'll spill everything to Malik's wife. Great story. Don't you think, Em?" Franny said.

"If it's true, I guess it makes him look rather unscrupulous in an altruistic sort of way. But how can we prove it's true? And even if we could, how does it prove Malik and Suzanne set Sam up?"

Grant sighed. "Exactly what I told Franny. It doesn't."

"But it's a start, Em. Another nail in the coffin lid."

"Sure. I appreciate it."

"We're not done," Franny said. "We'll get that bastard, Emma. You'll see."

"Thanks for trying."

I returned to the baby name book. Demarast . . . Denorah . . . Diane. At some point, I dropped off the slippery edge of consciousness. I plunged deep, reveling in the still, encompassing escape.

Lost as I was in the insensate darkness, I was oblivious, at first, to the danger at my door.

·FIFTY-ONE·

In my dream the pounding was Tyler, playing builder man with his bright plastic tools. He brought the red hammer high overhead and smashed the side of the building with a grunt. A single brick dislodged in a haze of dust. Dried mortar rained from the hole.

I tried to tell him to stop, that he shouldn't hurt our house, but I couldn't speak. When I opened my mouth, mothlike creatures burst forth. They flew off, dispersing my thoughts on the wind.

Rearing back, Tyler smashed the façade again, harder this time. The sound set my teeth on edge and raised a seismic tremor in my bones.

The noise that followed seemed innocent at first, almost playful, like a handful of pebbles tossed down a sandy hill. But it soon grew louder and more menacing. Bricks popped free and plummeted to the ground in a choking fog of blinding debris.

The building wavered as if it stood on rickety knees, and I felt a horrifying groundswell.

I screamed for Tyler, but my words were lost in the deafening implosion.

There was a brief, thrumming silence. And then the screams and pounding began again. "*Ayudame, por favor!* Help me, please!"

I snapped awake, heart thrashing. Wrapped in Sam's plaid cotton robe, I went to answer the door.

Bori stood in the hall with bare feet and pale horror etched on her face. Her voice was tinged with hysteria.

"*Es la muchacha. Tienes que venir conmigo.*"

I asked what was wrong. Was Adriana hurt, sick?

She told me no. The little girl was unharmed, but I had to come. She couldn't explain it. I had to see for myself.

I cinched Sam's robe tighter. "Where are Dr. and Mrs. Malik?"

She told me they had gone to a concert. The rest of the story emerged in tortured bits. Before she moved in, the Maliks had made her agree to a litany of rules. At the top of the list was a prohibition against entering Adriana's portion of the apartment at night. Once the child went to bed, Bori was banished to a small room off the kitchen, where she was to stay until morning. She was not to leave the room, not to have any dealings with the child at all, unless it was a dire emergency, unless the child got seriously ill or there was a fire. If there was an emergency, Adriana had a panic button that would trigger an alarm in Bori's room.

Often, Dr. Malik and his wife went out for the evening, she told me. They wore the finest clothing. Her mother had worked as a seamstress, so she knew. Mrs. Malik would take hours to get ready. Like so many things, this made Dr. Malik angry. Things were never perfect enough for him, never the way he liked.

Tonight, there was a dinner before the concert. Bori had been told to feed the little girl early and see to her bath. By six o'clock, Adriana was in her room, and Mrs. Malik instructed Bori to go to her room immediately and stay there.

Too fearful to disobey, she'd followed the order. She hadn't even dared to venture out to get something to eat. She'd tried to pass the time listening to the small radio the Maliks had provided. There was no television, no books or magazines. The evening stretched long and lonely, and her stomach growled with emptiness. But she was grateful for a decent place to live. Glad to have a job.

Anxiously, she peered up and down the corridor. She was worried, she said. If they found out she'd disobeyed, the Maliks would fire her.

I asked what it was she wanted me to see. If the girl was all right, I really shouldn't be going to their apartment.

She took my hand. Her eyes sparked with pleading.

I said maybe she'd be better off with one of the people who worked in the building or someone from hospital security. But she insisted it had to be me. I had asked her to let me know if there was anything strange going on in the house. There was, but she couldn't explain it. There was no way to put such a thing into words.

· FIFTY-TWO ·

Our baby monitor boasted a four-hundred-foot range, though given our postage stamp–sized apartment, I'd never come close to testing that limit. I switched on one of the receivers in Tyler's room and tucked the other deep in the pocket of my robe.

Reluctantly, I trailed Bori up the stairs. By the time we slipped through the Maliks' front door, my apprehension had spawned near panic. What if someone saw me and told the Maliks I'd been snooping around? What if Dr. and Mrs. God happened to come home early and find me there?

I urged Bori to hurry. Show me what it is, I told her, and then I have to leave.

At the door to Adriana's suite, Bori paused. She drew a ring of keys from the pocket of her jeans and unlocked the dead bolt. I was startled to see that the child was contained like a prisoner.

The girl's furious screams split the air as soon as Bori opened the door.

"Let me go! Let me out of here!"

The walls and ceiling had to be soundproofed. I hadn't heard a thing from the hall. Then again, tonight I hadn't heard a sound from upstairs through the ceiling. Either I'd been too fast asleep, or perhaps they'd somehow blunted the noise through the floor as well.

Bori switched on the light. *Mira,* she said softly. Look.

I blinked hard, barely able to believe my eyes. Steel shackles bound the child's wrists and ankles. Heavy chains connected them to the posts of the canopy bed. Adriana's struggles to break free had worn bands of paint from the posts, so in grim parody, the thick dowels looked shackled as well. Had she somehow managed to free her arms or legs, a steel belt circling her waist was chained to the bed frame. A steel collar girding her neck was fastened to a grommet in the wall.

The child's dark eyes stretched with astonishment.

"I'm your neighbor from downstairs, Adriana. My name is Emma. Are you okay?"

Stiffly she pressed against the headboard. "Don't hurt me. Please. I'll be good."

"Of course I won't hurt you."

She held out her hands. The skin around the shackles looked raw and swollen. "Please get them off," she whimpered. "They hurt so much."

Bori was talking quickly, jabbering in fear. Adriana had pressed the panic button. The alarm had an intercom, and the girl had said she smelled smoke. She couldn't believe her eyes when she saw the child this way. It had to be the devil's work, she said. Only *el diablo* would treat a child like that.

The chains were fastened by heavy pickproof locks. The steel bands around her wrists, ankles, neck, and waist were hinged and required a key.

"Do you know where they keep the key?"

"Somewhere in the playroom."

Bori was nodding, wringing her hands. It was good that I could speak to the girl. She had tried, but they hadn't been able to understand each other. Dr. and Mrs. Malik spoke Spanish, but the child did not. They had made it clear they didn't want her to learn.

I asked her to come help me search for the key. We looked under cushions and toys, beneath the books and behind the pictures. I pried out the grates covering the speakers and the air-conditioning ducts and checked above the moldings and recessed lights.

Bori's voice grew increasingly more desperate. *No hay nada!* There's nothing.

The carpeting was wall-to-wall, but I lifted the corners to be sure, and the heavy sound-deadening pad that lay beneath it. I checked the bathroom as well, searching in the toilet tank, under the soap and shampoo, in the medicine chest, and beneath the sink.

Through the monitor, I heard Tyler murmur in his sleep. I stiffened, fearful he might wake up and find me gone. But his breathing soon settled back in restful rhythm.

When I returned to the bedroom, Adriana was whimpering in a weary delirium. "Please get me out of here. I don't feel well. I have to go to the bathroom."

"Are you sure they keep the key in the playroom?" I asked.

"Yes. After Daddy locks me up, I hear him go in there. There's a ding sound when he puts the key away."

"Ding?"

She nodded. "Like when you hit your fork against your plate."

Dark hollows bloomed beneath her eyes. She'd suffered her fill of nightmarish solitude. I told Bori to stay with the girl while I continued to search.

Back in the playroom, I looked for anything that might make a metallic ringing sound. I felt all around the ballet barre. I removed the shades, harps, and finials to peer inside the lamps. I examined the stereo system.

If only I could contact Ms. Kresge from Child Welfare, but it was after hours and I didn't know her home number or her cell. I considered calling the police. But this wasn't my house or my little girl. If they refused to get involved, we could lose precious time. Malik might return in the meantime, and imprison the girl somewhere else.

Or worse.

I scanned the room again. I ran my hand over the hem of the drapes, and along each slat of the blinds. Suddenly, my eye settled on the popcorn machine.

Hurrying there, I ran my hand along the back and sides. Straining, I moved the heavy frame a few inches to be sure the keys were not hidden underneath. Doing so, I tipped the machine slightly. The flap on the spigot lolled open. There, on the underside, the key was taped.

Unfastening the locks, my hands trembled. As each of the shackles fell open, the little girl sighed with relief and rubbed the soreness from her pale, delicate skin.

"Oh, thank you," she said. "That's so much better."

"I'm glad."

"But they'll come back soon. Daddy will lock me up again."

"No. We won't let that happen."

"He'll kill me for getting loose. He'll beat me. Please. You have to get me out of here."

She was right. I couldn't leave her here at her monster father's mercy. If I did, whatever happened would be on my hands.

"All right. We'll go."

Beneath the long pink nightgown, her slim chest

heaved with relief. "Thank you. Thank you so much. I'll just go grab some clothes." She dashed into the walk-in closet.

Bori kept chattering. Where would we take the girl? What would we do?

In an instant, Adriana was back, carrying one of her shapeless dresses, underwear, and shoes in a tidy bundle.

"We'd better hurry. Daddy hates concerts. He always gets disgusted halfway through and makes Mommy leave early. They could be home anytime."

With that, I realized that I had no choice but to call the police. I couldn't simply run off with the child. She wasn't mine. They could charge me with kidnapping.

I was picking up the phone to dial emergency, when I heard a key clatter in the lock. Voices murmured in the front hall and slowly, they approached.

· FIFTY-THREE ·

Terror rooted me in place. Adriana raced to her bed-room door and closed it soundlessly. "There. Now they can't hear us."

"What if they come in to check on you?" I rasped.

She seemed utterly unfazed. "They won't. They never do once they chain me up. No one will come in until morning."

"Will they go right to sleep?"

She shook her head. "They watch the late-night shows on TV. They never go to bed until one or two o'clock in the morning."

"How do you know that if you're locked up in here?"

"They always talk about it at breakfast, about what Leno said in his monologue and who he had on. About some dumb old movie they watched after that."

My mind was racing. Tyler could wake up anytime. "I can't wait that long. I have to get back to my son."

She pointed to the mirror. "That's actually a door. It used to be the entrance to this apartment. They blocked it off, but it still works if you take out the screws. We can get out that way."

"But your parents—" I couldn't say the rest. The words, and the unthinkable possibility that they might happen to step into the hall and discover us, caught in my throat.

Holding her bundle of clothes, Adriana gestured for us to follow her. Bori hurried to follow. And seeing no other way out, I went along.

· FIFTY-FOUR ·

Tyler was fast asleep with his arms around Sebastian and Fred. The night-light cast his face in angelic glow.

I pulled the covers to his chin and kissed his forehead. "Mama loves you so much."

In the living room, I found Bori standing alone. "Where's Adriana?"

She told me the girl had complained of a stomachache and gone to the bathroom again.

I knocked. "Adriana? Are you okay?" I caught that same strange bitter chemical smell I had noticed in the hall.

"Much better now. Be right out."

Before I made it back to the living room, she stepped out into the hall behind me and shut the door.

"I'm going to call the police, Adriana. They'll make sure you don't get tied up like that ever again."

"Wait, Emma. I have to give you something."

"What?"

She approached me shyly and held out her arms for a hug. I drew her close, appalled by her bird-boned fragility.

She was so painfully thin; I wondered if her parents were withholding food.

"I'll never forget you," she said, clinging fast. "I was praying for someone to help me, and you showed up. It's like a miracle from God."

"I'm glad to help. And the police will help you, too. Now I need to call, so they'll come." Her odd scent was making me queasy. I struggled not to recoil.

Her grip tightened. "I'm scared."

When I stroked her back, my fingers bumped over the xylophone of ribs. "I understand. But you'll see. It's all going to turn out fine."

She started weeping. "Why is my daddy so mean? How come he doesn't love me?"

"Some people just don't know how to be sweet and kind, Adriana. Maybe he never learned."

"What about my mommy, then? Why doesn't she make him be nice?"

Leaning back, I blotted her tears with the sleeve of Sam's robe. "It's complicated. Too hard for me to explain right now. Now let me make that call."

She doubled over, clutching her stomach. "Ow! It hurts something awful. I think I'm going to throw up."

"Let's get you to the bathroom."

Her hand flew to her mouth as I urged her down the hall. Quickly, I grabbed the knob to open the door. As it swerved in, the pain registered. And in shock I faced a raging wall of flames.

· FIFTY-FIVE ·

"My God! Hurry! We have to get out!" My hand screamed with pain, burned raw by the scorching metal knob.

Adriana stood watching. She was slack-faced, as if in a trance.

I grabbed her arm and pulled, but she wouldn't budge.

"What happened, Adriana? How did the fire start?"

Her chin crumpled. "I tried to light the pretty candle and it fell. Don't hurt me. Please!"

"Of course I won't. Don't worry. Come on! We have to get out of here."

I shouted for Bori to take the girl so I could get Tyler. She urged Adriana to run, but the child seemed oblivious.

The flames were leaping into the hall. I slammed the door to cut the fire's air supply.

Incredibly, Tyler had not awakened. I scooped him out of bed, cradled him in my arms, and headed out through the thickening smoke.

Bori's cries stopped me at the door. She was pleading with Adriana to leave, trying to warn her of the lethal danger in a language the child could not comprehend.

I told her to pick up the girl and carry her out. I listened to the struggle as she tried. The child flailed like a demon, trying to escape Bori's grasp. Bori lacked the size and power to overwhelm her.

Clutching Tyler, I raced toward the sounds. The smoke was thickening, burning my eyes, making it hard to see. Catching Adriana by the wrist, I dragged her toward the door.

"Stop. Let me go. Don't touch me!"

"We have to get out now!"

"No! I don't want to."

"You must. Now hurry. We have to call the fire department and sound the alarm. There are other people in this building. We have to warn them."

She dug her heels in, making it harder to move her. Bori grabbed her other wrist and pulled.

Quickly! she pleaded, coughing. *Rápida!* Hurry! The fire is growing.

Suddenly, the little girl crumpled to the floor. When I leaned down to pick her up, I realized she was laughing.

"Listen to me," I said sharply. "This isn't a joke, Adriana. You have to stand up and walk."

"Fire, fire, burning bright," she chanted in a playful singsong. "Fire, fire, burn all night."

"We have to get out now!"

I told Bori to grab her legs. Holding Tyler awkwardly, I took her wrists. Down the hall the first of the flames teased beneath the door frame.

My throat was raw, eyes streaming tears. "Enough!" I passed Tyler to Bori, amazed that he was still asleep. Then I held Adriana with her back to me, pinning her arms and legs as best I could, and made for the door.

The hall was clear of smoke, and I drew a greedy breath. We were racing toward the stairs when he appeared.

· FIFTY-SIX ·

"What's going on here?" Malik's voice was a thunder-ous boom, his face florid.

The little girl struggled free of my grasp and threw her arms around him. "She took the safeties off and made me leave, Daddy. It's all her fault."

Safeties?

Disengaging from her embrace, he scowled at the girl. "I smell smoke, Adriana. What have you done?"

"Nothing. It was an accident. I swear it."

"Tell the truth!"

"I am. Don't hit me, Daddy. I'm begging you, please!"

Bori cowered against the wall, cradling my son.

Lena Malik stepped out of the stairwell next. Her eyes were downcast, her hands behind her back like a penitent. "Everyone's all right, Douglas. No harm done. Now, take the fire extinguisher and put it out."

"No," I said. "The right thing is to get out and call the fire department. Fire can be tricky. They know what they're doing."

"Douglas knows what he's doing." Her voice was eerie, a dead mechanical drone.

With practiced moves, Malik opened the wall-mounted box and freed the extinguisher from its mountings. I had left the door unlocked. Filling his lungs, he opened it and rushed inside.

I took Tyler from Bori's arms. "Do as you please. We're getting out."

Lena Malik brought her right hand around. She looked vaguely surprised to discover that it held a gun.

"Sorry, Mrs. Colten. I'm afraid you need to stay here."

Bori gasped.

"Are you crazy? Put that thing away!" I turned away, trying to shield Tyler, setting a futile hand over the swell of my unborn girl.

"We simply need to talk awhile, Mrs. Colten. I'll explain everything so you understand completely what we're dealing with here."

"Fire, fire, burning bright," Adriana chanted. "Fire, fire, heart's delight."

"We mustn't ever speak those rhymes, my darling," Lena Malik said gently. "You promised. Remember?"

"Fire, fire, burning bright. Strike a match and curtains light. Whoosh!" Adriana's hands flew up.

"Now, Adriana. Remember what the doctor said? You have an illness in your head that makes you think strange things."

The child was schizophrenic, I thought. Kitso pitso, in Tyler's words. Everything he'd said about her had been true.

"It's like a very bad cold in your brain. When your mind plays tricks, you mustn't trust it. You must tell Mommy or Daddy, and we'll help you to stay in control like we do at night with the safeties."

"Fire, fire, rising higher; lovely flames that stop the liar;

kill the sigher." The child was wild-eyed, sinking in a crazed delirium.

"Stop!" her mother demanded. "You mustn't touch fire, Adriana. You mustn't even think or speak of it. It's like a bad drug. Fire makes you very, very sick."

"Pretty blaze that eats the liar. Fire, fire, heart's desire."

"She doesn't know what she's saying, Mrs. Colten. Adriana has an emotional illness. She's had a difficult time adjusting to the move, the new school and all. I never imagined it would be such a trial. I wanted her to have a fresh new start. And she will. You're going to get better and better, aren't you, princess? We'll hang a pretty painting of you over the mantelpiece and take movies at your dance recital and buy you lots of beautiful shoes and dresses and before you know it, you'll be done with that silly illness and you'll grow up to be the loveliest young lady of all."

My heart squirmed and I clutched Tyler closer. "I understand. If you let us go, we won't say anything. She's your child, your business. Not ours."

Malik came back. Taking in the scene, his look darkened. "Adriana, come here at once!"

"Fire, fire, kill the liar. Burn the string and melt the wire. Pretty flames that lick the sigher."

Malik grabbed the girl. He restrained her arms and held a hand roughly over her mouth. "Inside. All of you. Now!"

· FIFTY-SEVEN ·

Malik ordered us to sit on the couch. Bori cowered be-
side me with her head bowed, hugging her knees. My eyes
skittered nervously, seeking some way out. I rubbed
Tyler's back, praying he'd stay asleep until this nightmare
was over.

God worked with crisp surgical precision, barking orders as he did. "Close the blinds, Lena. It's obvious that the
smoke detector isn't working, but take out the batteries to
be sure. And open the window to air the place out."

While she did as he said, Adriana twirled about, chanting. *Fire, fire . . .*

"You won't feel a thing, Mrs. Colten. Much as you don't
deserve my concern after all your unthinkable interference,
I'll see to that."

Tyler stirred. With a trembling hand I soothed him back
to sleep.

"I told you, we won't say anything. Just let us go." Despite the terror, my voice sounded eerily calm.

Malik did not answer me. "Of course, we'll have to

move out. The building won't be habitable for some time after the fire takes its toll. But I think it would be wise in any event. Adriana will be happier in a house in the country. Somewhere in Connecticut perhaps, where we'll have more privacy."

Turning to the little girl, he held out his hand. "Give me the matches, Adriana."

The child went coy.

"Now!" Malik roared.

The little girl fought like a demon as he wrested the matchbook from her hand.

His wife blinked slowly. "Wait. What are you saying, Douglas? Didn't you put the fire out?"

"Temporarily, yes."

"What do you mean, temporarily? What are you going to do?"

"Take care of this unfortunate situation. What do you think?"

"Are you out of your mind? You'd kill them all? You'd hurt a little boy?"

My heart was hammering. "No one has to get hurt. Just please let us go. That will be the end of it. I swear!"

Malik sighed. "I shouldn't have listened to you, Lena. I knew it was unwise to place the child in a situation like this, but I let you talk me into it. She's been getting worse and worse since we moved here."

"We had to leave Cleveland, Douglas. You said so yourself. People talk. What happened at the school would have gotten out eventually."

His eyes bugged. "You're the one who talks, Lena. You're the one who fantasizes and denies and has stubbornly refused to place the child where she belongs. I'm the one left to mop up after your mistakes, as usual."

From his pocket he drew a syringe and a vial of clear

liquid. "This is a powerful sedative. Fast-acting and rapidly cleared from the system. You'll simply go to sleep."

I held Tyler tighter. "No, please!"

Pouting, the little girl rubbed her arm. "Flame that makes the hurt expire. Lovely, lively fire, fire."

He filled the syringe and pressed the plunger until a fine quicksilver plume spurted through the needle. Slowly, he strode toward me.

"No, Douglas. You can't. You mustn't. They're trying a new medicine. She'll get better. This will all be behind us. You'll see."

"Strike a match and see the flame rise, blind the children's shiny eyes."

Lena Malik's hands fluttered like skittish birds. "Stop that, Adriana! You mustn't say such things."

"Still the children's hurting cries."

"No, my darling! Hush!"

Malik pushed up the sleeve of my robe and dabbed my arm with antiseptic, as if he were worried about infection, as if I were a patient in his care.

I tried to squirm away from him, but I couldn't. And I couldn't escape the cold metal eye of Lena Malik's gun.

Tyler stirred. "Mama?"

"Hush, sweetie. It's okay." With a quaking hand, I stroked his hair.

Adriana smiled. "Still the children, by and by. Fire, fire, heart's desire."

Cringing, I felt the stick of the needle. Heat surged as the sedative coursed through my veins.

"Don't . . . hurt . . ." My voice, everything, was growing dark, winding down.

Crushing weariness consumed me. I was sinking beneath it when the room went bright as blazes and the walls shook with one mad, deafening blast.

· FIFTY-EIGHT ·

Things kept getting away from me. The sun slid like a runny egg down the face of the sky and dripped into the river. People spoke to me in gibberish upside down. At my feet, a plump purple dinosaur danced, but when I looked again, the dancer was a dangerous-looking man in noose tight jeans.

The crib was huge, the walls a soft cornflower blue. The zebra lying beside me smelled like juice. My mouth was impossibly dry, as if I'd been sucking on chalk. When I tried to ask for water, I sounded drunk.

"Here, sweetie."

I gripped the straw and drank greedily. Slowly, things edged into clearer focus.

"Sam?"

He smiled with wet eyes: a human sun shower. "Welcome back, sleepyhead. And about time. You've been out for most of two days."

"Tyler?"

"Look, Mama. Sebastian and Fred are resting, too!"

So that explained the zebras. The black-and-white jumble on my pillow was his prized pair of stuffed Dalmatians.

The next questions were answered before I asked them. The baby kicked in a way that made me know she was all right. The sound rose on the television, and Barney the purple dinosaur sang his cloying refrain: *I love you, you love me, we're a happy family.*

"Malik?" I croaked.

Sam's eyes shifted uneasily toward Tyler.

Mrs. Kalisher came up behind him. "Good to see you feeling better, Emma darling. You know, Tyler dear, I was just thinking I could use a little snack. Why don't we go to the cafeteria and get some ice cream?"

"Vanilla?"

"Definitely."

"Four scoops?"

She took his hand. "We'll talk about that on the way."

I waited until they were out the door to ask again. "Malik?"

"His wife confessed as soon as the cops showed up. She said she'd had no choice but to shoot Malik, to stop him from hurting you and Tyler. She said she'd suspected he wasn't right in the head for quite a while, that her little girl's mental illness was hereditary. She knew he was driven, ruthless. But until she saw him inject you, she couldn't believe he'd actually go so far as to kill someone who got in his way."

"Adriana set fire to the school in Cleveland?"

"She's been setting fires since she turned five. The one at the school was the worst, and Malik was determined to keep it hushed. He donated five million to buy their silence. But according to his wife, Malik kept worrying that it would catch up with them somehow if they stayed in Cleveland. He became convinced that it was dangerous to stay there, more and more paranoid. Somehow, he got it in his head they'd be safe in New York. But naturally, as soon as they moved here, his delusions followed along."

"What happened to Adriana?"

"Child Welfare took her. She'll be tested and placed in a therapeutic environment until she's able to live in a less structured setting without hurting herself or anyone else. That's what should have happened a long time ago."

I shuddered at the thought of what could become of people, and too often did.

"Lena Malik?"

"She's being held without bail. I suspect she's going to have to get used to living in much, much smaller quarters for quite a while."

"Where did Suzanne fit in, Sam?"

He shrugged. "Lena Malik confirmed that her husband and Suzanne had been involved. I don't know why she was willing to make those ridiculous charges against me, but I'd guess it was for Douglas the daddy figure."

"Could be. Or maybe she's just a garden-variety sociopath who makes a hobby out of wrecking lives."

"Suze?"

I glared at him, but only because I was still far too exhausted to lunge out of bed and wring his neck.

"Doesn't matter what you call it. It's like you said, Em. She's a snake."

Everything washed over me in a jumble of confusion. Purple dinosaurs, stuffed Dalmatians, the terrifying unpredictability of the human brain. I stroked the tummy bulge that contained my baby daughter. Having a child or being one was a most courageous roll of the cosmic dice. When you really thought about it, it was truly amazing anyone ever took the plunge.

"So it's over," I said.

Sam kissed me lightly on the forehead. "That part, yes."

· FIFTY-NINE ·

She arrived bright and early on her due date, and we named her Charlotte Faith. Soon after we brought her home, Tyler insisted we have a party for her zero birthday, and of course, this called for plenty of ice cream and cake.

My sister, Charlotte, came with her family. Jared's arrhythmia had been treated successfully, and they were still in a celebratory mood. My parents flew in for the occasion, as did Sam's sister's family. With all of them plus Mrs. Kalisher, Siena and Amity, LeeAnn, and Bori, who was now working at Little Ranger as the aide for Jake, our minuscule apartment was busting at the seams. We left the door open, and people milled about in the hall. At the last minute, Franny had been forced to bow out by the sudden arrival of her new daughter. Like our little girl, she had weighed in at seven pounds, six ounces. Franny and Grant had named her Emily Jane.

I couldn't believe how tiny my infant daughter seemed or how enormous Tyler had suddenly become by comparison. He was working the crowd in his Superman cape, taking inventory. "That's my mama and my daddy and my nana and my Auntie Frieda and my Auntie Charlotte and my Krypto Superdog and my peanut butter sandwich and my M&Ms."

My father stood beaming with an arm around my nonexistent waist. "He so reminds me of you at that age, Emma."

"He does?"

"Never forget what a bright, verbal little thing you were. And you always had to have everything in its proper place."

"I did?"

"Plus mischievous." My mother chuckled. "And then some. How many three-year-olds can claim to have cracked up the family car?"

"Excuse me?"

Three decades of distance had blunted the horror so they could tell the tale as an amusing little joke. A boy in my nursery school had come down with pneumonia. We lived nearby, so my mother had volunteered to deliver the hand-drawn Get Well cards the class had made. Since he was contagious, Mom had stopped on their driveway and left me and Charlotte, who was then an infant, in the back of the car. She'd taken the keys and put on the parking brake, but in the couple of moments it took her to walk to the door and ring the bell, I'd unlatched my seat belt and disengaged the brake. The driveway was steep, and the car went careening down the hill and across the street, where it was stopped by an oak tree. By some miracle, we hadn't been hurt, but the car was history.

"How come you never told me that before?"

My mother shrugged. "Of course we did, though we tried not to make a big thing of it. For months after it happened, you were so terribly upset. You had trouble sleeping, nightmares. You kept apologizing, saying you were a bad girl. We told you it wasn't your fault, but you were convinced it was."

"And I was Tyler's age?"

"Yes, Emma. You were three."

So maybe that was the trauma that haunted me still. Maybe I'd been convinced that the malevolent ghost of past trespasses would come back and punish me. For the sin of totaling my parents' car as a toddler, maybe the cruel fates would damage my little boy. Crazy as that sounded, it made perverse sense to me. I could all but hear the tumblers click into place.

We sang "Happy Birthday," and Tyler blew out the candles on his sleeping baby sister's behalf.

Sam cut the cake. "Here, tiger. You get the first piece."

Tyler ferried his plate toward the bassinet. "My baby sister should have it. It's her birthday."

"She wants you to eat it, sweetie. She's too little for cake. She's not allowed to have anything but milk for a while."

"No ice cream?"

"Nope."

"No pasta? No pizza?"

"Only milk."

"Yuck."

At that moment, all I could think was that life didn't get any better. And yet it was poised to do just that. With Malik's death, Norman Stryker had returned to chair the Department of Cardiovascular Surgery. Sam would be chief surgical resident next year and, from all indications, a fellow with Stryker after that. He'd been fully reinstated, the charges against him dropped. Though I could only guess the reason, "Suze" had changed her story completely. Sam hadn't assaulted her. It had all been a silly misunderstanding.

As if that were not enough, the hospital administrators, perhaps in guilty response to the false accusations they had believed, had promised to move us two flights up to a three-bedroom apartment. Workers were painting it now, and refurbishing the ancient kitchen with new cabinets and appliances. It would be ready for us in a couple of weeks. Little Charlotte and Tyler would have their own rooms. We'd have a much larger living room with a tiny terrace that overlooked the park. There was even a fireplace. Fire regulations didn't allow us to use it, but on cold winter nights I could snuggle with Sam and pretend.

I was surrounded by people I loved. Everyone was healthy and thriving. There was no dark cloud looming overhead. And soon, very soon, we'd have built-in bookshelves, not to mention closets galore.

I smiled at the thought of extra closets. It most certainly did not get any better than that.

Don't miss the page-turning suspense, intriguing characters, and unstoppable action that keep readers coming back for more from these bestselling authors...

Tom Clancy
Robin Cook
Patricia Cornwell
Clive Cussler
Dean Koontz
J.D. Robb
John Sandford

Your favorite thrillers and suspense novels come from Berkley.